THE BLOODY, BLOODY BANKS

ANDREW RAYMOND

HB HUNTERHILL BOOKS

CHAPTER ONE

THE SUN DANCED over the surface of Loch Lomond, the water glimmering in a thousand different directions, as Robbie the kayak instructor pondered who in the group he would kill first.

'I mean, that's easy,' he said, taking a long hit on the joint. 'It's obviously Connor.'

'Obviously,' Hazel agreed.

The group, along with their instructors, had all the water within half a mile of the tiny Luss pier to themselves. There wasn't a lot happening on the water early on a Tuesday morning.

Perched on paddle boards, Hazel and Robbie kept their distance until they had finished the joint. Standing on the boards helped with monitoring their group. Although a more accurate description for what they were doing would have been "vaguely aware that no one was yelling for help, or actually drowning."

Hazel snapped her fingers and held her hand out. 'You going to pass that, or what?'

Robbie checked that no one was looking their way, then passed it to Hazel. He had been hogging it and hoping she wouldn't notice.

This was why Hazel preferred getting stoned on her own.

As soon as she had taken a hit, she held the joint behind her back, though most of the group was too spread out, paddling away in various directions, to notice the smell lingering in the air.

The group was from an American financial services firm based in one of the trendiest buildings in Glasgow city centre. A dozen of the company's up-and-coming brokers on a supposed "team-building" day that had so far consisted of everyone grumbling about getting wet, and a tedious health and safety presentation from Robbie earlier on.

That was when he had first become aware of Connor Blaine, who fancied himself the alpha of the group. He had mocked the health and safety rules mercilessly. A thirty-year-old broker who was well on his way to earning six figures a year, and acted like he was a character on *Succession*.

Robbie could hardly relate. While he sported a carefree, bohemian appearance of mostly second-hand clothes, Connor epitomised an air of entitlement, poncing across the pier in a pair of sockless loafers, displaying little regard for any activity that didn't make him the centre of attention.

At the age of twenty-five, Robbie found it perfectly reasonable to picture himself twenty years from now, still getting baked every day, watching *Star Wars* for the millionth time. How could anyone *not* want to do that every day?

He wondered how much he could really take before smacking Connor across the coupon with a kayak paddle. He could picture Connor's gormless face slapping the wooden planks on the pier, before casually rolling him off into the water with his foot, and letting him tumble into a watery grave.

Robbie complained to Hazel, 'I mean, look at him...' He gestured in Connor's direction.

Connor had put down his paddle so that he could take a selfie for Instagram. He tapped into the text field, *"Roughing it vibes on Loch Lomond."*

"Roughing it" had so far consisted of breakfast at five-star Cameron House just up the road.

Robbie went on, 'He's at it again...' He then shouted across the water, 'Connor! Hold onto your paddle. At *all* times!'

A good hundred yards away, Connor barked back, 'My oar's wonky.'

Robbie corrected him, 'The paddle. What's wrong with it?'

'It's wonky. Look! The bits at the end are pointing in different directions.'

'The blades are offset.'

Connor stared back blankly.

Robbie explained, 'You said earlier that you were experienced at kayaking, so I assumed you would be more comfortable with offset blades. I can change the angle if you want?'

'No, no, it's fine,' Connor replied. He eyed the paddle blades as if he knew what he was talking about. 'It must be, like, a little more onset that I'm used to.'

'You mean *off*set.'

'Yeah. Whatever.'

Robbie gave up and turned away with a sigh. He asked Hazel, 'You going down the Dog House tonight?'

She rolled her eyes. 'Yeah, because I just love having Sky Sports News pointing at me from three different directions, and listening to Lewis fucking Capaldi with his shouty falsetto.'

Robbie looked a little hurt. 'I quite like him. Seems a nice dude.'

Hazel grumbled, 'Don't you want to go to Sleazy's or something? Balloch's fucking dead, man.'

'Glasgow's just as bad, Haze. Have you seen Sauchiehall Street recently? It's got Waterstones, Primark, and the rest is empty units for takeaway food and discount clothes shops. There's just a bad vibe in the city centre these days. Feels less safe. Have you seen all the gangland stuff going on? The neds run riot around Union Street.'

'Yeah, cos there aren't any neds in Balloch...' Her expression changed to something more serious. More considered. 'Mind what I was saying about who you might kill. What if it was for real? Not just talking who-would-you-like-to-see-die-for-shits-and-giggles, hypothetical, would-never-actually-happen-anyway. What would someone have to do to make you *really* want to kill them?'

'Fuck me. Should I be worrying about you, Hazel?'

'No, I'm serious,' she said, flicking away the end of the joint. 'Do you think someone totally normal like us could end up killing someone? What would it take? What about a bunch of people?'

Robbie pushed out his lips as he mulled it over. 'Nah,' he finally said. 'I couldn't kill someone. Don't have it in me. You?'

Hazel replied, 'In the right circumstances? Someone did something to my family?' She paused. 'I could see it.'

Robbie puffed. 'Remind me to never hog a joint from you again...' He was distracted by the sight of Connor with an arm outstretched, phone in hand, in prime selfie position, turning his head just so for the perfect angle.

Robbie yelled to him, 'Connor! Grab your—'

It was already too late – even as Connor lunged for the paddle that was tipping up to vertical and sliding into the water.

In his panic, he then fumbled his phone out of his hand, which sank like a stone.

Connor's colleagues applauded him sarcastically.

'*Nice job, Mr Bean!*'

'*I don't think you can upload to TikTok from the bottom of the loch, Connor.*'

Connor cursed, 'Shite!'

As he fished about wildly for his phone, the kayak rocked from side to side.

Robbie quickly paddled over to him. 'Forget the phone. It's gone. Grab your paddle, mate.'

Connor didn't realise that Robbie only ever used "mate" as an insult. Reserved for clients that he thought were arseholes. His little cheat way of swearing at them to their very faces.

The paddle was designed to float on the water, so Robbie didn't have any urgency about grabbing it for Connor.

Still looking helplessly for his phone, Connor reached out for his paddle.

Or what he thought was his paddle.

Robbie peered towards the object as it broke the surface of the water. 'What is that?' he asked himself.

Connor had a good piece of it in his hand, and instantly knew that something was off.

Too thick. Too heavy.

Connor froze. At first in confusion. He couldn't tell what he was looking at. It was too pale to be wood.

Robbie's mouth hung open. 'Um...that's not a paddle, mate.'

By the time Connor lifted it above the surface of the water, he knew what it was.

A spine-chilling, ear-piercing scream erupted from

Connor's throat, ripping over the serene waters and echoing across the beach and through the village. The sheer terror in his cry brought everything to an abrupt standstill. The very air holding its breath in response.

Connor dropped the object as if it had suddenly become charged with a thousand volts. In a frenzy of panic, he thrashed his arms and legs wildly. The violent motion capsized his kayak, plunging him into the chilly waters he now dreaded.

He'd always had a thing about swimming or floating somewhere really deep. Couldn't handle it. Like standing at the top of a building – he could look down from a hundred storeys up, no problem. But get him to look *up* and his legs would turn to jelly.

His screams only intensified, as more and more of the objects surfaced all around him, bumping gently against his body like sinister buoys heralding an unspeakable horror.

But they weren't buoys. And they certainly weren't kayak paddles.

CHAPTER TWO

DCI JOHN LOMOND was halfway up Beinn Dubh –
overlooking Luss on the western shore of Loch Lomond
– and feeling amazing. It was late morning in May and
the sun was out. The infernal pace he set himself had
turned him into a red-cheeked sweat box, but he was
feeling amazing nonetheless.

At the same point two months earlier, his legs had
been anchors, and his lungs burned. Now he was striding
confidently past climbers that were dressed head to toe in
premium outdoor gear. They'd paused to take photos of
the bluebells that had flowered and carpeted huge tracts
of the hillside.

Lomond couldn't contain a smug grin to himself once
he passed them. *All the gear and no idea*, he thought. *No
effort. Taking breaks whenever they can.*

Although feeling a little superior, he had worked
hard. Three months ago he could barely walk the length

of Helen Street car park. Now he was flying up hills that were in actual walking guides. And not guides called things like *Easiest Walks for Folk Who Can't Be Arsed*. They were hills in the moderate to difficult range.

Once he had passed the walkers in the expensive gear, he felt guilty. He would have been wearing the same gear as them if his salary could stretch that far. But even on a chief inspector's salary, Lomond balked at stumping up £400 for a waterproof jacket. For that kind of money, he expected the jacket to give your feet a wee rub when you were done. Fetch you a pie and a pint.

He was still wearing the same gear as when he had walked around Loch Garry three months earlier. It was looking a little worse for wear now. Determined to get himself back in shape, when he hadn't been hitting the bikes at his local gym or hillwalking, he'd been grinding himself into a fine powder with a work schedule that would have overwhelmed someone half his age.

He had climbed Beinn Dubh multiple times now, and was on track to take six minutes off his previous best. His lungs were clear. Legs feeling strong.

He hadn't eaten fried food for weeks now, cut out sugar almost entirely, and had even invested in an expensive blender to make smoothies – whizzing up oats, five kinds of frozen fruit, and a protein powder to help with muscle recovery after a long walk.

When he reached the peak, there was a couple Lomond's age sitting having a picnic, taking in the view.

Lomond gave a simple nod hello, then took out his

phone to check the half dozen messages he'd heard ping through when he was on the lower slopes.

On such a clear day, the view across the wooded islands that peppered the breadth of Loch Lomond was nothing short of breathtaking. The view pleased him, but the time on his watch was actually *satisfying*.

The picnicking couple were surprised to see Lomond turn and go back down almost immediately. They couldn't help but think it a waste to get all the way to the top and hardly spend any time there. But it wasn't about the view. Lomond just wanted to know he was getting faster. Which meant he was fitter. Improving.

He left the peak feeling good about himself, and didn't hear what the couple had said quietly to each other about him.

'That guy looks like he hasn't slept in a week.'

'I know. I could see the bags under his eyes from here.'

LOMOND WENT DOWN the same way he came up, avoiding the boggier sections the loop circuit many walkers favoured. If he had gone the boggier route, he never would have heard the scream.

It rose from the foot of the glen like something monstrous. So sharp, and it went on for ages. It wasn't someone merely testing out the echo around the hills. It was the sound of true horror.

But it didn't stop there.

Two further screams carved a path up through Glen Luss, reaching Lomond a few seconds after they had happened.

Lomond thought someone must have been chewed up by a jet ski. Except, there had been no jet skis on the water. The sound of those carried for miles, and Lomond had a full view of the loch.

By the time he got to the foot of the hill, he could hear police cars approaching from Dumbarton.

As he reached the wooden footbridge leading to Luss – crossing the busy, high-speed A82 – two patrol cars raced beneath him at breakneck speeds.

Looks like today's a work day, after all, he thought.

CHAPTER THREE

Both Pardeep and Jason had phones clamped between cheek and shoulder.

Jason nodded towards Detective Superintendent Linda Boyle's office. Detective Inspector Willie Sneddon was leaning over her desk, making *calm down* gestures with his hands.

Jason asked, 'Who do you think they're talking to up there?'

Pardeep didn't give the office so much as a glance. 'Weekly phone conference with the board of Melrose White.'

'They're still requesting that?' said Jason in surprise. 'The dude's a crook who's got millions in the bank and he's been missing for six weeks. He doesn't want to be found. How much longer are they going to make us chase our tails over this guy?'

'As long as Melrose White have close ties to the First

Minister, and the First Minister keeps pressing her thumb very firmly on top of the Chief Constable's head.'

Jason pointed to the whiteboard across the room where the other outstanding cases for Major Investigations were piling up. 'We've got honest-to-God crimes that need cleared. Instead, we're wasting our time on some runaway millionaire.'

'Aye, countdown until Melrose White realise there's actually a billion-quid black hole in their accounts, and George Melrose is the one who's run off with it.'

'You think that's what's going on?' asked Jason.

'Put it this way, he's either showing up in a penthouse apartment in some non-extradition-treaty country, or he's being found in a suitcase in his underpants with his throat slit. A guy with that much money, and that many enemies, can't stay hidden too much longer. In the meantime, the Melrose board are going to keep demanding answers from the Det Sup. Which means we're going to keep wasting our afternoons making–' Pardeep broke off, as the line on the other end of his call came back. After a brief pause, he sighed. 'Okay, thanks anyway.' He chucked his phone down and made an *I rest my case* gesture. 'More dead-end phone calls.'

Having endured ten minutes of silence at the other end of the phone, Jason checked the screen. 'Aw, you have *got* to be–' He looked at the ceiling in anguish.

'What is it?' Pardeep asked.

'They already hung up. God knows how long I've been sitting there on hold to fucking no one.'

Pardeep flashed his eyebrows up. He knew that if Jason was swearing, they really must have been on a hiding to nothing.

'Where the hell are Ross and Donna, anyway?' Jason complained. 'How come they don't have to sit here and put up with this nonsense?'

Pardeep replied, 'Ross has got another filler day with Organised Crime. As for Donna? Who knows.' He checked on both sides, then leaned a little towards Jason. He lowered his voice conspiratorially. 'I've been hearing things.'

Jason leaned in too. 'What sort of things?'

Pardeep shrugged. 'That Professional Standards have got something cooking with her.'

Jason's jaw just about hit the floor. Even tangential mentions of Professional Standards being involved with anyone on 'the shop floor' like Donna was a big deal.

'What like?' asked Jason.

Pardeep sat back in his seat again as he saw Willie descending the stairs from Linda's office. 'Tell you later.' He did an upward nod of his head at Willie. 'Anything we need to worry about, boss?'

Willie huffed as he unwrapped his Bacon Breakfast baguette from Greggs that he had been looking forward to for over half an hour. Now stone cold as he got stuck into it. 'Load of bollocks,' he said, shooting out a clump of ketchup-stained bread in the process. 'Play with fire, you get burned.'

Jason asked, 'What do you mean?'

Willie paused until he finished chewing a little more. 'He was called George "Butcher" Melrose for a reason, Jason. A man like that tends to make a few enemies along the way.'

'You still think he's dead?' asked Pardeep.

Willie nodded knowingly. 'Oh, aye. No doubt. Floating in the Forth near that third home of his, if you ask me.'

'Nah, the third home's on the hillside in Greenock.'

Willie spluttered a laugh. 'Imagine having the cash for a third home and thinking, aye, I'll build it in Greenock.'

'Imagine just living in Greenock.'

Jason asked, 'Do you know where Donna is, Willie?'

Unseen by Willie, Pardeep gave Jason a quick shake of his head, like he shouldn't have been asking about it.

Willie answered, 'None of your fucking business. Now get back on the fucking phone, the pair of youse.' He turned around when he heard the swing doors at the office entrance opening. 'Oh, aye. Look who it is. John McClane himself.'

Swaggering in through the office was Detective Sergeant Ross McNair, dressed down in black jeans, slim black t-shirt, and a trendy collarless black biker jacket. 'Just getting some *actual* police work done, boys. You know how it is.'

Pardeep and Jason had to bite their tongues. There was a relaxed atmosphere among colleagues in DCI Lomond's Major Investigations Team, which extended to a gentle ribbing from anyone *to* anyone on the team. Even to Lomond himself. But Ross had taken quite a pasting from Willie since being seconded to the Organised Crime unit, and a couple of detective constables didn't want to lay it on too thick to their superior.

Willie, however, had no such concerns. 'I looked out the window earlier expecting to see you in a dirty white vest with a bullet wound in your shoulder, running after a couple of white Range Rovers stuffed full of bags of smack.'

Ross took a seat at his desk, which was almost empty – he hadn't done a lick of work there for a week. 'Are you kidding? I've been sitting in briefings and reading paperwork for the last three days.' He did a quick three-sixty of the office. 'I know it's the gaffer's day off, but where's Donna?'

Willie grumbled, 'Christ, you too. Never mind where Donna is. You're back on John's clock now, and you're an hour and a half late from your morning briefing with the bloody London Road Cowboys. So pick up your phone and get to work.'

Just then, Linda appeared at the foot of the stairs while Ross had diverted everyone's attention.

Jason and Pardeep quickly lowered their phones.

Ross, feeling bolshy with his newfound position, asked, 'Do you know where Donna is?'

Linda retorted, 'I'd rather you paid a bit more attention to folk that are actually official missing persons, Detective Sergeant, seeing as you're sauntering in an hour and a half late. Don't you worry about Donna. I've just had word from John that he's found George Melrose.'

'John?' asked Willie.

'Where is he?' asked Pardeep.

'Who? John or George Melrose?' asked Linda.

'Either,' said Jason.

'They're both in Luss.'

'Alive or dead?' asked Ross.

'Dead,' said Linda. 'Melrose, obviously.'

'Where was he found?' asked Willie.

'Well...' She tried to figure out how best to describe it. 'Technically, he's been found in several places.'

CHAPTER FOUR

THE TINY CONSERVATION village of Luss was on the western bank of Loch Lomond. Home to only two hundred and fifty people, it saw over three quarters of a million visitors every year. A lot of them abandoned their cars along the main thoroughfare of Pier Road, robbing locals of parking spots outside their own houses. Recently, the local council had stepped in and built two car parks that bookended the village. Despite massive signs warning of the repercussions, dozens of tourists every day still illegally parked on Pier Road. Their brazen entitlement and disrespect towards the locals were rewarded with eye-watering parking fines. Waiting for the tourists to return to their vehicles and discover the tickets had become a minor sport for the locals. Always good for a laugh.

Pier Road itself had a magical, ethereal quality to it, with its traditional cottages covered in ivy and creepers, and front gardens bursting with hedges and flowers. Add in the old-fashioned streetlights, and the only evidence of the current century was the locals' cars – now parked in their rightful places.

But all of that quaintness and gentility seemed far away down at the beach. Normally, the imperious sight of Ben Lomond across the water dominated the view from the beach. But it was proving to be anything but a normal day in Luss.

A detective sergeant and detective inspector from Dumbarton stood next to Lomond, surveying the carnage that police divers from the Dive and Marine Unit had been fishing out of the loch for the past two hours.

Lomond turned around when he heard his MIT colleagues – everyone but Donna – being ushered under the blue and white police tape by a constable guarding entry to the crime scene.

Lomond gave an anxious cough, even though his lungs and throat were clear. He felt emasculated standing there in hiking shorts while everyone else was dressed in proper work attire.

Willie didn't waste any time sticking the boot in. 'What is this?' he called from a distance. 'Dress-down Wednesdays or something?'

Lomond nodded, ready to take the pelters he had been expecting for the past half hour. 'Yeah, yeah, laugh it up. I'm the one that's been standing around controlling your crime scene on my day off.'

'How come you're here, boss?' asked Pardeep.

'I was up Beinn Dubh,' Lomond pointed to the hill behind them overlooking the village, 'when I heard this almighty scream from the beach. By the time I got down, a couple of patrol cars were arriving, so I knew something was up.'

Ross's eyes were everywhere, taking in the grimness of the scene. A single lonely tarp was laid out on the sand, where the limbs found so far had been bagged. In the background, a police boat floated gently on the water, as a senior Marine officer leaned over the side, supervising and directing the ongoing dive.

Linda asked, 'Who found it? Or them?'

'Connor Blaine,' said Lomond. 'A lad on the water, with a group in the kayaks.' He tried not to laugh. 'He screamed so hard he passed out.' He pointed to Robbie and Hazel, giving statements on the pier to a pair of constables. 'Cheech and Chong over there had to fish him out of the water. They called an ambulance for the poor sod. He was hyperventilating.'

The others fought hard to contain their laughter, too.

The Dumbarton cops chuckled along nervously, trying to fit in with the hot-shot Glasgow unit.

It couldn't have been more wrong to laugh in such a moment, but it wasn't laughter about the actual crime. In a job as dark as working Major Investigations, tiny moments of levity were sometimes the only thing that made the job bearable.

It was in that moment of respite that Pardeep and Jason noticed how knackered Lomond looked. He might have lost a good stone and a half, but he wasn't looking well for it. His face had thinned down, but there was still a bit of loose stuff at the bottom of his cheeks. He had lost his natural stockiness, as if he'd been stuck in a machine from a sci-fi movie and set to shrink ten per cent. And as he hadn't been lifting any weights or doing anything to keep his strength up, his arms were now looking thin from the elbow up.

Linda led the way, introducing herself to the two Dumbarton detectives. 'Detective Superintendent Linda Boyle,' she said, shaking the men's hands so firmly they almost stumbled forward.

The detective inspector was well aware of who she was.

'Pleasure to meet you, ma'am,' he said.

The compliment didn't mean much to Linda. She was used to hearing it whenever she attended crime scenes. For a rural-ish DI, Linda Boyle was about as senior as he was going to encounter.

Linda turned her attention to Lomond. 'What have we got?'

'So far...' said Lomond. 'Both arms. One leg. One torso. And just the one head, you'll be pleased to hear.' He pulled back the tarp that was covering the gruesome find.

Drawing out the profanity, Linda said gravely, 'Fuu-uck me. And we're sure that it's...'

Lomond pushed his lips out as he nodded. 'It's him, all right.' He crouched down to indicate one of the evidence bags containing a hand. 'That's Melrose's wedding ring. And before you point out that someone might have just put Melrose's ring on someone else's hand...' He reached over to another bag, this one containing an arm but no hand. 'Those are the tattoos of the dates Melrose's kids were born.'

Linda puffed. 'George "Butcher" Melrose gets butchered. The newspaper editors will have a field day writing headlines on this one.'

'Plus, there's this...' Lomond moved one of the bags that was covering another, revealing a decapitated head that was light grey with streaks of blue. 'He's been in the water a while, and we'll get DNA to confirm of course, but that is definitely George Melrose.'

Linda crouched down next to him to get a closer look at the face. 'Shite.' She squinted, trying to see something on the forehead through the condensation inside the bag. 'What is that?'

'Aye. That's something else.'

She straightened out the bag. 'Does that say what I think it says?'

'Aye. I had a look before it was bagged.'

'Well, then this is even worse than we thought.'

CHAPTER FIVE

FEELING like he was missing something, Jason asked, 'Why is this bad? We've just cleared a high-profile missing person case.'

Pardeep replied, 'And in the process, upgraded it to a high-profile murder case.'

'Isn't that good?'

Pardeep smiled at Jason's naivety, deferring to someone more experienced to explain.

Lomond said, 'The point, Jason, is that a case like this is all downside. Solve it, and it's expected. Drag your feet, and the whole world will have an opinion. Especially the orks in Mordor, and *especially* the top brass in Disney World.'

To the uninitiated, Lomond might have sounded like he had just suffered a brain injury. But to those within his Major Investigations Team, it was a quick shorthand of nicknames that had become engrained in the patter of the officers.

Both nicknames had come from Lomond.

Mordor was Police Scotland's administrative headquarters in Dalmarnock, where Lomond's nemesis Chief Superintendent Alasdair Reekie kept watch on the Greater Glasgow area like the evil Lord Sauron in *Lord of the Rings.*

Lomond had dubbed Police Scotland's corporate headquarters as "Disney World". Not that the converted Tulliallan Castle, where the Executive Team were based, bore any resemblance to the sunshine and glamour of Disney's Cinderella Castle. But to listen to the fantastical theories and flowery buzzwords and politics that emanated from Tulliallan's gloomy, dark stone walls, it all sounded like nothing more than fanciful fairy tales to old-school officers like Lomond, Willie, and Linda.

The Dumbarton DI cleared his throat nervously, like he'd been standing there waiting, building up to something. 'Now that you're on the subject, ma'am,' he said to Linda, 'I wanted to ask, like, is there any chance that we might,' he gestured to his young DS, 'you know, maybe take on...'

Linda smiled. The poor sod didn't even have the guts to finish his question. 'Detective Inspector...' She trailed off, waiting to hear his name again.

'Minto,' he replied.

She leaned forward with a pained expression. 'I'm sorry, I'm not getting it.'

The poor bastard actually had to resort to spelling his name.

Now that she had his name, Linda pointed to the collection of bagged body parts in front of them. 'Detective Inspector Minto. You're standing in front of the remains of one of the country's most famous, and vilified bankers, possibly ever. This murder's going to be covered on multiple continents. When I get back to Glasgow, I fully expect to have voicemails waiting for me from – among others – Interpol, Europol, the FBI, and the Metropolitan Police Commissioner. Are you asking me if I should direct their enquiries...to the Dumbarton police switchboard?'

The DI stammered for a bit before relenting. 'No...I suppose not.'

'Great. Then do me a favour. Grab the three constables that are standing about with their thumbs up their arses over there, and get them to taser the piss out of whoever's flying that drone up there. This is a crime scene, not a fucking Instagram reel opportunity.'

As the two Dumbarton cops left with their tails between their legs, Lomond turned to his team.

Suddenly realising who was missing, he asked, 'Where's Donna?'

'Christ,' Willie said, 'you as well? When did she become so popular around here?'

'Weren't we expecting her out by now?'

Willie looked around cagily. 'She's still in that thing.'

Lomond checked his watch. 'Still? That's not good.'

He took a deep breath, then reset. He ushered Ross, Pardeep and Jason closer. 'All right, guys. You'd better see this.'

It wasn't every day that the officers in MIT had to inspect a decapitated head, but today was that day. There was no time for queasiness.

'Jesus,' said Ross, forcing himself to not look away.

Jason seemed more intrigued than disgusted.

Pardeep crouched down. 'Does that say...'

'Yep,' said Lomond. '"*PAID*".'

'What does that mean?'

'Organised crime?' Jason offered, coming down for a look.

Ross remained standing. 'Debt was an avenue we were investigating at one time.'

'And we found no evidence of it,' Linda replied.

Lomond said, 'It's going to take days for the divers to do their thing. We might not even recover the remaining limb. By my reckoning, they've been in the water about a week, give or take. The way the limbs have risen to the surface suggests they were bagged together, almost certainly dropped in the water near where they came up. Maybe they were weighed down by something, but someone was out on the water about a week ago with those limbs.' Lomond pointed to the nearby houses on Pier Road. 'That means someone around here could have seen something. A boat out at night isn't unheard of. But we should concentrate on whatever vehicle was used to aid this little operation.'

Ross suggested, 'We could check ANPR and road network cameras in the area. There can't be many cars towing boats around at night.'

Lomond appeared to think better of this. 'Thing is,' he shook his head, 'towing a boat around at night attracts attention. Would they risk parking near here, offloading what must have been a very large and very heavy suitcase, and risk being spotted? Not exactly a lot going on around here at night. Someone would remember that.'

'What you thinking?' asked Linda.

Lomond put his hand out to Willie. 'Bit of paper and a pen, please.'

Willie fished them out.

Lomond scribbled something down quickly, but kept it concealed from the others. 'Ross? What would you do?'

Ross replied, 'The killer might have dumped them here, but that doesn't mean he parked near here. It's easy to row out or take a boat from one side of the loch to the other. They might have come from as far as Balloch.'

'Possible,' said Lomond. 'But there's a whole team of constables that are waiting for your instructions. What are you going to tell them?'

Feeling under the cosh, Ross shook his head slowly, trying to think of something. 'Check CCTV at the local marinas?'

Lomond showed them all the bit of paper.

On it, he had written, "*CHECK MARINAS FOR THEFT.*"

'Close,' Lomond said. 'If towing a boat around draws

unwanted attention, the killer might have skipped straight to stealing one instead.'

Jason said, 'But there's not exactly a lot of places to just plank a boat around here. Leaving it somewhere when local police could have been looking for it is risky too.'

'Except maybe he knows that half the boats around here are barely used all year. You just pick a boat that looks ancient. There's plenty of them in Balloch. Pinch one, take it to another marina for a few days. Simple.'

Pardeep added, 'So we check with Dumbarton police for any reports of stolen boats in the past week.'

'If the killer also took the chance of stealing the boat whilst in possession of a dismembered body. Getting caught pinching a boat is one thing. But murder's a whole other kettle of beans.'

Pardeep squinted. 'Don't you mean fish?'

'No, I don't mean fish. I mean *beans*. It's an ironic mixing of idioms.'

Pardeep grumbled, 'It's just a bit confusing...'

Lomond snapped at him, 'Can we get back to this?'

Ross was only too happy to move on. 'So we look for any boats stolen about two weeks ago. We can't check marinas until the morning, though.'

Lomond said, 'That's why tonight we're going to make a start on identifying where Melrose was actually murdered. That's where we stand the best chance of finding forensic evidence of who the killer is. For that, we'll have to go back to ground zero. Melrose's main place over the road at Lochgoilhead.'

Ross said, 'We combed through there last week, boss.'

Lomond picked up an evidence bag containing Melrose's right hand. He showed a set of keys hanging on a finger through a keyring. 'The killer had Melrose's house keys. If he's been there, we need to have another look. Because Melrose and the killer were there. And judging by the colour of the limbs we've got, I don't think it was long ago.' He asked Ross, 'Did you bring that bag with my shirt and stuff in it from my office? I look like a total idiot.' He gestured witheringly at his hillwalking clothes.

'Yep, it's in the boot,' Ross replied. 'Have you got a sec, boss?'

Lomond turned them away from the others. 'What is it? We've got a full day here.'

'It's just...my paperwork. You still haven't signed it.'

'Paperwork?'

'The paperwork I've been asking you about for the last three weeks.'

Lomond nodded as the penny dropped. 'Oh yeah, soon.' He turned to go back to the others, but Ross laid a hand on his shoulder.

'Sorry, sir, but DCI Hunt has opened up a spot for me.'

Lomond glanced at Ross's hand.

Ross removed his hand from Lomond's shoulder. 'I need this signed pronto for my secondment to get through HR in time, or Hunt's going to give my spot to someone else.'

'I don't know if you've noticed, Ross, but we've got multiple body parts of a high-profile missing person in this loch. I get that you're moving on to bigger and brighter things and that's great, but now isn't the time for paperwork.'

'It's just...'

'Why do you even want to be on Hunt's taskforce? Do you know how many emails a day I get from folk begging to be in Major Investigations? This is the Champions League, man. You want to walk away from that for the Organised Crime Taskforce? You want to swan around with nutcases like DI Ally Corrigan? Or do you want to get one step closer to Tulliallan? Is that it? Rub noses with the Executive Team? They bloody love a good taskforce, don't they? Get your face in the papers, looking like a hard man?'

By now, everyone else was listening. It was impossible not to hear every word, but no one dared look at DCI Lomond.

Ross replied, 'You really think those are the only reasons I'd want to leave MIT? How about to get some actual senior investigating officer experience? Some leadership.'

'You get leadership roles here,' Lomond grumbled.

'Oh, yeah. I really lead the charge to Greggs at lunchtime. It's exactly like Gordon says.'

Lomond made an ironic expression of being

THE BLOODY, BLOODY BANKS   31

impressed. 'Gordon, is it? First-name terms already? And what does Gordon say?'

'He says you don't know how to nurture talent. Because you think you're the only one who has any. In the first Sandman case, you just hired and fired.'

Lomond was temporarily stopped in his tracks. No one had ever pointed it out to him before, but he had to admit that DCI Hunt had a point.

Lomond tried a more measured tone to bring the temperature down a bit. 'Let me try putting this in sporting terms you might understand, Ross. When Roger Federer started out, everyone said he was the most talented nineteen-year-old in the world. But he struggled to win much his first few years. They said he had all the shots but didn't know when to play them.' Lomond pointed both forefingers at Ross. 'You've *got* all the shots, Ross. I'm just trying to show you when to play them. DCI Hunt? All he's going to do is show you a bunch of between-the-legs show-off shots that you're never going to need on the court.' He paused. 'Are you still following the whole tennis analogy?'

'I get it,' Ross said.

Trying to wrap the conversation up, Lomond said, 'I'm about to have the full weight of the Executive Team shining a spotlight on every move I make for the next forty-eight hours. Half the world's media is going to be descending on this village. Tomorrow morning, there's going to be a half dozen "Limbs in the loch" stories on the front pages, and we need to somehow control twenty-two miles of water with about a million entry points. Yes, your secondment paperwork is urgent. This is *more* urgent.'

Turning to the others, Lomond called to them, 'Willie and Pardeep! You're with Ross at Melrose's house. Jason, stay here and get this Dumbarton lot organised. I want Pier Street closed off all the way down to the Loch Lomond Arms, and get this beach secured. I want a tape line at both ends all the way down to the Lodge. And the moment you hear about anything else coming out of that water, you call me and Willie.'

Linda nudged Lomond aside. 'What was all that about with Ross?'

'Nothing. The usual. His secondment again. Maybe I should just take him off this thing once he gets back to Helen Street. His mind's clearly elsewhere already.'

Realising that Lomond was heading off in the opposite direction, Linda asked, 'What about you?'

'I'm going to Mordor,' Lomond replied, stalking off through the sand. 'As long as I'm losing a detective sergeant to Organised Crime, I need to know whether I should start looking for another detective constable as well.'

CHAPTER SIX

Donna's union rep, PC Nigel Skelton, shuffled his papers to straighten them. Before the murmuring among the panel died down, he reminded her, 'Stick to the facts. This is just a preliminary hearing. Try to leave emotion out of it.'

Donna scowled. 'What, because I'm a female officer I can't leave my emotions out of it?'

Nigel sucked in air. 'My background report did throw up that you have *something* of a reputation, Donna.'

She replied calmly. 'Just because I have strong opinions doesn't mean that I can't control my emotions. When male officers rant and rave, folk say that they're impassioned. When female officers do it, we're called hysterical.'

Nigel let it go, seeing that the panel chair was looking around the room for quiet.

Nigel and Donna sat together on one side of a long conference table, with the five members of the Professional Standards panel on the other. The conference room had windows looking out over a walkway next to the River Clyde, the bank strewn with rubbish and empty cider bottles. A glass wall separated the room from the long corridor of offices that lined the hallway outside, but the blinds had been shut for privacy.

A man sat alone in a solitary chair, clad in a navy suit, with cropped grey hair and exuding an air of self-assurance. The attractive traits from his younger days – the strong, square jawline, and balanced features – still defined his mature appearance. He gazed out the window without making eye contact with anyone around.

The panel chair lifted a hand and the room fell quiet. A name card on the table identified her as "Karen Gilchrist".

After running through the tedious requirements of such a hearing – who everyone was, how the hearing was going to work, who was taking notes, and what would be available to Donna afterwards, which Nigel had already explained to Donna in their prep meeting – Karen honed in her laser-like eyes on Donna.

'DC Higgins,' said Karen. 'As I'm sure your rep has briefed you, we are here today to discuss the background leading up to a raid carried out by DCI John Lomond's Major Investigations Team in July of last year at a property belonging to a Peter Lee. This was part of the investigation into the abduction of Jack Ferguson, which we now know to be linked to the so-called Sandman murders.' Karen looked to her left, where her deputy had notes prepared to summarise the background.

The deputy looked and sounded disinterested. His mind already wandering to when he might be able to leave for the day. 'DC Higgins,' he began, 'this Professional Standards panel has convened to investigate the circumstances surrounding the raid on Peter Lee's property, and how said address was acquired. As you know, this hearing is to lay out the scope of the Professional Standards investigation that we will be undertaking, as well as establishing if there is indeed a case to answer. And the first questions we will be examining are as follows. Were any improper or illegal procedures used to acquire Peter Lee's address in the Jack Ferguson abduction investigation? And was Peter Lee's Multi-Agency Public Protection Arrangements file – or MAPPA file – illegally unsealed, and its contents used in the Jack Ferguson invest–'

Nigel interrupted, 'Sorry, Mr Deputy Chair. I have to interject. DC Higgins and I had not been informed of this new line of enquiry.'

The deputy chair turned his palms upwards. 'Consider yourselves informed. This is what preliminary hearings are *for* Mr Skelton. Or should we have had a *preliminary*-preliminary hearing?'

Skelton's silence provided the answer.

'I thought not,' he said. 'As I was saying, if indeed a

MAPPA file has been unsealed without the proper clearances, this would be considered a major breach of professional standards and procedures.' He shuffled to a new piece of paper. 'Now to the second item on the agenda: the matter of Barry Higgins. Three months ago, as part of DCI Lomond's Major Investigations Team and the Specialist Crime Division's Organised Crime unit's joint investigation into money laundering – the so-called G1 Gelato money laundering case – a mobile phone came into the possession of DC Higgins after a covert sting operation on an ice cream shop on Great Western Road. The subsequent follow-up report from SCD discloses that DC Higgins had visited the Organised Crime unit at London Road station, and confessed that she knew the exact address belonging to a prominent, otherwise anonymous, contact found on that phone. Barry Higgins – who is DC Higgins' estranged father.' He looked at Donna. 'Would you accept that terminology, DC Higgins?'

Donna replied, 'I could probably use a few different terms myself, but yes. Estranged would be accurate.'

'The SCD report goes on to conclude that the reason DC Higgins knew the address of the anonymous phone contact was that she had spoken to Barry Higgins during the Jack Ferguson investigation. Mr Higgins claimed to know the name of a former prisoner at Barlinnie who could be germane to the search for Jack Ferguson. This former prisoner was Peter Lee. During the Jack Ferguson investigation, DC Higgins claimed that she had acquired

Peter Lee's address when her Barlinnie source, who had given her Peter Lee's name, suddenly remembered after the fact that he had Peter Lee's address written down, and texted it to her later. This text message has not been found, and nor has the phone on which it was received. Which DC Higgins has claimed was due to water damage to said phone. She also claimed not to know the name of the source who gave her Peter Lee's name and address. Are these claims true? Or did DC Higgins simply obtain all that information by opening Mr Lee's sealed MAPPA file? We already have an admission on record to Specialist Crime that DC Higgins knew the address of the anonymous phone contact, as that same contact was the person who gave her Mr Lee's name, which led her to Mr Lee's MAPPA file. Were other more senior officers involved in this? Was there a cover-up? Does there continue to be a cover-up, in light of the discovering that Peter Lee's MAPPA file is now missing, and is being treated as stolen...'

Donna tried hard not to let her jaw hit the floor. It was the first she was hearing of it.

The deputy chair concluded, 'With DC Higgins' cooperation, we hope to find answers to all of these questions. And based on our investigation, make recommendations for disciplinary and, if this panel deems it appropriate, criminal charges.'

Donna had been feeling all right until the word 'criminal' had been uttered.

The deputy chair gestured to the man sitting on his

own off to one side. 'DCI Hunt. If you'd like to join us, please.'

DCI Hunt sat at the far end of the conference table, his face a picture of determination and composure.

Donna gulped hard. Depending on what Hunt had to say, she might be on the road to finding out how well police officers are treated in jail.

CHAPTER SEVEN

KAREN, the panel chair, said, 'DCI Hunt, can you briefly describe DC Higgins' involvement in your unit's money laundering investigation?'

Hunt was unflappable. As the head of the revered Organised Crime Taskforce, he regularly shared a conference table with the Chief Constable and the Executive Team at Tulliallan. Not to mention the Justice Secretary. A bunch of glorified accountants and paper pushers from Professional Standards could never rattle someone like DCI Gordon Hunt.

Hunt said, 'Three months ago, Detective Constable Higgins came to my unit at London Road station, and informed my sergeant that she knew the identity of an anonymous contact found on a phone recovered from suspects in our money laundering case. A phone recovered by DC Higgins herself, in a frankly ballsy and ingenious move...'

Donna felt herself relax a little. It seemed like DCI Hunt had her back.

Karen tilted her head in a passive aggressive motion of dissatisfaction. 'DCI Hunt, if you could–'

No stranger to Professional Standards, Hunt was having none of it. He raised her hand to Karen. 'Excuse me, but my appearance here today was based on the assumption that I would be allowed to finish my sentences.'

Donna shot Nigel a glance of *holy shit, he just tore her a new one.*

Karen bristled, but said nothing.

Hunt went on, 'I'm not in a position to speak to any improper procedures that may or may not have been used in the Jack Ferguson investigation. But the Organised Crime Taskforce had no way of identifying the exact location of the contact found on the phone that Donna acquired. Without her assistance, Barry Higgins wouldn't be in custody awaiting trial, and drugs with a street value in excess of fifty thousand pounds wouldn't have been impounded. I know that hard facts like that might be an inconvenience to a panel with no experience of boots-on-the-ground policing, but in my opinion–'

Karen shook her head. 'Excuse me, DCI Hunt. The panel has made significant allowances for this, frankly, unorthodox intervention from yourself on DC Higgins' behalf. This hearing is simply not the time or place for opinions...'

While Karen kept talking, Hunt spoke right over her, stabbing his finger on the table for emphasis.

The pair raised their voices, vying for supremacy.

Hunt won out.

'In my *opinion*,' he said firmly, 'Detective Constable Donna Higgins is exactly the sort of officer Police Scotland needs on the street. All of the work she carried out during our joint investigation is bordering on commendable, and I would be proud to have her on my team anytime. I'm already taking on her colleague, DS Ross McNair, who has similarly sung DC Higgins' praises to me.'

Karen nodded with the bare minimum of patience. 'Thank you, DCI Hunt. Your *opinions* have been noted.'

On his way out the door, Donna made a point of mouthing 'thank you' to Hunt.

He nodded back.

When Donna was finally allowed to leave, she took a half step backwards when she found DCI Lomond waiting for her – pacing around like an expectant father at a maternity ward. Now dressed in proper work attire.

Noticing Lomond, Hunt lifted a hand slightly to say hello.

'Gordon,' Lomond said, then turned his attention to Donna. 'Well?' he said.

She quickly ushered him away towards the stairs. 'What are you doing here?'

'Protecting my investment,' he replied. 'Nice of DCI Hunt to put a word in.'

'Aye, he's been good,' said Donna.

'It's a good sign he's got your back. What are they saying on the panel?'

Donna found them a quiet corner away from prying eyes. 'It's not looking great. They made it pretty clear it was just the start of disciplinary hearings. And from the evidence they have, there's a case to answer.'

Lomond turned and sighed. 'Christ, Donna...'

'I don't know why you're upset. It's my head on the chopping block.'

'I'm annoyed because you should have come to me first on this, not Gordon Hunt. He's proper police is Gordon, if a bit of a boy scout. But you should have come to me as soon as you realised who that contact was on the burner phone. I could have fixed it. Hunt doesn't know how to get his hands dirty. Walks around with a bottle of fucking anti-bac gel, that guy. He might be putting the face-time in here, Donna, but he won't be able to unfuck this for you the way I could have.'

He was swearing more than usual. A bad sign, thought Donna. That meant he was mad.

'I didn't want to get you involved. They're all over this Peter Lee thing.'

'Don't worry about that.'

'They know everything.'

'They do not know everything, Donna, because the only people in that corridor with the MAPPA files that day were you and I.'

Donna paused. 'Can I ask you a serious question?'

Lomond waited.

She lowered her voice further. 'Did you destroy that MAPPA file?'

Lomond looked away, saying nothing.

'They just told me that it's disappeared,' she said. 'Treated as stolen.'

'Yeah, well,' he sniffed. 'Hard to prove that you unsealed that file, then.'

'You think it's *better* that it looks like I stole it?'

'It doesn't look like that, because you never stole it. It doesn't matter what they suspect, Donna. It's what they can prove. You need to trust that I know how these things work. I told you at the time that I would handle it and I did.'

'Have you thought about what could happen when this is over? Once some lawyer gets hold of this, it could throw out Sharon Belmont's conviction for the Sandman murders.'

Lomond put out a calming hand. 'That's not going to happen. I was the one who opened that MAPPA file, and they've got no way of proving their assertion that it was you.'

'I won't let you take the fall for this, sir.'

He snorted. 'So now we're *both* going down over this trying to save each other? There won't be any fall, Donna.'

'Someone at Professional Standards knew to go looking for that file. What if they have evidence–'

'They can't.'

'But what if they *do*? If they find out you stole that file and had it destroyed, they'll can you. For good. I don't know if I can protect you from what happens next. And that scares the shit out of me. When you got this MIT gig again, sir, you came back to Paisley to bring me with you. Without you, I'd still be chasing shoplifters around Braehead. I won't let you risk your career. I was the one who lied about how I found Peter Lee's address. It's on me.'

Lomond tried, but he couldn't hide the worry in his eyes. 'For now, I need you to park whatever you've got going on in your head. You know that switch I tell you and Jason to flick when we walk out of Helen Street each night? When we become who we really are, not just polis. I need you to do that now, because we've got a live one.'

Ever a junkie for action, Donna's eyes found their sparkle again. 'Oh yeah?'

'We found George Melrose in Loch Lomond. Pieces of him, anyway. I need you, Donna. Willie and Ross have found some things at Melrose's house. This is bigger than anything we've seen for a long time.'

Donna looked back towards the conference room as the Professional Standards panel slowly filed out. 'Then let's get to work.'

CHAPTER EIGHT

GEORGE MELROSE's house took up a prime secluded spot on a hillside in Lochgoilhead at the mouth of the loch, with stunning views all across the ten-acre grounds.

Willie and Ross had made multiple trips out there during the missing person investigation, but it was Pardeep's first time, having been sent to other pertinent locations around Glasgow. As the three men approached the grand nineteenth-century house, puttering along the thick-gravel driveway in a fleet Ford Focus, Pardeep leaned forward from the back seat for a better look.

'So this is the sort of place you live when you've got a few hundred million,' he cooed.

Willie demurred. 'It's all right. A bit ostentatious for my liking.'

Ross's eyes were everywhere, but he was less interested in the architecture and luxury that was on display.

'No obvious signs of disturbance so far. Looks pretty much as we found it last time.'

It had been three weeks since Willie and Ross had last been there to talk to Melrose's neighbours for any updates of visitors, or anything suspicious. The house grounds had been designed to grant total privacy. The winding, rhododendron-lined driveway blocked any view of the house from the main road.

As expected, Willie and Ross had found nothing.

Now, the men weren't sure what they were about to find inside.

The three got out of the car and began a careful inspection of the grounds, starting with a recce around the perimeter of the house itself. On previous visits, arrangements had been made via Melrose's personal secretary to gain access to the interior of the house. But they were in London on business. So an inspection from the outside would have to suffice.

Willie pointed to the gravel path that led around the back of the house. 'We'll start with the outside of the house, then work out from there. And mind your feet, boys. We need to assume that anything we find here could be a suspect's.'

While Willie went ahead himself, heavy footsteps scuffing on the gravel, Ross hurried a few steps to catch up with him.

Ross checked that Pardeep wasn't close enough to overhear. 'The gaffer was a bit on edge back in Luss, don't you think?'

'If you're looking to build a posse against John, you're asking the wrong cowboy,' Willie replied. 'But aye,' he conceded. 'A little temperamental, maybe.'

'He's getting out of control, Willie. He's working himself to death.'

'You've got no idea the sort of pressure he's been under to close this Melrose case. Do you think that's going to get easier or harder now that we've found him chopped up in Loch Lomond? *And* he's about to be down a DS?'

'Can't you have a word with him?'

Willie laughed.

'I'm worried about him,' Ross said. 'He's lost all this weight. He looks like shite warmed up...'

Trying to focus on the task at hand, Willie said, 'You're not wrong, Ross. But he's John Lomond. He can look after himself.' He pointed to an outhouse where gardening equipment was locked up. 'Why don't you check over there? I'll keep going round here.'

Taking the hint to drop it, Ross did as he was told.

From their place in the garden, the view across Loch Goil was incredible. Light drizzle fell as sunlight broke through heavy clouds above. It was one of those magical west coast days that squeezed in three different seasons, the light changing every few minutes.

Standing there, surrounded by beautifully mani-cured gardens and one of Scotland's most stunning lochs, it was easy to get swept up in the beauty of the surroundings.

But all of that was about to change in a hurry.

Pardeep followed Ross over, scouting around carefully.

'What sort of things would you look for in a search like this?' Pardeep asked.

Looking over the outhouse, Ross replied, 'Firstly, any broken windows or any obvious damage to the property. Signs of access from atypical directions. Maybe muddy footprints on the decking over there would tell me someone's come up from the beach and then over the boggy bit down at the perimeter fence. See if anyone's come through the gardens, flowers broken, soil disturbed, that kind of thing. You'd know it if you saw it, Pardeep.'

Willie looked back, glad to hear not only Pardeep trying to learn a thing or two, but Ross encouraging it. A lot of sergeants and inspectors didn't put in much effort to help the constables on their team. Not so on Lomond's MIT. There was no mentality of pulling up the ladders behind you. As Lomond was always emphasising, crimes were solved in collaboration, not because of one person's brain wave.

Willie looked through each of the tall windows in turn, stopping at the rear of the building. 'Eh, guys...' He waved to them to catch up, but kept staring through the window.

Ross and Pardeep jogged forward, anxious about Willie's demeanour. It wasn't fright. It was more like awe.

Still to take his eyes from the window, Willie asked, 'Either of you got a phone signal?'

'Mine's fine,' said Ross, eager to get a look at whatever Willie was seeing.

'We might need it.'

Ross was next to see it. 'Oh, shit.'

Pardeep, who had been languishing behind inspecting some footprints in a flower bed, hurried to get there.

Ross was staring just like Willie. 'Have you ever seen anything like this?'

Willie puffed. 'Never.'

Pardeep skidded slightly in the gravel as he came to a halt. The moment he laid eyes on the living room wall, he said, 'Whoa...'

Ross asked Willie, 'Do you think we can get through the conservatory?'

'Aye,' he replied.

He and Ross put on latex gloves, prompting Pardeep to quickly follow suit.

When Willie got to the conservatory door backing onto the main garden, he told the others, 'Best cover your ears.'

Pardeep asked Ross, 'What does he mean?'

Without any preamble, Willie elbowed through a pane of glass in the conservatory door, setting off an alarm that sounded like an air raid siren.

Pardeep clutched at his ears, then told Ross, 'Never mind.'

The three men put on their latex shoe covers before entering.

Willie and Ross walked carefully through the shattered glass on the tiled floor, considering each step carefully. They knew now that they weren't just dealing with a property linked to a murder victim. It was a crime scene.

The painful screech of the alarm soon faded as the three men were captivated by the sight that had stopped Willie in his tracks outside.

Above the fireplace on the living room wall, a message had been scrawled in thick red letters. Which, now that they were right in front of it, was undeniably blood.

Willie pointed at the writing, that looked like it had been applied to the wall with the palm of a hand. 'We're going to need blood work done. We shouldn't assume it's Melrose's.'

'And find out whose hand painted it,' Ross added.

In the hope of impressing with a contrarian theory, Pardeep offered, 'Maybe it was Melrose's.'

Willie said, 'I highly doubt that.'

Looking around the carpet, Ross shook his head. 'He wasn't killed in here, anyway.'

The carpet was cream, and in immaculate condition. But not so immaculate that Ross considered whether it may even be new and hiding a multitude of sins underneath.

The three men stood in a row in front of the fireplace. In equal parts dazzled. Awestruck. And baffled.

The message read: *"THE TAXMAN 1, POLICE SCOTLAND 0"*

'What the fuck *is* this?' asked Ross in wonder.

Willie took out his phone to call Lomond. 'By the looks of it, it's just the start.'

CHAPTER NINE

LOMOND AND WILLIE flashed their ID cards on the RFID reader at the entrance to the Major Investigations Team office on the second floor. Inside, they were were greeted with the intense murmuring of a full-house awaiting a major briefing. It was a twenty-strong team altogether, with five detective sergeants, and a ton of ambitious – and very capable – detective constables who had either stayed late, or come in very early.

As Lomond and Willie made their way through the bullpen of office chairs and desks, Lomond remarked, 'You'd think something big was going on...'

Willie replied, 'When you tell them you're doing the eight o'clock morning briefing the night before at quarter past seven, you tend to get a good response.'

The pair separated near the front of the room. Willie to his desk, Lomond taking up his usual spot in front of the whiteboard.

Lomond noticed a vacant desk at the front where Jason should have been sitting. Instead, only Pardeep, Ross, and Donna were in attendance at their desks.

Behind them was the unofficial back-up team that was always there but often working different cases to Lomond. It was only for something truly major and newsworthy that the entire floor was roped in together.

Lomond caught Willie's eye, then motioned to the empty desks along with a *where's Jason?* gesture.

Willie shrugged that he didn't know.

Lomond shook his head in annoyance. There were plenty of things that drove him mad, but not being on time was right up there.

He took a long look at the whiteboard, arms folded.

The room fell silent.

Behind him was written in large black marker "George 'Butcher' Melrose. Former CEO of Melrose White Investment Securities". Under that, all the essentials on the missing person case.

Lomond told the room, 'Look, you all know I don't do bullshit. I don't want to hear it, and I don't care to speak it. We all know that George Melrose wasn't the most popular guy in the world. There will be certain commentators in the media tomorrow – and maybe at this press conference I'm about to do – that will tell us that Melrose must have made a lot of powerful enemies. But we're not here to judge. In this case or any other. We're here to secure justice for whoever killed him. And stop them before they do it again.

Because so far, as the killer tells us, we are one nil down.'

He pointed to the assembled newspaper headlines about Melrose, from before and after he went missing. Among them was:

"MELROSE WHITE ON THE BRINK AFTER MORTGAGE MARKET TANKS"

"MELROSE WHITE BAILED OUT BY TAXPAYER"

"FURY AS BOSS OF FAILING BANK NETS £12.4 MILLION BONUS"

"£217 MILLION MISSING FROM MELROSE WHITE SAYS REGULATOR"

"GEORGE MELROSE 'MISSING' SAY POLICE"

"FRIENDS 'CONCERNED' FOR GEORGE MELROSE'S WELFARE"

"NO LEADS IN MELROSE CASE SAYS SENIOR GLASGOW COP"

'For those of you who weren't on my task squad, let me catch you up on our missing person case. George Melrose. Nickname of Butcher. So called for the way his company chopped up competitors in hostile takeovers. They would slash the work force, and sell off chunks of the company for huge profits. When Melrose absconded as chairman of his company with about two hundred million quid of taxpayer's cash, it soon turned into a missing person case. We established from everyone that knew him or did business with him, that this was not a guy short on enemies. The list of people with compelling motive to wish harm on Melrose consisted of most of his closest associates, and the complete contents of the phone book. And before any of the bloody millennials in the room start on me again that there isn't a phone book anymore, you'll just have to trust me that there was a lot of names in it. In short? George Melrose: unpopular guy. That was all six weeks ago. Between these four walls, and as the papers have been only too happy to point out, we've been chasing our tails since then. Until earlier today.'

Lomond wheeled the board around to show the other side, where he had organised pertinent points for the briefing. He pointed at each of them in turn, starting with a photo of the message on Melrose's living room wall.

'Someone's keeping score,' said Lomond. 'The Taxman, apparently. Thoughts?'

Willie said, 'It's a shite name for a start.'

Ross chimed in. 'You can't self-apply a name like that. That's cheating. At least let the papers come up with it first.'

On the verge of smiling, Lomond said, 'I don't disagree. Get into all of your prison sources. Check if anyone knows this Taxman name, or has heard of it. Is it the nickname of some kind of enforcer or hitman? I also want to know where George Melrose has been for the last six weeks. Is his disappearance connected?'

A voice at the back suggested, 'Maybe it's a coincidence.'

Lomond glanced over to Linda, who was standing near the foot of the stairs leading to her office. 'You should all know by now, coincidences drive me crazy. I don't believe in them. Not in this game. The limbs that I've seen are nothing close to six weeks old. Moira McTaggart over at Gartcosh agrees. She doesn't think the body parts have been in the water more than seven days. Where was Melrose before that? It seemed to us, when he was a missing person, that he had simply vanished off the face of the earth. But the killer went to his house in Lochgoilhead. Willie?'

Willie joined Lomond at the board, pointing out the various photos they had taken at the scene around multiple rooms in the property. 'We think it's unlikely that Melrose has been back to this house in the last five weeks. Out of ten other houses around the world, this was where he spent the most time. Security cameras were unhooked, hard drives stolen, so we've got nothing to look at. As you can see from these rooms, including all the bathrooms, there's no evidence that Melrose was murdered in this house or anywhere else on the property.'

Ross, arms folded, spoke up. 'Logically, the killer would have had to dismember the body – and there's really nowhere in the house to do that – then drive forty-odd minutes to Loch Lomond to dump the body.'

Donna, slumped slightly in her chair, asked, 'If Melrose was killed in the house, why not just dump the body in Loch Goil? Is there significance to Loch

Lomond? And if he wasn't killed in the house, why did the killer write the message there?'

Lomond watched carefully as a uniformed figure emerged from the shadows at the edge of the bullpen. It was Chief Superintendent Alasdair Reekie.

'The answer,' Lomond said, 'is noise.'

'Noise?' said Donna.

'Everyone knows Loch Lomond. It makes a lot more noise if Melrose is found there. Same with the message on the wall. The probably self-applied moniker. This killer's got big ideas, and they want to be heard. Wants us to know they're starting something. That's why I don't want a single word about this "Taxman" uttered. They're hunting for headlines. Notoriety. We're not going to give them the oxygen they want.' Lomond made a clenched fist. 'We need to be tighter than a nun's arsehole on this one. Got it?'

CSU Reekie shook his head like a parent to a delinquent teen.

Relishing the amused groans around the room, Lomond looked innocently towards Reekie. 'You can't say anything these days, can you, sir?'

Linda stepped forward hastily, eager to wrap things up. 'Thanks, John. Fortunately HR have gone home for the day, so I think that's enough to get started with.'

Lomond concluded by saying, 'DS Whyte, DS Johnstone, you're with DI Dagley as usual, who has your marching orders.' He raised both hands above his head before the hubbub got too loud. 'Folks, *folks*! I know we might all have certain feelings about the victim here. If I was down the pub right now I'm sure I'd find plenty of opinions about George Melrose. But we need to put all of those opinions aside. It's our job to catch this guy, and get him off the streets before he can do this again. That starts with each and every one of you. Tonight. Because the next victim might not be a George Melrose.'

Lomond took a marker and underlined the photo showing the scoreline painted on Melrose's living room wall. 'This message is my primary concern. Yes, our job is to find the killer. It's also to stop them killing again.'

Making his way through the bullpen past CSU Reekie, was a slightly flushed and out of breath Jason. He waved apologetically to Lomond who was holding his gaze, then Jason pointed at the notebook in his hand.

Remembering he was still finishing up a briefing, Lomond concluded, 'This message suggests there's more to come. By the end of tomorrow, I want to be at least two-one up on this bastard.'

CHAPTER TEN

WHILE THE MEMBERS of Major Investigations broke out into huddles with their respective sergeants and inspectors, Lomond joined his team at the front.

Detective Inspector Willie Sneddon. Detective Sergeant Ross McNair. And Detective Constables Pardeep Varma, and Donna Higgins – who Lomond couldn't help but notice was standing half a step back from the others.

Now joining them, was Detective Constable Jason Yang. 'I'm sorry, sir. I got here as fast as I could.'

Lomond replied, 'What I say next depends on what's in that notebook of yours that you seem so excited about.'

Jason was already thumbing through the pages which were densely annotated – many with sketches of faces, road layouts, and car registration plates. 'I was checking with some of the Dumbarton constables who were knocking doors earlier, and they said there were a lot of people not at home. Which struck me as odd, as it's been a nice sunny day, and there's a lot of retirees in the village. Anyway, I double-checked a number of the addresses they had, and they weren't checking the gardens in the back.'

Lomond scoffed in frustration. 'They never heard them knock.'

Jason showed him his notebook. 'I got three separate accounts of a dark-coloured Volvo estate parking near the pier late at night about seven to ten days ago.'

'I suppose a registration plate is hoping for too much.'

'It is. But get this...the latter of those accounts also described the car towing a dinghy trailer.'

'Tell me there was a dinghy in the trailer.'

'All three separate accounts say there was.'

Ross asked, 'What time of night was this?'

'The lady reckons it was about quarter past ten. The streetlights aren't for shit on Pier Road. They're like something out of a Dickens novel, so that's all I've got.'

'But it's a start,' said Lomond. He turned to Willie. 'Everyone is on this. Got it?'

'You got it, John,' Willie replied, hastily making way for Reekie, who moved languidly across the office to Lomond. He rushed for no one but the Chief Constable.

Reekie said, 'Informative *and* offensive. You're a man of so many talents, John.'

Lomond appeared congenial, obviously masking his true feelings. 'Thank you, sir.'

'Are you ready for this press conference?'

'You mean can I sit there and keep my mouth shut while you and Linda handle it?' He nodded. 'I've had some practice at this point.'

He'd also had a lot of practice at what he was about to do next: tell his boss that he was making a mistake, without making it too obvious.

'It's just...' Lomond began. 'Are we absolutely sure a press conference is the right way to go on this? It's a sensational case, and I don't see how we avoid getting dragged into the gutter on why we failed to find Melrose before this happened. Also, the hacks are going to keep throwing words like dismember at us on every question.'

Reekie bristled. 'This is too high-profile for a press release. We need to appeal for witnesses around Luss.' As Linda joined them, he asked her, 'Linda, anything?'

'I agree with John,' she said. 'But I don't see how we can avoid words like dismember, or limbs.'

Reekie said, 'We're trying to avoid a panic that some maniac vigilante calling himself the Taxman is out there chopping people up.'

Lomond countered, 'That's *exactly* what we've got.'

'Great, John. Maybe we could release some photos from Luss beach. Make sure the entire country vomits into their porridge. What about this car and trailer I just heard you talking about? We should get that out as loud and clear as we can, surely.'

Linda and Lomond were thinking the same thing. But he left it for Linda to give the polite answer.

'It's a little too soon to release that,' Linda said.

Reekie replied, 'But you've got a description.'

'That's exactly the issue, sir,' said Lomond. 'The description is too broad for the public. If we release what we have, we'll get inundated with information about perfectly innocent owners of dark Volvo estates. That takes up valuable bodies to run down go-nowhere leads that could be helping us search through CCTV footage from petrol stations and ANPR in and around the Loch Lomond area seven to ten days ago.'

Reekie rolled his shoulders, taking a defiant posture. In Detective Chief Inspector language, Lomond had just found about eight ways of telling Reekie his instincts were all wrong. To an outsider it might have sounded innocent enough, but Linda was eager to steer conversation swiftly away.

'What do you suggest, then, John?' she asked.

Lomond sighed, unsure. 'If you need a diplomatic answer, you should really ask a diplomat.'

'You are definitely *not* a diplomat,' Reekie assured him.

'Then you're asking the wrong person, sir. The papers are going to sledge us for failing to find Melrose before this happened. Let's do a statement straight to camera only, no questions.'

Reekie scoffed.

'That won't wash,' said Linda. 'We need to keep the press on our side. Starting with no questions will just get their backs up. Having said that, I think either way the public will be onside. Everyone hated Melrose. I think it's possible we'll even see a few opinion columns saying that Melrose got what was coming to him. I think we'll have the public's support.'

'Until one nil becomes two nil,' said Lomond, distracted by a text message coming through.

'Sorry, are we boring you, John?' asked Reekie.

'I'm going to have to get straight to Gartcosh after the press conference.' He showed him the message.

It was from Moira MacTaggart at Forensic Services.

"John, you'd better get over here. I've found something."

CHAPTER ELEVEN

BEFORE THEY WENT OUT for the press conference in a large purpose-built room on the ground floor of Helen Street, Reekie and Lomond were left alone while Linda fielded phone calls from Dumbarton detectives.

The TV networks and newspapers all had their major correspondents on hand, phones poised to record the audio, ready to fire off a slew of questions.

Reekie was as calm as you like, used to being in the media spotlight. 'You seem nervous, John.'

Lomond stopped pacing. 'I'm impatient, sir.'

'Gartcosh will still be there when we're done. I need a familiar face for the press. The public still love you after solving the Sandman murders.'

'That was a team effort.'

'They might love you a little less if this mess with Donna Higgins gains momentum.'

'Donna has my full support.'

'Of course she does. But eventually the evidence is going to come out, and her position will be untenable.'

'Donna helped save Jack Ferguson's life,' said Lomond, barely keeping a lid on his contempt for the man many on the force called "the Grand Arsehole". 'And she helped save *my* life three months ago at Lochinver.'

Reekie shook his head, as if he knew so much more than Lomond. 'Loyalty's such a bad reason to defend someone. You won't have a choice, John. I'll see to that. The girl's bad news. You should get rid of her while it's still your choice.'

'Girl? She's twenty-seven.' Lomond's expression steeled. 'And the Peter Lee MAPPA file isn't the only thing that might come up at Professional Standards.'

'What's that supposed to mean?'

'We both know that it was you who deleted Sandy Driscoll's MAPPA file from the system. Conveniently hiding one of the worst miscarriages of justice since Police Scotland formed. You managed to save your career, but it cost us days in tracking down Jack Ferguson. It's a wonder you didn't doom the poor lad.'

Reekie looked like he was about to erupt.

Lomond went on, 'Now, I can't prove that it was you. But Professional Standards might be able to access a digital trail that I can't. All they'd need would be a gentle word from someone to nudge them in the right direction.'

'You know, there's not a disciplinary enquiry in the

land that wouldn't find what you're doing right now to be extortion and blackmail.'

'Not at all, sir,' Lomond replied calmly. 'I'm not asking for anything in return for safeguarding Donna's career.'

Reekie was aghast. 'It's Professional Standards, John. I don't have the seniority to suggest what they should put in their coffee, let alone sway an active enquiry.'

'I think we both know that's shite. Sir.' He handed Reekie a tissue. 'You should wipe your forehead. Don't want to be sweating in front of the cameras. Makes you look guilty of something.'

Linda rejoined them, wondering why the air between the two men had changed so radically. 'That's us,' she said. She led them out to three chairs set up behind a long wooden desk.

Reekie held back a second. 'John,' he said, grabbing Lomond's arm before they got into view of the dozens of cameras awaiting them. 'Let me see what I can do.'

CHAPTER TWELVE

THE PRESS CONFERENCE was going without a hitch. Reekie had read their prepared statement, avoiding all hot-button words and downplaying the extreme violence of the crime. Instead, focusing on efforts for information from the public.

All Lomond had to do was sit there and direct everything to Linda or Reekie. At least, that was the plan.

Until Colin Mowatt of the *Glasgow Express* upended everything.

His baby face belied his thirty years, not helped by his floppy ginger hair and bright freckles.

In a reedy little voice, he held the microphone too close, which picked up and exaggerated his plosives. 'Yes, Colin Mowatt, *Glasgow Express*,' he announced pompously.

In the chasm between Mowatt's lofty opinion of

himself and how the rest of the world saw him, there was space to drive a double-decker bus.

Mowatt said, 'DCI Lomond, as the senior investigating officer, do you think you'll be able to give this your full attention while there's an ongoing Professional Standards enquiry into allegations of illegal information-gathering in your own team? Including in the Sandman murders?'

Lomond was too stunned to react at first. In a panic, he found himself saying, 'I'm not going to...that's not accurate—'

Mowatt was like a dog going after a bone. 'You're denying that there's an enquiry?'

Lomond stammered on. 'I, em...I won't, I *can't* confirm...'

Mowatt grinned, revelling in mowing Lomond down in full view of the national media. It was even going to be on TV. He could barely contain himself.

'Are you worried, DCI Lomond, that the outcome of this investigation may result in overturning convictions in the Sandman murders?'

Lomond had already known how serious the investigation was. But hearing the question framed that way in front of the press churned his stomach.

Reekie finally stepped in. 'I think what DCI Lomond is trying to express is that it would be inappropriate for any of us here to comment on any ongoing investigation at this time. Our full attention and our full resources are committed to this case.'

For the first time in his life, Lomond was glad to have Reekie around. He might have been an arsehole, but he handled questions like a seasoned politician. And John Lomond was definitely no politician.

Reekie swept Mowatt's persistent questions away with ease, and quickly wrapped things up.

Once the three were safely away from the cameras, Reekie's grace disappeared.

'Where the *hell* did that come from?' he fumed.

Lomond was too shell-shocked to articulate his thoughts. 'Sorry, I...I fucked that up.'

He wasn't going to get any disagreements from Linda or Reekie.

Linda asked, 'How has a little runt like Mowatt got wind of a Professional Standards enquiry? A fucking internal investigation?'

'There's only one way,' said Reekie. 'We've got a leak.'

Linda rubbed her eyes with a groan. 'John, do me a favour.'

'Yep,' said Lomond, still stung with embarrassment.

'You'd better pray that Moira's got some good news for you at Gartcosh.'

'And John...'

'Yeah.'

'I signed Ross's paperwork. As of tomorrow morning, he's with Gordon Hunt at Organised Crime. You'll get him back – if you want him – in six weeks.'

'Linda, I–'

'I don't care, John. There are four other detective sergeants in that MIT room. Pick one if you like. But you've got more than enough firepower with Willie, and the others need their stabilisers taken off anyway.'

Lomond lodged his tongue firmly into his cheek, saying nothing. He knew he couldn't hold back the tide any longer.

To nudge him over the line, Linda added, 'He'll be back before you know it.'

'Fine,' he relented.

'Give him a break, John. He's just a young guy with ambitions.'

'And I'm an old guy with a pile of limbs on a beach, and a leaky disciplinary proceeding. This is going to get worse before it gets better.'

CHAPTER THIRTEEN

UPON EXITING the M73 North at Gartcosh, the Scottish
Crime Campus emerged in full view amidst the vast
expanse of an almost deserted industrial park. By nine
o'clock on a cool May night, as Lomond approached, the
campus appeared in its full glory, bathed in the gentle
glow of subtle uplighting from the ground. It resembled
the grand headquarters of a cutting-edge tech giant
straight out of Silicon Valley. Police Scotland had come
in for its fair share of criticism over the years – for
botched enquiries, unworkable policies that had to be
embarrassingly reversed like banning facial hair, and
corruption within the Executive Team – but the one
thing they definitely got right was the Scottish Crime
Campus.

Built in 2013, at the cost of a mere £82 million, the
Scottish Crime Campus was a state-of-the-art facility
that brought together a host of key law enforcement

agencies, including the Scottish Police Authority, Specialist Crime Division, the Serious Organised Crime Agency, and Forensic Services – all working under the same roof for the first time.

The sprawling car park was only a third full by that time of night, allowing Lomond the rare opportunity of getting parked near the front door. Which would have been a near-miraculous achievement during regular business hours.

As much as Lomond respected the rarity of a publicly funded project coming in on time and on budget, not to mention the sterling work that went on there, he wished that the architecture would stop demanding attention. Everywhere you looked, there was some lofty idea on display. Like the ground plan based on the shape of a chromosome, an atrium roof designed to look like the bars of DNA sequencing, and bridges linking different floors inspired by DNA connections.

After signing in at reception, Lomond found himself temporarily lost going back and forth across one of the bridges before he got his bearings. Eventually, he found Forensic Services on the third floor.

Despite his numerous visits to the campus, Lomond had never actually set foot in Moira McTaggart's laboratory. At the end of a long corridor of closed doors that had narrow glass panels in them.

He knocked on Moira's door, unsure of what he would find inside.

She shouted for him to come in.

When he opened the door, he was greeted by the unlikely sound of The Beach Boys' *Smiley Smile* album. The current track playing was 'Good Vibrations'. Moira wasn't exactly known as the most expressive person on the force – you don't acquire a nickname like Moira Dreich for nothing. Lomond had pictured her as more of a classical music fan. Likely to be listening to something sombre. Sad. He'd had her down as a Franz Schubert person, or maybe Gustav Mahler, rather than listening to one of the most joyful and bombastic albums ever recorded.

Moira leaned over a microscope with several glass slides laid out meticulously. With her back to him, she told him blankly, 'Make yourself comfortable.'

Lomond looked around. He thought, *Comfortable? How?*

The only seating available was a tall stool, and Moira was currently sitting on it. The rest of the lab was spotlessly clean white surfaces with an array of equipment, computers, fridges and freezers that made Lomond terrified of touching a thing.

'You said you had something for me,' Lomond ventured, stuffing his hands in his pockets as he got closer to her desk.

She removed her protective goggles and stepped off the stool. 'Let me turn this down,' she said, lowering the volume on the speaker.

There was something incongruous about discussing a

dismembered body while listening to a track as jubilant as 'Good Vibrations'.

A scene-of-crime officer had rushed the body parts found at Luss to Gartcosh so that Moira could get started on examinations as soon as possible.

Moira walked to her desk at the side of the lab to fetch her paperwork.

Lomond knew that he should have been focused entirely on the investigation, but he couldn't help letting his eyes drift towards Moira's desk. There were three photos of the same man, but the photos looked at least ten years old. Ever eager to take a small detail and run with it, Lomond wondered if it was a dead partner. *Too young to be Moira's dad. Maybe a brother...*

Moira explained, 'I haven't had time to do much, as you can imagine. The divers found the other leg, you'll be pleased to hear.' She handed him a photograph taken during the examination of the limb.

'The foot's stitched back on,' said Lomond. 'Why would someone dismember a body then stitch the foot back on?'

'A question I asked myself,' Moira replied in her typical droning tone.

Lomond couldn't imagine what being stuck in the lab all day with her was like. But then, Moira had never exactly been one for small talk.

'It isn't Melrose's,' she said. 'The leg is, but not the foot. I could tell just by looking at it. Bone structure, shape. I'm not surprised it was missed at the scene. The differences are subtle, but they *are* different.'

'Is there any way of identifying whose it is?'

'I've already started running tests. But it's going to take a few hours. And there are no guarantees.'

Lomond took a closer look at the photograph of the leg. 'I'm no expert—'

Moira couldn't resist sniping, 'You don't say.'

'These stitches look...quite decent?'

'It depends on what your standards are, of course. It looks a bit to me like someone who understands the theory but hasn't had the practice. Definitely not a surgeon or medical expert.'

'Thank god,' Lomond muttered.

Then Moira seemed to change her mind. 'Or maybe the killer did it crudely to throw you off the scent.' Her eyes narrowed. 'You might even be dealing with a forensics expert. Who knows?' She held his gaze for a moment, then it vanished and was replaced with a sardonic smile.

Lomond smiled back. 'Very good, Moira. Very dry. No one appreciates your dryness the way I do.'

'Is that why they call me Moira Dreich?'

Lomond didn't know how to respond.

'It's all right, John,' she said. 'It's not exactly news to me. Contrary to popular belief, I do actually have a sense of humour. Deep down. I think this killer has one too.'

'How do you mean?' he asked.

'Oh, come on. A banker whose reputation was built

on mergers and acquisitions ends up with someone else's foot stitched onto his leg? George "Butcher" Melrose, butchered into pieces? You've got a very dark comedian on your hands. Not exactly my sense of humour, but everyone's a critic these days.'

'What about this blood from the wall?' asked Lomond.

She opened her laptop, which had the full works of a protective hard case, and a tempered glass screen protector. It could have been thrown off the campus roof and probably survive. 'That is going to take a little while too.'

'All this technology, Moira. Why does it take so long?'

Taking personal umbrage, Moira replied, 'I don't know, John. Let me see...The test is a Raman spectroscopy, which shines a light on a blood stain to measure the intensity of scattered light. The spectrum it reveals is as unique as a fingerprint, and is non-destructive to the sample, meaning we can repeat it over and over again. Which is often necessary with this process. I then have to analyse the spectrum to interpret the peaks and identify molecular vibrations in the sample. The position and intensities of the peaks tell me what's what. Forensic science isn't as easy as scanning a QR code on your phone to order drinks at a bar.'

Chastened, Lomond revised his objections. 'Okay, but when you say "a while", that means that the big hand's on the twelve and the little hand is on...?'

Moira gestured to a blood centrifuge machine across

the room. 'The sample's currently spinning at about three thousand RPM. Why don't you pop a finger in to stop it and ask it when it'll be done?'

Lomond paused. 'You know, I'm going to start getting everyone to call you Moira Shite.' He turned towards the corridor. 'Let me find a grotesquely uncomfortable couch somewhere. You can find me in "a while", I suppose.'

Once he was gone and Moira had her back turned to him, her face cracked into a tiny smile and she let out an almost silent chuckle. 'Moira Shite,' she mumbled to herself and shook her head. 'Cheeky git.'

CHAPTER FOURTEEN

LOMOND HAD CURLED up on an angular couch the colour of chippy curry sauce. He'd made a temporary pillow out of his suit jacket, rolling it up and stuffing it under his head.

His mouth hung open slightly, arm dangling off the side of the couch.

Moira almost felt bad for waking him.

'Wakey, wakey,' she announced, gently kicking his leg.

Lomond shot up, forgetting where he was for a moment. It took a few seconds to get his bearings. The couch was on one of the many bridges that crisscrossed above the ground floor. Down at reception, there only a low murmur of conversation from security staff finishing up night shift. It would be another hour before the building started coming properly to life for the day.

The first rays of sunlight were tickling the top of the Campsies, but only just.

Lomond shoved his shirt sleeve up to check the time.

4.58am.

'It should be illegal to be awake at this time,' he grumbled.

He felt like a computer that had simply been switched off at the socket instead of methodically shut down. Now Moira had plugged him in and he had to be up immediately and start running all sorts of programs, like Wipe Dribble From Corner Of Mouth, and Tuck Shirt Back In.

Moira was holding two cups of coffee. She nodded towards her office. 'Come on,' she said. 'I've got something for you.'

When they reached her office, she left both coffees on the tabletop far from where she was working. She tapped away eagerly on the keyboard, showing no interest in having a drink.

'Aren't you having one of these?' Lomond asked, rubbing a hand firmly over his shaved head.

'I don't drink coffee,' she answered distantly. 'They're both for you. You're going to need them.'

Lomond rubbed at the stubble that had come through. Coarse and dark, flecked with grey if given the chance to grow out more. But like his receding hair, he never gave it much chance.

He took a sip of coffee, which was scalding hot. He

couldn't even taste anything resembling coffee. It was just a mouthful of heat.

'Have you got a match for the mystery foot?' he asked.

Moira turned her laptop to share the screen with him. 'You're not quite that lucky. But I can tell you the foot was severed about three weeks ago.'

'Three? You're sure?'

'As sure as I can be.'

'So the Taxman went after the owner of the foot first.'

'But he wanted you to *find* Melrose first.'

'Why do you say that?'

She clicked to a file on her screen. 'This is why I woke you up. It came through twenty minutes ago. The divers found a safe about fifty feet down on the loch's surface, near where the limbs were floating. At the southern end, the loch is often as deep as a hundred feet.' She pointed to the map of the loch on her laptop. 'But the loch is a little shallower between Luss beach and Inchlonaig. The thing of note with the safe is that it had a buoyancy aid wrapped around it.'

Lomond did a double-take. 'Then why didn't it float to the surface?'

'Buoyancy aids come in different ratings. A lifejacket that's rated at, say, one hundred Newtons provides a minimum of ten kilos of buoyancy. Now, that doesn't mean that anyone wearing the jacket that's over ten kilos sinks. But it would protect a person in rough waters.' She highlighted the forensics photos on her screen, showing the floats found wrapped around the safe. 'These aids are rated at fifty Newtons. Enough to keep it pointing up a certain way–'

'But not so much that it would float to the surface.'

'Exactly.'

'That must have taken some experimenting to figure out. But why go to all the trouble?'

'My guess is because of this...' She pulled up another tab on her laptop, showing photos of the safe itself in more detail. 'This is a time release. At a given time, the safe door opens.'

Lomond scoffed, almost impressed at the Taxman's industry. 'That's why he needed the floats?'

'To keep the safe door facing the surface. Then, when the time release opens the door...' She made an *et voila* gesture.

'The limbs would float right out the door and reach the surface. So this was all by *design*?'

'Without a doubt,' said Moira.

'And you said that the foot was cut off three weeks ago.'

'That's right.'

Lomond needed a long pause to get his head straight.

Moira helped him along by saying, 'Your killer's got it all figured out, John. There's also nothing to say that whoever that foot belongs to isn't still alive. Somewhere.'

Lomond tutted as a message from Linda came through on his phone. He said, 'I'm not so sure about that.' He put away his phone, then took as long a drink of the scorching coffee as he could stand.

'Bad news?' asked Moira.

'I think the Taxman's about to go two nil up.'

CHAPTER FIFTEEN

LOMOND WAS TALKING to Linda as he strode to his car. 'You maybe don't realise, but when you send a man messages at five in the morning that just say "call me", it looks a little desperate.'

Linda's tone told him in an instant that she wasn't in the mood. Her already aggressive voice raised to be heard on her car speakerphone. 'Yeah, very good. I need you to wake up Willie and anyone else who'll answer. Looks like we've got another one. The word "paid" found on another body.'

'Where?'

'This one's on the torso.'

'No, I mean where has the body been found?'

'Gullane.'

'Gullane? As in East Lothian?'

'Unless they've moved it. Do you want me to check?'

'Jeez. You're crisp at this time of the morning. Do your kids get to enjoy this dazzling wit over breakfast?'

'I'm not sure what's funnier, John. Your clever jokes, or the idea that I ever get to have breakfast with my kids.'

Lomond hit the beeper to unlock his car, passing a group in cleaning overalls on their way in. 'Christ,' Lomond muttered. 'You know it's early when you're leaving somewhere before the cleaners have even started their shift...' Getting into his car, he asked, 'Right, where am I going?'

'Gullane Golf Club,' said Linda. 'Edinburgh MIT is already at the scene. I've told their DCI to expect you.'

Lomond waited for more details that never came. 'You sound a little off, Linda.'

'I'm trying to tread carefully with this one,' she replied. 'I assume by your nonchalant reaction that you didn't hear she transferred from Aberdeen.'

As soon as she said Aberdeen, Lomond's stomach did a cartwheel. Then a backflip.

He said, 'I, uh...' There was a long pause. 'I didn't realise.'

Linda could tell that he was trying to sound fine about it, but she knew that he simply couldn't be. 'She's been down six weeks already. This isn't going to be a problem, is it?'

'It was a million years ago, Linda.'

'And she broke your heart, John. I remember because I was there picking up the pieces for about six months afterwards.'

He shook his head to get rid of the anxiety that had consumed his body. 'Yes, thank you for reminding me. Look, we've got bigger things to worry about. I want to conference in Willie on my way.'

'Right, call me back when you've got him. I'll be in the office in five.'

'Can you at least tell me what to expect over there? More body parts?'

'Actually...'

Lomond's eyes widened in surprise. It wasn't often that Linda was lost for words.

She said, 'I really don't know what you'd call this.'

CHAPTER SIXTEEN

THE DRIVE from north-west Glasgow towards Edinburgh, and swinging up the East Lothian coastline, gave Lomond plenty of time to think. A little too much.

The M8 all the way via Harthill was like driving through the set of a zombie movie – there was barely a car on the road. With a clear road ahead, and his mind drifting to thoughts of the past, he ended up effortlessly touching ninety for a few miles before he realised his speed.

Lomond didn't know why he was surprised that she was ending up back in his life. It seemed to be the way with life. You might be done with the past, but the past is so often not done with you.

He already had the curious time-release safe found in Loch Lomond on his mind. But now, instead of focusing on the actual policing, he was distracted with all sorts of trivialities. How much would they end up working together? Should he tell his team that he and another DCI had a past? Wouldn't that just invite gossip the second his back was turned?

Not for the first time, he wished that Ruth Telford would just get out of his life for good.

———

THERE WAS a blanket of fog along the coastline from Musselburgh all the way to North Berwick. But it was at its thickest when the mossy-walled and tree-lined edges of the A198 opened up as the road split through the middle of Luffness golf course. The fog was low to the ground, hugging the flat landscape. The only visible landmark was the unmistakable cone-shape of Berwick Law, a good seven miles away.

Golf courses dominated the countryside there. Few places in the world had such a dense concentration of courses – as well as an abundance of wealthy locals to support them all. The most famous course of them all was Muirfield – or to give it its official name, The Official Company of Edinburgh Golfers. A club so elitist and misogynistic, it hadn't even allowed female members until 2017.

Golf had never interested Lomond. Though on the face of it, he would have made an ideal player. On the course, the only person you can really rely on is yourself. The actual action of hitting shots made up barely five per cent of a round. The rest of it was thinking and walking and self-recrimination. You had to accept the ups and downs, the knocks of fortune and unlucky bounces with equal grace. They were as much a part of the game as raw skill was. Like life itself, the game had a habit of knocking you down to size just when you thought you had conquered it.

What also put Lomond off was having to wear the ridiculous clothes that went with the sport. Anytime he had watched golf on TV, he thought the players looked like middle-aged dads dressed for a dinner out on holiday.

Then there was the dislike of having to be approved by a committee in order to join a club if you wanted to play seriously. Lomond subscribed to Groucho Marx's view on clubs, that he would refuse to belong to any club willing to accept him as a member.

Lomond took a deep breath, like he was preparing for a bungee jump or something equally terrifying. 'Please don't look good, please don't look good,' he said to himself.

He knew that it was petty, but the whole situation would be so much easier to process if she didn't look good. He took a quick look in the rear-view mirror.

He sighed. '*You* look like shit, John.'

Not only did he appear worse than he did a few months ago, but to someone who hadn't seen him in twelve years, he objectively looked quite unhealthy. The lack of sleep overnight had done little to alleviate the pronounced bags under his eyes. While his face had slimmed down, it still appeared puffy.

After a brief rise, the road turned into a long flat straight, with Gullane Golf Club on either side of the road. The club had no less than three separate courses that stretched along the coastline of Aberlady Bay.

Lomond looked for any obvious signs of police presence on either side of the road. Then he spotted the hivis tabards of a pair of constables by the second tee on Course No.2, right next to the road.

Two police patrol cars and a Serious Incident van were parked further up the hillside on the fairway of the second hole.

On the other side of the road near the clubhouse, a gaggle of greenskeepers huddled around their mowers and bunker rakes, exchanging rumours about what exactly had been found.

Further along the road, some locals walking their dogs had assembled. It was impossible to close the entire road, as it was the only throughway to North Berwick. It was a village of early risers, the retired with leisure time on their hands who thought that eight o'clock was a late start to a morning. They took residency of their village seriously. It wasn't uncommon for residents to barrack the many large groups of cyclists that came through in all the pro gear – gesticulating and reprimanding them for the supposed crime of speeding through the village at twenty-three miles an hour when it was a twenty zone. It might have seemed petty, but it was only because they took pride in where they lived. Which was understandable. It was the sort of place Lomond could imagine himself retiring to.

As he parked on the grass verge, the constables conferred with each other.

'Holy shit,' one said. 'That's John Lomond.'

The other stood up a little straighter. 'Right. Don't say anything embarrassing.'

The other muttered back, 'Piss off,' then gave Lomond a serious nod. 'Morning, sir.'

Lomond could tell that they recognised him, but he showed his ID anyway. 'Morning, boys. Where is it?'

One of them pointed. 'Up the hill, sir. He's on the second green.'

Lomond looked up the hill, where he could now see a group in smart office wear, along with a few in white forensics outfits. 'Have either of you seen it up there?'

'We were first on the scene, eh,' one of them said, obviously a local.

'Never seen nothing like it, sir,' said the other.

'What's happened to him?' asked Lomond.

The pair looked at each other. Neither wanted to answer, and they certainly didn't know how to put it.

'His, em...He's got...'

The other took over. There *was* no other way of putting it. 'Sir...his mouth's stuffed full of horseshit.'

Lomond shook his head. 'Honestly. This job.' He took another look up the hill. 'Is DCI Telford up there?'

'Yes, sir.'

Lomond nodded, taking another second or two before setting off. 'Right. Cheers.'

The one who had been unable to answer then said, 'It's an...an honour to meet you, sir! Let us know if we can do anything.'

'Right you are,' Lomond replied.

He didn't hear the other constable snort with laughter, doing a mocking imitation of his colleague. '*An honour to meet you?* Arse kisser...'

It took a few minutes to make it up the three hundred-odd yards to the green where Ruth's team were milling around. Along the way, Lomond noted a number of long scuff marks on the fairway. Like someone had been dragging their heels.

Ruth still had her back to him as he approached. Lomond repeated to himself, 'Please don't look good...'

When she turned around and he got a clear look at her face, he cursed inwardly. 'Damn.'

She didn't just look good. She looked even better than when they'd been together. Time had been kind to her to the same degree that time had been unfavourable to Lomond.

When she turned in profile, Lomond said to himself, 'Oh...my...god.' He wasn't commenting on the gruesome murder scene awaiting him – that was still out of sight. It was that Ruth was wearing the same Swissgear backpack she'd had back when they were together.

It was bulky and sat high on her narrow shoulders, laden with a heavy Police Scotland laptop, an assortment of stationery, and a water bottle among a ton of other things. Lomond had grown to loathe the sight of it.

She greeted him with a warm smile and a low-key wave as she stepped off the greenside. 'Long time no see, John.'

The sound of her voice immediately took him back the twelve years since their relationship ended. Despite having lived in Scotland most of her adult life, she had retained her smart, vaguely middle-England accent. It had always put Lomond in mind of rolling green farmlands, tweeting birds, and large oak trees. A childhood of comfort, where nothing was ever a struggle. Unlike Lomond, most of Ruth's life had been simple, without trauma or grief. The only people close to her she had ever lost were grandparents.

Lomond had long held the belief that lacking profound sorrow or intense grief by a certain age could become a problem. It wasn't necessarily good to have only experienced the positive aspects of life. Something that Lomond, as the son of an alcoholic father and an absent mother, had struggled not to feel envious about during his relationship with Ruth. It had been yet more proof of how different their worlds were – and how inevitable it was that she would never – and *could* never – truly understand what it was like to be John Lomond.

Years at the helm of Major Investigations teams had given her a manner of effortless authority without being aloof. The blank space of what she had been up to for the past twelve years only heightened the mystery around her.

Seeing her again after so many years overloaded Lomond's brain. The sight of her. The sound of her. The smell of her perfume.

And the sight of a dead man lying on the green next to the flag, flat on his back, his mouth gaping open, filled with something dark and lumpy.

The flag for hole number two fluttered gently in the breeze. The killer had used the existing '2' on the flag and, in a script reminiscent of what they had discovered at George Melrose's house, scrawled a message in blood that read:

"THE TAXMAN 2, POLICE SCOTLAND 0"

CHAPTER SEVENTEEN

'Who's more of a sight for sore eyes?' asked Lomond, gesturing to the body behind Ruth. 'Me or him?'

She smiled cautiously, as if she didn't want to let him know how warm it made her feel inside to see him again. 'It's been a while, John.'

'Too long?'

She looked skywards for a moment while she thought. 'You know when you sometimes *really* want a Chinese takeaway, and then the moment you get that first mouthful of chow mein you think, nah, I'm actually not in the mood for that?'

'You've known for at least half an hour that I was coming. Is that the best you could come up with?'

She smiled kindly. 'You look tired. How have you been?' Her eyes were probing as they met Lomond's. Digging about for a lie, or weakness. With Ruth, it never felt like merely a conversation. Always an interrogation.

Lomond knew what she was thinking. He looked shitty, exhausted. She no doubt assumed he was hungover. 'I'm not drinking if that's what you're asking.'

'That wasn't what I meant,' she protested, doing her best impression of innocence.

Lomond wasn't convinced. 'Of course,' he said, happy to let it go. 'I was surprised to hear you were back down.'

'Aberdeen was never going to be forever.'

'Yeah. Well. Sorry I never got in touch after your transfer. It's been pretty hectic down here.'

'Oh,' she said, surprised. 'When I spoke to Linda, she made it sound like you didn't know about it. And it was a promotion, by the way. Not a transfer.'

Now it was Lomond's turn to appear innocent. 'Of course.'

Ruth paused. 'Look, I want to be honest—'

That makes a change, Lomond thought.

'—I was a little nervous when I found out it would be you coming over. I'd like us to work well together.'

Lomond shifted his gaze towards the crime scene, then he checked his watch. 'I wasn't intending to do otherwise.' he said. It was as much small talk as he could handle. 'Do you want to tell me what we have?'

Ruth turned back towards the scene. 'Male, about sixty, sixty-five years old. No ID. Cause of death appears to be asphyxiation.'

'And there I was thinking the worst crime committed

on a golf course was plaid trousers.' Lomond motioned towards the body. 'May I?'

Ruth led him over. They held back a few steps to let forensics continue their work, erecting a tent around the body.

Lomond considered the scene, hands on hips. He had never seen anything else like it.

The victim was wearing silk pyjamas, which had ripped in whatever struggle had taken place. His mouth was crammed full of horse manure. The dark-brown, crumbly lumps flecked with undigested plant fibres and hay. Forensics were still spooning it out of his throat to assess cause of death, and check for anything else lodged in his airway. It might have been darkly funny if it wasn't also for the sickeningly twisted expression on the victim's face. Terror mixed with agony. It might have been dark and quiet on the course when he died, but he definitely hadn't gone peacefully.

Ruth explained, 'A greenkeeper who was mowing the fairway around quarter to five found him.'

Lomond screwed up his face when he noticed it. 'So that must be *his* vomit over there.'

She chuckled. 'A guy suffocated with horseshit but it's the vomit that you can't deal with?'

'It's too early for vomit.'

'But you're fine with the corpse?'

'I'm murder police, not a paramedic.'

Ruth looked back down the fairway. 'Did you see the scuff marks on your way up?'

'I did,' Lomond said. 'You think he was alive when he was brought up here?'

'That's what I'm starting with. If he was already dead, the marks would have been steady. Those are of varying, inconsistent depth. Like someone still putting up a fight.'

'He must have known what was coming, though.'

'Probably,' she said, taking a grip of both straps of her backpack.

He crouched down for a closer look. 'So, suffocation?'

'We think so.'

'Second hole. Second flag. Extra style points for using the two on the flag...Speaking of which. Moira McTaggart is going to need the blood on that flag ASAP.'

'Already on it,' Ruth assured him.

Lomond sighed. 'It's my killer, all right.'

He noted the victim had both feet attached. But he didn't need Moira's forensics skills to tell him who the victim was. He stood up. 'Well, this makes things a little clearer. And it explains the horseshit.' He made sure to avoid eye contact with Ruth.

She sighed in annoyance. 'The part where you know something I don't. Congratulations. Did you enjoy it? Can we skip to where you tell me what you know?'

He pointed at the victim. 'That's Dennis Dunbar. And any DCI who had worked here longer than the shelf life of a carton of milk, or didn't have a team of twelve-year-olds would have known that.'

'Fine. I'll bite. Who is he?'

'A lawyer – hence the horseshit, no doubt. Our killer seems to have a dry sense of humour.'

'What kind of lawyer?'

'The very exclusive, very expensive kind. Most recently to sex pests off the telly, and footballers accused of rape. You can throw in a couple of serial killers too. If a heinous crime's been committed, you can bet your arse that Dunbar will be defending.'

'There must have been a better way to make money in the legal game.'

'Not in criminal defence,' said Lomond. 'Nah, Dunbar loved it. The notoriety. The big speeches he got to make in court. I'm amazed this didn't happen to him years ago.'

Ruth said, 'So the list of people with motive to do this would be substantial.'

'I would have said as long as the phone book, but apparently no one knows what the hell that is anymore.' Lomond looked at Ruth's team. 'Your guys are even younger than mine.'

'I like it that way. They don't have any bad habits.'

'They look like a bunch of vegan students in Next suits.'

'It doesn't surprise me that you would make fun of a group of young, ambitious, fit and healthy officers. I picked these guys myself.'

'No kidding.'

'They don't show up with hangovers. They read

books, they study old case files. They want to do some good out in the world. Not play up to some decades-old myth of the loner detective sobbing into a glass of whisky every night, while some sad jazz record plays in the background.' As soon as she was done, she realised she had taken a cheap shot at him.

Lomond said, 'You haven't been around, Ruth, so maybe you don't know. But that's not me either. Not anymore.'

Ruth shut her eyes for a moment. 'I don't want to fight, John. Not here. Not now. We did enough of that already.'

'What is there to fight about?'

'I want in on this case.'

Lomond laughed. 'And I want a physique like Ryan Gosling. Seems that we both want things we can't have.'

She put out a defensive hand. 'I spoke to Ogilvy this morning.'

Of course, thought Lomond. It was just like Ruth Telford to rub it in his face that she was taking phone calls with the Assistant Chief Constable for the East.

Ruth continued, 'He says that it might be a good idea. To help get on top of this quickly.'

'Unbelievable.' Lomond rubbed his face in disbelief. 'You're back ten seconds and muscling in on a newsworthy case. And behind my back?'

'I don't know if you know this, but I have a one hundred per cent clearance with MIT in Aberdeen, and I've got the same here after six weeks.'

He faked an expression of being impressed. 'A whole six weeks? Wow. How many lost dogs and stolen bikes have you found in that time?'

'Very funny, but I had the same rate in Aberdeen for the last four years as DCI.'

'Aberdeen, eh. Hotbed of major crime, that place.'

'It actually has its fair share of complex cases, if you cared to look into it.'

'The only way to get me to care about Aberdeen is if Partick Thistle have an away game there.'

'You might not like it, John, but at this rate, I'm headed for Tulliallan in less than ten years. I *will* be the youngest ACC that Police Scotland has ever had.'

'Still working the angles. You haven't changed, then.'

'You never respected my ambition, John. That's what hasn't changed. You could learn a thing or two from me about that. How it's in your interests to spread the wealth a bit right now and do yourself a favour.'

'Now you're doing *me* a favour?'

'Of course I am. I saw the mess you made of that press conference last night. Linda and Reekie aren't going to be able to save you every day that this drags on. You hate that I'm a political animal, and I know how to play the game. But admit it. That's exactly the sort of person you need right now.'

'The bollocks I do!'

Before the argument escalated further, one of the SOCOs raised his hand for their attention. His voice oozed with disdain for what he perceived as the pair's lack of professionalism. 'If you've got a second, you might want to see this.'

His colleague tipped the victim's body up on his left side, allowing Ruth and Lomond a view of the victim's back.

'He wasn't just suffocated by the, em, manure,' said the SOCO. 'He was shot.' He paused. 'Right up the jacksy.'

'The *jacksy?*' said Lomond, shaking his head with laughter. 'What is this, an episode of *Dad's Army?*' He crouched down for a closer look. The moment he caught a glimpse of the wound, he recoiled. 'Fucking hell. He was shot...up the arse?'

Ruth let out a long, queasy puff. 'Jeez...'

'But no weapon?' Lomond asked.

The SOCO replied, 'Nothing yet. It looks like it was a handgun.'

Lomond thanked the heavens that he didn't do a job that involved figuring out what sort of weapon had been used to inflict an arse wound.

Reappraising the scene, he said, 'He's enjoying this. The Taxman. It's not just about doling out punishment. He had fun doing this.'

'You're sure it's a man?' asked Ruth.

'Bloody strong anyone who could carry or pull a fat heap like Dunbar up that hill.'

Ruth was more interested in the route back down the fairway to the main road. 'He must have parked by the side of the road. There's no other access, and the markings on the fairway fit with dragging Dunbar from there. Question is, did the Taxman take the gun with him? I don't think so.'

While she considered the path from the green back down the hill to the main road, seeing nothing but closely mown grass, Lomond remembered what it was about her that made him so sure she would end up in this position. The quick insight, sharp eye, and faultless logic.

She turned to Lomond. 'We should check for any drains on the road. If he ditched the gun anywhere, it would be in one of them.'

Now it was Lomond's turn to add some analysis. 'I can't see him taking the chance to shoot him out here. It's totally open ground. The sound would carry straight to the village.'

'What about the marks on the fairway? If Dunbar had already been shot, the marks would have been steady.'

Lomond paused. 'Unless the gunshot didn't kill him.'

Just thinking about the agony Dunbar would have been in made Ruth feel sick.

Lomond added, 'If Dunbar was already shot, this would be a good place to take him. No cameras around, no sightline from the road to here. You don't have to worry about him letting out the odd howl of suffering. And nobody's out here in the middle of the night, I assume.'

'No,' said Ruth. 'Dog walkers head for the beach if they're out after dark, they tell me.'

'I'd bet that Dunbar lives nearby. The killer wouldn't have risked a long journey with him alive in the back. We've already got a bit of a lead on a dark Volvo estate. It might have been used for transportation. Any word on time of death yet?'

Ruth glanced back at forensics. 'They reckon sometime around two-ish. Maybe one, but no earlier.'

'That makes sense. He couldn't have risked coming any earlier. At this time of year on a clear night it must still be a little light out here even at elevenish?' He looked around quickly. 'No streetlights along here. Very little light pollution.'

Ruth called over to one of her team. 'Jane. Two seconds.'

A woman in her mid-twenties hurried over. She had on a backpack as well, and looked like a junior version of Ruth. She even had the same hairstyle as her, scraped back into a functional bun. The same style sported by what few women were on the Police Scotland Executive Team.

'Yes, Ruth,' said Jane.

'John, this is DS Jane Erskine,' said Ruth. 'She's my right hand.'

Erskine held out a hand towards Lomond. 'I know all your cases, sir. I'm looking forward to working together.'

When Lomond glanced at Ruth, she looked away quickly.

He shook Jane's hand and made as polite a face as he could manage. 'Nice to meet you, DS Erskine.'

Ruth explained, 'John's managed to ID the victim. He's Dennis Dunbar and we think he's a local. I need an address for him.'

'Right away, ma'am,' Erskine replied.

Lomond said, 'She's looking forward to working with me. That's nice. But what does your DS know that I don't?'

Ruth replied, 'I know that you'd only accept sharing this case over your own dead body, but ACC Ogilvy said that between my clearance rate and your experience, we could put this Taxman thing to bed before his name leaks to the press.'

'Unfortunately for you, it's not ACC Ogilvy's call. And I don't need to split this case with someone to handle the press.'

'You know they'll have a field day when it breaks. And it's going to break later today. That's going to turn your next press conference into a feeding frenzy.'

'It might hold longer than today.'

'Don't tell me none of those greenkeepers are going to talk to the press when they come around here later. Tulliallan isn't going to tolerate a vigilante on the loose bumping off high-profile victims. And you know the Taxman already has a third victim lined up.'

'What are you talking about?'

'The mystery foot stitched onto Melrose's leg. It's not only Glasgow MIT that has connections with the Crime Campus, you know.'

'What's your point?' asked Lomond.

'Dunbar still has both feet. You're probably going to have a third victim by tomorrow. Three victims in three days. That's even more shit for you to eat from the press.'

Lomond took one last look at Dunbar as the forensic tent was sealed up. 'I could just give all the shit to him. He appears to have developed a taste for it.'

The pair of them smiled. Just being able to flex those muscles in Lomond's jaw came as a huge relief to him. It really was true that it was harder work to frown than it was to smile.

Jane hung up her phone, then called over to Ruth. 'Boss, I've got an address for a Dennis Dunbar. It's barely five minutes' walk from here.'

Ruth asked Lomond, 'Shall we?'

CHAPTER EIGHTEEN

DENNIS DUNBAR's house was a short walk away, across a few holes of course number two, and the opening hole of course one. The house sat among a long row of stately Tudor-style houses with direct views across the golf courses. While they may not have had the flashy exteriors of the modern, architect-designed mansions that were the preserve of the ultra-wealthy, the presence of tall security gates at the end of each driveway suggested that the owners placed a premium on privacy. Every garden was impeccable, maintained by professionals. The street was free of any parked cars, something that Ruth picked up on immediately.

'It must be hard for an outsider to park around here and go unnoticed,' she said.

Following close behind Ruth and Lomond, Jane agreed. 'If the killer took Dunbar from his house, he must have parked close to the house. We might get lucky with a neighbour who saw something.'

'But he would have been taken in the middle of the night,' said Lomond. 'Not much curtain twitching going on at those hours.'

Jane double-checked Dunbar's address, though there was no need. Lomond could tell which one it was from three houses away: it was the only one whose driveway gate was hanging open.

Dunbar's house was protected by high walls which were surrounded by low-hanging trees. As private as the other houses were, Dunbar's was a total mystery from street level.

Lomond made sure to enter the driveway ahead of Ruth. He didn't want her forgetting that she and Jane were just passengers on this case.

Jane slowed as she took in the sight of the magnificent grounds. 'How the other half live, eh.'

Lomond replied, 'I'd say this is more like the top five per cent.'

There were three cars in the driveway. A white top-of-the-line Range Rover with tinted windows, a Porsche Taycan estate, and an Aston Martin Valhalla. Within two seconds of seeing the Valhalla, Lomond was certain that it was the most beautiful car he had ever seen – maybe even the most beautiful *thing*.

'You weren't kidding that this guy was elite,' said Ruth.

The front door was wide open, allowing a gentle

breeze through the hallway. On a round marble table, fresh flowers fluttered in a vase.

Lomond paused, then looked back out to the driveway. 'The gate's open.'

'I *did* notice that as we walked through,' said Ruth.

'No. I mean, look around this place. It's like Fort Knox.' He pointed around the ceiling and to the first-floor landing. 'There are cameras all over the place. I counted at least five outside, too.'

'What's your point?'

'How did the killer get in without setting off what looks like a very sophisticated alarm system?'

Jane ventured, 'It can't be that hard to deactivate some cameras and an alarm, can it?'

'It's actually incredibly hard,' replied Lomond. 'Especially without access to the grounds. If we assume the killer climbed a wall or the gate to get in, he could have easily found a key or used Dunbar's fingerprint to open the front gate to get back out. After all, he couldn't scale a wall or a gate carrying Dunbar – even if he was drugged or passed out.'

Jane said, 'What if Dunbar knew the killer? Trusted him enough to open his gate to him in the middle of the night?'

Ruth nodded. 'That's possible.'

The search of the ground floor didn't take long. Everything was tidy and in place. No furniture knocked over. No signs of a struggle. Which only backed up Lomond's theory of Dunbar knowing his killer.

Upstairs in Dunbar's bedroom was a different story.

Drawers and cupboards had been pulled out and emptied, their contents strewn across the floor. Clothes, shoes, underwear.

While Ruth and Jane walked around the room looking for clues, Lomond stayed in one spot, panning around the room.

The bedcovers were pulled back, like Dunbar had been ripped violently from his bed. The beside table was on its side on the plush carpet, and the lamp was still on.

A camera tripod without a camera was set up, pointing towards the bed.

'Aye, aye,' said Lomond, inspecting it. Then he realised that there was a mirror on the ceiling above the bed. 'Ooft,' he groaned. 'If I looked like Dunbar, I would *not* want that thing up there. I don't even want to know what goes on in here.' He then stopped dead in his tracks. His voice turned downcast. 'Oh, shit,' he said.

Ruth turned around quickly.' What is it?'

Lomond pointed to a wicker basket sitting in the corner of the room. It was full of toys for young children.

Ruth sighed. 'Oh, Jesus.'

'Yeah,' he said, taking a shuddering intake of breath.

Either naive or in denial, Jane suggested, 'Maybe he's got young relatives.'

Neither Lomond nor Ruth bothered arguing.

'This might get ugly,' Lomond said.

'I don't get it,' said Ruth. 'In here – just one room – it looks like a basic burglary.'

Concentrating, Lomond's voice was distant. 'He didn't know what he was looking for. Maybe Dunbar was holding out over something. Wouldn't tell him.' He then set off next door to Dunbar's study.

'Where's he off to?' Ruth complained to herself.

She had never seen him working a crime scene before, and though she would never show it, she was finding it thrilling. More than anything, what she found attractive in someone was a mind at work. Everything else flowed from that. And she could see Lomond's mind lighting up like the sky above Edinburgh castle on Hogmanay.

In the study, a safe in the wall, hidden behind an oil painting of Aberlady Bay, was wide open. Inside was a computer hard drive, the safe's sole contents.

Lomond considered the safe, like a critic evaluating a painting. 'The killer knew what he was looking for. Dunbar must have been holding out in the bedroom, so the killer searched everywhere he could think of. He must have finally convinced Dunbar to tell him where the safe was. And the combination.'

Ruth said to Jane, 'Tell forensics to get up here quickly. We need to find out what's on that hard drive.'

While Jane retreated to the staircase landing to make the call, Lomond said, 'What's the story here, then? Punishing a lawyer who defends the guilty?'

'I'd say the mouth full of horse manure is pretty clear, John. You lie, you die.'

'It's too vague. Then I see those toys next door and...' He couldn't bring himself to complete the thought.

Ruth said, 'Presumably, the answer will be on that hard drive. It's clearly been left for us. Otherwise, why not take it?'

'Yeah, I'm looking forward to finding out, and also dreading it. Whatever its contents are, I'm sure the Taxman already knew before he got here.'

'What about a connection between George Melrose and Dunbar?'

Lomond pursed his lips. It was too early to be grabbing at one or even two theories. The list of reasons why the Taxman was killing, and who he was killing, was far too long to get attached to any one single theory at such an early stage.

'Anything's possible,' conceded Lomond. 'But that's the problem. I can tell you that Dunbar never represented Melrose. I knew Melrose's guy. The same guy who represents Frank Gormley. A real piece of work called Campbell Fotheringham. This is a lawyer who just lives to fuck with the polis. He's so rich, it's all a big game to him at this point.'

Ruth asked, 'Didn't Frank Gormley get out of jail last month?'

'Trust me,' said Lomond. 'This is not the work of Frank Gormley. He might hate the police, but he doesn't paint cryptic messages with blood on walls, or leave bodies lying around golf courses like pieces of modern art. As far as drug kingpins go, Gormley's got something close to a moral barometer. But all this isn't his style. I don't know why you care so much. In a few hours, you'll be back in Edinburgh with your feet up on a desk.'

Ruth said nothing.

'What don't I know, Ruth?' asked Lomond.

'You should talk to Linda,' she replied.

'Why should I talk to Linda?'

Before she could answer, Jane appeared suddenly in the study doorway. 'Ma'am, you were right. They've found a gun in the drain.'

Ruth made a *told-you-so* face. 'How about that.'

Lomond said, 'You know, I never actually disagreed with you about that.'

'They're sending a car for us,' said Jane. 'I'll get uniform to close up the house until forensics get over.'

Lomond stayed rooted to the spot. 'Why should I talk to Linda, Ruth?'

She laid a hand on his shoulder as she went past him. 'I just want you to know it wasn't my call. None of this is personal.'

Lomond's phone rang. Linda's name pierced out from the LED screen.

Her first words to him were, 'John, we need to talk. And you're not going to like it.'

CHAPTER NINETEEN

DS Ross McNair was woken by the sound of crying through the baby monitor a few inches from his ear on the bedside table. He had fallen back asleep at four, collapsed in a heap in the darkness. He had been lucky to land on the bed at all.

Isla's face was pressed into her pillow. 'It's your turn,' she groaned.

Her Northern Irish accent was even stronger when she was shattered.

Ross groaned in reply, 'I was up with him at four.'

'Yeah. And he was up again at half past.'

'Really?' A long pause. 'Shite.'

There was no avoiding it. Neither of them ever had to do two wake-ups in a row. That was the unspoken rule between them.

Ross peeled himself up off the mattress. He was almost at the bedroom door by the time he had opened either of his eyes, flapping his arms out in front of him, feeling for obstacles.

The crying had subsided by the time he reached Lachlann's bedroom. He was greeted by the sight of his baby son – who was a few weeks away from eighteen months old – on his feet, grabbing the bars of his cot, bouncing up and down, and giggling excitedly.

Trying to remain neutral and not engage, as the parenting books and YouTube guides said, Ross found himself struggling to contain a laugh.

Another sleep regression period was well under way. The four-month regression – where the wee one starts to roll over – just about killed Ross and Isla. Lachlann was waking up every ninety minutes. Ross had informed Isla one morning over strong coffee that he was pretty sure their child was using Guantanamo Bay-style sleep torture on them. After the nine-month regression, things evened out a little, and Lachlann started sleeping through the night. The worst mistake Ross made was assuming that it would last forever.

'Daaah-dee,' Lachlann cooed, then clapped his hands.

Despite the exhaustion, and dealing with broken sleep patterns again after months of blissful uninterrupted nights, Ross still managed to smile. Lachlann's boundless enthusiasm – and total disregard for time of day – was infectious. The sound and sight of his boy lit up his heart like a Christmas tree.

He picked him up. Through a long yawn, he said, 'How's my guy?'

Lachlann pointed at the window. 'Buh!'

'Yeah? Will I open the blinds?'

He did as instructed. The moment he yanked up the blackout blind, the room filled with sunshine that was so bright for the hour that Ross staggered back a step.

'It's going to be a beautiful day, matey,' he yawned.

'Yeah. Daddy's starting a new kind of job today.'

From seven o'clock, everything about Ross's mornings was an emergency. Making Ready Brek with mashed banana for Lachlann, tea and Weetabix for Isla, coffee for himself. While running back and forth between Lachlann's high-chair, servicing him with more porridge, and picking up the spoon that Lachlann felt compelled to toss across the room every thirty seconds, Ross emptied the dishwasher that had been full for twenty-four hours already, refilled it from the disgusting pile he had abandoned in the sink at ten o'clock the previous night, put the washing in the machine on another fast cycle as it had been sitting in the drum overnight for the second night running, and now it stunk to high heaven.

By eight o'clock in the morning, Ross had got more done than he would in entire days when he was twenty-five. When he looked back, he wondered what the hell he was doing for fifteen years of his life. He had probably spent entire weeks browsing Netflix, trying to find something to watch. The thought of doing that now was unthinkable. If there was no plan for what to watch, it was easy to load something from his or Isla's list, seeing as they had accumulated well over fifty movies and documentaries they planned to watch. Which was a waste of time anyway, seeing as they were both fast asleep within fifteen minutes of putting anything on the telly.

Happiness sprang up in ways that he could never have anticipated before Lachlann's arrival. Happiness to twenty-five-year-old Ross was crashing on the couch with some lager, watching *Match of the Day* on Saturday night, then falling asleep after a late-night Papa John's pizza. Now, happiness was discovering that the next load for the washing machine was only a single bed sheet and some towels, rather than fifty items of Lachlann's tiny clothes – and fifty items that would somehow have all magically turned inside out during the wash.

Ross and Isla had both been up for nearly twenty minutes before they actually spoke to each other about something non-Lachlann-related. 'What time did you get in last night?' asked Ross, grabbing and quickly dropping some toast from the toaster that was too hot to handle.

'Half one,' Isla replied through a yawn, turning on the cold tap for him.

Ross winced as he put his hand under it. 'Why so late?'

'A table of eight walked in at ten o'clock. I seriously considered murdering them all and leaving them in the walk-in freezer.'

'At least in prison you'd get some sleep.'

'Aw, don't say that.'

'I'm joking. It's worth it, eh.' With Lachlann finishing off his porridge on his own, Ross took the rare opportunity to grab Isla from behind and kiss her on the neck. 'I love you,' he said.

In his highchair, Lachlann pointed at Isla. 'Maah-mee!'

'I know, buddy,' said Ross. 'We love mummy, don't we? Mummy's the best.'

Isla kissed Ross on the cheek. 'I can't believe I have to go back in already. I'm sorry.' She picked Lachlann up from his high-chair, which he didn't appreciate.

Ross comforted him with a kiss on the head. 'It's all right, little man. You just have to go into nursery a little earlier today. Daddy and mummy have got work.'

Isla told Ross, 'Good luck today. A day without John Lomond. However will you manage?'

'What's that supposed to mean?'

'Come on, you love him, really. Oh, did you ask him if he wanted my friend Catriona's number? Did you remember?'

'Isla, I was trying to get him to sign my paperwork. It wasn't at the forefront of my mind.'

'Well, can you ask him today?'

'I'm not going to see him. Remember? I'm out in Cowcaddens today.'

'What if I just text him, and–'

'*Don't* do that. Please. Just leave it. For a little while.'

On her way to the front door, Isla said, 'Look at you. My man, working Organised Crime.'

Ross shook his head. 'Don't say it.'

On the way out, Lachlann leaned over Isla's shoulder, waving his hand. 'Bah-*bah!*'

Ross waved back with a huge smile. 'Bye, bye, matey!'

Isla grabbed her house keys and opened the front door. 'I'm not going to say it.'

Then, after she pulled the door shut, she shouted through the letterbox to him, 'Be careful!'

CHAPTER TWENTY

LOMOND HEADED across Dennis Dunbar's staircase landing to take the call. 'What won't I like, Linda?'

She sighed. 'ACCs Niven and Ogilvy have decided to combine our and Ruth Telford's Major Investigations Teams for this case.'

'Why would Niven do that? This case originated in the West Division. You know, the one he's temporarily in charge of.'

'Are you forgetting that Niven has just come out of A Division as Chief Superintendent? He might only be warming the next guy's seat, but I hear that Niven and Ruth Telford went out for curries twice a month when they were in Aberdeen together. And Ogilvy...well, he wants someone from the East Division in the game.'

'So Ruth's got two assistant chief constables in her pocket. That was always the difference between her and I. I never cared about having curries with a chief super.'

'No,' said Linda. 'But I can tell you that the odd bottle of wine for your DSU wouldn't go amiss.'

Glossing over the joke, Lomond said, 'She doesn't care about justice, Linda. She cares about who she's photographed with. Where her name ends up. The politics.'

'The politics demand that this case be wrapped up tidily. And quickly. It might not seem like it, but there's a mutual benefit to be had here.'

Lomond paused, trying to digest his disbelief. 'You're actually *in favour* of this?'

'John, let's be real. The press conference was a disaster. And Reekie and I don't have the time to hold your hand. It doesn't look good having the Chief Superintendent fronting press conferences. It elevates things in a case we're trying to keep as quiet as possible. Unfortunately, we're chasing a killer who is anything but quiet.'

Lomond was almost scared to ask the next question. 'Tell me she's not SIO.'

'No. Niven argued for it, but I talked him down. You're Senior Investigating Officer and will remain so. Unless Niven changes his mind, or you screw up in some massive way. Like, I don't know, an independent enquiry finds that you and Donna Higgins conspired to break the law in the Sandman investigation.' Linda paused to give him time to respond.

'It's going to be fine,' he said. 'Nothing happened. Donna didn't do anything wrong.'

Linda puffed. 'Okay, then. I'm sending over Pardeep,

Jason, Donna, and Willie. You and Ruth will brief from Edinburgh, then we'll see what's what.'

'What about Ross?' asked Lomond.

'He's starting at OC, remember? It's his first day.'

'Of course. I forgot.'

At the foot of the stairs, Ruth waved Lomond down. 'John, hurry up. I've got a patrol car waiting.'

'Yeah, be right there,' he called back, starting down the stairs.

Before Lomond ended the call, Linda said, 'Tell me I have nothing to worry about with this hearing.'

He replied, 'You have nothing to worry about.'

After close to two decades of working together, lying to Linda never got any easier.

CHAPTER TWENTY-ONE

Ross STOOD across from the Passport Office on the corner of Milton Street and Renton Street in Cowcaddens, pulling up the map on his phone. He pinch-zoomed in and out, alternating between the map and what he was standing in front of. He couldn't believe he had the right place.

It was a single-floor building with tiny windows covered by venetian blinds – all of them pulled shut. It looked like it had once been some kind of manufacturing facility. The building had been next to the site of the former *Sunday Post* offices before they were knocked down a few years ago, leaving an empty patch of wasteland that had been turned into a cheap car park. Cheap, as there were no guarantees your car would still be there when you returned.

The map checked out, and Ross set about finding the

front door. Then he realised there wasn't one. The only entrance was around the back. That was when it started to make more sense.

The ten parking spaces at the back of the building were occupied. The cars looked like they belonged on the set of *The Fast and the Furious*, low to the ground, with sound systems that could be heard from several streets away, and had preposterous popping and cracking sounds from the exhaust.

Multiple security cameras covered the entrance, and Ross had to give his name through an intercom before someone buzzed him in.

The interior reminded Ross of a derelict high school. Seventies lino peeling up off the floor. Broken doors hanging off their hinges, and fluorescent strip lights flickering above.

There was no reception area. Just a long corridor, and the sound of laughter somewhere near the end of it.

'Hello?' Ross said timidly, knocking on the door frame that opened into an expansive but dingy office space.

Now it started to look more like there was police work going on there.

There were whiteboards covered in mugshots, and names and dates, and desks with laptops. There were no desktop computers there. The site was only temporary.

There were five officers in plain clothes, none of them paying any attention to Ross.

In a corner of the room, two men were playing pool.

While bent over the table taking a shot, one of them said, 'Welcome to Renton Street. You must be DS McNair.' As he stood up, he added, 'Shaun's replacement.'

'I...I'm not sure. I don't know Shaun.'

'Shaun Webster.'

Ross shrugged. 'Em, possibly?'

The officer's friendly demeanour vanished. 'Then you must be in the wrong place. Because Shaun Webster was fucking irreplaceable.'

Baffled at what he had stumbled into, and not wanting to antagonise the officer further, Ross let it go.

He looked around the room, getting a feel for what the taskforce was working on. One of the whiteboards had a picture at the top and centre of a man with close-cropped hair and narrow eyes. It was the expression of a man both trying to stop anything getting out, or letting anything in. Ross didn't recognise him, but he looked exactly like the kind of guy he expected the Organised Crime Taskforce to be investigating.

At the centre of the room, a female officer was sitting with her back to the conversation, drinking coffee from a mug that had years of discolouring down the outside. She was scrolling through *The Citizen* website – a notorious Glasgow magazine run from a kitchen table in Yoker that specialised in crime and gangland stories. Free from editorial insight, it was full of mostly nonsense and gossip, but thanks to its network of underworld sources, it occasionally landed on a real story that no one else had.

She had platinum-blonde hair and dark pencilled eyebrows. She looked tall and athletic even sitting down, and had an unnaturally uniform skin tone from frequenting a tanning salon. Such a look in a testosterone-fuelled environment such as a Police Scotland taskforce populated by alpha males and lads, guaranteed trouble. Ross could imagine the sort of comments that went on when she left a room.

'You must be DS McNair,' she said, her back still turned. 'Ally Corrigan.'

Not only was she one of the youngest in the room, she was by some distance the youngest detective inspector that Ross had ever met.

'Ah, you're DI Corrigan,' Ross replied. 'We spoke on the phone.' He pulled out a chair and sat down at a long communal table that bisected the office.

Ally looked over her shoulder. 'Who said you could sit down?'

Ross looked at the others in the room, who just stared back at him. He was on his own.

For a moment, Ross leaned forward, about to get up.

Eventually, Ally said, 'I'm fucking with you.' She turned to her colleagues who were already smiling. 'He was actually going to get up.'

The others laughed with her, leaving Ross feeling like he was back in school again.

He might have had a cool choppy haircut and trendy

clothes, but when he was a kid, Ross McNair was not cool.

Small talk dispensed with, Ross stole a look over at Corrigan's desk. She had a small monitor showing the security camera footage from the front door.

Ross cleared his throat, nervous about interacting further after his first humiliation. But he didn't have a way of getting her attention, as she still had her back to him.

'Were you the one who buzzed me in?' he asked.

'We all know every person who's coming at any given hour,' she replied. 'We might be of different ranks in here, but we're all responsible for keeping the place safe. A lot of dangerous people would pay good money to know we're out here.'

Lomond had warned Ross it would be like this. A tight group of hard bastards who thought of themselves as "part polis, part Jason Bourne". Living life on the margins, outside the normal rules and regulations of Police Scotland. A law unto themselves.

The elite Organised Crime Taskforce led by the legendary DCI Gordon Hunt.

But Ross couldn't see him anywhere.

Bored by *The Citizen*, Ally tossed her phone down, then spun around in her chair. 'Why do you want to be in OC, Ross?'

Trying to fit in with the other alphas in the room, Ross leaned back in his chair, pretending he wasn't nervous. 'Well, I grew up around a lot of bad people. A pretty rough scheme. I saw what they did to the neighbourhood and the people. I didn't like it. I want to put folk like them away. You know, not just one bad guy at a time like we do at MIT. I'm talking about entire networks. Like OC takes down. And I want to start making moves into undercover work. I want to make a difference. A *real* difference that regular folk can see on their streets day to day.'

'You want some action, then?'

Ross hesitated.

Ally said, 'It's all right to admit, Ross. It's why half of us are here.'

'I do want some action,' he admitted.

'And you think you have the stomach for how we do business?'

Ross pushed his lips out and nodded. 'I reckon so.'

She smiled, and it wasn't a kind one. It slowly disappeared. 'Do you like sausages, Ross?'

Certain another joke was about to be made at his expense, Ross floundered.

'Shall I repeat the question?' asked Ally.

He relented. 'Sure. I like sausages.'

'What if I showed you how they were made? What went into them. The reality. Because you don't think about it, do you? You think they taste good in a roll with some tattie scone, right? But the reality? That's something else entirely.'

To change the script, Ross nodded at the whiteboard. 'Is that a current investigation?'

'Old, but ongoing. Regular OC back at London Road deal with the day-to-day stuff. Us? We're on the hunt for Shaun Webster.'

'Who is he?'

She pointed to the picture of the man on the whiteboard. 'The best undercover officer this taskforce ever had.'

'You lost an undercover officer?'

'We're still trying to establish what's happened.'

DCI Gordon Hunt suddenly strode into the room. Everyone straightened their backs and said in unison, 'Good morning, sir.'

'Morning, everyone,' Hunt replied, distracted. He threw his newspaper down on his desk, which pressed up alongside the other officers' desks. Despite the obvious respect everyone had for Hunt, if there was a hierarchy in the taskforce, Hunt was clearly not fussed about it. Ross had never seen a DCI just sitting amongst his team that way.

Hunt looked Ross up and down. 'You must be Lomond's boy.'

Ross hated everything about the sentence, but in the circumstances he didn't have much choice but to agree. 'Sir.'

'Ally's going to take you out.' He told her, 'I've set a meeting for you with Kenny Fan at the Sichuan Feng on Sauchiehall Street. He's expecting you any time before eleven this morning. You know him?'

Ally said, 'I know that he was Shaun's contact, sir, but I never met him. How do you want me to play it?'

'Find out if he's heard anything from his Chinese contacts about Shaun. The rest of you, I need you to ship out back to London Road. Chief Superintendent Reekie wants to look under your fingernails.'

A mixture of 'Aye aye, boss,' and 'Fuckin' hell' were the replies.

While everyone gathered their things and took their last drink of coffee, Ally asked from across the room, 'Ross, what car's yours?'

He stammered, 'Oh, I...eh...I didn't take it here. I got the subway to Cowcaddens.'

She scoffed. 'Fuck me, he doesn't even drive.'

'No, I drive. I've got a car. I just didn't take it. My wife needed it to drop my wee boy at nursery.'

She scoffed again. 'Christ, kids too. It just gets worse.'

Ross was getting tired of being a punching bag. 'Excuse me?' he retorted.

'Forget it. We'll take mine. The red Golf GTI. And wash your hands. I only got the car valeted this morning.'

Ross let out an incredulous sigh. Before he could reach the tiny sink in the corner of the room, DCI Hunt stepped in, holding Ross back. 'Go on ahead, Ally,' Hunt told her. 'Ross needs to sign some paperwork. He'll be out in a few minutes.'

Corrigan left with the others, the sound of their guffawing laughter at the end of the corridor echoing all the way back to the office. Ross was in no doubt that it was at his expense.

Ross complained, 'Sir, DSU Boyle signed my paper-work personally–'

Hunt pointed to a chair. 'Sit down, Ross.'

'What's going on, sir?'

Hunt's voice was grave. 'This isn't about your paperwork.'

CHAPTER TWENTY-TWO

HUNT TOOK up a spot leaning back against DI Corrigan's desk. He drummed his fingers on the tabletop for a few seconds before speaking again. 'I need someone I can trust. Someone outside my team. Someone new. That's why I wanted someone from John's team. I know that anyone who can handle DCI John Lomond for almost a year can handle pretty much anything.'

'I'm all ears, sir,' Ross said.

Whatever Hunt had to say, he still hadn't made up his mind that he was going to say it. Not out loud at least. 'What do you know about Shaun Webster?'

'Other than the fact your entire team apparently loathes me already because I'm taking his spot, not much.'

'That's everything? No rumours around Helen Street?'

'To be frank, sir, what goes on here is a mystery to almost everyone. Being buzzed in here earlier was like stepping into the wardrobe and going to Narnia.'

'We work privately for good reason, son. An Organised Crime taskforce is too much power to entrust to people. Not just me or my guys. Anyone. On a long-enough timeline, everyone gets corrupted by what it offers. The longer you work in it, the more you figure out the angles – and work out just how much you can get away with. Shaun Webster was one of those people. He was the best undercover officer the force has ever had, in my opinion. His work put away dozens of high-level thugs and gangsters, and taken millions of pounds' worth of drugs off the streets. Not to mention spared innocent people from human trafficking, sex slavery, and god knows what else.' Hunt paused, reluctant to go on.

'What happened to him?' asked Ross.

'To understand that, you first have to understand what Shaun Webster lost. Or more accurately, what OC has taken from him. When he agreed to go undercover, we took his entire life from him. What was left of it.'

'What do you mean?'

'It was before your time, but eleven years ago Shaun lost his wife and daughter in a car crash. He was the only survivor. Doesn't even bear thinking about what that must do to you. He threw himself heavily into work when he came back from leave. He begged for the under-cover assignment. Said he'd walk from the entire job if I didn't give him it.' Hunt sighed. 'I didn't want to lose him. So I did. These guys...they love the action. I mean, you've seen them. They're all convinced that they're the only thing standing in the way of Glasgow turning into Beirut. I look at some of them and it's like they're playing a video game. Except it's real. And it's their lives on the line. But like I say, they love the action. And Shaun loved it more than anyone.' Hunt pulled out a chair and sat in front of Ross. 'What I think happened – and educated guesses are all anyone has – is that Shaun got found out. He had worked his way up with Barry McKenna's people. Serious bloody people. They were on the cusp of a huge heroin deal, then Shaun stopped calling in. We assumed that he'd just gone dark because the deal was imminent and it wasn't safe for him to make contact. These guys are so paranoid. Always checking where everyone is, who they're talking to. So I let it go. A few weeks went by. Then it was a month. Then it was six.'

Ross's eyes bulged. 'He's been out of contact for *six months*?'

Hunt pulled out a cigarette and lit it. 'Yeah,' he said through a long exhalation of smoke.

'And you think he's still alive?'

'I don't know anymore. No one does.'

'Chief Superintendent Reekie must be all over you for answers.'

'And the rest. We haven't told Tulliallan yet.'

Ross didn't want his shock to come across like insubordination. 'Sir, if the Chief Constable or anyone in the Executive Team finds out, won't there be hell to pay?'

'For starters,' Hunt admitted. 'They'll burn the Task-force to the ground, along with my career. They're a bunch of secretaries, Ross. DCI Lomond and I have always been on the same page about that. It's why I trust you to come here and help me.'

'Help how?'

'You're my last chance to find Shaun. The last throw of the dice.'

'He's been missing for six months. Why the urgency?'

'Because sooner or later his body is going to appear somewhere, and I'm going to have no story for where he's been. I'm running out of time.'

Ross stood up and walked around. 'Sir, you know that I'd be honoured to join the Taskforce. But I've got a wee boy at home. I don't know if I could handle going under-cover with headcases like Barry McKenna so early in–'

'No, no, no,' said Hunt, raising his hand in defence. 'I don't want you to take Shaun's place. I want you here. Inside.'

Ross paused. 'I don't understand.'

'I want you to go undercover. In my team.'

'What? You think someone in your own taskforce is responsible for Shaun Webster going missing?'

Hunt took another drag of his cigarette. 'It's possible.'

'Based on what?'

Hunt leaned forward on his knees. 'Telling even a trusted associate what I'm about to say would be risky. I'm putting my trust in a stranger purely because John Lomond said that I could trust you with anything.'

Ross stopped his pacing.

Hunt said, 'Detective Inspector Ally Corrigan is a wild one. Exactly the sort of officer I described earlier. She's been going off the rails the last year. I heard rumours about possible rogue operations she was running, but nothing solid that I could confront her with. I think Shaun may well have found out something about her. I need someone on the inside to find out if she's telling me everything she knows about Shaun's disappearance.'

Ross put his head in his hands. 'I thought this was a secondment. What the hell have I walked into?'

'Son, we're police officers, not the army. But one of our own is behind enemy lines. And we have to go in there and get him.'

'You want *me* to go and get him – what your Taskforce has been unable to do for the last six months?'

'I want you to get the information. You won't be in harm's way. I promise.'

Ross let out a heavy sigh. Doing a favour for someone like Hunt – and tangentially, CSU Reekie – would be a very smart career move. In return, Hunt was asking for a lot – and Ross suspected, not telling him the whole story. At least not yet.

But it was Organised Crime. And this was his way in.

Ross said, 'When do I start?'

Hunt replied, 'Right now.'

CHAPTER TWENTY-THREE

WILLIE, Donna, Pardeep, and Jason were already impressed by the sight of Fettes College and its grand driveway at the end of Fettes Avenue in the Comely Bank area of Edinburgh – it looked like something out of *Harry Potter*. But they were equally impressed by the home that Edinburgh's Major Investigations Team had acquired for itself in the newly refurbished Fettes Avenue Station.

Once a seventies red-brick, flat-roofed eyesore, the station was now a modern marvel. An ode to glass and steel. Helen Street might have had the prestige of being the most secure station in the country – where major terror suspects and high-profile arrests were detained and questioned – but the new Fettes Avenue was without question the most desirable place to work.

'No wonder Telford transferred here,' Pardeep gushed as the group walked through the car park.

'It wasn't a transfer,' replied Willie. 'It's a big promotion. John says she's being groomed for Tulliallan.'

Donna said, 'I don't know how they swing these cushy positions.'

'Kissing all the right arses,' Pardeep said.

Willie added, 'That, and a hundred per cent clearance rate for year after year.'

'She really did that?' asked Donna.

'It's Aberdeen,' Pardeep replied. 'Who gives a fuck?' He waved his hand disdainfully at the building in front of them. 'And who gives a fuck about Edinburgh either? Take away the castle, it's just Argyle Street with a bunch of Americans kicking about, and it takes five times as long to walk anywhere.'

Jason, conspicuously quiet until now, could no longer hold his tongue. 'You really think Glasgow's that much better than Edinburgh?'

'Stack up any Glasgow equivalent that Edinburgh has, and I'll tell you why Glasgow's version is better.'

'How about the Edinburgh Festival for starters?'

Pardeep grumbled, 'The bloody Festival...fuck me. Five million shows every year, and about three that anyone actually wants to go see. Plus, everyone actually *from* Edinburgh hates the Festival. Glasgow's got the Comedy Festival, which actually makes folk laugh. And you've got TRNSMT at Glasgow Green, though they seem to have something against vowels for some strange reason.'

Jason tried again. 'Okay, how about Leith? It's

cosmopolitan, chic, but still salt-of-the-earth working class.'

Pardeep looked disgusted. 'You call yourself a Glaswegian? Are you seriously going to put Leith's hipster-wannabe, gentrified pizza bistros up against Partick? A place that still has an actual identity? Or does Leith win because it's got a Zizzi's?'

'What about football teams?' asked Donna.

Pardeep's disgust now turned to horror. 'Are you actually kidding? Hibs and Hearts up against Celtic and Rangers? Tell me you're kidding!'

Donna laughed with Willie. 'Can't believe he fell for that one. That was too easy.'

Pardeep's aversion to all things Edinburgh didn't soften once they got inside the station. When their wait at reception moved into minute two, Pardeep couldn't resist mentioning, 'Typical east coast welcome, I see...'

Donna remarked, 'Pardeep, I think you might have a problem.'

'And what would that be?'

'I think you're a racist.'

'Racist against folk from Edinburgh?'

'Can that be a thing?' asked Jason.

'Sure sounds like it,' said Donna.

Willie had heard enough. 'Just stop it the lot of you. We need to work with this crowd. Show some profession-alism, for fuck's sake.'

Next to reception, DCI Lomond swung open a door. 'Right, you lot,' he announced. 'In here.'

He had his sleeves rolled up and wasn't wearing a suit jacket as he usually did.

As they went upstairs, each of the team removed their jackets too.

'Why's it so hot?' asked Willie, who had picked a bad day to opt for a three-piece suit. Even peeled down to his waistcoat he was still cooking.

Lomond gestured at the abundance of glazing around them. 'The whole place is designed to be carbon neutral. Energy efficient windows and the like. The place holds heat like a Dutch oven.'

Jason was so hot, he didn't think twice before saying, 'I've been on maternity wards that are cooler than this.'

As soon as he said it, he regretted it. He shut his eyes.

Lomond, leading the way, said nothing, but the others didn't know where to look or what to say.

Jason was beside himself. Of all the people to crack a joke to about a maternity ward, Lomond wasn't the one.

Willie moved conversation on as quickly as he could. 'So what's this lot like?'

'Honestly?' said Lomond. 'It might look like bring-your-kid-to-work day up there, but you can't argue with their stats. They get the work done.'

When they reached the fourth floor, Jason made a point of keeping Lomond back.

'Sir,' he explained. 'I didn't mean to—'

Lomond patted Jason on the shoulder. It was like patting the side of a mountain. 'Forget it, son. Really. We've got more important things to worry about.'

CHAPTER TWENTY-FOUR

Ross ARRIVED in the car park halfway through some ongoing banter. Like someone walking into a movie halfway through, he didn't really understand what was going on.

Not wanting to appear prudish, Ross chuckled along, hoping someone would notice that he didn't mind the avalanche of homophobic and sexist remarks being lobbed around. Most of it by Detective Inspector Ally Corrigan.

The rest of the team hung on her every word.

'New guy,' she shouted to Ross. 'You're with me.'

A wave of wolf whistles went off, along with a call of 'Hands off the boss, Ross.'

Ross didn't know what to do. He had never experienced a dynamic between constables and a detective inspector that was so far beyond banter, it was bordering on harassment.

When they were both in the car, Ally checked, 'Did you wash your hands?'

Ross lifted them up. 'Spotless.'

'Great,' she said, starting the engine and immediately over-revving it. 'Don't even think about touching the stereo. I've got the levels just the way I want them.'

She pressed play on the steering wheel, which put on Dr Dre's 'The Next Episode' at ear-splitting levels. When Snoop Dogg's opening line came in, the bass was so loud and thumping Ross was convinced there was a pneumatic drill hammering under the car.

'Hold on,' Ally said, then set off at a terrifying speed along Milton Street for Dobbie's Loan to avoid the chronic traffic on the M8 above.

Ross, who was still putting on his seatbelt, was thrown back into his seat.

Trying to maintain some degree of cool, he asked, 'What's up first, Ally?'

'Micky D's. Fucking famished, mate. I was legless last night.'

'Oh yeah? What time did you get in?'

'Fuck knows. Three? My phone battery died when I was in Distrikt, and the guy I went home with didn't have a clock anywhere.'

Ross nodded. 'Cool.'

Ally made half a glance in his direction, then scoffed to herself.

She spent the rest of the journey to McDonald's drive-through in Finnieston nodding her head in time to the hypnotic beat, spitting every lyric without missing a word.

Ross sat there mesmerised, feeling like he had truly arrived. He put his window down like Ally had, and nodded along with the music – though not quite as enthusiastically. For a few minutes he forgot that he was police.

Ally ordered two double bacon and egg McMuffins, and a supersize vanilla milkshake. Ross couldn't believe that someone so svelte could pack away such a sizeable breakfast.

When she handed him the large, heavy bag and the tall cup, Ross said, 'You really *are* hungover.'

Ally held an expectant hand out. 'I'll eat on the move. McMuffin, the milkshake, then the other McMuffin. In that order. Got it?'

'No problem,' said Ross, recoiling at the smell of the food. Like most teens, he had regularly tanned Big Macs and fries, but stopped after he met Isla. After a five-year break, he tried a Big Mac again, and felt like crap for the next six hours. Ross passed her the first McMuffin. 'So how does this guy know Shaun Webster?'

Ally tore into the McMuffin like she hadn't seen food for days. Speaking with her mouth full, she said, 'A contact from when Shaun was sent to infiltrate Barry McKenna's crew.'

'Hang on. I thought McKenna was Edinburgh.'

'He was. Until Frank Gormley was put away for a decade and change for fraud and money laundering. In

Gormley's absence, the whole criminal landscape's gone to shit. Anyone who's been out in the city centre recently can testify to that. The sad truth is that having Frank Gormley around kept things on an even keel. Since he was put away, you've got a bunch of small-time guys fighting to become big time. That's the problem with a vacuum. There's always ten other guys waiting to fill it. Best-placed to do that was Barry McKenna. He had the muscle, the connections, and he damn well sure had the funds. He's made big gains across the central belt. Mostly in the north of Glasgow. Gains that were thanks to an alliance he made with some Chinese nationals that have been operating out of an office in...' She gestured for Ross to complete the sentence.

It took him a moment. 'The Sichuan Feng?'

'Exactly,' said Ally. 'Getting solid intel about the Chinese from an informant inside the restaurant helped strengthen Shaun's legend for being undercover.'

'Legend?'

Ally rolled her eyes. 'His cover story. The information Shaun supplied the gang to make him sound credibly not a cop. Having inside info on the Chinese made Shaun more valuable to McKenna. That whole landscape is about to change, though, seeing as your old boss helped get Gormley out the jail.'

Ross said nothing.

'Yeah,' said Ally, 'the word's out on that now. Word on the street is that something crooked went down in Barlinnie between Gormley and your man Lomond.'

Ross retorted, 'You have no idea what Gormley gave us in return. A kid's life was at stake.'

'And how many kids' lives will be at stake now that he's back on the streets? Next time you see Lomond, tell him I hope it was worth it.'

Wanting to get off the subject of Lomond, Ross asked, 'How do you get inside a gang like McKenna's?'

'Shaun got in tight with one of their crew after saving them from a hiding outside a pub in Hamilton.'

'That was lucky.'

'Not really. It was us that gave the guy the hiding.'

'You jumped a guy?'

'Me and the other guys made Shaun look like a hero. From then on, he worked his way up. It took months. He was the best. I mean, they had no clue. They had him doing drop offs and they didn't bat an eyelid.'

'Drop-offs?'

Ally rolled her eyes again. 'Christ, you *are* green, aren't you? The days of some stoners turning up to your door looking to score are long gone. No dealer's going to keep that amount of gear lying around. The more you get caught with, the longer you're going away. And the reality of dealing is that eventually you're going to get popped. When it happens, you want to be carrying ounces, not kilos. With a drop-off, you text a number, you make arrangements to meet a car that picks you up on a quiet street somewhere, and the deal happens in the car. That way, you never have to have more than what we consider to be "a bit of personal" on you at any time. Bear in mind, these guys are driving around in a fucking Toyota Yaris or a Renault or something. Driving around in a blinged-up Mercedes is just asking for trouble these days. You could walk right by a deal happening in the street. Just looks like some guy getting dropped off by his uncle or something. It's easy. Deal in the car, money exchange, then back to pick up whatever's next. Done. It's like sending out Ubers but with drugs.'

'That's almost impossible to stop,' said Ross.

Ally adjusted the rear-view mirror. During all her rapping and knocking back McMuffins and milkshakes, she had still been able to notice a white van two cars behind them in the long queue bound for Charing Cross.

Ross asked, 'How close did Webster get to McKenna?'

'The last I heard, he was very near the top. I think he came to like it. You've seen the other guys. They're alphas. Big swaggers on them, tight t-shirts, big arms. Shaun was a total alpha. Big gym guy. I think he was on juice but he always denied it. The picture in the office doesn't do him justice. He was a thick neck mother-fucker. Guys like that, they want to be around other alphas. So the top guys, they warmed to Shaun once they got to know him. They could tell he was one of them. They started taking him out to clubs. Weekends to Amsterdam. Hard partying. A lot of coke. A lot of girls. He loved it. But he forgot he was there to do a job.'

Ross wasn't sure about whether he should ask his

next question, *Do you think Webster's alive?* Instead, he rephrased it.

'What do *you* think happened to Webster?'

Ally slurped up the last few drops of her milkshake with the straw. 'I don't know. Maybe dead. It could be that he's just gone quiet to protect his cover.'

'But for six months?'

Ally looked with relief in the rear-view mirror as they finally made it through the traffic lights. The white van behind them had turned left instead of following them straight towards St Vincent Street. 'I worked with Shaun for two years before he went undercover. That guy's been through more in his life than you'll ever know. All sealed on his file. But I know what you're thinking.'

'What am I thinking?' asked Ross.

'You think Shaun's gone rogue. Joined McKenna's crew for real.'

'You must see that there's a chance of that.'

Ally admitted, 'I do.'

CHAPTER TWENTY-FIVE

In the Major Investigations Team office, the stark contrast between Fettes Avenue and Helen Street was further evident. Work spaces were tidy, chairs tucked in behind desks. Lomond knew that if his team had been put in the same building, within a week the place would have been littered with greasy Greggs paper bags, stained mugs, Irn Bru on the carpet, and paperwork spilling onto floors. The Fettes team didn't have anything personal out on their desks. No photographs, Post-Its with silly jokes on them, or little trinkets. All they had was work, stationery, energy bars and bottles for making protein shakes. It was like working in a Police Scotland show-room – the absolute pinnacle of how Tulliallan wanted offices to run. The only issue was that every DCI like Lomond said it was impractical or impossible to replicate in older buildings.

Of course everyone at Helen Street worked with

THE BLOODY, BLOODY BANKS   149

determination to catch criminals, and they worked long, thankless hours. But the Fettes team were so much more efficient and organised about the way they worked. They were the Japanese rail network: always on time, clean and tidy, did everything by the book, and never suffered any disasters. While Helen Street was ScotRail: often late, a little disorganised, outdated inside, and a few too many drunks hanging around.

At Helen Street, it was sometimes six and half a dozen whether a plug socket would work. At Fettes Avenue, everything worked perfectly.

When Lomond brought the team into the office, Ruth led a round of applause that prompted quizzical looks among the Glasgow group.

Pardeep said quietly to Jason, 'I can't tell if we're being celebrated or made fun of.'

DCI Telford held court at the front of the room, bringing her hands together like a primary school teacher about to announce something exciting. 'Okay, guys,' she said with bright eyes. 'I know this is a little unorthodox for us all, but I want to tell you I'm super invested in this process.' As further spontaneous applause broke out from Ruth's team, she nodded away. 'Yes, indeed. Now, John and I are fully aware of the impact two chief inspectors can have on a case. Wires can get crossed. Conflicting messages etcetera. So I want to be really heard on this point, Fettes Avenue team: it is our role to provide whatever help John and his team require. For my guys, I know this is going to require a period of adjust-

ment. We're all very tight aboard this particular investi-
gatory ship...'

Willie and Lomond exchanged a glance of '*what the
fuck is she babbling about?*'

For Lomond, he was at least used to it. She had
always talked that way as long as he'd known her. Like
she'd learned the English language from a Public Rela-
tions textbook and *Talk Shite for Dummies.*

'Let me introduce the team,' she said, then gestured
for DS Erskine to go first.

'DS Jane Erskine,' she said, only getting half out of
her seat and waving at waist height. If she and the two
detective constables she was with had been siblings, she
would have been the slightly older, wiser sister who read
lots of books, while the two boys spent all day outdoors
climbing trees or playing video games.

As she moved to sit down again, Ruth lifted her head
expectantly. 'Jane? Remember?'

Then, with obvious embarrassment at having to do it,
Jane said, 'My pronouns are she/her.'

'Christ,' whispered Pardeep to Donna. 'It's DCI
Telford's mini-me.'

'Same haircut and everything,' Donna replied.

'Don't. I can't even look at the hair. It's freaking me
out.'

The next to stand up was a male officer. Thin and
pasty, with what Lomond thought of as an embarrassment of facial hair. It was an insult to facial hair to even
call it a beard. It was an accident.

'DC Ian Lambie,' he said in a reedy voice. 'My pronouns are he/him.'

Donna whispered to Pardeep, 'Looks like an actual wee lamb, doesn't he?'

Pardeep had to restrain spluttering laughter. Lambie looked so innocent, Pardeep could picture him jumping around the office like a spring lamb whenever a lead came through.

Last was another male officer who was the cleanest-cut plain clothes Lomond had ever seen. In a clearly well-educated Edinburgh accent so stiff that he sounded starched, he said, 'Hi there. I am Detective Constable Fraser Foster...'

Willie muttered to Pardeep, 'It's like if Marks and Spencer made an android.'

Pardeep replied, 'He could make a choir boy look like Johnny Rotten.'

'Definitely plays rugby.'

'Aye. Cricket an' all.'

'Aye, no doubt.'

Foster then surprised the Glasgow team by adding, 'You can use whatever pronoun you want for me as long as it's not an expletive.' He chuckled earnestly, then added, 'I'm just honoured to have the chance of working with you all. I'm looking forward to learning a thing or two.'

'Shite,' Willie said quickly to Pardeep. 'I feel bad now.'

'Seem an awright bunch,' Pardeep replied.

Ruth wore a look of satisfaction now that her pupils had impressed the important visitors. 'Without further ado, I'll now hand you over to DCI Lomond.'

He took up Ruth's spot in front of the whiteboard, which was already full of case particulars relating to George Melrose and Dennis Dunbar's deaths. But instead of standing off to the side, Ruth lingered just behind Lomond, as if he might need her at any moment.

He shot her an irritated glance, but she either didn't pick up on it, or didn't care to move.

He started by introducing his team, which set off a wave of overlapping handshakes. Once they were over, Lomond turned to the whiteboards. Except Ruth was in the way. Once she got out of the way, Lomond pointed to the information on Melrose.

'Victim number one is George "Butcher" Melrose,' he said. 'Dismembered, limbs discovered in Loch Lomond near the beach at Luss harbour. In the last twelve hours or so, the dive unit have uncovered a safe in the water. The safe door had a time release. When the door opened yesterday morning, the limbs came to the surface. We could spend ages on these facts alone. Why not just weigh the limbs down? Dump them in a bag with a bunch of rocks?'

Too eager to realise Lomond was being rhetorical, DS Lambie called out, 'The killer wanted the limbs to be found.'

'Quite clearly,' Lomond replied, trying to be polite. 'There's also the complication of a mystery foot that was stitched on Melrose's leg. That foot has yet to be identi-fied, but we're hopefully going to get something on that later today. I can tell you that Moira McTaggart at Gart-cosh thinks that the amputations were done with proper medical equipment. We're not talking about someone going at Melrose with a hedge trimmer here. This killer was prepared. Professional.' He turned his attention to the forensics photos from Lochgoilhead. 'This message was found in Melrose's living room, written in blood. We're still waiting for a possible ID on that blood, but I can tell you that Moira has at this stage ruled out the blood being Melrose's.' Lomond checked his watch. 'And about fifteen minutes ago, she ruled it out as being Dennis Dunbar's as well.'

Willie said, 'So we're potentially looking at a further two victims already out there.'

'Possibly,' said Lomond. 'Another possibility, as awful as it might be, is that those two unknown persons are still alive. One missing a foot. Another missing a heck of a lot of blood. And if we don't get on top of this thing soon, they could have a damn sight worse coming their way.'

CHAPTER TWENTY-SIX

As Ross and Ally inched towards Sauchiehall Street, with only two cars at a time managing to putter through the traffic lights each cycle, Ally said, 'Say Shaun *has* gone rogue, I can't say I'd blame him. What's his reward if he stays undercover? A bit of extra pay that lasts a few months, maybe a wee holiday somewhere nice for a fortnight. Meanwhile, the guys he's helped send down – like Gormley – are out in a matter of years, and when they get out, they'll spend every penny they have to track his sorry arse down. There's no money you could give me to do what Shaun did.'

Ross respected the honesty, but he was staggered that a detective inspector in the elite Organised Crime Taskforce would have such apathy for the job – and have such empathy for a fellow officer hypothetically turning rogue.

Ally checked the time on the dashboard. 'You know

you're the first guy to come through OC that didn't tell me how hot I was within an hour of meeting me.'

Ross felt his cheeks go red.

Ally was unquestionably attractive. In a glamour model way. But ever since he met Isla, he just wasn't capable of thinking that way about other women. He simply wasn't interested. Isla was it for him. She was his person. End of.

Ally explained, 'Every room I've walked into since I was sixteen, guys have been trying to shag me. It's like a superpower I've got. You're all so led by your dicks.' Then, as casually as someone might offer someone else a sweet, she blurted out, 'You want a go-around? We're heading to Sauchiehall Street. We could park up in Sauchie Lane.'

Ross gulped. Was she for real?

His voice cracked as he said, 'I'm married.'

'You sure you're not gay? I mean, I'd be surprised. Normally I can tell.'

Ross didn't respond.

Ally pressed on. 'You're telling me you don't want to shag me? Just because we're working together? Because you think you shouldn't? Be honest. You *don't* want to shag me?'

Ross was frozen. He was trapped in a potentially career-ending incident if he said the wrong thing. 'This is crazy, Ally. And totally inappropriate.'

'Suit yourself. But in case you're ever wondering, that's what a sure thing looks like. And you should have taken it. Because you're never going to get anything else from me.'

'I get it,' said Ross. 'You think that the only way to survive in a taskforce like this is to act like you're one of the guys. You can do this sort of stuff every day, but you'll never get their respect.'

Ally turned her back to Ross. 'Do you see a zip there?'

'No.'

'So I definitely don't look like I zip up the back?'

Losing patience, Ross snapped, 'No!'

She shook her head in disbelief. 'You think I go around begging officers to shag me?'

'Then what's this about?'

'I had to make sure you weren't like the others. I was pretty sure already. Now I *know*.'

'And how am I not like the others?'

'You didn't want to shag me for one thing.' Ally paused, wanting to choose her words carefully. 'You want into the Taskforce permanently, right?'

'More than anything.'

'The other guys? They're morons. But they do their job well because they think simply. All they want to do is workout, shag, watch the game, and kick in doors. They're only marginally above the morons they're trying to arrest and put in jail. DCI Hunt's a decent guy, but he doesn't have the guts to do what's required to get the job done. I mean, I respect the things he's done, but he's a fossil as far as crime prevention goes. It's a different world now and he's not built for it. DCI Lomond on the other hand...'

'Yeah, well, I came here to get away from John Lomond.'

'Why? He saved that wee boy's life and put away Sharon Belmont.'

'The team did actually,' Ross clarified. 'In any case, the whole Sandman conviction is up in the air thanks to DCI Lomond's disregard for rules.'

'Are you serious?'

Ross shuffled in his seat. 'You didn't hear this from me, right. But there's a disciplinary hearing about something that went on in the investigation. I don't know exactly what. But Lomond is involved. And if the hearing doesn't find in MIT's favour, it could be the start of a process that ends with Sharon Belmont's conviction being overturned.'

Ally ran her hand over her mouth. It was time to lay her cards on the table. 'The lesson from that story isn't "don't take risks". The lesson is "don't get caught". Professional Standards don't understand that not everything is black and white out here on the streets. Especially with Organised Crime. I respect guys like Hunt and Lomond, but if you want to make major plays in this Taskforce, make no mistake. You've got to keep up with me and have my back, no matter what. That means you're going to have to forget about what you know – and what you *think* you know – about right and wrong, and justice. In the short amount of time you're with me, that's going to be hard to understand sometimes. So I need to know that you're onboard with what we're trying to do here.'

'And what is that?'

'Keep the streets safe, no matter the cost. Are you with me?'

Ross said nothing as the road cleared ahead. Most of the traffic was joining the M8 below.

But without any hesitation, Ally slammed on the brakes and pulled up the handbrake. Traffic behind came to a standstill. She leaned across Ross and opened his door.

'My way or the highway. Your choice. But if you stay, you do exactly what I say and without questioning my methods. You're here to help me find Shaun Webster, and I will do absolutely *anything* to make that happen. You understand?'

Ross gripped the sides of his seat. 'What the hell are you doing?'

She wasn't just blocking the road ahead. They were on the crossroads of the St Vincent Street flyover, and blocking the long queue of commuter traffic that had built up behind the lights. When the lights to their left changed, Ally's Golf GTI was blocking the path of even more traffic. Within a few seconds, a cacophony of horns rang out across Charing Cross.

Ally didn't seem to register any of it. 'Well?'

Ross exclaimed, 'Just drive, would you?'

She leaned forward to enter Ross's line of sight.

'We're going nowhere until you answer. We can stay here all fucking day for all I care.'

Ross's head flicked from left to right. The traffic lights changed again, which turned the car horns into surround sound. 'Another minute of this and the guy in that truck is going to kill us both.'

Ally snapped her fingers in his face. 'Hey! Do you understand?'

'Yes! Yes! I understand. I'll do whatever you want me to do to find Shaun Webster. Just drive!'

Ally dropped the handbrake, then jerked the steering wheel hard, using momentum to close Ross's door for him.

She pulled into the bus stand on Holland Street. The reprieve from the Golf's loud engine brought an eerie silence to the car. 'Would you ever participate in the torture of a drug addict to maintain your cover? How about sit comfortably in a room while someone who owes a debt is raped?'

Ross thought for a moment, mouth tight. 'Yes.'

'Bullshit,' Ally replied. 'But I tell you what. I'm going to give you a chance to prove yourself to me. OC isn't for everyone, Ross. I've seen plenty of guys like you. They've got the slim-fit suit, the lashings of aftershave, the stubble. You want to be like them. You want to be like those morons back at the office. They might be as dumb as a box of rocks, but you can't read their eyes. The eyes always give you away. And yours are soft, Ross. The second a real gangster looks in them they'll know: you've got something to lose. You want to know how I do it?'

'How?' Ross asked.

She held her hand out, palm up. 'You take everything you care about, everything you love, everything that makes you happy, and you put it in there.' She closed her hand and made a fist. 'Then you wrap it up tight, and lock it away somewhere. If you don't, you're going to end up hurt out here.' She stared at him. 'Do you trust me?'

Ross answered, 'Absolutely not.'

'Good,' she said. 'You're starting to learn already.'

When she got out of the car, a bus driver behind blasted his horn, then held his hands up in disbelief.

He hung out his window. 'Ho! This is buses only.'

Instead of showing her badge, Ally turned around and calmly told him, 'Fuck off.' She started walking.

'I don't understand,' said Ross, catching up with her. 'Why aren't you ditching me?'

'Because I still want to find Shaun, and I think you can help me. If I'm going to have someone from John Lomond's MIT reporting back to Hunt on my every move, I might as well get something out of it.'

Ross looked back, as the bus driver leaned on his horn.

Ally strode on, smiling. Impervious to everything around her.

Ross thought, *what the hell have I got myself into?*

CHAPTER TWENTY-SEVEN

LOOKING AROUND THE BRIEFING ROOM, Lomond felt more than ever that he was missing Ross. Willie, Donna, Pardeep, and Jason were always reliably smart once he had already asked something of them. But without Ross, Lomond was left to fill in the blanks.

'The problem we have,' he explained, 'is too many possible motives and suspects. George Melrose wasn't called "Butcher" for nothing. And whoever killed him this way was trying to make a point. It's not our job to decide whether Melrose deserved to die. But someone out there clearly thinks that he did. We don't have time to send resources out to chase down dozens of leads. We unfortunately needed a second victim to help narrow things down.' Lomond edged along the whiteboard to the details on Dunbar. 'With the discovery of Dennis Dunbar in Gullane, we now have that. What we need to establish is whether anything connects Dunbar and

George Melrose. Any commonalities. Did they do business together?' He turned to DCI Telford, who showed no signs of contributing. Or anyone else, for that matter.

Walking back and forth in front of the whiteboard, he said, 'He's punishing them. Humiliating them. Whatever's driving him to do this is personal. You don't just naturally acquire this depth of feeling, to act this way. To do these things. Whenever people hear of some paedophile being released from jail, they talk about doing things like this. But no one actually does it. The Taxman does. He takes action, while everyone else talks. Making that leap from talk to action requires something dramatic. A catalyst. He didn't choose to do this, I don't think. He was compelled. Thinks he's doing the right thing. In a world of chaos and violence, he turns the sin against the sinner.'

Jason asked, 'You think there's a religious component to these?'

'Possibly,' replied Lomond. He stared at the personality traits he had noted on the whiteboard, then appeared to dismiss them all in one go 'I don't know. I'm reaching.'

Continuing her role of teacher, Ruth scanned the group. 'Any other questions so far?'

DC Foster asked, 'Is there any evidence that Dunbar was murdered because of one particular case, or his overall career?'

'Great question, Fraser,' Ruth said. 'In short, we don't know yet.' She picked a forensics photo off the board. 'But this hard drive found in Dunbar's study certainly paints a compelling picture. Before we get into the hard drive's contents, we know that the killer was looking for this. John and I's suspicion is that Dunbar was threatened and eventually gave up the drive's location.'

Donna asked, 'Was there any blood found in the house? Or do we think the gunshot happened at the golf course?'

Ruth replied, 'Another great question...'

Lomond tried not to let on how irritating he found Ruth's affirmations. She had no doubt read in a book or heard at some management seminar to praise a question before answering it.

Ruth continued, 'There was no blood found at either the house or the golf course. So what we're starting with is the gunshot being fired in whatever vehicle the Taxman was using. I believe John has an update on that to come. Before that, however, we need to talk about what was found on Dunbar's hard drive.' Her head dropped in a moment of solemnity. And it was genuine. 'The contents are grim. We're talking thousands of images and videos of sexual exploitation of minors. John, you have a little more experience in this area.'

Arms folded with tension, Lomond stared at the ground. There was no getting rid of the images he had found on the drive from his mind. 'They're as extreme as anything I've ever come across. As well as being a very wealthy lawyer for decades, it appears that Dennis

Dunbar has been a deeply depraved paedophile for just as long. There are images going back twenty years. And that means that some poor bastard at Gartcosh has got the unenviable task of going through each image and compositing images of faces and what they might look like today. Because anyone who was involved in Dunbar's activities...' He broke off, almost trembling with anger for the victims. 'Let's just say I could understand someone taking the law into their own hands in this case. In a rather messed up way, knowing what I know now about the Taxman's victims, it's going to be hard for members of the public not to cheer the guy on once this gets out.' Still caught playing the terrible images in his head, Lomond added, 'In another life outside of the police, I might actually have been one of them. For now, we're going to try keeping a lid on these details.'

Jason raised his hand – as he always did before asking a question in a briefing.

'Yes, Jason,' said Lomond.

'Sir, was there anything else on the hard drive? Related to his work?'

Ruth said, 'Why do you ask, Jason?'

'It's just, the manure in the mouth. That speaks to someone who believes Dunbar has told lies rather than committed sexual crimes. As shocking a find as the images and videos are, it could end up being a huge mistake going down the wrong rabbit hole.'

Lomond flashed his eyebrows up. 'It's a fair point,' he said to Ruth.

'And we have discussed that, Jason,' she said. 'This is just a jumping-off point for now. What we do have, as far as evidence goes, is the gun.'

The moment she heard it, Donna thought that it sounded wrong. She whispered to Pardeep, 'Why would he leave the gun?'

Thinking the same thing, DC Lambie called out, 'It seems a bit off that he would leave the gun, don't you think?'

'Maybe,' said Ruth, 'What we have in our favour is the NABIS database. For those of you unfamiliar with it, that's the National Ballistics Intelligence Service. Gartcosh tests every gun that arrives there, and every available data point on that weapon is uploaded to NABIS. From there, we can tell if weapons have been used during prior illegal activities, and build a picture of where it might have been. But like the blood from Melrose's house and the mystery foot, it's going to take a little while.'

DS Erskine raised her hand while still taking feverishly fast notes. 'Ruth, just quickly on that point...' She put down her pen. 'What if the barrel of the gun has been replaced at some point? Wouldn't that give a different ballistic signature? Render the data from NABIS irrelevant?'

Ruth conceded, 'Yep, that's possible. We could also get Gartcosh to strip the gun down for DNA.'

'There's nothing on that gun,' said Lomond. 'Forensics dusted it already. In any case, the Taxman's not going to forget to wipe it down before he chucks it.'

'Of course not. But I had a case in Aberdeen where a member of a crime gang was abducted and tortured. Part of it was being pistol-whipped. Later, when we found a suspect with a weapon, Gartcosh were able to strip the gun down to its tiniest component parts. They then swabbed every part for sweat and blood to capture any DNA that might be within the magazine or the chamber. Just wiping down the exterior of a gun isn't enough now. Even a rag soaked in bleach and run all over the exterior contact points. They found microscopic particles of the victim's blood and sweat which were previously hidden. It's a relatively new test. If you don't know about it, I doubt the Taxman is aware of it.'

Lomond had to admit he was impressed. Ruth's one hundred per cent clearance rate was becoming less of a mystery.

Lomond nodded enthusiastically. 'Let's get Moira onto it. Donna, you handle that.'

He looked around the room, getting a feel for how everyone was reacting to the briefing. He wanted to end on a note of optimism, to start building momentum. 'These are all potentially valuable results.' He tapped a murky photo of a dark Volvo estate taken from CCTV near the A82 that was pinned to the board. 'But until Moira gets us some news, we're going to concentrate on this vehicle. We know that it was seen in the Luss area around the time we think George Melrose's body was dumped in Loch Lomond. If we can link that vehicle to Gullane also, then—'

Ruth winced audibly, then acted surprised when Lomond stopped talking. 'Sorry, John. But I thought we were putting the Volvo lead on the back burner.'

Lomond turned his head slightly in confusion. He asked, 'Could I talk to you for a moment? Privately?'

Ruth showed him the way to her office, set away from the communal area. It was largely sound-proofed by a long window visible to everyone in the briefing room.

Ruth retreated behind her desk. She knew what was coming.

'Put the Volvo lead on the back burner in favour of what?' demanded Lomond.

While Lomond didn't give a shit how many eyes were on him at that moment – and it was every pair of eyes in the office – Ruth tried to give off an air of calm authority.

She said, 'Until we get something we can move on from Moira, we should divert our resources to our existing cases.'

Lomond stared at her with incomprehension. 'Are you outside of your *mind*? Did you fall and hit your head in the last thirty seconds? We're two days in on a serial killer case and you want to *divert* officers to another case?'

She tried to smile. A mere impression of one. 'Please

lower your voice. I never could talk to you when you're like this.'

'Like what?'

'Hysterical. You're being hysterical.'

'Because you're handling this case like a politician. Two days in, you don't sit and wait for information to fall into your lap.' He remonstrated towards the office doors. 'It's our job to go out there and get it.'

The Fettes Avenue team didn't know what to do with themselves. The Helen Street team, however, made no secret of being in rapt attention to the argument. Like children who grow up in a house of frequent arguments between mummy and daddy, raised voices and violent gesticulations didn't bother them.

Calmer now, Lomond said, 'I don't actually begrudge the way you weaselled your way onto my case. I get it. I mean, Lord knows I could never do it. You always played the game. But do I need to remind you that I'm SIO here?'

'No,' she said.

'Good.'

'Sorry, no, as in you're not SIO.'

Lomond paused. It was like someone had just told him that two plus two didn't equal four. Baffled rather than angry, he asked, 'What are you talking about?'

Ruth lifted her head defiantly. 'I spoke with ACC Ogilvy earlier. He and Brendan...sorry, ACC Niven, agree that given the stormy waters currently lashing

Helen Street's door, it would be wise to lower your visibility. On this case. For now.'

Lomond heard a loud ringing in his ears. A throb of angry blood that had nowhere to go. Now it was like someone had told him that two plus two equals yellow. He wanted to scream. He wanted to put a fist through a wall. But all he could do was smile. 'I knew this would happen. Fuck the victims. Fuck the public. And fuck whoever's out there in the hands of this maniac! As long as we keep our budget under control and up our clearance rate, right Ruth?'

'It's the most responsible way to handle it.'

'I told Linda that the difference between you and me is that I never cared about having curries with the chief super.'

'No, John,' she replied. 'The difference between you and I was that you thought it was okay to start drinking at ten in the morning on your day off.' She waited a moment for the barb to truly land, then she added, 'Don't you get it? The days of men like you running departments are going to be over soon. No one wants to be led by the tortured, damaged detective with a drinking problem. It's over.'

He replied, 'You haven't been around, Ruth, so you don't know. But that's not who I am anymore. It's not who I've been for quite some time now. I've changed. I'm not surprised you don't like the man standing in front of you now, because I'm not the same as when we were together. The John Lomond you want is the sad, pathetic drunk I was back then. You never really loved me. You only loved me when I was broken. The moment I fixed myself, you were out the door. And I thank god, or Buddha, or Partick fucking Thistle for the day that happened, because two months after you split, I met Eilidh.' His eyes piercing, and heart rate thumping, he stabbed a finger on Ruth's desk. 'And *that* was the beginning of my life. Not us. And it ended when...'

Christ, he thought. *Now's not the time to get into all that.*

He had plenty more to say. But before he could, his phone rang.

MOIRA MCTAGGART CALLING.

Pissed off at having to delay his argument, he sighed. 'I have to take this.' He turned away from Ruth. 'Moira.'

'John,' she said, as blank as a sheet of paper. 'Are you busy?'

Normally, such a question in the current circumstances would have prompted some withering put-down, but his blood was still up and he just wanted the protein of whatever Moira had to tell him. 'What do you have, Moira?'

'Your mystery foot is no longer a mystery. I've got an ID. But you're not going to like it.'

CHAPTER TWENTY-EIGHT

THE SICHUAN FENG restaurant was across the street from the burned-out O2 ABC venue. 'To Let' and 'For Sale' signs stuck out all along the street. A few takeaway places maintained by passing trade from nearby offices were struggling on. But for the most part, Sauchiehall Street was dead. It was just after half nine in the morning, and there was hardly anyone around. Even the homeless had abandoned it because of the lack of footfall.

A traditional Chinese music playlist was on in the restaurant, but there was no one around inside.

Ally said, 'Hello? Kenny?'

Kenny Fan, a modest Scots-Chinese man in his late fifties with small round glasses, hurried through the restaurant, waving his hands as if he was trying to stop them introducing themselves. His accent was pure Glaswegian. 'Hello, you must be from the fridge company.' Before Ally and Ross could object, Kenny put a finger to his lips, then gestured for them to keep up the pretence. 'Thank you for coming at such short notice. I wanted to get the work done before the other staff came in.' As he led them through the restaurant, he rolled his hand in the air, encouraging them to play along.

'Yeah, no problem,' said Ally, confused.

'Happy to help,' Ross added. 'What seems to be the issue?'

Kenny said, 'It's probably best to show you…' He took them through the double swing-doors to the kitchen, then pointed out the walk-in fridge. 'Yeah,' he explained a little too loud for normal conversation, 'I came in this morning and it just wasn't that cold in here…'

When Ally and Ross went in, it definitely felt cold.

Once the door closed behind them, Kenny sighed in relief. 'I'm sorry about that.'

Ally said, 'What the hell is this?'

Kenny raised his hands in apology. 'They have the whole place outside bugged. It was either here or the walk-in freezer.'

'Who's bugged it?' asked Ross.

Kenny pointed wildly at the door, trying to keep his voice down. 'The bosses! They put in microphones to hear what's being said.'

Ross turned to Ally. 'Is this what we came here for? Tinfoil hat stuff?'

'Wait a minute,' Ally told him, then asked Kenny, 'Who is *they*?'

Kenny lowered his voice. 'The Chinese. Native Chinese. Here illegally, organising crime for bosses back in Shanghai. They have people all over Europe. Paris, Rome, Berlin, all the major cities. They make millions in every city, and it all goes back to Shanghai. My boss here, Mr Wenbo, he's in charge of Glasgow. Very paranoid.'

Ally asked, 'Are the Chinese running a station here?'

After a long pause, he nodded his head affirmatively.

'A station?' said Ross. 'What station? What's going on?'

Ally explained, 'For some time now, we've known that Chinese officials have been using locations around the city to gather intelligence and monitor Chinese citizens living abroad. It's a crackdown against dissidents and students operating pro-democracy groups on Facebook, and people who fled China because they feared for their safety.'

'But where does the threat come from for the Chinese living here? They're on foreign soil.'

'The threat isn't here. These people have families back home that could be thrown in jail in retaliation. The Shanghai crime bosses work hand in hand with the Chinese government. In return for their cooperation and help of the crime bosses overseas, the Chinese government turns a blind eye to all the drug money flooding back from Europe to Shanghai.'

Kenny added, 'They also use places like here to organise pro-Chinese propaganda. Especially with students. There are so many in the city now.'

Ross said, 'Someone on my old team's parents were first-generation immigrants. They died a few years ago.'

'If they were still alive, I'm sure they would know all about these places. The man that owns here and many others, he has big political influence. He runs a host of fake charities that wine and dine politicians like the First Minister, the Justice Secretary, as well as senior officers in Police Scotland.'

'Why?'

'To buy influence. It allows them to continue their anti-democratic activities. Legitimise them. They donate huge amounts of money and give lavish gifts to protect their operations. If they knew I was speaking to you, I would be killed. One hundred per cent.'

Ally added, 'Hence the secrecy. But Kenny, I'm not here about that. Which I think you know.'

'Shaun is still missing?'

'Yes.'

'Oh no...'

'There's a lot of people very worried about him, and my boss thinks that you might be able to help. You were Shaun's informer, right?'

Kenny was clearly spooked. Even with the fridge door closed he was reluctant to raise his voice above a whisper. 'He wanted to know what was going on between the Chinese and Barry McKenna. We would often meet in the multi-storey car park at St Enoch Centre. When he stopped contacting me, I just assumed our business was over.' Kenny shook his head. He wasn't sure he could continue. 'I'm breaking all of my rules talking to people I don't know. But Shaun said if anything ever happened to him that I could trust you and DCI Hunt.' He eyed Ross suspiciously. 'No one else.'

'You can trust him,' Ally assured him. 'Was Shaun worried something was going to happen to him?'

'Not that I know of. But everyone around here is pretty spooked. I tried to warn him.'

'What about?'

Kenny's reticence was clear, so Ross leaned forward and touched him on the shoulder. 'There's no one else here but us, Kenny. You're safe. For now, it's just words.'

Kenny scoffed. 'There's no such thing. Words will get you killed. That's why we're talking in here.'

'You think your boss is going to kill you?'

'No, not Mr Wenbo.' Kenny gulped. 'He disappeared three weeks ago.'

'Have you reported it?'

Kenny chuckled darkly. He said to Ally. 'He must be new.'

'He is,' she replied.

Ross glanced down, letting Ally take over.

'Your boss,' said Ally. 'Was he in the middle of any business with McKenna?'

He mumbled, 'It's not McKenna.'

'How can you be sure?'

'I don't know.' He paused. 'I heard a rumour about some vigilante that's on the loose. People are disappearing left and right. They say he's going about killing people.'

'What people?'

'Business people. Gang bosses.'

Ross felt compelled to speak up again. 'If there had been any bodies in the last few months, I would know about it.'

'All I know is that people are disappearing and they're not coming back.'

'What else have you heard about this vigilante?'

'My boss told me about him. He goes after criminals. Like fucking Batman or something.'

'What's his name?'

'Nobody knows.'

'Where's he from?'

'Nobody knows.'

Ally laughed. 'Sounds really solid, Kenny. A man with no name, no background, who leaves no bodies. Let me get my entire team on this right now. In fact, I could get it on *Crimewatch*. They can just show a black screen for three minutes.'

Ross, however, wanted to hear more. 'Tell me everything that you *do* know.'

'All I know is from Mr Wenbo, and that isn't much. Nothing solid, anyway. Mr Wenbo heard from a guy who worked for a guy, type of thing,' he rolled his hand in mid-air, 'about a man whose family was killed by gangsters, then went on the rampage for revenge. The way Mr Wenbo told the story, I don't exactly blame the guy.'

'What did he say happened?'

'It was some regular working guy who owned a small hardware shop in a rough neighbourhood. Somewhere on the outskirts of Glasgow. No one really knows. Anyway, business gets tough, and he can't keep the place afloat. No one will give him a loan – except for the local loan sharks. When he's late for the second time on repayments...' He thought about how best to describe it. 'Let's just say he was dealing with people who are not exactly open to negotiating. So one night, they bundle him off the street into a van. He's taken to a warehouse in some industrial estate. They keep him there for days, but for a regular guy, he's tougher than anyone they've ever come across. Mr Wenbo once took me to his boxing gym. There were all these young guys, leathering the punch bag as hard as they could. Mr Wenbo called them idiots. It doesn't matter how hard you can hit, he would say. It's what you can take. Well, this guy, he takes more than anything these gangsters ever handed out to anyone. By day four, he's dangling by a thread, but he's still alive. They've broken bones, burned him, electrocuted him, everything you could ever imagine and worse. Still he refuses to pay. But the gangsters aren't done with him yet. The worst is still to come.'

Ross asked, 'What came next?'

'They let him go.'

'That was their worst?'

'I'm coming to that bit.' Kenny hesitated. 'The worst part is when he gets home. Battered, broken, and beaten, he finds his wife sobbing, telling him there was a fire at the shop the night before. Destitute, and already living hand to mouth, the wife can't take it anymore. She hangs herself in the garage.'

Ross sighed. 'Jesus...'

Ally said nothing.

'Wait, there's more,' Kenny said. 'In the aftermath of the wife's suicide, the man can't cope, and has no business left to pay the bills. With nowhere left to turn, the man lasted another week. Then *he* hung himself in his garage, the night before the wife's funeral.'

Ross looked at Ally in confusion – then at Kenny. 'Hang on, I thought the guy–'

'That was all twenty years ago,' Kenny clarified. 'The vigilante isn't the dad. The vigilante is the man's son. He was eleven years old at the time. But he grew up, and he never forgot. Now a man, he starts tracking down every person responsible for the deaths of his parents. They're all dead. He wages war on the entire gang. But that isn't enough. He then expands his mission. Avenging the wounded, the dead, and the grieving. Administering his own brand of justice for those the system has failed. He's determined. And he's never going to stop.'

Ross let out a long puff of air, trying to take it all in. His mind was racing. Taking everything Kenny had just told them, he placing it metaphorically over everything the Taxman had done so far. It wasn't a perfect fit, but the two stories lined up pretty well. Keeping his cards close to his chest, Ross simply said, 'It's quite a story.'

'That's one way of putting it,' Ally added. 'A load of bollocks if you ask me.'

'Call it whatever you want,' said Kenny. 'That's what Mr Wenbo told me. And I believe it.'

'Why have I never heard of this guy before?'

'Because the people he kills are already ghosts. He's not been going after the real top, top guys. Until now. So I hear.'

Ross asked, 'Did you tell Shaun about this vigilante?'

Ally interjected, 'You mean this urban legend.'

Ignoring her, Kenny answered, 'I was going to tell him. We had a meeting planned. But he never showed.'

'You're sure?'

'St Enoch Centre multi-storey. Same as always. I went floor to floor from the ground up. He wasn't there. Trust me. It's hard to miss a Volvo estate. The back end always stuck out in the parking space. There wasn't a single one in the entire car park. Then I started worrying that–'

'Wait, wait, wait,' said Ross. 'What did you just say?'

'About what?'

'You said a Volvo estate. That's the car Shaun Webster drove?'

'Yeah. So?'

'What the hell does *that* matter?' asked Ally.

'Just trust me on this,' Ross replied. 'What colour was it?'

'Black,' said Kenny.

Ross didn't breathe for a few seconds. Taking everything he knew so far about Shaun Webster, the Taxman, and Kenny's mysterious vigilante, a picture started to form in Ross's mind.

'I need to make a phone call,' he told Ally.

Once he was outside on Sauchiehall Street, he knew there was only one person he could call.

CHAPTER TWENTY-NINE

Now that they had an ID on the owner of the mystery foot attached to George Melrose's leg, the two Major Investigations Teams rushed across the car park, fanning out to their respective cars.

Ruth told everyone, 'Lee Vickery's on parole, and had instructions to stay within Glasgow. The chances he's been taken beyond Glasgow are slim. A missing foot is going to cause a pretty big mess. We'll head towards the city as a start. Any other moves we make, we'll figure out on the way.'

Pardeep and Jason would be in Willie's car like before, but there was an awkward moment when Ruth's team broke away to their own car.

Ruth slowed to a stop as she realised. 'I'll need to go with you, John.'

He made sure the others didn't hear him. 'Are you kidding? I wouldn't share a–'

Ruth cut him off. 'Insert sardonic and likely offensive metaphor. I'd rather you saved your damaged brain cells for the investigation rather than sniping at me.' She pointed at her junior colleagues. 'We need to use the travel time to coordinate strategies here. The Executive Team made some changes last year to multi-area investigations like this one. We should really review the operating procedures.'

'It's a murder enquiry, Ruth. We're not building IKEA furniture. We don't need a bloody manual.'

'So what do you want to do? Look like a total weirdo by driving to Glasgow yourself? Which would also be professionally negligent. I mean, what are you going to do if Moira sends through a text while you're driving? What if she needs a reply to something?'

'Fine,' Lomond relented, then shouted, 'Donna! You're with us.'

Already halfway into the back seat of Willie's car, Donna sighed in disappointment.

'Hard luck,' said Willie. 'That's going to be like driving with Mary, Queen of Scots and Elizabeth the First.'

Jason was the only one to laugh. He clapped his hands. 'Good one, Willie.'

Remarking on the glazed expressions on Pardeep and Donna's faces, Willie said, 'Oh for god's sake, read a history book, you two.'

Ruth asked Lomond, 'Why is she coming with us?'

'As of this morning, I don't have a detective sergeant, and Donna is the closest thing I have to one.'

'DC Varma has far more operational experience.'

Lomond replied, 'If you knew Ross McNair, you'd know where I was coming from.'

Donna dashed to Lomond's car. She was dreading the drive back now. Everyone had seen the argument between Lomond and Ruth. No one else knew the history, but it was obvious that something had gone on between them – whether professional or personal.

In the driver's seat, Lomond passed his phone to Donna in the back. 'Get onto Helen Street CID and see if they can dredge up something on Vickery. Also try Bobby Jenkins at the Scottish Prison Service. Vickery's not long out of Castle Huntly but he should still be on parole. SPS should have a last-known for him. He's been clean since he got out, so if Bobby doesn't have anything, try Mill Street. Vickery's last arrest before Castle Huntly was in Paisley.'

Donna already had the phone up at her ear. 'On it, sir.'

Still putting her seatbelt on as Lomond ripped out of the car park onto Fettes Avenue, Ruth took her laptop out of her ever-present backpack. She pulled up Vickery's record.

'What do I need to know about Vickery that isn't in this file?' she asked.

'He's a piece of shit,' said Lomond. 'They wouldn't let me put that in last time.'

His mugshot showed a skinny little runt. Pushing forty-five, he was forever with bruises on his face as long as Lomond had known him. He had sunken, faraway eyes, and his head was the shape of an upside-down triangle, his chin coming down to a point from a massively wide forehead. The way he looked at the camera lens made him seem as if his head was quite literally empty.

But Vickery was no harmless fuck-up – as Ruth was discovering.

'This guy's a real piece of work,' she said. 'Crimes go back all the way from the age of thirteen. Most recently locked up for...' She grimaced. 'Dear god...' Even a hardened DCI like Ruth was shocked. 'Culpable homicide of a baby? Is this right?'

'Sadly, yes. It was my enquiry. Given what he was locked up for, it's no surprise what the Taxman wants with him.'

'What happened?' asked Ruth.

'I was at Mill Street in Paisley. The first one that really got to me since the original Sandman investigation had gone cold. It was four years ago. A nine-month-old baby, Tyler, was reported to social services after concerns were raised by neighbours who had seen bruising and heard crying for days at a time. But they failed to follow up. That Christmas morning, police were called after complaints of screaming. Those turned out to be from the mother, Shannon Muldoon. The officers found Tyler in his cot. He'd died from internal injuries two days earlier. We arrested the dad, Lee Vickery, on suspicion of murder.'

Ruth asked, 'It says here his was the only arrest. What about Shannon?'

'She and Vickery were notorious shoplifters in Paisley, feeding their habit. They were in and out of Mill Street all the time. In the week running up to Christmas, Shannon had found a scratch card in the street and won three hundred quid. She spent the next week on a crystal meth bender and hadn't noticed a thing. She was asleep when we arrived.'

'If Vickery was arrested for murder, why the culpable homicide charge?'

'It was all we could get in the end,' said Lomond. 'What we had was circumstantial. For instance, three days earlier, Lee had sold Tyler's pram to Cash Converters. The bastard already knew what he was going to do. But any decent defence lawyer would just argue that the sale was temporary to help pay a utility bill, and that he was going to buy the pram back as soon as he had the money, etcetera.'

'That's a tricky one,' said Ruth.

'He'd also claimed to friends that Tyler couldn't be his because the baby had fair hair, and both he and Shannon have dark hair. Lee got obsessed with the idea that he was acting as father to some bastard, and Shannon was screwing around behind his back.'

'But that's not how hair colour works. It can jump generations.'

Lomond nodded wearily. 'I know. We tried to tell the idiot even after he was arrested, but he wouldn't hear a word of it. He hated that wee boy for totally imaginary reasons. Vickery was just...sick. Never showed a shred of remorse the whole time. Just doubled down on denials, said he never did anything wrong. The bastard wasn't even upset. It meant *nothing* to him.' He broke off, shaking his head in disgust. 'I can still see those photos of the baby in the living room. None of them in frames. Just sitting in a pile. He looked a lovely wee thing. You forget, don't you...that guy screaming outside a pub late at night. The two neds pulling clumps out of one another's hair at the Four Corners. The junkie passed out on a sheet of cardboard. They were all babies once. They all laughed. They all cried for their mothers. It means we're all the same. At the start, anyway. Then somewhere along the way, you turn into someone like Lee Vickery. Someone capable of hating an innocent baby.' He paused. 'There was a point where I was alone with him in the interview room. I shouldn't have been, of course. But I was. I thought about strangling Vickery right there. Wouldn't that have been right? Fair? Just? Prison never seemed enough for him.'

'So you cut a deal?'

'I had to,' said Lomond. 'The lawyers hammered out the details. It was either culpable homicide or the possibility that he walked a murder charge. We didn't have a timeline. And we didn't have anything to pin it directly on Lee.'

'Didn't Shannon want to give a statement that Lee was violent?'

'She refused. That was the final nail in the coffin. He was given thirteen years. After nine months, he was transferred to Castle Huntly because of overcrowding elsewhere. They didn't think he was a risk because the murder was quote "a one-off". Can you believe that?'

'It's the system we're in, John. We either accept it or go home.'

'An open prison, Ruth. For killing a baby. Cases like that make me question whether the Taxman isn't doing the world a favour.'

Donna, still on the phone, caught a glimpse of Lomond in the rear-view mirror. She could see how serious he was. How deeply the case still affected him.

Ruth exhaled. 'I'm going to pretend you didn't say that.'

Donna hung up, then told the two DCIs, 'Last we have, Vickery's of no fixed abode. We're going to have to try known associates.'

Ruth asked Lomond, 'Do you think he's still alive?'

He replied, 'I doubt it. But we've got to at least try.'

'What's the plan, then?'

He thought it over. 'Shannon Muldoon.'

Donna said, 'She didn't stay in touch with him, did she?'

'Yeah,' said Ruth, 'that sounds like a long shot.'

Lomond demurred. 'She always denied involvement, and she never made a single statement blaming Lee for

Tyler's death. She always said she would have done anything for him. I'll bet you they kept in touch when he was inside.'

Ruth said, 'I'll get onto Helen Street to track her down.'

'She'll be in Paisley,' said Lomond. 'Same place, probably.'

Donna was about to pass Lomond his phone forward when it started ringing. 'Sir, it's Ross.'

Lomond sighed. 'Christ, what does *he* want?' He told Donna, 'Put him on speaker.'

CHAPTER THIRTY

Lomond's reply at the other end was brusque. 'Three hours, Ross. That's how long you managed in OC without me.'

'John?' said Ross, struggling to hear him. 'Are you in a car?'

'Aye. It's a nice day, so I thought I'd drive the team down to Largs for a Nardini's.' Lomond paused to let the sarcasm sink in. 'Yes, I'm in the car. What do you want?'

Ross replied, 'I might have something on that Volvo estate.'

After recounting Shaun Webster's background and disappearance, then Kenny's story about the vigilante and his secret meetings with Webster, there was silence at Lomond's end. Long enough for Ross to question if Lomond was still there.

'You don't have it,' Lomond finally said. 'Not yet anyway, but it's a start.'

Donna couldn't help herself. She leaned forward. 'Ross, mate, it's Donna. The fact that a dark Volvo estate was seen near Luss, and Webster drove a black Volvo estate, doesn't necessarily implicate him as being the Taxman.'

Ruth weighed in as well. 'Ross, DCI Telford here.'

Ross paused. 'Um...nice to meet you?'

Lomond said, 'Long story, Ross.'

Ruth continued, 'Webster could be dead and the Taxman's driving around in Webster's car.'

'That's what I was thinking,' Ross replied. 'Hey, maybe the foot attached to Melrose's leg is Webster's?'

Lomond cut in. 'Don't try to play catch up, Ross. You're twelve hours behind us. That foot's been ID'd. We're on our way to try and intercept the rest of him now.'

'It's not a Chinese male called Mr Wenbo, is it, by any chance?'

A long pause followed.

Lomond then said, 'Are they making you drink over there, Ross? Some sort of initiation thing or something? What the hell are you talking about?'

'Shaun Webster's informer, the manager of this Chinese restaurant, says that his boss, a Mr Wenbo, has gone missing.'

'Well, he's not the foot, but Moira's still working on blood found at the second crime scene.'

'There's been another Taxman murder?'

'In Gullane over in East Lothian this time. Victim

had a mouth full of horse shite.'

Ross recoiled at the thought. 'Jesus...Thing is, if you're still looking for an ID on the blood, then it could be Webster. He was in deep with Barry McKenna's crew. What if Webster got mixed up in something real and the Taxman has mistaken him for an actual genuine gangster?'

'Or maybe Webster's gone rogue. There's a lot of money to be made in these gangs. A dirty Organised Crime cop would fit the Taxman's MO for a possible victim.'

'What do you want me to do?' asked Ross.

'*You* to do? Absolutely nothing. You're off the case. You're off the bloody team, Ross. We'll handle this.'

'You can't, though,' Ross replied. 'I've got the inside track on Shaun Webster. DCI Hunt dotes on the guy. He's not going to hand you over a confidential under-cover file on him if the implication is that Webster's some kind of vigilante murderer.'

'Hold your horses, Ross. You need some compelling evidence to even start down that path. Much more than a similar car to what a witness saw near the Luss crime scene. I get that it seems a coincidence, but let's not get carried away.'

'What do you need?'

Lomond had an idea. 'How about you do some digging on Webster, son? Everything you can find out about him. Addresses, contacts, family. You could get access to files on him that Hunt will never give me.'

'Hang on...Now you want me back investigating the Taxman case with MIT, but remain undercover here with OC while I do it?'

Lomond replied casually, 'Aye, that'd be great. Right, better go. Cheers.'

Then he hung up.

Ross stood on the pavement, stepping aside as a motorised street sweeper puttered past, spraying fag ends and dust over his shoes. Flicking the mess off his shoes, Ross gave a weighty sigh. He was now going undercover for two different DCIs, and had unwittingly negotiated his way back onto Lomond's team.

———

BACK IN LOMOND'S CAR, Ruth's phone pinged with a message. 'Right,' she said. 'I've got an address on Shannon Muldoon. Do you know where Murray Street is?'

'You could say that,' replied Lomond. 'I lived around the corner on Caledonia Street for five years.' He checked the time on the dashboard. 'We can be there in about twenty minutes, I reckon. Fifteen if I drive *really* dangerously.'

Ruth stared back, unimpressed.

Lomond replied, 'Joke.'

For the first time since Gullane, he had managed to make Ruth smile.

CHAPTER THIRTY-ONE

LOMOND, Ruth, and Donna went to Shannon Muldoon's door, while the others waited in the two cars parked on Caledonia Street.

It was a tenement building overlooking the main road, and used to have a prime view of St Mirren's Love Street stadium across the road before they knocked it down.

Lomond kept pressing the buzzer to Shannon's flat in 2/1. 'She's probably passed out.'

Ruth said, 'Have you tried buzzing another flat?'

Repeatedly buzzing 2/1, he said, 'Thank god you're here, Ruth. I would never have thought of that. There's no answer.'

Then, one of the neighbours Lomond had tried finally answered. 'Hello?'

'Police,' said Lomond. 'We need access to the building.'

The woman buzzed them in.

On the way in, Ruth muttered, 'Doesn't hurt to say please, John.'

On the second-floor landing, Shannon Muldoon's neighbour was standing in her doorway.

'You looking for Shannon?' she asked.

Lomond showed his badge. 'We are.'

'She won't be long. She went out to the Londis on the corner for her drink. Same time every day.'

'Thanks,' said Lomond, about to turn and confer with Ruth and Donna.

The woman was still standing in her doorway. 'Are you here to do something about the noise?'

Back in Paisley and on familiar ground fielding anti-social behaviour, Donna stepped forward. 'What noise has there been?' she asked.

'Screaming at night,' the woman said. 'As late as three a.m. sometimes.'

'Multiple people or just her?'

'Just her. I can't remember the last time I saw anyone else up there with her.'

Lomond pulled Donna away. 'We should catch her on the street. Less chance of a scene.'

The woman said, 'I try to look out for her, you know. It's not her fault. She's just a wee soul.'

They found Shannon in the Londis on the corner, about to buy what Lomond always described as the Holy Trinity: booze, fags, and a scratch card.

She was coming down the cereal aisle when she locked eyes with Lomond. She froze.

So did he. 'Shannon?' he said.

Ruth raised a hand of appeal. 'It's all right, Shannon. You're not in trouble.'

Aye, right, Shannon thought. Two plain clothes intercepting her in the middle of the Londis? She dropped the bottle of Glen's vodka she was holding and bolted for the door.

Lomond yelled to Donna, who was in the vegetable aisle and not expecting trouble. Shannon was quicker off the mark, and was out the door before Donna could grab her.

But Shannon didn't realise that the three detectives weren't alone. Going in the opposite direction to her flat, she ended up running straight towards the Ford Focus of DS Erskine, DC Foster, and DC Lambie.

To everyone's surprise – especially the Helen Street boys in Willie's car – it was Lambie who threw his door open first and set off in pursuit.

His gangly legs flailed around like an octopus taken out of water, but he had some speed on him for a skinny lad. He caught her up in no time, then grappled her around the waist and hauled her down.

Shannon yelped and kicked and screamed on the ground. 'Ah've no' even done nothin'!'

The others closed in on the chaotic scene, Lomond first, who surprised his Glasgow colleagues with his speed.

Fighting to control his suspect, and in a desperate bid to exert his authority, DC Lambie yelled out the thoroughly non-textbook line that would be repeated back to him for many months.

'Ma'am...*do not* resist me!'

His colleagues following closely behind, along with the Helen Street team, almost broke down with laughter.

Lomond and Ruth ran to them and peeled Shannon away from Lambie.

Out of breath, Ruth wheezed with a laugh. 'Less chance of a scene, eh, John?'

'Come on upstairs,' Lomond grumbled to Shannon. 'We need to talk.'

CHAPTER THIRTY-TWO

SHANNON'S FLAT was everything you would expect from a long-time alcoholic and drug addict. Every surface was covered in a patina of tobacco, cannabis, and dirt. There were stains on the carpets that defied the wildest guesses as to what they were. Filthy clothes littered the floors. There were empty cans and bottles everywhere, most of them used as ashtrays at one time or another.

The curtains were pulled shut in every room, but the living room where Shannon took Lomond, Ruth, and Donna was particularly dark.

Shannon had been ranting the entire way there. Mostly about how she didn't have the vodka she'd gone out to buy.

'All ah've got is wine,' she drawled, 'and that's no good, cos ah've been oan cider aw morning. Disnae agree wi' me.'

She had been drinking since early morning, when stomach cramps had woken her. Since then, it had been all about the countdown to ten o'clock. Lomond knew that wait all too well.

Shannon grabbed a bottle out of a cupboard and opened it. For an alcoholic to leave a full bottle stashed away, there had to be something seriously wrong with it. The taste was somewhere between cider vinegar and boot polish. But it was enough to take the edge off.

Shannon collapsed down into the deep crevice she had mined into the couch over the years. 'Whit's this aw aboot?'

The three cops stayed standing. There was nowhere to sit, except right next to Shannon on the two-seater couch.

Lomond took the lead. 'We're here about Lee, Shannon. We're trying to find him. It's very important.'

Shannon lowered the wine bottle from her lips. Slowly. 'Lee?' She held Lomond's gaze.

Lomond knew what was coming. He waved for Ruth to get out of the living room doorway. 'Quick! Out the way...'

Shannon shot to her feet, hand clamped over her mouth. A dozen staggered footsteps got her to the toilet just in time. It was impossible to escape the horrid sounds in the tiny flat. Shannon sounded like she was hacking up oil.

Lomond got on the phone to Pardeep downstairs.

'Fetch a bottle of Glen's vodka from the Londis for her. I need her lucid, not staring down a toilet pan.'

'This is ridiculous,' said Ruth. 'Your plan is to get her drunk? How do you expect to get anything worthwhile out of her in this condition?'

Lomond replied, 'We don't need a signed statement from her, Ruth. I'm not asking her to perform a heart bypass. All I need is an address.'

Ruth continued to let her feelings be known by pacing around in front of the window with her arms folded.

Shannon returned a little worse for wear, groaning under her breath. 'Fuck's sake, man. Mixin' ma drinks.'

'I've got some Glen's on the way up the stairs for you, Shannon,' Lomond told her. 'About Lee.'

'What's so important about findin' him?'

'I can't go into details...But we have hard evidence that his life is at risk.'

Shannon sat on the couch again and lit a cigarette. She leaned forward, on edge in every way. 'Ah've no seen him for a while. Last ah heard he was dealin' a bit when he got oot the jail. Is that whit this is aw aboot?'

Impatient for progress, Ruth stepped in. 'There's a man who appears to be targeting people accused of crimes, Shannon. Hurting them. Lee was the one accused of causing Tyler's death. We think that might be a motive.'

Shannon stared back and picked absently at a fingernail. The mere mention of Tyler's name was all it took to send her spiralling towards another bottle. 'It wisnae Lee's fault,' she said softly.

'Is that why you refused to testify against him?' asked Ruth.

Shannon asked Lomond, 'Who the fuck's she?'

Ruth replied, 'I'm DCI Telford. And we need answers, Shannon. Do you really think I won't be able to find something incriminating in this flat to bring you to Helen Street to tell us what we need to know?'

'Ah'm gawn naewhere!' Shannon fired back.

Lomond lifted a defensive hand towards Ruth. 'Hang on, no one's talking about taking anyone anywhere. This is informal.'

'Ah've no done nothin'.'

'Not according to your neighbour,' Ruth said. 'I could have you down to Helen Street like that,' she snapped her fingers, 'on an anti-social noise complaint.'

'Noise? Whit fuckin' shite is this? Ah make nae fuckin' noise in here. When ah cry masell tae sleep at night, ah dae it intae a fuckin' pillow. Awright?'

The sadness of the statement was lost as Shannon's complaints rumbled on. Lomond turned fully towards Ruth and mouthed almost silently in aggravation, 'What are you doing?'

There was a knock on the front door, then Pardeep brought in the bottle of Glen's.

When Shannon started knocking it back with a trembling hand, Ruth retreated to the window again. 'This is pathetic...' she grumbled, making no attempt to hide it from Shannon.

Seeing red, Shannon barked back, 'Whit dae you know, eh? Think you're aw that cos you've got oan a suit? How many weans huv *you* lost?'

Lomond had heard enough. He beckoned Ruth out of the room. 'Cool out,' he muttered to her.

Ruth was only too happy to leave, barging past Donna.

'I'm sorry about that,' Lomond said.

'Fuckin' should be,' Shannon replied. Her hands were shaking so much she abandoned her cigarette, mashing it into the coffee table that was pocked with similar ash marks.

Lomond sat next to her. He tapped her vodka bottle. 'Take a bang of that. It'll level you out. The next half hour will be as bad as it gets. You'll be fine after that.'

She took a long drink from the bottle. As long a drink as most people would have of cool water on a hot summer day. 'Cheers, John,' she said.

He joined his hands together. 'I lost a baby too, you know.'

'Is that right? Fuck's sake.'

'Aye. Complications with the birth,' he said. 'Lost my wife as well...'

Donna looked on in amazement. Neither she nor any of the others in Helen Street MIT had heard Lomond open up much about what had happened. Yet there he was, laying it all out to some Paisley ex-junkie alcoholic. It was strange, Donna thought, how much more comfortable he was talking to someone like Shannon than his work colleagues.

Shannon croaked, 'Ah'm sorry, John. That's fuckin'...aye.'

'The noise at night,' Lomond said. 'You mustn't realise you're doing it. Big drinkers like you are always passed out by midnight. I always was, anyway.'

'One at the latest,' Shannon said.

'Aye. I've been there,' Lomond agreed. 'The neighbour said the screaming's as late as three in the morning. It's nightmares, isn't it?'

'Ah don't know,' she said. 'Ah cannae remember nothin' in the morning.'

'Do you remember anything about where Lee was living?'

Calmer now, and straightened out from the vodka taking effect, she said, 'Dennistoun. He had a wee place above the laundrette on Alexandra Parade. 109 Gartland Avenue.'

Lomond nodded at Donna, who was writing it down. 'That's great,' he told Shannon. 'Thanks.'

As he got up, he added, 'Shannon, do yourself a favour. Keep moving forward. Live your life. Forget about what happened.'

'It's no' that easy,' she replied.

'I know. But you'll be amazed at what you can live with. What you can forget.'

Shannon had another drink.

When Lomond left the living room with Donna, he found Ruth standing in the hall. She'd been listening to every word.

CHAPTER THIRTY-THREE

OUT ON CALEDONIA STREET, Donna waited for the inevitable confrontation between Lomond and Ruth. She'd had a private preview upstairs. Now the rest of the Major Investigations Teams would get the full show – and this one wouldn't take place behind an office window.

Everyone was out of their respective cars, waiting for details of what had gone down in Shannon Muldoon's flat. Willie, Pardeep, and Jason expected a DCI Lomond swagger along with an affirmative clap of the hands that they'd got it, then shoot off to find Lee Vickery. Edinburgh MIT's guys didn't know what to expect. They were on foreign turf, and had no idea who Lomond had even been talking to.

Ruth was first to emerge from the tenement close.

Lomond followed quickly behind. 'What the hell was that, Ruth? You threatened her.'

'I was moving things along,' she claimed.

'Have you experienced good results getting in an alcoholic's face like that? You're wanting to arrest her over a *noise* complaint? Are you completely incapable of thinking about your clearance rate for five minutes?'

Ruth flashed a look towards her team, standing around DS Erskine's car. Suddenly, they all became fascinated by the Fountain Gardens park across the road. And the Bombay Deli takeaway. Anything for an excuse to look the other way.

Donna stood a few steps behind Lomond, lingering near the close door, unsure of what to do.

Ruth turned her back on the others, managing to lower her voice more than Lomond. 'When I'm writing up the notes on how we ended up encountering Shannon Muldoon in the corner shop, I have to mention the neighbour who led us there. And I'm obliged to mention the noise complaint said neighbour made at the time.'

'Obliged?' spat Lomond. 'What, you can't just look the other way? It doesn't help anyone writing up Shannon Muldoon for anti-social behaviour. Except you. Because all you care about is dotting every i and crossing every t, so that when Tulliallan opens the books on you, you're clean as a whistle.' He thrust a thumb at his sternum. 'I want to help people. You're only interested in helping yourself.' He was about to give her a chance to reply. Instead, he thought of something else that reloaded his outrage. 'I used to think your ambition was good for victims, Ruth. That was always your defence. But after seeing how you treated Shannon, I know now.'

Ruth's eyes widened with indignation, as if they'd been operated by a switch. 'What do you know, John?'

'You're not good police, Ruth,' he answered. 'You don't understand people because you've never lost anyone in your entire life. You don't understand suffering and misery and pain, because you grew up in a house with seven bloody bedrooms. You've never been hungry for a thing in your life, except personal advancement. You think that's what people do. Most people are just trying to *escape* something. To get away from a bad situation, like not having enough money. Living in a shit-hole like Shannon Muldoon. Or grieving for a dead child. Most people aren't like you, Ruth, because they've got too much other shit to deal with to have the luxury of being like you. That's what you never understood about me. Why you can't understand that someone like Shannon shouldn't spend hours giving a statement against the man who killed her only child, because it will take months to get to trial, she'll sit in a witness box for days, and in the meantime she'll spiral and probably drink herself into a grave before Lee Vickery sees anything like real justice. All you see is the letter of the law. But the law's not only made up of letters, Ruth. It's made up of people.'

Ruth didn't bother to reply. She could have. She had been captain of the debating team at university. The reason she didn't reply was that she knew from what she had overheard in Shannon's hallway that Lomond had got an address. And that was far more important than winning an argument with John Lomond.

Lomond yelled to the others, 'Follow me! We're going to Alexandra Parade, 109 Gartland Avenue.' He told Willie, 'Get a response team out. I mean, it'll be probably be bloody Wednesday by the time they get there, but I've got absolutely no idea what we could be walking into here.'

CHAPTER THIRTY-FOUR

LOMOND CHARGED OUT OF PAISLEY, quickly leaving Willie and DS Erskine's cars behind when he ran a red light next to the old Racecourse. Formerly a dozen football pitches on an enormous patch of grass next to the M8 flyover by Glasgow Airport, every time Lomond went past there he got a chill: it was the scene where the Sandman's second victim Leanna Donnelly had been found many years ago. All the goalposts and pitch markings were long gone, but it would always make Lomond feel the same way – even when the area was inevitably developed for yet more housing.

Ruth had gone off in DS Erskine's car along with DCs Lambie and Foster, who were in the back seat of the Peugeot 308 hatchback. Ruth's height meant that she had slid her seat back, squeezing the even taller DC Lambie.

'Got enough space back there?' she asked him.

'Yes, I'm fine,' he lied, trying not to grimace in discomfort.

Ruth couldn't stand to be anywhere near Lomond after his outburst on Caledonia Street. She didn't even want to breathe the same air as him. Being back with her own team was her only consolation.

She said, 'I know you must be wondering about the squabbling you just witnessed back there. DCI Lomond's under a lot of pressure right now.'

The others left it for DS Erskine in the driver's seat to respond. 'We understand,' she said.

'The thing is,' Ruth went on, 'John and I were once an item. A very long time ago. It didn't end particularly well, so I believe that's what is feeding some of the animosity on display. Like a puppy, you can train him over time. Give him a day or two.'

The young detectives were used to Ruth's candidness. Like an over-sharing parent who thinks that if they tell their teenager about their personal life, they'll find them more approachable.

In Willie's car, the discussion was briefer.

In the passenger seat, Pardeep said to Willie, 'Shagged, then?'

'Aye,' Willie replied. 'Definitely shagged.'

Meanwhile in Lomond's car, Donna had some rare time alone with him. He was concentrating on driving, weaving through the traffic across the flyover like he was in a video game.

Something about being alone with him made Donna feel bolder in her conversation.

Clutching her seatbelt as Lomond continued his rally moves, she asked, 'Do you want to talk about what happened back there?'

His hands gripped the steering wheel, eyes flitting from windscreen to side mirror to check for obstacles, then to the rear-view mirror to check that Willie and DS Erskine were keeping up – they weren't even in view anymore.

'No,' Lomond answered. 'Everything's fine.'

'You didn't sound or look fine.'

He snorted at her punchy response. 'Are you trying to be more like a DS in Ross's absence, Donna?'

'Someone's got to,' she replied. 'Willie's always going to have your back, but he's not exactly the type of man to ask another man how he's feeling.'

'What's next? You want to give me your pronouns like DCI Telford's team? Shall I pull over so I can talk about my feelings?'

Donna's eyes were dead ahead. 'I think your feelings are the last thing you should be talking about driving at this speed.'

'DCI Telford and I don't see eye to eye on a number of things,' he explained.

'Like what?'

'She thinks I'm an arsehole. I don't.'

Donna smiled and shook her head. It was pointless trying to get anything further out of him on the matter.

They spoke little until they sped through the criss-crossing junctions around the Royal Infirmary, speeding towards Alexandra Parade. Lomond threw the car into the opposite lane to overtake every single car he could, and jumped the lights at the Wishart Street junction, etching out solitary seconds of progress at a time. They all added up. But Willie was a good minute behind. DS Erskine was even farther back, as Ruth insisted she stick to the speed limit and the rules of the road.

She explained, 'What DCI Lomond forgets is that if you crash and hit someone, it's your career and mine as SIO that go out the window.'

Lomond made even more time by tearing along the empty bus lane for a few hundred yards.

The old Wills tobacco factory on the right side of the Parade – now some ghastly modern office space – marked for Lomond the real end of the city centre, and the start of the east end of Glasgow. From there, it kept getting rougher and bleaker until you reached one of the city's roughest areas: Cranhill. Child poverty and alcohol misuse there were miles higher than the national average. Much more memorable in Lomond's mind, however, was that he'd once had the shit kicked out of him there.

Time made a big difference. Twenty years ago, when quizzed on the city's roughest areas, a young PC John Lomond could have said Anderston. But that had all been regenerated. The past knocked down and built over. It might have looked different, but those that had been there still remembered.

Life may well go on, but it goes on with ghosts from the past trailing behind.

Donna held onto her seatbelt again. This time preparing to take it off and get ready to run with Lomond. 'What do you think the chances are of finding anything here?' she asked.

'I think they're pretty decent,' he replied. 'It's what we're going to find there that's troubling me.'

'If Lee Vickery's there, he's not going to be alive, is he?'

'No chance. The foot came off two weeks ago. I'm sure that was just the beginning of the end. The Taxman's not going to let us save one. Not yet, anyway. You saw what he thinks of a crooked banker and a paedophile lawyer. There's no telling what he's capable of doing to a guy responsible for the death of a baby. I think whatever you have in your head, double it, and you'll still be nowhere near. But at least you'll be a bit better prepared.'

CHAPTER THIRTY-FIVE

LOMOND DIDN'T WAIT for the others when they reached 109 Gartland Avenue. He wasn't about to sit around in a matter of threat-to-life.

There were sirens somewhere nearby from the uniform response that had been called in, but Lomond didn't want some new PC going through the door first and getting in harm's way. Ruth's operational procedures might not have agreed, but Lomond saw it as his responsibility to deal with whatever the Taxman had done to Lee Vickery.

Lomond ran to the tenement door which was unlocked, the latch pushed up. He paused momentarily. *The Taxman's work?* he wondered.

There was no time to consider it further.

Donna chased after him, the pair taking two stairs at a time until they were at the second-floor landing.

The moment Willie's car reached the address, Willie,

Pardeep, and Jason all piled out and followed them inside, eager to protect their gaffer and colleague.

When DS Erskine pulled up behind their abandoned cars on the deep pavement, Ruth made no move to rush inside.

When Jane did, Ruth put out a hand to give her pause. 'What are you doing?'

'Going in,' Jane replied.

'They don't need more bodies up there.' Ruth got out the car casually, leaning on the roof as she took her phone out.

Her adrenaline pumping from the race across the city, Jane paced about, eyes hunting for what window would have been Lee Vickery's flat.

She told Foster and Lambie, 'We should be up there.'

The two DCs shrugged impotently. They weren't about to ignore their DCI for someone only two years older than them, and made a DS less than four months ago.

Upstairs, Lomond and Donna were creeping quietly towards Vickery's flat.

Lomond tapped Donna on the side, then pointed to the heavy-duty silver tape running along the foot of the door frame.

Donna gestured to the two other doors on the landing. 'Neighbours?'

Lomond shook his head. 'They're both "to let". There were signs outside.'

In the rush, Donna hadn't noticed them.

Lomond peeled the tape away slowly. The rancid smell hit them as soon as there was a gap under the door.

He tried the door handle. Softly. Then pushed it.

The door opened. It had been left unlocked.

The smell gathered force like a tsunami wave when they entered the hallway. It was dingy and dark. All the doors closed. Chunks missing around the bottom of them where they'd been booted over the years, or had furniture thrown at them. A junkie's flat suffers a lot more than a regular citizen's.

Following the smell, Lomond put his forearm to his nose. He pushed the bedroom door open and recoiled from the scene in front of them.

Not because of any gratuitous blood or violence on display. As murder scenes went, it was one of the quietest Lomond had encountered. What affected him was the arrangement of the body, and what had been done to it.

Lomond took out a small torch from his inside jacket pocket. The leap from darkness to harsh white light was jarring to their eyes.

He grimaced as he lowered his arm. 'It's just like baby Tyler,' he croaked.

Lee Vickery was on his back, lying on filthy bedsheets, surrounded by squalor. He'd been handcuffed to the metal bedpost. He was emaciated and wearing only an adult nappy. His severed foot had been bandaged. Cigarettes had been put out on his arm, and there were bruises up and down each limb, most of which appeared to be broken. The bed was covered in every bodily fluid imaginable.

'He looks like he's been starved for weeks,' Donna said.

'I'll bet you anything it was methadone overdose.'

'What makes you say that?'

'Tyler died after being given a huge quantity of methadose syrup. It's ten times more concentrated than compounded methadone. Lee had been selling it from his and Shannon's flat. It's red, and when it's bottled it looks similar to babies' Calpol. When Tyler was unwell, Lee had refused to give him any Calpol, but Shannon insisted he needed it. Lee ended up giving Tyler the methadose syrup.'

'By mistake?'

'So his lawyer would have you believe.' Lomond shook his head. 'He knew what he was doing. Shannon was still high from her meth binge. Lee was pretty lucid. Moira reckoned Tyler died in his sleep. It might have been the only peace the wee soul ever knew.'

Donna and Lomond turned around as a floorboard creaked in the hall.

Lomond remarked, 'Did you stop for lunch on the way or something?'

Ruth said, 'Rules are there for everyone's safety, John.'

'I know the rules well so I can break them effectively. You know who said that?'

Knowing it was the wrong answer, she said, 'Charles Manson.'

'No,' replied Lomond, 'it was the Dalai Lama.'

'Terrific. Next time you're on trial for dangerous driving, you can call him as a character witness.' Turning her attention to the scene, Ruth said, 'Rooms like this are why you couldn't pay me enough to be in forensics. Bloody hell.'

Lomond shone the torch around the bed, then up the wall.

The torch illuminated graffiti-style writing on the wall.

'Hmm,' he said, tilting his head slightly as he contemplated it. 'Now that *is* interesting.'

"THE TAXMAN 2, POLICE SCOTLAND 1"

'Whoa,' said Donna.

Ruth asked, 'Why has he given us a point?'

'It's a change. Change is good. It means something about this one stands out from the others.'

'But why would this be a win for police but not the Taxman?'

'I'm sure we'll get to that.' Lomond put his hands on his hips, surveying the rest of the room. 'He's loving this. Loving the questions we'll be asking ourselves.'

'You don't think it's relevant?' asked Ruth.

'Of course it is. But to me, the scoreline's not even in the top three most interesting things about this murder scene.'

Donna asked, 'What's your top three?'

He crouched down to shine his torch on Lee's various injuries. 'These are just like Tyler's. As in, almost exactly.'

Ruth said, 'It was four years ago. How do you remember?'

Lomond stood up again. 'How could I forget?'

Donna said, 'But how could someone know where all of his injuries were?'

'The trial?' suggested Ruth.

Lomond said, 'A juror remembered the exact placement of injuries four years after the fact, somehow tracked down a man on parole who has no known address, and did this? Along with the other murders? I don't think so.'

'What's the alternative?'

Lomond paused. 'That's almost too scary to comprehend.'

'Why?'

'Because it has to be someone who had access to the original investigation file.'

Donna added, 'They would also need to have intimate knowledge of Lee Vickery. Even we struggled to find this address.'

Lomond nodded. 'Someone deep on the inside.' He stared at the scoreline on the wall. 'I think the Taxman is a police officer.'

CHAPTER THIRTY-SIX

DONNA STARED BACK AT HIM, dumbfounded.

'What?' exclaimed Ruth.

He nodded again. 'I think he's a police officer. And, if I'm right, that's means all bets are now officially off.' He turned to Donna. 'Get the others up here. And grab any uniform if they're here yet. We need this room secured.'

Once she had gone, Lomond said to Ruth, 'You're not disagreeing with me.'

'It's possible.'

'It's *likely*.'

'It's possible,' she repeated.

'He knew Tyler's injuries inside out.'

'*You* knew Tyler's injuries inside out.'

'What's that supposed to mean?'

Ruth paused. 'Never mind. This is a nightmare.'

'You thinking about the headlines?'

'How are you *not*? There could be a maniac cop

running around out there.' She shook her head as the implications piled up. 'This will go all the way to the Chief Constable.' For the first time, she lost her cool. '*Shit!* Why did I take this *bloody* job?'

Lomond said, 'They say that the only thing worse than not getting what we want is getting it. You wanted to be in charge. Now you are.'

Ruth turned and left the room.

While he was alone with Lee Vickery – something that Lomond would have paid good money for when Lee was alive – he crouched next to the bed.

He whispered in Lee's ear, 'Enjoy hell.'

A light went on in the hall, sending a shaft of light towards Lomond.

Ruth stood backlit in the doorway. She called his name aggressively, the way someone calls on a dog for going somewhere it shouldn't. 'Come downstairs. I don't want you alone in here.'

Lomond stood up.

On his way past, he said, 'Today was a good day for justice. Maybe the Taxman's onto something.'

Waiting until Lomond was gone, Ruth tapped out a text message.

"*Need to talk asap.*"

The recipient was "*COLIN MOWATT - GLASGOW EXPRESS*".

CHAPTER THIRTY-SEVEN

Ross LOITERED on the edge of the car park of Police Scotland's administrative headquarters in Dalmarnock. He paced around in the same few square metres, arms folded and eyes fixed on the expansive glass entrance. After a ten-minute wait, DCI Gordon Hunt emerged – and he didn't look happy.

He shoulder-checked each side, making sure that no one was paying attention to their impromptu meeting. From a short distance away he said, 'For future reference, DS McNair, my officers ask questions when they text me. They don't demand things from their SIO like "I need to see you." You must have learned that from DCI Lomond.'

Ross replied, 'In the circumstance, I thought urgency was more important than civility.'

'Yeah, well, civility is just one of the many differences between John and I.'

'That's strange. He seemed to think you two were alike.'

He chuckled, allowing his annoyance to subside. 'Maybe once. A long time ago.' He glanced back at the glass cuboid building glistening in the sun. 'Look, Ross, I'm in a meeting with CSU Reekie. What's all this about? Ally busting your chops already?'

'No,' said Ross. 'We need to talk about Shaun Webster. I've come into some information that's potentially very damaging. I'm new here. I don't know how this all works when an officer has to come to his SIO about another officer.'

'You man up and talk to them, Ross. What else *would* you do?'

Feeling free to speak frankly, Ross said, 'I've had SIOs in the past that wouldn't like what I'm about to tell you.'

'Then it sounds like I should hear it.'

Ross looked down at his feet for a second. 'Before I finished up at MIT, we started an enquiry into the Loch Lomond limbs murder.'

'Yeah, I saw your man's press conference. Car crash stuff.'

'Well, one of our lads got a lead on a vehicle spotted near the crime scene around the time the body was possibly lobbed into the loch. It was a dark Volvo estate.' Ross waited to see Hunt's reaction.

There was none.

'Is that meant to mean something to me?' asked Hunt.

'Shaun's informer that DI Corrigan and I spoke to this morning said that Shaun drove a black Volvo estate.'

'So you think that Shaun is your murderer?' Hunt snorted, waiting for Ross to admit he was joking. 'You've actually pulled me out of a meeting for this?' Hunt turned to go back inside. 'John Lomond told me you were a serious officer, Ross. Don't waste my time with pish like this.'

Ross called after him. 'I think either Shaun Webster is the Taxman, or he's one of the Taxman's victims.'

Hunt stopped in his tracks. When he turned around, he had a haunted look on his face. 'The Taxman?'

'That's what he calls himself. We found a message written in blood in George Melrose's home in Lochgoilhead. It was a scoreline. The Taxman one, Police Scotland nil. DCI Lomond was called to a second scene in Gullane first thing this morning. The same scene. Different score. The Taxman is up two nil now.'

Hunt's mouth hung open. 'Fuck.'

'I think we need to sit down and talk, sir. I don't think you've given me the full story on Shaun Webster. Am I right?'

CHAPTER THIRTY-EIGHT

WHILE ROSS GOT a couple of coffees from the snack van parked on one of the few remaining patches of wasteland off Reid Street, Hunt sat on the kerb, staring vaguely around the ground. He shook his head gently like he didn't understand.

Ross sat down next to him and handed Hunt his coffee. It was too hot for Ross to hold, but Hunt had no such issues with his leathery hands, tough and worn like a joiner's.

'What do you want to know?' asked Hunt.

'I need to know everything. From the start.'

Hunt snorted. 'The start...It's hard to say when some things start, isn't it?'

Ross resisted the urge to say something else. He knew that in his position, Lomond would have waited. Let the 'witness' decide to talk for themselves. They gave up so much more when you pushed a little less.

'What did Kenny say?' asked Hunt.

'He told us about a vigilante that's been working people over. For what sounds like a while now. He thinks his boss at the restaurant, Mr Wenbo, has been taken by this man. Kenny said that Wenbo told him about a man that's been targeting people in organised crime, but has now expanded the scope of his targets.'

Hunt hung his head down. 'Jesus...'

Ross lowered his head to meet Hunt's eyes. 'Sir...I want to talk to you before I take this to DCI Lomond. But I *do* have to take it to him. Today.'

Hunt took a sip of coffee, then a deep breath. 'When you've been in the job as long as I have – and John has – it changes you. It also changes different people in different ways. John thinks the system is something you have to trick your way through, finding loopholes, stretching rules until they break – or just flat-out ignoring them altogether.'

'How did it change you?' asked Ross.

Hunt's eyes narrowed as he looked across the street at nothing in particular. 'When I joined the police, I thought I could make a difference. That's no longer the case. We can't actually win, Ross. You'd understand that if you sat for an hour with these accountants-in-uniforms in that glass coffin over there. The game's rigged. We're a body that operates according to the rule of law, fighting people who have nothing but contempt for the law. That's not a fight you can ever win.'

'Unless you get rid of some rules.'

'I think Shaun believed the same thing. But nothing's changing anytime soon. All that's left is to try and keep the streets as safe as possible. Keep the peace. That requires compromise. John Lomond doesn't know the meaning of the word. It can be painful, but it's worth it for the greater good.'

Ross said, 'John cut a deal with Frank Gormley to get intel that saved wee Jack Ferguson's life. He knows when to compromise.'

'That was a deal with the devil to ward off his own guilt. John had already been shunted off the Sandman case and was a wreck for years after. I remember meeting him the summer after he came back from his leave of absence. It was like talking to somebody who'd gone to war. This faraway look in his eyes. The voice was quieter. When the Sandman came back and he was put on the case again, that deal with Gormley was an act of desperation. You try bringing the same deal to Lomond on a case that isn't his and see what his answer would be. He'd tell you to take a running jump.'

'Is this your way of telling me something about Shaun Webster?'

Hunt peeled the plastic lid off his coffee and swirled the contents around. 'Shaun had always been highly strung. He came from a very stable background. Decent family. Nice house out in Giffnock. The parents are still out there, I believe. In their nineties. We've staked out the house and questioned the parents, but...' He rolled a forefinger next to his head. 'The grey cells are gone. I even checked medical records. They're not faking it. Even if Shaun had been there and told them where he was going, they still couldn't help. They've got carers coming in three times a day. Somewhere...Shaun got lost. It was Reekie and I's plan to have him infiltrate Barry McKenna's crew. We had been chasing our tails with organised crime for so long, we decided we were really going to do it right this time. No more wasting sources or informers for stashes worth five, or even six figures. It was time to cut the head off the snake. To do that, we needed to plant someone deep – I mean really deep – inside a major crew with major muscle and major cash. I'd never seen someone slip into a double life as quickly and as easily as Shaun did. I mean, he actually enjoyed it. Those guys he was hanging out with, they bought his cover totally. Then...well, it all went sideways.'

'What happened?' asked Ross.

Hunt stared intently at the ground. 'He was in deep with McKenna. Really high up. But there were some things along the way that caused me concern in Shaun's reports.'

'Like what?'

'You need to understand how far you need to go to prove yourself when you're new in a gang like McKenna's. You can't show weakness for even a second. These guys, they'll cut your throat over fifty quid. They don't give a shit, Ross. I mean, we walk about this city and think of life being a certain way. But walking the very same streets, going into the same shops, up and down Buchanan

Street or wherever, these guys are living in a totally different world. They're prepared to kill and *be* killed. They've built up a huge stack of chips, and they've put it all on the square that says "GANGSTER". Shaun had to act that way. And it broke him.' Hunt shook his head. 'The things he saw, son. Jesus...One time, he went round some guy's flat in Royston with a couple of McKenna's guys over an unpaid debt. They stomped on the guy's head like it was a watermelon. I saw Shaun three days later. He was still traumatised by it. Something shifted in him after that. Stopped making calls with McKenna's people. Missed meetings. And then people in McKenna's crew started going missing. Small-time guys to start with. Ally heard about it through the grapevine and told me. Shaun denied that he had anything to do with it. Then he started missing check-ins with me, around the same time that one of McKenna's young dealers was found in an alley off Hope Street, beaten to a pulp. There was a still from CCTV nearby that caught the assailant.'

'Shaun,' said Ross.

'Yep. I had to take it to Reekie to make sure the case was given to us, so we could bury it. I managed to get a sit-down with Shaun, to talk him down whatever he was going through. But he couldn't hear a word I was saying. He was railing against the force. How pointless it was what we were trying to do. I told him, you know, this isn't the way to do it. I was scared he was going to end up in jail. But there was no reasoning with him. Shaun was gone after that meeting. After that, he broke off contact altogether.'

'That was six months ago?'

Hunt nodded. 'Ally heard about him battering people left and right. He was out of control.'

'How much does she know?'

'A little. Not everything.'

'What about Reekie?'

'He knows everything. I didn't have a choice about that.'

'And Tulliallan?'

'Nothing.'

'Sir,' Ross said, deadly serious. 'I really think you should tell them the truth. Me and Helen Street MIT might not be enough to rescue this for you.'

'This is my pension, my family's future...everything is tied up in this. That's why I brought you in, Ross. Not to find Shaun. But to bring him back from whatever he's become. He's out there operating with no regard for the rule of law. And if I don't get him back...' He broke off, considering his options. 'Reekie and I might have to put shotguns in our mouths.'

It didn't come as a great shock to Ross. Over the last several hours, his barometer on what was shocking had moved significantly.

Still, it was a terrible load to put on someone: *get a result or I'll have to kill myself.* Ross knew that Hunt had a wife and teenage son at home, so for him to say something like that, he didn't doubt the extremity of what Hunt was facing.

Ross did the only thing he could do. He reassured him, 'It won't come to that, sir. I'm sure of it.' He cleared his throat. 'But I need to ask you a direct question. Do you think Shaun Webster could be the Taxman?'

Hunt looked up. 'It was George Melrose that MIT pulled out of Loch Lomond, right?'

'Yeah.'

'You said that MIT found a second victim this morning. In Gullane?'

'That's what John told me.'

Hunt paused. He couldn't even look at Ross. 'Was it Dennis Dunbar?'

Ross couldn't think of a reason not to tell him. It would be plastered all over the news by early evening. 'Yeah, it was. How did you know that?'

Hunt exhaled.

'How did you know that, sir?'

'It's him, Ross,' Hunt said, looking down. 'Shaun Webster's the Taxman. Come back to the office with me and I'll show you the proof.'

CHAPTER THIRTY-NINE

LOMOND AND RUTH were in front of the whiteboard in Helen Street's MIT office, when Lomond remembered he wasn't SIO. As the others conferred, all milling around and talking over one another in one large group, Lomond took the opportunity to ask Ruth privately, 'How do you want to play this?'

Ruth had her back to the office, scribbling down notes that she wanted to cover in her briefing. 'Sorry?' she asked, still writing.

'Do you want me to stand at the side or something?'

Ruth put her pen down then pulled Lomond aside, into the shadows of the unlit area of the office. 'We need to talk.'

'I think I've said everything I–'

'Let me rephrase,' she said. '*I* need to talk.'

He scoffed. 'That's just bloody cheating. Everyone

thinks of the perfect comeback an hour after a fight. But if you want to use it, then go ahead.'

She shut her eyes and took a breath. 'John, can we just start again? Please? I didn't take this enquiry on because I wanted to hurt you or your career. I'm here to help. I get that you don't like my approach. That's fine. But what the hell happened to *us*?'

'It's irrelevant,' he said. 'All that matters is solving this case.'

In their first few hours together, it was impossible for her to see anything but the old him. Now, she could see who he was. She said, 'You think that taking better care of yourself, not drinking, running up hills, and making peace with the past has cured you.'

Lomond began saying, 'How did you–'

'I talked to Linda when we got back. She told me you've been working eighteen-hour days. That you're still frazzled after what happened with the first Sandman investigation. Those years in the wilderness in Paisley after I went up north.' She paused. 'And she told me about Eilidh.'

Lomond looked away towards his team. Then down at the floor. Anywhere but Ruth's eyes.

'I'm so sorry, John. I didn't know.'

'Well...thank you. But it doesn't really change anything.'

'Actually, it does,' she said. 'I understand a little better why you don't follow proper procedures for driving. Or go charging into properties where a murderer might still be present. You're happy risking you and your team's safety because you're trying to fix the world one enquiry at a time. But there's no way of making the world just, John. It's like emptying a loch one teaspoonful at a time. Except, it's always going to rain. That loch is never going to empty.'

He had no retort. No argument. No defence.

Standing close to her, he remembered how head over heels in love with her he had been. He also knew, deep down, that she was right. He was never going to find happiness – true happiness – if all he had was work.

Ruth said, 'You lead this one.'

'Are you sure?'

'You're more familiar with Vickery. And you're on home turf.'

It was a small gesture, but one that he appreciated.

Lomond brought proceedings to a start with a clap of his hands. 'Right,' he announced. 'The Taxman two. Police Scotland one. For some reason, he's decided to give us a point. Why?' He tapped the whiteboard where he'd stuck Lee Vickery's mugshot. 'Whatever the reason is, it must be to go with this fella. Lee Vickery. Convicted of culpable homicide of baby Tyler. Pulled a cushy sentence in an open prison then was released back into society. But he didn't last long. Turns out the Taxman had plans for him. The injuries found on Vickery's body match those found on Tyler. This was about vengeance.'

DC Jason Yang raised his hand. 'Sir, assuming that Vickery was murdered as some kind of statement about his own crime, why has the Taxman given us a point? George Melrose and Dennis Dunbar both did terrible and illegal things. But their murders were chalked up to the Taxman.'

Lomond answered, 'We don't know yet, Jason, is the short answer.'

From the mezzanine above, Detective Superintendent Linda Boyle looked on with a mixture of fascination and tension. Wondering how long before Lomond and Ruth exploded again.

'But,' added Lomond, 'the fact that the Taxman has been able to replicate the injuries from Tyler onto Vickery, presents a very disturbing picture. I have a theory that the Taxman is possibly a police officer. Maybe even someone senior, but definitely someone with access to the original police report on Tyler's death.'

DS Erskine raised her hand, assuming everyone on Lomond's team did it. 'Sir, what about Vickery's foot? Tyler's foot wasn't cut off.'

Ruth started to answer 'Well, that—' Realising she had cut Lomond off, she stopped. 'Sorry, John. On you go.'

Lomond said, 'We can only assume that the Taxman required the murders so far to be connected in some way. Dennis Dunbar's blood on George Melrose's living room wall. Vickery's foot stitched onto Melrose.'

Jane replied, 'Why not just cut off a finger?'

From behind her, Willie answered, 'Everything the

Taxman's done so far has had meaning. He wouldn't have cut off Vickery's foot if it didn't have meaning.'

'I agree,' said Lomond. 'Though we do have one other connection between the victims that's come to light in the last hour. Ruth?'

She turned to a table next to Lomond and picked up an evidence bag with a piece of paper in it. 'This was found in Lee Vickery's flat a short while ago. It's paperwork from Dennis Dunbar's office, arranging a meeting between Dunbar and Vickery next Wednesday. It seems that Vickery had a minor drugs charge a month ago which mysteriously vanished from all records. Following Dunbar's involvement, the charges were suddenly dropped. No case to answer.'

'That doesn't make any sense,' said Donna. 'I think it's fair to say Dunbar represented some pretty questionable characters, but how did a piece of...' She reworded on the fly. '...a guy like Vickery afford Dennis Dunbar to help him on a minor drugs charge? We all saw the state of that flat. Sure, Vickery had some gang connections back in the day, but nothing since he got out.'

Perched on a tabletop edge, Lomond said, 'That we know of.'

DC Lambie and Foster started conferring. 'Something weird going on there...'

Soon, everyone was speculating with whoever was beside them.

Ruth raised her hands for quiet. 'Okay, we're going to do this textbook. The most efficient thing we can do is continue searching for the one piece of evidence that I believe remains our strongest lead. That dark Volvo estate.'

The reaction from Lomond's team was far from cele-bratory.

Ruth's team didn't yet grasp the full tedium of what they were about to be asked to do.

Ruth explained, 'We have a list of cars in the Greater Glasgow area, and we're going to check every single one of them off.'

Donna whispered to Willie, 'That's going to suck up the next five days chasing empty leads.'

'A car like that isn't fleet. It'll have been stolen. It's a dead end.'

'Why don't you tell her that?'

Ruth's ears pricked up. She lifted her chin like a teacher who had caught someone chatting in class. 'Tell me what, Donna?'

She fired a nervy look Willie's way, then back at Ruth. 'It's just...Don't you think there's a good chance the car's stolen?'

A voice far back at the office entrance said, 'It's a very good chance.'

Emerging from the shadows was Ross.

'DS McNair,' said Ruth. 'How nice of you to join us. Is Organised Crime not all it's cracked up to be?'

He lifted a manila folder into the air. 'Depending on how wide a net you want to throw, there's anything from thirty-three, to one hundred and twenty-seven vehicles in the Glasgow area that fit the description of the Volvo seen in Luss. It's not a car from the fleet. Shaun Webster picked it up himself through a gangster in Barry McKenna's crew. It was stolen. It's a dead end.' He tossed the folder down on the desk where Willie and Donna sat. 'That's *not* a dead end.'

'What is that?' asked Ruth.

'Proof,' he said. 'That the Taxman is an undercover police officer gone rogue. Detective Sergeant Shaun Webster of the Organised Crime Taskforce. This dossier that Webster put together months before his disappearance lays out his entire plan.' He paused. 'It also tells us who he's going to target next.'

CHAPTER FORTY

RUTH SET EVERYONE TO work on chasing down leads on the Volvo. Like a bunch of salesmen sent off with a call list, the detectives got busy dialling and crossing off names.

While the office hummed like a call centre, Ross showed Lomond and Ruth the dossier by a desk at the whiteboard. He walked them through it.

'I spoke to Hunt earlier,' he explained. 'Turns out, he and Reekie knew that Shaun Webster had gone rogue a long time ago. I mean, walked right off the reservation. Running his own ops, battering dealers, all sorts. Before that happened, Webster had written up a dossier for Hunt, detailing his strategy – if you can even call it that. Part of that dossier, he mentioned some names that had been prominent in the news. This is just a copy I've made. Look at the highlighted names.'

Ruth and Lomond huddled around the file, quickly scanning the names.

Ruth read them aloud. 'George Melrose...Dennis Dunbar...Lee Vickery...'

'They're even in the same order,' Lomond added.

Ross said, 'Look at the next names over the page.'

Ruth turned the page. After a long pause, she said, 'Shit.' She showed it to Lomond.

'Oh, bloody hell.' Lomond backed away from the desk. 'Well, if these are the next names and the Taxman gets to them before we do, that'll be a major riddy. No wonder he's keeping score between himself and Police Scotland.'

Ruth screwed her face up in confusion. 'A "riddy"?'

'Aye. A riddy.'

'Just repeating the word doesn't help, John. What does it mean?'

Ross put her out of her misery. 'A red face because something embarrassing's happened to you.'

'Thank you, Mr Weegie Cultural Attaché,' said Lomond. 'It's bad enough that the Taxman is running rings round us, but going after these guys is just trying to rub our faces in it.'

'We'll need to issue Osman letters immediately,' said Ruth.

'Yep,' Ross agreed.

Osman letters were issued to people where there was evidence of a 'threat-to-life', but the police didn't have enough evidence to make an arrest. So-called after businessman Ali Osman, who was shot dead following the police acquiring information that his life was at risk by an unknown assailant. Information that, if communicated, might have saved his life. In some circles of organised crime, being given an Osman letter was considered a badge of honour.

Lomond slapped him so hard on the arm that Ross juddered. 'Good work, Ross.' He then turned to the office full of MIT officers on phones. 'Okay, everyone. Phones down. Listen up.' He waited a few seconds for them to hang up. 'For those of you who don't know DS Ross McNair,' he gestured at Ross, 'his talents outside of policing might not extend further than maybe a shared third place in a Martin Compston lookalike contest, but while he was here at MIT he was actually very valuable.'

Lomond might have taken a few detours to reach anything resembling a compliment, but Ross was grateful nonetheless.

Lomond added, 'He moved over to the Organised Crime Taskforce this morning, and has come crawling back to us already.'

Ross retorted, 'You mean rushed back to save your enquiry.'

'Christ, twelve hours without a suit and he's firing pelters at his old gaffer.' Lomond handed the floor over to him. 'You know this better than me, DS McNair. Take it away.'

Ross took up Lomond's normal position in front of the whiteboard, holding the dossier in his hand. 'This is a dossier written by Organised Crime Taskforce under-cover officer DS Shaun Webster. Six months ago he went silent while on an op inside Edinburgh drug kingpin Barry McKenna's gang. Two years ago, Glasgow's Frank Gormley was put away for money laundering and fraud. Since then, Barry McKenna has been the main beneficiary of Gormley's absence, making deals with Chinese nationals and other foreign national crime gangs to eat up Gormley's old territory. From what Webster's SIO, DCI Hunt, has told me, after years of living a double life, Webster snapped. It's been six months since he last called in.' Ross stuck a picture of a black Volvo estate onto the whiteboard. 'An informer of Webster's saw him multiple times driving this vehicle. The same kind we know was close to the Luss crime scene when we think George Melrose was dumped in Loch Lomond. It looked like a possibility that Webster may have been a victim of the Taxman himself. Until I was handed this.' Ross tossed the dossier down on the table at his side. 'This dossier was written by Webster last year, detailing his work within Barry McKenna's crew. A few pages in, Webster rants about recent miscarriages of justice, and criminals he feels escaped quote real justice. He goes on to describe what he calls fatal flaws in the Taskforce's approach and leadership strategy. In this section, he names George Melrose, Dennis Dunbar, and Lee Vickery – in that order – as people who have profited from the quote failed system. He then also names Frank

Gormley and Damien Reid. We think these two might be next.'

DC Lambie said, 'We all know Gormley, but who's Damien Reid?'

Lomond replied, 'Willie, you want to field that one?'

The mere mention of Reid's name seemed to do a number on Willie. He remained sitting down. 'Damien Reid is one of the foulest pieces of work I've ever come across. And John and I have seen our share.' He said to Ross, 'Your man at OC, DCI Hunt, he was one of the first boots on the ground on that one. We were all constables back then, of course. This is going back seventeen years. It messed up all of us for a while. Reid had convictions for all sorts by that point. He was on probation for domestic abuse, and arson which targeted his ex-partner, Amber Fulton. For his curfew order, he gave probation officers Amber's address, despite his previous conviction and suspended sentence. No one checked with Amber if she consented to her address being used, and they never visited her for a risk assessment of the house. If they had done that, they would have found the threatening letters Reid had been sending Amber while he was away. But the probation officers were more worried about Reid's apparent links with right-wing extremist groups in Shotts prison while doing a two-year stretch for robbery and assault.' Willie's voice cracked. 'A few weeks into his curfew order, he went to Amber's house for her birthday, high on amphetamines and booze. Next morning, answering calls of a disturbance, a police officer found

Amber, along with the bodies of her two teenage sons, and Amber's parents, all dead. Reid had attacked them with a claw hammer. A whole family. Wiped out in one night.'

There was silence.

For those who knew the story, it was hard to hear it again. Reid's face had peered out from the front pages of newspapers for weeks, as the full horror of what he had done came out during his trial. For the younger officers like Jason, DC Lambie, and DC Foster, who didn't know, their hearts broke.

To give Willie a break, Lomond took over. 'I can't think of anyone the Taxman would like to get his hands on more than someone like Damien Reid.'

Donna was the sole voice of dissent. 'But Reid was given a life sentence. He was to serve at least twenty years, wasn't he?'

Willie was still adrift in painful memories of the case. All he could manage to say was, 'Aye.'

'He's not technically got away with anything, has he? He committed a heinous crime, and was convicted. Why would the Taxman want him?'

'Because it's not enough,' said Lomond. He broke into a sardonic chuckle. 'He chopped up George Melrose because he chopped up companies. He filled Dennis Dunbar's mouth full of horse shit. He inflicted the same injuries on Lee Vickery, as Vickery had inflicted on his baby son. The Taxman isn't lobbying for stricter sentences, Donna. This is proper Old Testament, eye-for-an-eye type stuff.' His attention was broken by Linda standing at her desk, taking a phone call. She then marched over to her printer, ripped something out of its drawer, then headed for the stairs. As she descended, he managed to complete his thought. 'Who deserves to die? A murderer? A rapist? A thief? You've got two guys who each hit someone in the face on a Saturday night. One falls over and nothing else happens. The other one falls and cracks their head open. One of those guys is going to prison. But is one of them really more deserving of prison than the other guy?'

'Of course he is,' said Pardeep.

Jason shook his head insistently. 'No, it's called moral luck, and philosophers have been debating its anomaly for centuries. Look at the Catholic Church and the idea of limbo. It used to be that unbaptised babies who died didn't get into heaven. Then, one day, the Church just changed its mind. Did some sort of portal open up between heaven and earth where this new decree was communicated?'

'I think we've gone off topic a bit,' Ruth warned.

'The point is,' said Jason, 'the Taxman is removing moral luck from the equation. *He* is deciding. *He's* judge, jury, and executioner, because in his mind, the justice system as it stands isn't up to the task.'

At the table next to him, DS Jane Erskine silently swooning, having written him off as some gym-junkie meathead.

Linda was now at the bottom of the stairs and waving

Lomond over. Whatever she had to say wasn't for everyone's consumption yet.

She said to him quietly, 'Moira McTaggart has got a positive DNA match on that gun found in Gullane. It's got traces of Shaun Webster's sweat on it. We've got a hit on ballistics as well. The NABIS database has linked the weapon to several robberies and attempted murders thought to have been ordered by Barry McKenna.'

'So it *is* Webster,' said Lomond.

DC Lambie, who had been studying a police report on his laptop throughout, raised a timid hand. 'Sir, this might be known...em, knowledge already...'

'Known knowledge,' said Lomond. 'That's the best kind, Ian.'

Used to Lambie's nervy demeanour, Ruth nudged him along. 'Try us, Ian.'

His lifetime habit of slouching in his seat wasn't laziness or wishing to appear nonchalant. He was trying to make himself smaller and less visible. With all eyes on him, he sat up in his seat. 'I was just looking at the Damien Reid file, and I couldn't help noticing who the first officer at the scene was. The officer who found the Fulton family.' He handed the laptop over to Lomond.

The moment Lomond saw the name, he said dismally, 'Of course.' He showed Ruth the screen.

She read it aloud for the others. 'PC Shaun Webster.'

The confirmation knocked the wind out of Ruth. She handed the laptop back to DC Lambie with a mouthed,

'Good job.' She told the others, 'At least we know who we're chasing now.'

Linda shut her eyes, dread flooding through her body. 'What are the chances the press won't find out it's a cop who's killing all these people?'

Lomond replied, 'I think my dad would have described it as "a baw hair's breadth away from zilch."'

He was proven right far quicker than he expected.

From the back of the office, a voice boomed out of the shadows, like a bear growling from inside a cave.

'Linda!'

Out of the shadows strode Chief Superintendent Alasdair Reekie. He put a pin in his obvious fury. He barked, 'You, John, and Ruth in your office. *Right* now.' He marched up ahead, leaving a trail of confusion in his wake.

Before following the others to Linda's office, Lomond told everyone, 'Well, I've still got a job for at least the next ninety seconds. Until that changes, let's open up the books on Shaun Webster. I want his life story and every arrest he ever made by the time I come back.'

When Lomond reached Linda's office, Reekie was already in the grips of a full-on meltdown.

'What the shitting hell is *this*?' he fumed, brandishing a printout of the early edition front page of the *Glasgow Express*.

The headline read: "*VIGILANTE KILLER 'THE TAXMAN' ON KILLING SPREE*"

Lomond didn't immediately feel his stomach flip, as

the Taxman's name was always going to get out eventually. The nausea flooded through his stomach when he saw the subheading. It was no surprise why Reekie was climbing the walls.

"Outrage as senior cops 'hid truth' from public."

'See those little quotation marks?' Reekie seethed.

'I do, sir,' replied Lomond.

'That's a quote from a senior source within Police Scotland. You get one chance to answer this honestly, John. Did you talk to Colin Mowatt?'

Perfect, thought Lomond. *Of course it had to be written by Colin bloody Mowatt.*

'No!' Lomond exclaimed. 'I didn't talk to that little ginger weasel. If he tried to give me a tenner, I'd cross the street.'

'Well, somebody gave this quote,' said Reekie. 'This has leaked already, of course. Good luck on your way home tonight, because the place is crawling with press outside.'

Linda assured him, 'It'll be a good while before anyone goes home tonight, sir. I assure you of that.'

'The only saving grace is that we brought in Ruth to firefight this. You should prep for a press conference early tomorrow.'

'Of course,' Ruth replied. She didn't need to be asked twice to appear in front of the national media.

'The press is going to rip us apart and make stock out of our bones,' Reekie snarled. 'Let's at least have something to tell them tomorrow morning, eh?'

Once he was gone, Lomond scoffed. 'That was quite funny. The stock thing. I didn't think he had something like that in him.'

Without even a flicker of a grin, Linda said, 'This isn't funny.'

'I agree,' said Lomond. 'First, someone leaked about Donna's disciplinary hearing, and now this. What's the angle?'

'There's always someone who loves to act like they're in the know,' said Ruth. 'Someone with the inside track. Let Tulliallan worry about this. We have to stay focused on the job.'

'Speaking of which,' said Linda. 'What's your next move?'

Lomond asked Ruth, 'Have we got one?'

They all went back downstairs, with Ruth taking centre stage. She clapped her hands. 'Okay, people! Here's where we're at...'

Lomond shut his eyes in annoyance. There was no other phrase in modern usage that irritated him more.

Ruth continued, 'This dossier of Shaun Webster's might not be gospel, but it's the best chance we have right now of getting ahead of him. Two priorities going forward. One, Frank Gormley.'

Lomond said, 'I'll talk to Frank. He'd probably rather hear it from me that someone wants him dead.'

'Two,' said Ruth, 'Damien Reid. If we want to find Shaun Webster, we need to find these two.'

Linda, who had been hovering behind Lomond and

Ruth, leaned in. 'Damien Reid's serving a life sentence in Barlinnie. How is Webster going to hit him?'

'He's been surprising us so far,' said Ross. 'If the stories I've heard about the Taxman's activities are true, it's not outwith the realm of possibility. If anyone can get to someone inside Barlinnie, it's the Taxman.'

Ruth said, 'We should get Reid under supervision.'

'Protect him?' Lomond spat with disdain. 'We should tie him to a tree in Glasgow Green with a big fuck-off spotlight on him. Lure Webster out.'

Ruth looked at Linda for a read on what he'd said.

Linda told her, 'Oh, he's more serious than you would like about that.'

Lomond said, 'This is going to take more than just picking up a phone to find out where Reid is and get access to him.'

Ruth said, 'I might be able to make a few calls.'

'Do it quickly,' said Linda. 'We don't have a lot of time left before Webster strikes again.'

CHAPTER FORTY-ONE

LOMOND PARKED around the corner from Frank Gormley's enormous pad in Newton Mearns, because he knew there was no way Gormley would let an unidentified car inside the property. He hadn't become Glasgow's number one gangster – and stayed there for nearly two decades – by being reckless.

Gormley recognised the face on his CCTV monitor that was perched in its usual spot on his work desk. He smiled and said to himself 'Johnny boy...'

'Frank, it's John,' Lomond said into the intercom. He held up the Osman letter to the camera lens. 'I've got something to give you.'

Gormley buzzed him in without a reply.

Lomond's feet crunched on the red gravel. It had been laid out so that it was impossible to reach the front door without stepping on it. Motion-detector security lights lined the house perimeter, as well as cameras, and spikes along guttering and drainpipes. It was a fortress.

Gormley greeted Lomond at the front door in a pristine white Lacoste tracksuit. It was gleaming. A far cry from the Barlinnie inmate uniform of a red polo shirt and blue jeans that Gormley was wearing last time they met. He had a tan from a recent golf holiday in Florida, and his usually small, beady eyes had softened since he'd got out.

He ran his hand through his beard which he had grown out to a fashionable length. His short, wiry grey hair remained, pushed straight back, as if the world was rushing past him at an incredible speed, while he remained at the centre, implacable, and effortlessly in control.

Gormley smiled, pointing out the letter in Lomond's hand. 'You know how many of these I've had over the years? I should keep a big stack of them by the door here next to the Domino's menus.'

'This one's a little different, Frank,' said Lomond. 'Can I come in?'

Gormley reluctantly stepped aside.

'Is the family in?' Lomond asked quietly.

'Naw,' said Gormley, striding towards the living room – a sprawling open-plan area that had been tastefully furnished with ornate rugs and ornaments, and the walls covered in modern art paintings that had hidden meanings neither man cared to find out.

'The wife's taken the weans out,' Gormley explained. 'Make it fast. I've got two years I'm trying to make up for.'

'You've got about eight more to yourself as a free man thanks to me,' said Lomond.

'You want me to thank you for sticking to your word?'

Lomond handed him the Osman letter.

Gormley skipped to the only part that mattered. 'Is this McKenna again?'

'No. Like I said this one's a little different.' Lomond gestured to the couch. 'Can I sit down?'

'Go ahead.' Gormley remained standing.

'What do you know about the Taxman?'

Gormley looked almost dazed. 'I wasn't expecting that. The Taxman? Why not just tell me the fuckin' Easter Bunny's coming after me. The Taxman's shite. End of.'

'I've got three dead bodies at Gartcosh that would say otherwise.'

'I don't care what some two-bit dealer's fed you, the Taxman doesn't exist.'

'One of the victims was Lee Vickery.'

Gormley lodged his tongue into his cheek while he contemplated the news. 'Huh.' He glanced towards the bar, which was amply stocked with bottles in an array of ambers and browns. One of the finest whisky collections in the country. 'What can I get you?'

'Water would be great.'

'I'll get a bottle from the fridge—'

'Really, tap's fine, Frank.'

'I don't drink water from the tap anymore. And I don't let anyone else do it. I had a pal who was a plumber. He's deid now. Used to tell me horror stories about what you find in household pipes. He never drank tap water either. He said if everyone in the country had seen what he had, they'd do the same.'

Lomond nodded. 'Bottled it is, then.'

While Gormley was gone, Lomond heard him taking a phone call but couldn't make out the conversation.

Gormley returned with Lomond's water, then fixed himself a glass of Highland Park. 'So who in their right mind wants to kill a nobody like Lee Vickery, and also turn their sights on a King Kong motherfucker like me?'

Lomond turned his hands up to demonstrate full disclosure. 'He's polis. Undercover.'

'He's *polis*?'

'Organised Crime Taskforce.'

'That's Hunt's outfit, isn't it?'

'Aye.'

Gormley cackled. 'He must be *shitein'* it!'

Lomond couldn't help but admire the attitude. Absolutely nothing fazed Gormley. Not even an officially declared threat to life. 'Hunt's had better weeks.'

'Is it true he's shagging that DI of his? Some bird called Ally?'

'I don't know anything about that.'

Gormley pouted. 'That's what I heard on the inside. What's this guy's deal, anyway?'

'The short version is undercover cop goes a bit mad and turns vigilante.'

'Who else has he hit?'

'The first was George Melrose.'

'No way. That's a big scalp for your first one.'

'Then Dennis Dunbar.'

'I heard stories about him years ago. Bad ones. Prick.'

'I was going to say monster, but aye, also a prick.'

'And then Lee?'

'That's it so far. But I'm sure number four won't be long coming.'

Gormley pondered it over his drink. 'Melrose, Dunbar. Those are big players. What's Lee doing in there?'

'It looks like he's been targeting people he thinks have got away with certain crimes. He then turns the crimes against the accused. It's hard to argue with the bastards he's taken down.'

'Strong words for a Chief Inspector.'

'It's just us, Frank. We can be real with each other. Melrose cheated thousands of folk out of their life savings. Dunbar was a paedophile who defended the indefensible. And Lee Vickery killed a baby.'

Gormley's voice went down an octave. His head lowered, sombre. 'Aye. I heard about that. To think I shook hands with him. I mean, that was before he did that, of course.'

Lomond paused. 'You knew Lee Vickery?'

'Seeing as he's toe-tagged, I might as well tell you. He used to run for me. Pills mostly. Or smack. Had to let him go in the end.'

'How come?'

'He was skimming. If they stay with you long enough, the runners always end up skimming you. I never took it personal, like. And his bird was pregnant at the time, so I thought better of chibbing the prick.' Gormley turned his glass in his hand, mulling something over. 'But I'm glad. Sounds to me like he got what he deserved. I'd never lay a hand on ma weans. The wife's always on at me, you're too soft on them. I cannae help it. My da knocked lumps out of me. Just made me hate the prick. It's lucky Lee was out of my hands by the time he did in that wee tot. I'd be in Bar-L on a murder charge for sure.'

'Seems that the killer had the same idea.'

Gormley knocked back the rest of his drink. 'Well... whatever his reasons, we *made* him.' He gestured to himself and Lomond. 'Probably collateral damage in the mayhem we cause.'

'It's easy to get behind someone who kills bad guys,' said Lomond. 'But he has to be stopped. There has to be rules, otherwise anyone could be a savage.'

Gormley nodded in agreement. 'A line has been crossed. Let *me* be real now...' He put his hand out in Lomond's direction. 'You do what you do. I do what I do. And at the end of the day, there can still be a respect there. You don't mess me around, and I try to avoid causing you trouble.' He chuckled. 'To an extent. Where business permits, know whit ah mean.'

'I miss the old days,' said Lomond. 'One crew was really in charge. Everyone knew where the fault lines were, and you never crossed them. Then everyone got greedy.'

'Tell me about it. That's why I like to keep the peace. It's more profitable.'

Lomond sank down some of the bottled water, then shook it. 'Mind if I take it with me?'

'Nae bother,' said Gormley, escorting Lomond to the door.

'If you want, Frank, I could at least ask about a safe house for you? If you're worried about the kids.'

Gormley let a hand fall onto Lomond's shoulder with a thud. His hand was like an anvil. 'I couldn't hide, John. Couldn't do it. I'll take my chances.' Gormley put his hand out. 'Are you forgetting something?'

Lomond shook his head rapidly, like he wasn't thinking straight. 'Oh aye, sorry.' He handed him the Osman letter.

Gormley found the wording amusing. 'It's funny. As if I don't have a threat to my life every other day.'

'That's the job we've chosen,' said Lomond.

Gormley leaned into the porch and laid the letter on top of a pile of junk mail, then said, 'Cheers, John. Take care.'

LOMOND MARCHED into the MIT office and shuffled out of his jacket. 'Donna,' he called out. 'Get me everything we have on Frank Gormley. Associates, informers, contacts, business partners, everything.'

'So you had a productive meeting, then?' asked Ruth, who was patrolling the area in front of the whiteboard.

'Lee Vickery was one of Gormley's dealers,' said Lomond. 'He just came right out and told me.' He threw his hands up as if the conclusion was obvious.

'Right...and...so what?'

He grimaced. 'It's that foot.'

DS Erskine and the other Fettes Avenue officers looked up from their call sheets. They were still ploughing through an interminable list of Volvo estate owners in the Greater Glasgow area. Meanwhile, their Glasgow counterparts were being given the far sexier assignment of digging into an organised crime boss's past.

DC Foster leaned over and whispered to DC Lambie, 'Why do they get all the fun jobs?'

Lambie grumbled in response. 'We're glorified call centre staff right now.'

Lomond said to DS Erskine, 'You were right, Jane. Why cut off Lee Vickery's foot and stitch it onto Melrose? There were a ton of other ways Webster could have left a trail to Vickery.'

Ruth said, 'No one disagrees, John. But what do you want to do with it?'

Lomond looked to Ross, who looked right back at home at his old desk, surrounded by Pardeep, Jason, and Willie.

'We need someone to fill in the blanks between Gormley and Lee Vickery,' said Lomond. 'Find out what really happened with them. He says he let Vickery go because he was skimming. Vickery wasn't some apprentice not up to the job. He stole from Frank Gormley.'

'Why is that so special?' asked Ruth.

'Because that would make Vickery the only man in history to steal from Frank Gormley and live. There's something else going on here.' Lomond's eye caught Ross, who appeared to be having a brainwave. 'Who are you thinking, Ross?'

He sighed. 'It's a mate. An old mate. He's a screw at Barlinnie.'

'Great. Set up a meeting.' Lomond turned, thinking that was the end of it.

'It's not that simple,' Ross told him. 'We play in the same five-a-sides league. And we don't talk work. Ever. He asks nothing of me, and he trusts I'll never ask anything of him. It's the only way it works.'

'Well, it doesn't work for me,' Lomond retorted. 'Make the call, Ross. Tell him I need someone who can give me the skinny on Gormley and Vickery. Pardeep, Jason: get me any and all connections you can make to Gormley and each of the victims. Take one victim each, and get digging.' He turned to Ruth. 'Gormley's the key to this thing. I just know it.'

'What can I do?' asked Donna.

'You're coming with me,' said Lomond. 'Field trip.'

CHAPTER FORTY-TWO

THE FIVE-A-SIDES PITCHES were all booked up for the evening league matches. Joiners, bankers, doctors, teachers, window cleaners and workies alike all came together to play the beautiful game. Although, the way the game was played at Goals on Great Western Road, next to the golf driving range, there wasn't much of an emphasis on beauty. Beer-bellied guys charged about like rhinos in polyester and overpriced football boots, playing out fantasies of being Messi or Ronaldo. For many of them, each week brought one single hour of football on an artificial pitch to forget about whatever was going on in their lives. Can't pay the mortgage? You can always take pleasure from skinning some hapless call-centre operator playing for Maryhill United.

Ross was no different. He played five-a-sides because he never had to think about work for a single second.

Now he was going there for the express purpose to *do* work.

The pitches were right next to the dual carriageway, where Great Western Road straightens out for the fast run-in to Clydebank. A golf driving range was on the premises as well. Floodlit too. Whenever the chaos of shouting and refs' whistles died down, there was a constant, faint *thud* of golf balls being hit off astroturf.

That night, there was the added strangeness of roaring dinosaurs thrown into the mix from Jurassic Par – the dinosaur-themed crazy golf course adjoining the driving range. Whoever had been on for closing had messed up, as they had forgotten to switch off the mechanical dinosaurs' sound effects. They had, however, switched off all the lights. Which meant that every minute or so, a Tyrannosaurus would let out a huge roar in the darkness.

Ross wandered between the various pitches, all named after famous stadiums around the world. The San Siro. Nou Camp. Hampden Park. Eventually, he found the Stade de France pitch where Ronaldoughnuts were playing Is Your Motherwell.

The player Ross had his eye on was all over the pitch like a lost dog, running in circles. He was pouring sweat despite having barely touched the ball.

At full-time, and with Ronaldoughnuts on the wrong side of a thirteen-three thrashing, there was a mix of good humour and a bit of afters about an unnecessary late tackle.

Behind the chain link fence barricading the pitch, Ross called out, 'Hey, Danny!'

Danny walked over because he was incapable of jogging. Wondering what Ross was doing there not dressed for football, he asked, 'You injured?'

Ross said, 'Not playing till Sunday.'

'What brings you out here, man?'

'I need a favour.'

Danny looked disheartened. 'Give me a sec.' He grabbed a towel from his backpack then bid hasty good-byes to his teammates.

Danny led them over to the neighbouring Maracanã pitch that was shutting down for the night. 'You remember our agreement, right?'

'I do. But this is a favour I really need.'

'You know how many pairs of eyes I've got on me right now just because we're talking? There's a lot of connected guys out here.'

'I know. All I need is a name for someone inside.'

'Who?'

'Someone who has the inside track on Frank Gormley.'

Danny kicked at the ground. 'Fuck's sake. You're going after him again?'

'It's not like that.'

'Cos you'll no' get anyone to grass on Frank bloody Gormley inside the jail.'

'Don't worry about what I need from them.'

'What you need from them reflects on me, too. I take

my job seriously. They respect me because I respect them. I don't fuck them about like the other guards do.'

'I'll keep you light years away from it.' Sensing reluctance, Ross said, 'I hate to say something like you owe me...but you *owe* me, Danny.'

Danny knew he wasn't wrong. Ross had saved his life when he told Danny about a plot in the jail to knife him. When they searched the inmate's cell, they found a butcher knife seven inches long.

'I might know someone,' Danny said. 'But if you pull any shady shit, never contact me again. You get me?'

'I get you,' Ross replied. 'Who's the contact?'

'I'm going to put you in a room with a guy called Billy McDonald. He's all right. But you shouldn't go in there expecting anything out of him.'

'That's what I told my gaffer,' said Ross. 'He says he's got a plan.'

CHAPTER FORTY-THREE

DONNA AND LOMOND pulled into the car park of the *Glasgow Express* offices at Anderston Quay beside the River Clyde, where it passes under the Kingston Bridge.

Donna said, 'Remind me again why I'm the one going in and not you?'

'For two reasons,' Lomond explained, 'Number one, I'm your boss and number two, because I'm telling you. For all further enquires, please review reason one again.'

In reception, Donna did as Lomond had instructed: held out her ID, then asked to speak to Colin Mowatt.

The receptionist kept her waiting several minutes. Long enough for Lomond to come marching in. Tapping his watch and gesticulating, he shouted across the deserted reception area, 'What are you doing, Donna?'

Having been slouched in one of the many couches that lined the glass windows, Donna sat up. 'They said he was busy working. So I thought...' She trailed off as Lomond steamed past the receptionist.

'Detective Chief Inspector John Lomond,' he said, showing his badge. 'Tell Colin Mowatt we're coming up.'

The receptionist held out a hand towards him. 'Hey...you can't go up there.'

As he waited for the lift to come down, Lomond had eyes only for the LCD display showing the floors ticking down. 'If you're calling security to stop me, you'd better send more than a couple of guys.'

Upstairs, the offices were a sedate affair. Most of the final copy for the late editions – such as Mowatt's Taxman story – had already been filed.

The moment Lomond and Donna entered, Lomond felt a reporter's hand touch him on the shoulder. An attempt to hold him back, along with a weak cry of 'Hey, you can't be in here...'

Lomond rolled his shoulder, as if getting rid of a fly. 'Did you just lay your hands on a Chief Inspector?'

'Looked like that to me,' agreed Donna, still travelling at full pace.

At the end of the office, standing alone by his desk, Colin Mowatt saw the commotion and panicked. There was nowhere to run to.

Sounding friendly, Lomond said from a distance away, 'Colin! Good to see you. What's new?'

Mowatt raised his hands, trying to keep Lomond back. 'Hey, I don't make the rules. That was a legitimate quote, on the record.'

'I'm sure it was,' said Lomond.

Behind, Donna saw a solitary security guard appear at the office entrance.

Lomond lowered his voice. 'Just give me the name, Colin, and we'll be out of here. That's it, mate.'

'I can't do that,' Mowatt said.

'Of course you can. You just think back to whatever disloyal police officer you spoke to earlier, and you tell me their name. Or I make tonight really horrible for you.'

Retreating behind his desk, Mowatt said, 'I learned long ago...don't ever wrestle with a pig. You end up covered in shit, and besides, the pig likes it.'

'You've got the source. You've got your story. Well done, Ed fucking Sheeran. But you can still give me their name.'

Mowatt looked affronted. 'Give up a source? What do I look like to you?'

'Do you really want me to play that game?'

Before Lomond could fire off any insults, Mowatt interjected, 'Never mind. Stuff like this is why you're in bother to begin with. Police think they can do whatever they want. Applying your own rules as you see fit. You're no better than the Taxman.' He looked Donna up and down. 'Neither are you. I remember you from the Jack Ferguson story.'

Donna corrected him, 'It was an investigation, not a story.'

'You look different. Meaner about the eyes these

days. Is that Lomond rubbing off on you? Or is it more like you're rubbing him off?'

Mowatt had barely finished the last syllable when Donna threw him up against the window. The force of the shove and Mowatt's weedy cries for help brought the office to a standstill.

The editor, who had been on the phone until a few seconds ago, finally noticed the scuffle going on. She shouted from her office door, 'Get your hands off him this instant, or I'll change our front page to a shot of you grappling with a journalist.'

Lomond pulled Donna back and away from Mowatt.

She straightened out her shirt with a brisk tug at the hem. She pointed to Mowatt's computer screen. 'You misspelled grisly in the opening line.'

Mowatt waited for Donna and Lomond to leave before making the correction.

CHAPTER FORTY-FOUR

RUTH WAS STANDING over DS Erkine's shoulder, getting an update on the Volvo estate situation, when she saw Lomond and Donna returning.

'Where have you two been?' she asked.

'Don't worry about it,' Lomond replied. He headed straight for Willie's desk. 'Any progress?'

Willie said, 'Jason's been working on Gormley's links to George Melrose. Pardeep's been on Dunbar.'

'And you've been checking everything? There's no detail that could be too small.'

'They're on it, John. I've been double- and triple-checking what they've got.'

Pardeep had earbuds in, and was making feverish notes.

Lomond assumed he was on his phone, hands-free. Although Pardeep wasn't actually saying anything.

'Jason?' asked Lomond. 'What's the story so far?'

Jason had been twirling a pen at lightning pace up and down his fingers while examining a spreadsheet on his laptop screen that looked like the world's most impossible Sudoku. He tossed the pen down and brought his ergonomic chair from tilted to straight. 'I figured that finances were the best place to start with Melrose. He was doing illegal things, but within a respected business. So if he had any business with Frank Gormley, there had to be a paper trail somewhere. I went back through the case files on Gormley's money laundering enquiry. He might have been put away for rinsing the cash he made illegally, but a huge amount of it went into legitimate investments. I mean, his advisors had built him a decent portfolio by the time he was convicted. One of those investments was to something called the Ascot Group. They're the holding company to one of Melrose's ponzi schemes. It's all very technical, and once you actually dive into the numbers...' Jason puffed his cheeks out.

'Are you telling me Frank Gormley invested money with George Melrose?'

'Yeah. Along with about five hundred million quid of other people's money too.'

'How much was Gormley in for?'

Jason picked up his pen and pointed through the notes he had made on a pad. 'If the numbers are right – and I'm almost certain they are – then Melrose took Gormley for at least one point four million.'

Lomond did a double-take. 'Pounds? Not dollars?'

'Pounds.'

Willie added, 'Even if it was dollars or euros or bloody rupees, it's one point four million reasons to cut the guy up.'

Lomond nodded in Pardeep's direction. 'What about him?'

Willie answered, 'Progress has been a little slower on Dunbar. It's not like we're drowning in paperwork on the guy. Everything we got from the house in Gullane was personal. Sordid sex stuff. He was Barry McKenna's guy. Killing your rival's lawyer would be a scalp, sure. But it would be a huge escalation, and invite attacks on Gormley's close associates in retribution. That's the last thing he needs when he's trying to reassert control on his former strongholds.'

Lomond retorted, 'Unless Dunbar had more skin in the game than we realise.'

Pardeep shook his head in amusement and took out his earbuds. As soon as he switched off the bluetooth, the audio he had been listening to came out of the laptop speakers.

It was the nasally voice of a Glasgow hardman. Lomond hadn't heard the voice for a long time, but he certainly recognised it. The man was in the middle of a rambling anecdote about his glory days when he was on top.

Lomond was aghast. 'Are you listening to a bloody *podcast?*'

Willie snapped at Pardeep, 'You told me you found an insider.'

Pardeep panicked as he realised how it all must have looked. 'Sorry, boss. It's YouTube. I found this channel for Barry Groves.'

Lomond, face still tight with confusion, went over to see the laptop screen. 'I've seen it all now...Barry Groves has got a YouTube channel. Christ, look at him...'

Willie came over. 'He's looking well, actually.'

The man had short gelled hair, and was wearing a tight black t-shirt. Trying to still dress young despite his nearly sixty years.

Pardeep said, 'It's just him behind the desk, telling stories about his gangster days. It's pretty captivating stuff. He does some shorts of himself just walking around Glasgow.'

'Oh, aye,' said Lomond. 'I'm glad we could find you something to while away the hours, Pardeep. You can binge your way through them all until we get – I don't know – a vigilante serial killer on the loose.'

'He's not just talking about the old days,' Pardeep explained. 'He's gossiping about what's going on now. He's careful with what names he bandies around, and he doesn't actually mention Dunbar by name–'

'Then how did you end up on the channel?'

'Either Groves is mucking about, or maybe he's not very bright. It's kind of hard to tell listening to him. But one of the tags he put on the video when he uploaded it was "Dennis Dunbar". That's how I found the channel. Groves maybe thinks the tags are only visible at his end.'

Pardeep scrolled back through the timeline he had noted down. 'Listen to this.'

Groves was already in full swing, loving the sound of his own voice. "*So as ah says earlier, there was this show-down meeting planned between Frank and Barry. Things had been escalating for a while since Frank had been locked up. So Barry got his lawyer in tae arrange the meet. It was gonnae happen at Harthill Services, so halfway between Glasgow and Edinburgh. You know how it is, naebody wants to give an inch, so it has to be as close to halfway as possible. So Frank rocks up there at the arranged time. The lawyer's there all suited and booted, aw the rest of it. Then the lawyer goes aff tae take a phone call. While he's away, a guy wi a sawn-off tries tae blast Frank. But the weapon jams and he's no' got a back-up. The guy has tae make a run for it. The gunman's no' been found yet. But it's only a matter of time before you see some action in response.*"

Pardeep said, 'This was uploaded eleven days ago.'

Lomond asked, 'How are we only hearing about this now? From him?'

'I checked. There were no emergency calls placed at the scene. No reports made. The shooter never got off any shots. I've requested CCTV from the area–'

'There won't be anything,' said Lomond. 'You might see the vehicles arriving, but there's no way they'd set a meeting between Gormley and McKenna in full sight of CCTV. It was a set-up. We've now got reasons for Frank to kill Melrose and now Dunbar, too.'

Willie said, 'That leaves Lee Vickery. We've at least got a link between him and Dunbar.'

'But what we need,' said Lomond, 'is between *Gormley* and Vickery.'

Ruth pondered it all. 'You said that Gormley told you Vickery had been skimming cash from his deals for Gormley. Isn't that reason enough?'

Lomond was adamant. 'Frank wouldn't cut a leg off and do all the other stuff relating to Tyler's death over someone skimming from forever ago. What was done to Vickery is more personal than that.'

Ross speculated, 'Maybe that's why there was a point given to Police Scotland for that one, rather than the Taxman.'

'True,' said Lomond. 'In any case, Frank would have dealt with someone stealing from him back then if he was ever going to. He wouldn't wait all this time.' He shook his head. 'Nah...if we want something on Vickery, we need this source to come through for us.' He asked Ross, 'Are we set for tomorrow yet?'

'Tomorrow morning,' said Ross.

Linda called down from her office window. 'John! I've got a PC Ryan Venables in reception asking for you. Says it's urgent. Desk sergeant says the guy's scared out of his mind.'

CHAPTER FORTY-FIVE

PC VENABLES WANTED MORE privacy than talking openly in the MIT office, so Lomond and Ruth took the constable to an interview room downstairs. He was still wearing his uniform, having got off shift barely ten minutes earlier.

Ryan was barely able to make eye contact with Lomond or Ruth. He was biting his lower lip.

'Just relax, Ryan,' Lomond told him. 'We're not recording anything here. You're not under caution. Why don't you tell us what this is all about.'

Ryan took a deep breath. The exhalation came out shaky, trembling. 'It's the picture that came through a few hours ago. The one for circulation. Shaun Webster. I recognised him as soon as I saw it.'

Ruth shunted forward in her seat. 'You've seen Shaun Webster?'

'Yeah.'

'How long ago?'

'About three weeks.'

Lomond's eyes widened.

'Walk us through it in your own time, Ryan,' said Ruth.

He looked up with terrified eyes. 'Could I maybe get some water? I'm just...I'm worried I've made a terrible mistake.'

Deferring to Ruth as SIO, Lomond got up for the water just outside the door in a cooler. When he returned with the water in a disposable cup, Ryan drained it in one go. The coolness of it came as a relief on a muggy evening, and after a long day covering many miles on foot.

'Start from the beginning,' Ruth said.

'I'd just come off a twelve-hour shift. It was about nine in the morning. I was driving around the back of Glasgow Airport – you know, Barnsford Road – to get home, when I saw this guy walking along the wee pavement bit that's next to the airport perimeter fence. Do you know what it's like around there?'

'I know it,' said Lomond.

'I've never seen anyone walking along there. You'd have to be walking from St James Interchange, and there's just a grass verge there. Even once you get onto Barnsford, it's still ages to get to Inchinnan or maybe Renfrew. You get the odd runner or dog walker on the Abbotsinch Road side of the airport cos the football pitches are over there. But not on Barnsford. So I gave the guy a close look on the way past, when I realised he was wearing his dressing gown. Like, one of those heavy towelling ones. And he's got on slippers. I kept driving for a bit, but something made me go back. There was just something not right about the guy. I thought, maybe he's unwell, or done a runner from somewhere. I didn't think he was going to hurt someone. I was worried he might hurt himself, because at the back of my mind I was thinking, it's a few miles to Erskine Bridge. Plus he was holding a bottle of wine. A bit of me thought, all right, it's morning. He's on a bender here. Got a bit confused or something. But...he just didn't seem right. So I turned around and went back, so I could get a look at his face. He seemed like he wasn't in a good place. I was worried he was so drunk he might try something stupid at the airport, or stumble into the road. I mean, folk drive so fast along that road...'

Lomond and Ruth were on the edge of their seats – desperate to push Ryan on to greater detail, but reluctant to break his flow.

Ryan continued, 'The guy was sort of mumbling, ranting under his breath. He just looked...mad. His hair was sort of short but all over the place. He hadn't shaved in a while. I figured, this guy needs a bit of help. So I pulled over into a lay-by and approached him. He started kicking off at me. Don't come any closer, leave me alone, all the rest of it.'

'What was he ranting about?' asked Lomond.

'Specifically,' Ruth emphasised.

Ryan shook his head. 'Just all...mad stuff. They cut me loose. Made me disappear. I don't even exist anymore. Stuff like that.'

Lomond and Ruth exchanged a look.

'I didn't know what to make of it. I was going to call 999, but he freaked out when I told him.'

Lomond said, 'Did you ask where he lived?'

Ryan was still in panic mode. Not listening properly. 'I hardly knew what the guy was going to do, did I?'

'It's all right, Ryan,' said Ruth. 'Calm down. You're not in any trouble.'

Aye, yet, thought Lomond.

Ruth asked, 'Did he give you an address, or any description of where he lived?'

'He said that he'd walked about two miles.'

Lomond said, 'Tell me you drove him.'

Ryan said nothing.

'Ryan. Tell me you picked him up and dropped him somewhere.'

Ryan protested, getting a little louder, sensing that he was about to get the blame. 'I was knackered, all right! What was I meant to do? It's not like he was talking about topping himself, or waving a knife around. He was softly spoken. The only thing that riled him up was when I talked about calling the police to take him somewhere.'

Lomond excused himself and ran as fast as he ever had up the stairs to MIT.

'Ross!' he yelled as soon as he entered the office. 'I need you.'

Lomond rummaged through his desk drawers, pulling out a heap of crap that had been in there for years. Packs of pencils, empty notepads, and a tattered *Glasgow A-Z*. He let out a cackle of pleasure when he pulled it out. 'Pay attention, young man. I'm about to show you something you can't do on Google Maps.'

Donna, Pardeep, and Jason couldn't help but look over to see what was going on. The Fettes Avenue officers, too.

Lomond took out a pencil from one of the packs and made an asterisk at the rough point on Barnsford Road where Lomond thought Ryan had encountered Shaun Webster. He then considered the scale of the map and what he knew of the distances from living in nearby Caledonia Street years before. He then drew an arc around the airport and surrounding streets.

Ross said, 'Not to be pedantic, but you *can* actually do that on Google Maps.'

Lomond was too wired into his theory to notice the comment. 'That's everywhere within two miles from that star on the map. I need you to take this to Hunt or take a photo of it on your phone or something. I know that Hunt has ransacked every property that the taskforce has to check for traces of Shaun Webster. But where was Webster placed before the Taskforce?'

Ross said, 'He was with regular Organised Crime, working out of London Road.'

'Find out if they ever had a safe house within this marked area on the map.'

'Will do,' Ross said.

'Back to work, everyone,' Lomond told the others, then wondered why Ross hadn't left yet. Clutching at straws, he said, 'Please?'

'It's not that,' Ross replied. 'I'm still with DCI Hunt and OC, sir. I need to go back. Like, *actually*. I mean, I'm happy to help here, except...'

'Except?'

'I don't think I should be coming back here after Barlinnie tomorrow.'

Lomond seemed disappointed, then was quick to say, 'No. Of course. I mean, look, we've got a whole other crew from Edinburgh here. It's not like we're running light without you.'

As Ross turned to leave, Lomond held out his arm. 'Hey, Ross...'

He stopped. 'Yeah.'

'They could give me full MITs from Edinburgh, Aberdeen, Dundee, and Inverness. I'd still take you over the lot of them.'

Ross smiled. 'Cheers, boss.'

'You've had a big day. We need an even bigger one tomorrow.'

CHAPTER FORTY-SIX

BY THE TIME Ross got home, both Isla and Lachlann were fast asleep. He peeked in on Lachlann, taking delicate footsteps across the landing. The days of him waking up from the most minor of floorboard creaks were over, but Ross's paranoia remained. He and Isla had only recently started turning the television up loud enough to no longer need subtitles.

During paternity leave, he and Isla had watched most of *Game of Thrones* with the TV muted, such was their fear of waking Lachlann once they had finally got him to sleep.

Ross lingered by Lachlann's bedroom door. Few things in life brought him as much comfort as the sight of his son sleeping.

He was only able to relax about all things noise-related when he was in the kitchen. From there, Lachlann was one floor and three closed doors away.

It felt like it had been days since he'd last been home. It had been one of the fullest days in his career so far. Fortunately for him, he had married a chef. Isla had left the remnants of a luxurious fish pie in the fridge, still in the casserole dish. All he had to do was throw it in the oven for twenty minutes.

He was exhausted, but his mind was racing too fast to be able to sleep. He wanted nothing more than to sit down with the fish pie and watch an episode of *Top Gear*. He knew it was garbage, and the supposedly improvised banter was obviously scripted, but it did the only thing that Ross demanded from a TV show: it let him forget about work.

He placed the baby monitor on the coffee table and settled down with his very late dinner. But before he could get the first forkful up to his mouth, he heard a sharp *ping* from outside.

It had come from near the garage. Like a stone or a pebble striking the metal door.

Ross muted the TV then froze, waiting for any follow-up noise.

He was about to sit back again and turn up the volume, when the sound repeated. Slightly louder this time.

Ross put down his dinner plate with a sigh. Of course it was going to be nothing. It always was. But since Lachlann had arrived, he felt compelled to check any and all possible disturbances. Especially as they were in a new-build detached house in a large housing estate. The noises sounded like someone might be trying to establish if someone was home. Ross figured all he had to do was switch the kitchen light on and make himself known to whoever was out there.

He went to the back door, scuffing his feet intentionally on the top step to make some noise. The minor motion was enough to trigger the security light at the back of the house.

Then, the same ping sound came from somewhere near the garage around the corner of the garden.

He was still in a good position halfway across the back garden. If anyone did try to jump him, the security lights on either side of the house would come on long before they could reach him.

Then it happened. The security light pointing at the path alongside the garage flicked on. Ross's heart rate spiked. In the comfort of his own home, defences down and exhausted, his usual preparedness for a possible attack had gone out the window. He didn't have anything within reach that he could use as a weapon, and he didn't want to turn his back on the assailant to get something from the kitchen.

He took tenuous steps towards the sound, calling out in a whisper. 'Whoever's there, clear off!'

The garden was silent again.

Ross took so long to get to the corner of the garden, the security light turned back off.

He was in darkness.

Was the assailant standing still? Trying to lure him closer?

Ross got the answer when he peeked his head around the corner.

The light came on once more.

On the ground were three small stones lying in front of the metal door on the side of the garage.

While he crouched down to inspect the stones, the security light above turned off again.

Ross checked in all directions. There was no one there.

This time, when he stood up, the security light didn't come on.

It was the same story at the back door.

Ross waved his arms, but no motion would trigger it.

From inside the kitchen, a voice whispered, 'Don't bother.'

CHAPTER FORTY-SEVEN

HE WAS DRESSED head to foot in black. Almost like a soldier. Cargo trousers, a dark fleece, and a balaclava. He was tall and wide. With an enormously wide neck.

The man waved Ross inside. 'Or would you rather I lock you outside while your family is in here?'

Now he was in the thick of it, at least some of Ross's training kicked in.

Ross put his hands up. 'Please. Okay. I'll give you whatever you want. I don't want any trouble.'

'You don't want to implore me to leave Lachlann alone?'

Something primal shifted inside Ross at the mere hint of harm to his son.

'That's what the textbook says, isn't it,' the man said. 'Don't make appeals to empathy. You might end up triggering an escalation to the crisis. By mentioning a child, you bring them into the altercation.'

There was a flicker of green light from the baby monitor on the kitchen worktop, along with the sound of Lachlann stirring in his cot.

Ross was mouth breathing. Heart thumping. Hands clammy. But he was still thinking clearly. 'What do you want, Shaun?'

He peeled off his balaclava. 'This is surplus to requirements now.'

Ross kept his hands out in front of him, gesturing for Webster to keep back. 'Whatever's happened, whoever's angered you, you don't have any fight with me or my family. I'm just an honest cop.'

'Apparently you're my replacement,' said Webster.

'Hardly.'

'I should say so. I ambushed you with a garage security light and a couple of stones. You're no undercover officer, that's for sure.'

Webster sounded very in control. Measured. Little emotion in his voice. This wasn't about revenge, or some kind of attack. It was an assignment.

'Is it true what they're saying about you?' asked Ross.

'I've no idea what's been said about me.'

'That you lost it. Went rogue.'

Webster scoffed. 'Of course that's what they said. Don't get me wrong, I've had my moments. I had a bit of a hard time recently. Broke down a bit. But I am *so* clear in my thoughts now. In what I have to do.'

'What do you have to do?'

'A better way of looking at it is what *you* have to do for me. To stop me going up those stairs one night.'

Lachlann made more noise now. He was turning over. The beginnings of a whimper that Ross knew all too well. The whimper he made at night when he was about to start crying.

Ross shut his eyes. 'What do you want, Shaun?'

'Help me get Damien Reid. Or I start to take things away from you.' Webster stared at him. 'Look at me and tell me I wouldn't do it.'

'I believe you, I believe you. But I don't know how I can help you get to Reid on the inside.'

'He's not going to be inside, Ross. That's why I need your help. This is probably the only chance I'll ever have to get to him. It happened very quietly, but Reid was moved to Greenock not long ago. They put him in Chrisswell House. Do you know it?'

'Can't say I do.'

'It's where they put long-term prisoners to progress into an open prison. Damien Reid. In an open prison. After everything he did to that family.'

A single cry pierced out from the monitor, followed by gentle sobs. If Ross had been in bed and heard it, he would have gone in to check on him.

He said, 'If you're asking me whether the justice system is fucked, you won't get any argument from me. But what you're doing isn't the way to fix it.'

'It's the *only* way to fix it, Ross. Can't you see that?'

As Lachlann's cries got louder, Ross shifted his weight from foot to foot in aggravation.

Webster said, 'He's fine. Stay where you are. We're nearly done.'

'What do you want me to do?'

'Reid's going to be taken on a day trip into the city centre. Your taskforce will be there too, trying to catch me. When you see me, you do nothing.'

'Nothing?'

'You don't stop me. You don't try to catch me. If you do either, Lachlann and Isla die. It's as simple as that. Do you trust me?'

'Trust the guy threatening my family?'

'The thing is, Ross. You're moving among shadows that you can't even see. In a game you don't understand. Don't try to figure it out. You're a pawn, just like me. And pawns can only move forward. And never back.'

With that, Webster left.

Ross let out a huge sigh of relief. He locked the back door then dashed upstairs.

Lachlann was standing up in his cot, face wet with tears and a bereft expression of '*Where were you, Daddy?*'

Ross picked him up for a cuddle and shushed him gently. 'I'm sorry, buddy. I'm sorry...'

Isla appeared in the doorway, struggling to open her eyes. The faint night light on the floor seemed brighter than the sun. 'Where were you?'

'Sorry,' said Ross, his heart still thumping like a jackhammer. Somehow he was able to improvise a lie. 'I had to go to the toilet in case I ended up with him for ages.'

Isla traipsed back to bed, pausing on her way past the bathroom. She wondered why, if Ross had just been to the toilet, the cistern was silent. But she was too tired to give it a second thought.

Ross cuddled Lachlann harder than ever. He whispered to him, 'I'll never let anyone harm you, ever. I swear on my life. I'd do anything for you, little man. Anything.'

CHAPTER FORTY-EIGHT

FOR THE BIGGEST prison in Scotland, Barlinnie wasn't a tall building. Driving along Smithycroft Road, it was easy to miss it. But once you were on the nameless street leading to the main car park and entrance, it seemed to grow exponentially.

The visible part from the main road looked somewhat modern. That was the apple in the pig's mouth. At its heart and its bones, Barlinnie is and always would be a Victorian-era jail. As soon as you made a right through the car park and turned the corner, the unmistakable white-barred, tiny windows on the top floor came into view. Other than the blue signs on the tall wall warning of CCTV, it could have been a scene from the 1800s.

In the car coming down the nameless road, Lomond remarked, 'You look tired. You feeling okay?'

'Yeah,' Ross said, sipping a double-shot espresso. 'Rough night with the wee man.' He had found it hard to sleep after Webster left. Mostly, he dozed in bed while Isla snored. Ross had never been happier to hear her snoring. It told him she was safe.

Ross asked, 'What happens if he doesn't want to talk?'

Lomond could barely hide his smile. 'I've arranged a little convincer.'

Inside, they were taken to C wing, where Ross's prison warden mate Danny had found them a source.

His name was Billy McDonald. He was doing six years for robbery, the same sentence his dad had served in the exact same wing.

Ross combed through McDonald's personnel file, while Lomond paced back and forth. 'He's not exactly got grass written all over him, does he?'

'We'll see,' Lomond replied, distracted by the inmate being brought their way.

He had long hair down to his chin, and thick-rimmed glasses. He lurched along while inmates hurled insults at him from their cells.

Ross said, 'It's lively in here in the morning.'

'Most dangerous time of day,' Lomond said. 'Everyone's hungry, and they've had all night to bring bad blood to the boil.'

'Why have they put us in a room so close to the wing?'

'Because I asked for it.'

'Everyone can see who's coming in and out.'

'That's the point,' said Lomond.

The door opened, and an inmate came in.

It wasn't Billy McDonald.

'Melvin,' Lomond announced, like he was greeting an old friend.

The prison warden handed him over, and Melvin sat down across from Ross.

'Chief Inspector.' Melvin was barely thirty, but already had a reputation that could clear a room just by him walking into it. There were a lot of words for what Melvin Dooley was. The one that followed him around the most was "grass". In everyday Glasgow life, it was still a contentious label that many would do anything to avoid. For Melvin, he had made a career out of it.

He'd been a petty thief his whole life, forever the slightly-too-fat one who was the first to be made fun of. With little currency of his own, Melvin turned to grassing up anyone and everyone he knew – there was no crime too minor – to curry favour with cops and cut deals. Now he was inside, he did exactly the same with prison wardens.

When Melvin approached the pool table, everyone split.

The only thing that had kept him alive so long was the platoon of wardens that followed him around. Melvin was their guy, because he told them everything they needed to know about who was selling mobile phones, or banking heroin or cocaine.

'What's all this about?' Melvin asked.

'Absolutely nothing,' said Lomond, still watching the glass door that led to the wing. 'Sit there and be quiet.'

'What? You said you had something big in store for me.'

'I do. It involves sitting there and being quiet. So far, you've only done half of what I've asked you. Button it.'

It had only taken five words out of Melvin's mouth for Ross to decide that he thoroughly disliked him. There was nothing specific that he could have pointed to. It was just Melvin's entire...being. His tone of voice. The gormless expression he always had. The buck teeth. The prison uniform polo shirt that was forever riding up and exposing the lower third of his belly. It was no wonder Melvin was a grass, because he had absolutely nothing else going for him.

Ordinarily, Ross might have rooted for someone of Melvin's appearance. A bit dorky. Probably lonely. The problem was that Melvin was such a total arsehole. To everyone he ever met. If he ever got in an argument and couldn't think of anything clever to say, he would simply repeat back the other person's last statement in a whiny voice – as if that somehow magically won him the argument. He would steal your last Rolo. When his mum took him to the supermarket, he would throw packs of Abernethy biscuits on the ground really hard, so that they would shatter, but it would be impossible to tell that they were broken until you opened them at home.

In other words: a *total* arsehole.

Then there was Billy McDonald. By all accounts a

stand-up guy. If a little scary in the context of working in a betting shop, where it was highly possible that one day Billy would be pointing a shotgun at your face and telling you to empty your cash drawer.

The wardens dropped him off, leaving Lomond and Ross to deal with him.

The second he saw Melvin, Billy turned away.

'Fuck's sake, man,' he complained. 'What is this?'

'Settle down, Billy boy,' Lomond said, pulling out a chair for him. 'My intention is to make this easy for all of us.'

'Yeah? Well, my intention is to not miss breakfast, so let's make this quick.'

Lomond pulled up his chair next to Ross. 'Word has it that you used to run with Frank Gormley's crew.'

'Not exactly a big secret around here.'

Melvin cut in. 'You can say that again–'

Without looking at him, Lomond made a mouth-shut motion. 'Melvin. Clamp it.'

'Suit yourselves...' he huffed.

Lomond said, 'Did you hear the news this morning?'

'Aye. My cellmate's got a wee telly.'

'Then you know about this Taxman murderer that's loose.'

'Aye. Fuckin' mental. He seems pretty sound to me, man. Doing in paedos and bankers. Guy's legit.'

'Then you know we found a third victim yesterday as well. One we haven't named yet.'

'Aye.'

'It was Lee Vickery.'

Billy considered this for a moment. 'Good riddance, if you ask me. Bastard had it coming.'

Lomond deferred to Ross.

He leaned forward. 'It's just...we know you two used to run together. For Frank Gormley.'

'This all came out in my trial. If you're here to get me on the record against big Frank, jog fuckin' on, gents.' He gestured at Melvin. 'And take this bawsack with you.'

'We're not looking for you to grass anyone, Billy,' said Ross. 'All we need to find out is if Lee Vickery was up to anything against Frank.' Ross paused. He could see the gears starting to turn in Billy's head. 'Lee's dead, Billy. And Frank's on this nutcase's hit list. If we don't find him soon, it could be lights out for big Frank.'

Lomond added, 'You're not grassing on Frank. You're grassing on Vickery. What's the harm in that?'

'It's the principle,' Billy replied. 'Something you know nothing about.'

Ross said, 'What's big Frank's people going to say when they find out you could have helped us catch the man trying to kill him? Not a good look.'

Billy thought it over, then he smirked at Ross. 'You're fae a scheme, aren't you?'

Ross nodded. 'Aye.'

'Aye, I can tell.'

Lomond tried not to react as surprised as he genuinely was. He'd had no idea.

'You never lose it,' said Billy. 'So what turned you into a fuckin' pig?'

Ross's heart sank. He'd thought he was onto a winner.

Billy stood up. 'Goodnight, gents.'

Lomond spoke over his shoulder. 'I'd think twice before going towards that door, Billy.'

'And why's that?'

'Because I've told those wardens out there not to unlock the door to this room until you tell us something valuable.'

Ross added, 'Lovely glass walls in here. You can see right in.' He checked his watch. 'Breakfast is just a few minutes away. Which means every thug in C wing with an axe to grind is about to walk past this room to get their breakfast tray. You know what they're going to see? You, in a room with a couple of polis, and Melvin "Supergrass" Dooley. Do you think you might be asked the odd question about that later in the showers?' He turned to Lomond. 'Or are they a private bunch in here? Not known to fight about some gossip?'

Lomond said, 'Whatever you've got, you better give it to us fast before those cells open.'

Billy shook his head. 'Pricks.' He huffed and puffed, but he finally went back to his seat. 'What do you want to know?'

CHAPTER FORTY-NINE

LOMOND ASKED, 'What was Lee Vickery up to since he got out of prison?'

Billy crossed his legs, tapping his foot rapidly in midair. 'Last I heard he was going to turn against Frank. Lee was up on a drug charge that would've sent him back to jail. Until that knob Reekie took care of him.'

'Reekie?' Lomond shuffled in his chair. 'What did Reekie take care of, Billy? What does that mean?'

'He helped get Lee out the jail. Sent a letter of recommendation to the parole board and everything. It was a favour to big Frank.'

'Frank didn't want anything to do with Vickery after the murder charge.'

Billy moaned. 'Look, man. I'm just telling you what I know. Frank leaned on Reekie to get Lee out on parole. Then Lee got found with some weed or some pills or summat. Then at the cop shop, some rich lawyer showed up for him. He called in some favours and got Lee off the drug charge.'

'Frank sent in his lawyer?' asked Lomond.

'Nah, this was Barry McKenna's lawyer. McKenna was back on the defensive. Things were bad enough between Frank and McKenna, but McKenna made it worse by getting his lawyer to arrange a meeting between the pair of them. A sort of peace summit. War is bad for everyone kind of thing. Frank's lucky he got out alive. Somebody told me there was a shooter and his gun jammed. Safe to say, Frank wasn't best pleased. What made matters worse was McKenna sending word that next time he's going to chop Frank's foot off. His right foot, because McKenna knows Frank had a trial with Partick Thistle back in the day. Had a killer right foot. McKenna was just trying to aggravate him.'

Lomond sat back with a smile. He'd heard everything he needed to know – and more.

Billy's body language screamed anxiety and impatience. 'Come on, now. Fair's fair.'

Lomond chapped on the window to the wardens, who had their backs turned. 'He's good to go,' he told them.

On his way out, Billy snarled at Melvin, 'Utter one word of that and I'll make a skipping rope out of your intestines.'

Ross chapped on the window to signal to the

wardens who had brought Melvin along. 'He can go too.' He made sure that Melvin was taken away out a side door, out of sight.

When Lomond and Ross were left alone, Lomond rocked on his heels with satisfaction. 'Vigilante justice, my arse. This is about gangsters, Ross. It always was. We just didn't see it.'

'Now what?'

'We need to bring in Shaun Webster. Bad enough that all this Taxman stuff has got out into the papers. If he manages to hit Damien Reid, we can all start updating our CVs.'

Lomond turned to leave.

Ross followed suit, but also said, 'John...'

Lomond stopped and turned round. 'Yeah?'

All Ross could think of was Lachlann crying through the monitor the night before.

Still waiting for a response, Lomond asked, 'What's going on, Ross?'

Somehow he forced a smile. 'Nothing,' he said, waving it off. 'I was going to ask your opinion on something...but it's gone.'

As an honest man, every deceit is magnified and multiplied. Every pore in Ross's body felt like it was screaming, *I'm up to no good. It's a mistake to trust me.*

It was as he struggled with those thoughts in just a brief walk through the car park that Ross realised that Shaun Webster had been living that feeling for years. It served as a reminder of the gulf between them.

He had wanted to be a part of the Organised Crime Taskforce for so long, he couldn't really remember the reasons why he wanted to join in the first place. When DCI Hunt had asked him the previous morning, he'd made up his answer on the spot. The truth was starting to reveal itself to Ross. That he wasn't cut out for OC. And he certainly wasn't cut out to be any kind of replacement for Shaun Webster.

During their walk across the car park, Lomond said, 'Something's been bothering me since last night about what Ryan Venables told Ruth and I.'

'What about it?'

'He said he met Webster about three weeks ago. We know the Taxman was active back then. Not just abducting and killing, but planning. Logistics. Avoiding detection. Covering tracks. Does the man he described sound like the sort of man capable of pulling off what the Taxman has?'

Ross replied, 'Not from what you told me and the others. You have another theory?'

'Let's look at the victims list now. We've got George Melrose: stole Frank Gormley's investment cash. Dennis Dunbar: helping Lee Vickery stay out of jail, and in the meantime set Frank up for an attempted assassination. And now Vickery as well.'

Struggling to keep track of Billy's testimony, Ross asked, 'So how does he say it went down?'

'Frank put pressure on Reekie to get Lee Vickery

released early, as a favour to Frank. The question there is why did Frank want Vickery out?'

Ross answered, 'He wanted to kill him because he found out Vickery had cut a deal with McKenna to switch allegiances. But then Gormley could have just hit him in jail. It's easier than outside.'

'True,' Lomond admitted. 'It's easy to chib someone in jail. But it's not easy to do the things that happened to Vickery. There's no time for torture inside. I think Frank wanted more time with him. Wanted to make him suffer.' Lomond stopped walking. 'So how does Damien Reid fit in with all this? He's the one guy you can point to and say, he has absolutely no connection to Frank Gormley whatsoever. Frank always made a point of avoiding celebrity inmates like Reid. Actual evil psychopaths. Frank's a gangster. He's got nothing to say to a serial killer or a rapist.'

'Are you asking why is Damien Reid on Webster's list?'

'I am. It's making me question if we should pull out of the Reid thing. I don't like how it's sitting.'

Ross tried not to jump on it too fast, as it might provoke suspicions. 'We can't do that, surely. Reid's an evil bastard, sure. But we've got a threat to life here. We can't ignore it.'

Lomond shrugged. 'Maybe we should. Maybe the worst that happens is the Taxman gets another kill. We're following our noses here, but we don't really understand why Reid's the target. Forcing our way in might make things worse.'

'That's exactly the point,' said Ross, a little too stridently against Lomond's position. 'If we don't know what the shot is here, you can end up doing more harm than good. We don't even know where Reid is.'

Lomond took out his phone to check the ID of who was calling. 'Yeah, speaking of which. That's Ruth now with something on that.' He put her on speaker, 'Ruth, you're with me and Ross. How goes it?'

'I've had confirmation of Reid's location today. You're not going to believe it.'

'Where is it? Shotts still? Greenock?'

'They're taking him on a day trip. He's going into the city centre later today.'

'A day trip? Christ on a bike...' Lomond sighed. 'He knows. Webster must know. It's a prime chance to take him in the open.'

'You don't seem to have as much of a problem with my political connections when they help your enquiry.'

'You came through,' he admitted. 'I'm man enough to say so. Thank you.'

'I appreciate you not asking me where it came from.'

'All that matters is that we know. Now we have to get ready.'

'What about you, Ross?' asked Ruth. 'Will you be suiting up with us?'

'No, I need to get back to OC,' he replied. 'DCI Hunt wants a piece of whatever this might be with

Webster. I think he's worried if he's not there, that some-thing bad might happen.'

A twinkle in his eye, Lomond said, 'An Organised Crime Taskforce hunting one of their own undercover operators, who's trying to slay a notorious killer in Glasgow city centre in broad daylight. What on earth could go wrong?'

CHAPTER FIFTY

DCIs Lomond, Telford, and Hunt sat together in an unmarked surveillance van in Drury Street. In front of them was Renfield Street – one of the busiest streets in Scotland, and the main one-way arterial that ran through the very heart of Glasgow city centre. The van was white with fluorescent chevrons on the back, along with the word 'CONSTRUCTION'. The entrance to the cobbled lane was coned off, and a sign saying 'ROAD AHEAD CLOSED' put up.

The officers were huddled around a large computer screen that was hooked up to the CCTV feed of the area. Ruth's contact, who had leaked her the information of Damien Reid's whereabouts, told her to expect Reid on Renfield Street, as there were shops that he planned on going to there.

Ross, Ally, and Donna were in another van behind,

and had the same CCTV feed as their superiors. There was an open channel to each other via radio, but for now, everyone was pensive, watching the screens carefully.

Lomond said to Hunt, 'I meant to say thanks, Gordon, for letting me have Ross a lot of yesterday. And this morning.'

'I just want to put a stop to all of this today,' said Hunt. 'I saw some video of the press outside Helen Street this morning. Looked hoaching.'

'Yeah. Haven't seen it that bad since the Jack Ferguson thing last year. It's all a feeding frenzy. You just keep your mouth shut. Don't feed the trolls.'

'Then you're a better man than me. I saw that Colin Mowatt quote too. Little prick.'

'He's the least of our problems right now.'

'I don't know how you dealt with all that press with the Sandman enquiry. Not just the press. Everything.'

Lomond knew that Hunt meant the murder scenes themselves, but was talking around it. It was a sign of respect. Feeling out what Lomond was comfortable with talking about.

Ruth kept her eyes on the CCTV feed, not showing any obvious interest in the conversation, but was actually listening intently. What Lomond had been like and what he had seen during that period was a mystery to her.

Hunt went on, 'How did you deal with it?'

Lomond was nonchalant. 'You know, I saw this trailer on Netflix recently. Some American thing about real cops, real murders sort of thing. They've got these talking heads, and the cops are talking about the terrible cases they've had. And one of them's talking about a particularly bad one. He says that he couldn't talk to his wife about the case, it was so horrible and all the rest of it. Then he starts crying.'

Hunt groaned. 'Give me a bloody break.'

'I know, right. That's the job. How did I cope? By not talking. Everyone says these days, let it all out. Talk about it. Sometimes talking about it can be the death of you. It's your job to swallow it. To take it and bury it.'

Ruth found herself reappraising her judgement of Lomond. It reminded her of how long they had been apart. And how different he was now. The Lomond she knew back then wouldn't have had a shade of the self-awareness that he had just displayed – and had been displaying since returning from Edinburgh.

Trying to move conversation on, Hunt asked, 'How's the rest of your team getting on without Ross?'

Lomond smirked. 'I'm pretty sure Donna hates seeing him working alongside someone else. Especially someone like Ally Corrigan.'

'Jealous much?'

'Nah. It's only ever professional between Donna and Ross. But I think it's a bit like seeing an ex holding hands with someone new. You don't necessarily want the person back. You just don't want them to have anyone else.'

Ruth said, 'Here we go.' She pointed to the screen as a man and a woman dressed in casual, anonymous clothes walked down Renfield Street towards Union Street and the busy crossroads hub of Central Station.

A few steps ahead of them was a man wearing a navy baseball cap, and a light-grey tracksuit.

Hunt sucked in air. 'Christ...it's actually him.'

'It's so strange seeing him just walking the streets,' said Lomond. 'No cuffs.'

Back at Helen Street, Ruth's team and the rest of Lomond's were surrounding a projector screen that had been erected in front of the whiteboard. DCs Lambie and Foster were on their own computer screens, monitoring individual angles of the street.

Willie, Pardeep, and Jason stood in front of the projector alongside DS Erskine.

'I've always wondered what a monster looks like,' said Jane.

'Now you know,' Willie replied. 'They look pretty much like human beings.'

Back in the van in Drury Street, Hunt picked up the radio and told everyone, 'Eyes open, people. We're up.'

THE CONDOR SECURITY van used to transport Damien Reid had parked up at Buchanan Galleries. There was always a moment of anxiety for the guards when an inmate was taken out the back and allowed to walk around without cuffs. If they were going to try a bunk, they often did it fast, at the start. But Reid just stood there, turning his face up and breathing in the air. A multi-storey car park still felt pretty exotic to a man who had been caged as long as he had.

He walked through the Galleries, the two guards following closely behind. But not so close that it looked like the three of them were together. There was nothing to identify the male and female couple as prison escorts.

99% of the time, the guards didn't even know who they had in their custody. They were nobodies. To them, Damien Reid was simply Damien. No surname. They weren't told. They never knew in advance who they would be guarding, so there was no chance that attacks could be planned.

Reid's face had been all over the news when he'd gone on trial, and even more so when he was sentenced – as the full horrific details of what he'd done were made public. The only pictures ever released of him showed him with short hair and clean shaven. Now he had medium-length hair tied up into a man bun, and he had grown a beard, as well as lost over two stones in weight – he'd been a stocky guy back then. Now he was trim and looked like a fitness enthusiast in his tracksuit and cap.

The guards had assumed that whoever 'Damien' was, he couldn't have done anything that bad. After all, Damien had not long moved to Greenock and was in Chrisswell House – the first step towards moving to an open prison, and then release.

There he was, shopping for sports clothes, stopping at KFC for an early lunch. He offered the guards some of his chips and they took them.

They had no idea that they had taken chips from a monster.

CHAPTER FIFTY-ONE

Ross TUTTED as he watched Reid looking over his shoulder as a teenage girl passed him.

'Makes your blood boil, doesn't it?' said Ally. 'What you'd give for five minutes alone with him in a room with no windows, and no cameras.'

Donna kept looking back and forth between the computer screen and the various composites of Shaun Webster and the alternative disguises he may have. Wearing glasses or sunglasses, or with a baseball cap or a beard, or both.

'What do you think he'll try?' asked Donna.

Ally replied, 'Gun, surely. There's no time for the sort of theatrics he's been using until now. I doubt he cares about that. All he wants now is the target.'

The versions of Webster's face were imprinted on Ross's brain. Any time he thought about it, he saw Webster standing in his kitchen the night before.

Ally reached out, putting her hand on Ross's thigh. 'Can you stop that?'

He realised he'd been drumming his leg up and down, a tightly wound ball of anxiety and stress. 'Sorry,' he said.

Donna looked quizzically at Ally's hand. The way it had lingered a second or two longer than necessary.

Ross's brain was on fire with endless possibilities of what might happen. He had no idea what Webster expected of him, other than a vague notion of helping him get away with murder right under the noses of Ross's colleagues and superiors and about a hundred cameras. The safety of his family was at stake, but it wasn't like he could just burst out of the van and trip Damien Reid up while Webster ploughed an entire magazine of bullets into his chest. There was no point in saving his family if it meant him being hauled up for murder. There might not have been an aiding and abetting charge in Scottish law, but the principle of 'art and part' liability meant that if Ross was deemed an active participant in Webster murdering Reid, then Ross could face the same charge as Webster, and only a slightly lesser sentence.

Donna turned her chair away slightly, subtly shielding her phone screen from view as she texted Lomond.

"Was Ross alright this morning? he seems edgy. not like him."

A few seconds later, Lomond replied: *"I was thinking the same thing."*

Damien Reid and the two guards – Martin and Flo – were halfway down Renfield Street when another teenage girl passed Reid. The girl was too busy texting to notice him.

On his way past, Reid muttered something to her. It was out of the guards' earshot, but it was bad enough to make the teenage girl look at him in disgust, then start walking the other way. After ten seconds, she checked over her shoulder and was relieved to find that Reid wasn't pursuing her. She got straight on the phone to the police.

The guards on the street pulled Reid up.

'Ho,' said Martin, grabbing a handful of Reid's tracksuit. 'What the fuck was that?'

Reid's grin was miles wide. 'Bit of harmless fun.'

'Harmless?' Flo seethed. 'That girl was upset after you spoke to her.'

Reid pulled his arm out of Martin's grasp. 'What? I didn't even touch her. You can't say bugger all these days.'

Being careful not to make a scene, Flo warned him, 'Another word, and we're back in the van. You hear me?'

Reid flicked his head in Flo's direction, saying to Martin, 'Is it rag week or something?'

Martin shook his head in disgust. 'Keep walking.' He pushed Reid on, towards the crossroads at Central Station.

The huge video screen above the station, facing up Renfield Street, was a solid bright yellow. Bright enough to grab his attention for a second. That was all he needed to read the bold black words that ran the full width of the screen.

Martin tapped Flo on the arm, pointing out the screen while Reid swaggered away.

Some members of the public had noticed it too. Pretty soon, most of the pedestrians on the street were looking at it, taking pictures of it on their phones.

To those that hadn't watched the news, they asked others what the fuss was about, and what did it mean.

The screen said:

"THE TAXMAN 3, POLICE SCOTLAND 2"

CHAPTER FIFTY-TWO

LOMOND FRANTICALLY PULLED up an angle from the CCTV that showed the screen.

Reaction from Helen Street was already coming through over the radio.

'*Are you seeing this, sir?*'

'*Is it too late? Did we miss something already?*'

'*What is going on?*'

Lomond snapped, 'Will everyone shut up a second...'

When he got an angle on the video screen, Hunt leaned over for a look. He immediately took up the radio, communicating with the armed response team that was in vans along the top of the bus lane on Union Street, ready to pile out.

In charge of any armed response from Authorised Firearms Officers, DCI Hunt told them, 'AFOs stand by. Repeat, stand by. We could have something incoming on Reid.'

'Isn't it a little premature for armed response?' asked Lomond.

'It's the city centre, John,' he replied. 'I'm not mucking about.'

Ruth said, 'The last scoreline was the Taxman two-one up, right?'

'Right,' said Lomond.

'Why the jump to three-two?'

Stressed and trying to keep control of his composure, Lomond replied, 'I don't like this. I think we're about to get hit.'

In Ross's van, the three of them were glued to the screens. All leaning forward, putting mental question marks against every single figure on the screen.

Ally asked, 'Do you see anything?'

Donna replied, 'If I see anything, I will *not* be shy about it.'

Ross flexed his hands. They had gone cold and clammy. His stomach was in knots, and his breathing was erratic. He knew that Webster couldn't be far away.

Donna shook her t-shirt from the collar to generate some cool air. The van was a sauna with all the electrical gear running in an enclosed space shared with three people. Remarking on one of the angles on Renfield Street, Donna said, 'There is literally no weather that these food-delivery riders won't wear a big puffy jacket, is there?'

Ross couldn't reply. Couldn't even make a joke as a distraction.

'Are we watching him or not?' Ally wondered aloud.

'There's, like, four others,' said Donna. 'Look. They're all dressed the same, all on electric bikes. Throw a rock anywhere in the city and you'll hit one.'

'That's why it would be a good disguise,' said Ally.

But their attention was soon whipped away from the suspicious rider.

IT WAS BARELY a minute after the last altercation, when Reid made another comment – to a young woman this time.

'Piss off, you creep,' the woman snapped at him.

Reid cackled to himself as the woman issued urgent warnings to other women nearby.

Reid was loving it. Rubbing the guards' faces in it was half the fun. He didn't particularly care about being brought back earlier. He'd had his KFC, bought a few games for the Xbox, stocked up on some eye candy. A good day all round.

The red mist descended on Martin. He charged at Reid and threw him up against the shutter of a closed shop next to Greggs. The crash of the shutter, along with the visuals of a fight, meant that plenty of eyes soon landed on Reid and Martin.

Flo tried to pull the pair apart, and even got some help from a passer-by, who had no idea who he was getting involved with.

While Donna and Ally were looking at that, Ross saw a delivery rider wearing a balaclava sitting at a red light.

Although Webster had warned Ross not to get involved, it occurred to Ross that if he could somehow get away with helping – even in a minor way – then it could only help in safeguarding Isla and Lachlann from harm. The question was how to do it.

The idling delivery rider gave Ross an idea.

Pointing to a camera angle on the other side of Union Street, he picked out a male that looked the most like Webster that he could see. It didn't have to be perfect. Just a convincing possibility.

It was a male wearing a black woolly hat, a black hoodie, and sunglasses. A perfect candidate for Ross's needs.

He said, 'Hang on, I think I see someone. Look...is that him? I think that's Webster.'

Ally and Donna watched the man carefully. From the angle they had, it was hard to tell.

'I should get a closer look,' said Ross, getting out his seat.

'You're not going out there, are you?' asked Donna.

Lomond was on the radio. 'Donna, Ross, Ally, one of

you get out there and get control of Reid and that bloody guard. He's going to blow this whole op!'

In the background, Ruth argued, 'What if Webster sees?'

Ally said, 'Send Ross! It's only one guy, and he's new to OC. Shaun doesn't know him.'

Lomond made the call straight away. 'Ross, get out there. Tidy this up.'

Ross couldn't believe his luck. Lomond had given him an excuse to get out on the street. He opened up the back door and started running the moment his feet landed on the cobbles.

CHAPTER FIFTY-THREE

THE SCUFFLE between Reid and Martin was almost over by the time Ross reached them. He was nearly poleaxed by a bus and a taxi as he charged across the street while the lights were still green for traffic.

Flo had managed to prise the pair apart. Now she and Martin hauled Reid around to go back up Renfield Street and back to the van. Reid's day out was definitely over.

Unwittingly, they had pulled Reid around to now face the delivery driver with the balaclava.

Still slowing his bike down, the rider slid off his bright orange delivery backpack, then dismounted the bike before it had come to a complete stop. Seamlessly, he pulled out a Glock pistol from the holster under his jacket. There was no time for Martin or Flo to react.

All Reid saw was the balaclava-covered face and the

gun outstretched towards him. He cowered against the window of Greggs, covering his head.

Ross ran straight towards the rider with the gun, while armed response stormed over the road. There was a deep, bassy shout of, 'Armed police! Drop the weapon!'

Martin and Flo whirled around instinctively, seeing the shooter, then Ross, then armed response.

Webster didn't pause or hesitate. He only had eyes for Damien Reid.

Which meant that he didn't notice Ross sprinting up behind him.

Ross wasn't even thinking. Not on any meaningful level of cause and effect. When he'd leapt out the van, all he could think of was helping Webster somehow. But as he got closer, pure instinct kicked in. With so many eyes and cameras on them, there was no way for Ross to get away with aiding Webster's attempted hit.

Halfway across, Ross mentally caved. He knew he couldn't do it. He was aware of small children nearby with parents and grandparents. Webster's notion of justice aside, as well as the threats against his family, Ross had to preserve life at all costs. Even if it was a monster like Reid.

Ross tackled Webster from behind, throwing his arms around Webster's waist just as the gun fired. The impact of the tackle redirected a single gunshot into the window of Greggs. The glass shattered over Reid, showering him in razor-sharp shards. His face was cut to shreds. He tried to crawl away, his only route through the rest of the glass.

The crack of the gunshot sent people scattering all around, prompting a wave of panic all across the crossroads and around the front of Central Station. For those who hadn't seen what happened, they ran simply because everyone else had.

While Ross and Webster were entangled on the ground, DCI Hunt put out a call on the radio. 'If you've got a shot, take it.'

Lomond snapped, 'What? You can't order them to shoot in this scenario.'

'We need to take him out before there's a foot-chase through the city.'

'Gordon,' Ruth warned him, 'that's madness. Tell them to stand down!'

Lomond went on, 'You're going to get Ross killed!'

It was too late for objections. The lead AFO saw only a glimmer of an opportunity and fired a single shot at Webster.

With Ross and Webster still tussling, the bullet landed in Webster's upper back.

He threw his head back, recoiling in pain. Trying to wrestle Webster onto the ground, Ross ended up blocking the AFO's chance at a second shot. With adrenaline – and agony – flooding through his system, Webster heaved Ross aside.

The AFOs radioed, 'No clear shot! No clear shot!'

Using Ross as cover, Webster scrambled away into the melee he had created.

There was screaming everywhere. Bodies crisscrossing. There was no way the AFOs were going to fire into a crowd like the one Webster had disappeared into.

Ross clambered to his feet, then set off in pursuit. He struggled to turn his shoulder-mounted radio on while on the run. 'He's heading for the station...'

Webster clutched his right shoulder as he dashed towards Central Station. There was no exit wound. He had no plan for what followed. As Ross had done, he trusted his instincts – which took him down the escalator, where it was quieter. Where word of the violence upstairs had yet to filter down.

Galloping down the stairs, shoving aside anyone who slowed his progress, he headed for the low-level platforms.

Seconds behind him, DS Ross McNair was in pursuit.

CHAPTER FIFTY-FOUR

WHEN THE GUNSHOT WAS FIRED, Lomond threw open the back door of the surveillance van. Ruth ran out after him, trying to stop him, but her pleas fell on deaf ears.

By then, Donna was already gone, shouting Ross's name desperately as she picked her way through the static traffic. The entire crossroads at a standstill.

She followed the stream of armed officers who stormed through Central Station. Far ahead, at the top of the first escalator down, she saw Ross pushing his way through the crowd.

Behind her, she heard her name being yelled by Lomond. Distracted, she turned slightly. When she turned back again, there was a man twice her size running towards her. She couldn't get out his way in time. He clipped her shoulder with his on the way past, which felt to Donna like she had run into a brick wall. She shook off the pain then kept going.

On the run, Lomond asked, 'What the hell is Ross doing?'

Getting back to full pace again, clutching her shoulder, Donna replied, 'God knows...'

AFTER THE SECOND ESCALATOR DOWN, the air turned cool, as a wave of drafts from the tunnels below billowed up from the platforms.

Ross raised his voice to its maximum volume, yelling, 'Stop! Police!' as a warning to the innocent people ahead. The urgent cry rang out along the narrow tiled corridor, with its uncomfortably low ceiling.

As Webster continued sprinting ahead, still clutching his handgun, pedestrians heading in the opposite direction hurriedly rushed aside to clear a path for him. The sight of someone running with a gun in broad daylight in Glasgow was shocking and surreal to everyone nearby. Glasgow was a knife city. It didn't really do guns. And when violence did spill over, it was rare for it to happen in crowded, public spaces like Central Station.

Down in the damp, dingy lower levels of platform 16, a train was idling. As the door emitted a sharp warning beep, Webster made a desperate lunge for the nearest doors. But he didn't make it in time. The conductor had given the all-clear to set off.

As the train set off, Webster bolted along the platform. He managed to keep up for a few seconds, then the train accelerated faster than even Webster could run.

As the train pulled clear, the tunnel returned to a pure darkness, ready to swallow up Webster and anyone else who went after him.

Webster leapt off the end of the platform and sprinted with all his might. He pumped his arms as hard as he could. But his lungs were burning, and his legs were giving out. He looked around, expecting, hoping, that Ross wouldn't make the leap off the platform too.

Ross might have lacked Webster's confidence, but he knew he didn't have a choice. The armed officers were trailing behind, struggling to match Webster's pace, laden with bulletproof gear and their submachine guns which required both hands on the weapon at all times.

Webster's heart sank as Ross made the leap off the platform. He knew now that Ross wasn't going to stop. He also knew that his fate had been sealed when he failed to kill Damien Reid.

Webster and Ross ran for another minute, until it became apparent to Webster that it wasn't just Ross in pursuit. There were armed officers coming. But not just from behind. They were ahead, too.

DCI Lomond had directed them down through Argyle Street low-level.

Webster was surrounded.

He slowed to a halt. There was no way out. No secret doors. No fire escapes. No drainage grills.

Ross heaved for breath. His five-a-sides football had

made him nippy in twenty-metre sprints, but he wasn't cut out for extended runs. The only thing that had kept him with Webster was sheer determination.

'It's over, Shaun,' he wheezed. 'Put the gun down.'

Webster peeled off his balaclava. He was breathing hard, but nothing like as hard as Ross.

'I did what I had to do,' Webster puffed. 'If you'd been in my shoes you would have done the same.'

'I'd question that, myself.' He gestured for Webster to hand over the gun. 'Come on, Shaun. They're coming. It'll be better if you're not still holding that when they get here. What you do in the next minute could take years off your sentence. It might even save your life.'

Webster scoffed. 'I'm not doing any time, Ross. Haven't you been paying attention? This was it. The last dance. And I let him get away.' His shoulders slumped. He fought back tears. 'I found them, you know. The Fultons. Do you know what Reid did to them?'

'I read the report,' Ross replied.

Webster yelled, 'Reading the report doesn't get you there, Ross! It doesn't get you within a *mile* of what he did to that family. That's who you just saved.'

Ross showed Webster his hands, and started taking tentative steps towards him. 'I spoke to Kenny, Shaun. I know that you've been through a lot. And seen a lot.'

Webster lifted the gun up again, aiming it at Ross.

Ross kept coming, but slower. 'My gaffer. He lost his wife and child too. I'm sure he would sit down and talk if you wanted to.'

Tears fell from Webster's eyes. 'Doesn't make any sense. Does it? So meaningless. One minute, we were singing a song in the car. Then...' He broke down at the memory of it. 'It should have been me in the back seat with her. I should have slowed down going through that green light. Just in case, you know. Some bloody guy in a truck, half asleep from driving all night. He ploughed right into the back half of the car. They didn't stand a chance.'

'I'm sorry, Shaun,' said Ross. 'I don't think many people could have coped with that as well as all the stuff with your mum and dad. Kenny told me about that too.'

Shaun wiped the tears from his face with his upper sleeve. 'What are you talking about?'

Ross paused. 'Your dad's hardware shop. The one that burned down.'

'My dad was a teacher. What the fuck are you talking about?'

Ross looked beyond Webster, seeing the white lights of the approaching AFOs.

They didn't shout for fear of endangering Ross. From their perspective, he looked in control of the situation.

But a train was coming through from Central. The officers yelled warnings to get off the tracks.

There was plenty of space on either side of the tunnel, but word still hadn't reached the drivers that there were police in there.

Ross looked over his shoulder as the lights of the

oncoming train grew brighter. The sound of its engine louder.

The armed officer behind yelled for Ross to get out of the way.

He shouted at Webster, trying to be heard over the thundering and screeching of the train. 'Let me bring you in, Shaun!'

'It's over, man,' Webster shouted back. Then he took one step forward, putting himself in the path of the oncoming train. The driver blasted the horn when the headlights illuminated Webster seconds before impact.

Webster knew where he was standing. What would happen next. It was where he meant to be.

He put the gun under his chin and pulled the trigger.

His body didn't even have time to hit the ground.

Ross turned away and shut his eyes as the train smashed into Webster.

As the armed officers ran towards him, Ross could hear the call going out over their radios.

'*The suspect is down. Repeat, the suspect is down...*'

CHAPTER FIFTY-FIVE

Ross GOT a round of table slaps and low-key applause from his colleagues when he walked into The Three Judges pub on Dumbarton Road at the foot of Byres Road. He was quick to shut down any celebratory mood. He had spent the last two hours at Helen Street giving a statement of everything that had happened. Apart from Shaun Webster's late-night visit to his house. With Webster dead, Ross should have been in the clear, but he didn't feel like he was.

Everyone seemed keen to congratulate him on snaring the Taxman, but Ross wasn't so sure. He also wasn't looking to celebrate in the aftermath of an undercover officer's suicide – especially when his two former colleagues in DCI Hunt and DI Corrigan were present.

Ross joined the others at the back of the pub. Lomond was holding court, running off stories about the old days, drinking a Diet Coke. Ruth sat next to him with a gin and tonic.

The moment Ross sat down, Ally put her jacket on and finished her drink standing up. She had put on more perfume since Ross had last seen her.

She held him by the shoulders. 'That was a brave thing you did today, Ross.'

Ross pursed his lips. 'I'm sorry about Shaun, Ally. I did everything–'

She rushed to reassure him. 'I know. You don't have to explain. What matters is that it's over. The Taxman's done and dusted. I just wish it hadn't been Shaun.'

Trying to lighten the mood, he said, 'You have to explain where you're going. It's not even nine.'

'I've got a date, if you can believe it. I was going to cancel, but honestly I just want to go talk to someone about anything other than work.'

DCI Hunt chimed in from behind. 'Of course she's got a date. It's another day, after all.'

She rolled her eyes, trying to appear modest. 'See you tomorrow,' she said.

Pardeep dragged Ross away from the senior officers, before he was suckered into work chat. 'Get over here, you handsome bastard.' He ruffled Ross's hair, but it was so stiff with gel that it barely moved.

Donna slapped him on the thigh when he sat down next to her. She leaned over to him to whisper, 'Out of the office and with a drink in her hand, DCI Ruth Telford actually appears somewhat human.'

Ross pumped his head backwards in surprise. 'Jesus...Looking very comfortable next to the gaffer there.'

Donna made a show of sucking her lips in.

Ruth carried over a round of drinks on a tray, then returned it to the bar via the jukebox near the front door.

Lomond didn't see her sneak away to do it. His first indication was hearing a familiar opening electronic drumbeat. The intro synths and clean guitar strums couldn't have been more 8os.

He was already smiling when he recognised the song – 'Space Age Love Song' by A Flock of Seagulls. Then its signature guitar line kicked in. He started laughing as he watched Ruth dancing in step to the music to get back to the table. The others cheered her on – as well as a few strangers – which only egged her on more. Three gins in, and she was feeling light on her feet.

She got a round of applause when she rejoined Lomond, sitting next to him. 'You remember it, then?'

'How could I forget,' he replied.

'Where does this song take you?'

He didn't have to think long. 'The QMU. You were dancing on your own to this in the middle of the dance floor.'

'God, I forgot about that.'

'Your hair was longer. Your head was bowed down and you were waving it around. Just lost in the music.'

'You came over to dance with me, didn't you?'

'Yeah, I felt bad for you dancing on your own. It felt appropriate, given the lyrics.'

'I never really listen to song lyrics. I think half the time I'm not singing the right words. Tell me what it's about.'

'I think it's about a guy who meets a woman, and they can't be together. For a lot of reasons. They had a brief time together, then it fell apart, but she really got to him, you know. Really affected him. I think it's about that feeling, when you realise you're just...falling in love with someone. Like sliding down a chute. You just let it take you. It's the best feeling in the world. That first flush.'

Ruth held Lomond's gaze. For a second she thought he was actually going to try and kiss her. She broke off eye contact. 'I'm tipsy,' she said.

Lomond examined his glass of Diet Coke. 'I'm not remotely.'

She smiled. 'I never said before. You've done really well. Getting yourself together.'

He nodded politely.

'I mean it. Because when we were together...'

'Yeah, it wasn't a great time for me. Apart from you. You were the only good thing in my life back then.'

'You've come a long way, John. I should have trusted you more when you said you would change.'

Lomond held his glass up to take a drink. 'I know.'

CHAPTER FIFTY-SIX

AT THE OTHER end of the table, well out of earshot, Donna nudged Ross, indicating Lomond and Ruth in close conversation.

Donna said, 'They're looking quite cosy.'

'Don't,' said Ross. 'It's like thinking about your parents having sex. It's like, just lie to me. I don't want to hear about it. Tell me about storks or immaculate conceptions. Talking of cosy, what about them?' He nodded towards Jason and DS Erskine, who were pressed shoulder to shoulder, laughing and joking between themselves.

'Look at her,' said Donna. 'Already dreaming of being held in those big muscular arms tomorrow morning.'

Ross chuckled. 'Aye, she wishes. Jason'll be at the gym by half past six.'

Donna laughed, then immediately winced. She

clutched her shoulder.

'You okay?' asked Ross. 'What happened?'

'It's nothing. I got shoulder-charged in Central when I was running after you.'

'Aw, mate! I'm sorry.'

'You will be. I'm walking next time.' She tried to pick up her glass, but it was too painful. 'Ah, shite. I think I've made it worse.'

Ross put his arm around her. 'Come on. You're going to A&E.'

'I'm not sitting there for four hours to be told it'll heal on its own.' She looked along the banquette, watching everyone sharing jokes and telling stories. Pardeep and Fraser, and one of the more surprising friendships that had sprung up in Ian and Willie. And Jane and Jason.

Lomond nipped down the length of tables and leaned over Donna's seat. 'Everybody all right?'

She explained, 'I was just saying to Ross. Jane's good police.'

'Oh aye. They're a good bunch.' He leaned closer. 'Her and Jason's a bit of a turn up for the books, no?'

'She would be good for him,' Donna said. 'He needs to think a little less about work. It's all he does.'

'Aye, right enough,' Lomond said, keen to change the subject. 'Did you get your statement down okay, Ross?'

'Yeah. All good.'

'What did Webster say in that tunnel?'

Lomond scowled. 'Donna.'

'No, it's okay,' Ross said.

Pardeep and Jason and the others leaned in.

Ross gulped, still thinking about Webster threatening him the night before. And the weight of that secret he'd been carrying all day, and now it had been removed from his shoulders by a single self-inflicted gunshot. 'I don't know,' he began. 'He said there was no point going on because he'd failed to get to Damien Reid.'

Jane suggested, 'You can't look for logic or reason in someone like that. He was lost a long time ago.'

Ross squinted as he thought back. 'There was one thing…I was trying to empathise about his past, and all these terrible things that had supposedly happened to him – what this informer had said the Taxman had gone through. His family's hardware shop had been burned down by local gangsters, and it ended with the mum committing suicide, then the dad topping himself the night before the funeral. This was twenty years ago. Apparently the son became the Taxman. I asked Shaun about it, but he denied the whole thing.' He glanced towards the group of Ruth, Willie, DCI Hunt, and DCs Lambie and Foster, out of earshot at the far end of the tables. 'I don't know,' said Ross. 'It's probably nothing.'

Lomond said, 'I don't know how much stock you can put in that Kenny Fan story. DCI Hunt heard a million versions of that story he told you. He reckons the Taxman's a spook story. A myth. Shaun was just using it to fit his own purposes. Which as a very unwell man.'

When Donna winced again trying to pick up her glass, Ross said, 'That's it. I'm putting you in a taxi.'

She was in too much pain to argue anymore.

Ross waited with her outside, replying to messages from Isla who had been enquiring when he might come home.

He ended up calling her, rather than spending the next ten minutes texting. It was one of the things he missed about his relationship with Isla now they had been together for a while. They never chatted on the phone anymore.

'I'll be home soon,' he said. 'I'm just getting Donna into a taxi. She's hurt her shoulder.' After a pause, he told Donna, 'Isla says get well soon.'

'Thanks, Isla,' Donna replied.

When the taxi pulled up, Ross lingered by the back door. Maybe it was his brush with death, or getting out of the terrifying contract with Shaun Webster, but he felt compelled to say something he'd meant to say for a while.

'You know, Donna, about these hearings,' he said. 'I don't mean to pry, but I hear things. About you. And the gaffer. I just wanted to say,' he lowered his voice, 'if you need me to, like, say something. A lie, even. I can do that—'

Donna put a hand on his chest. 'Stop talking. Stop talking immediately, please. You bloody excellent pal. But I don't want to hear that. There's no way back for me, Ross. They're going to boot me. The only thing that could make that worse is getting my best mate booted too.'

Ross nodded, relenting. He backed away. 'Okay. Let me know how you get on?'

'Aye,' she said, groaning as she got in.

She was thinking about what Ross had said about the Kenny Fan story about the Taxman. And the fire in that shop.

The taxi driver hadn't even made it to the Expressway when Donna leaned forward in her seat. 'Actually,' she said, 'make that Helen Street police station.'

CHAPTER FIFTY-SEVEN

On his way back into the pub, Ross bumped into Hunt who was leaving.

Hunt smiled at him. 'Welcome to OC.'

Ross looked confused.

'I spoke to John,' Hunt explained. 'Shaun's old spot as DS is yours if you want it. You know I need a DS. It comes with a salary bump and a lot more freedom.'

Ross was polite but noncommittal. Deferring to talk it over with Isla.

A little stung by anything other than immediate acceptance, Hunt said, 'Okay. But just so you know, that's what an opportunity looks like.'

Lomond watched them from inside. He waited until Hunt was gone before he joined Ross.

He was sitting on one of the many bollards on the pavement to stop traffic cutting over it.

Lomond said, 'A little birdie told me Hunt is sleeping with Ally Corrigan.'

The allegation didn't seem to shock Ross. 'I couldn't say.'

'They both leave within fifteen minutes of each other. She's on water so she's not too drunk for a date later. A date with who?'

Ross smiled. 'Never stop working, do you?'

Lomond shrugged.

'He told me you freed me up.'

'I shouldn't have stood in the way of your career,' Lomond admitted. 'When you get to my age, son, you sometimes forget what it feels like to be hungry.'

'You must be relieved,' Ross said. 'Shaun Webster draws a nice big line underneath all of this.'

'Aye.'

Ross eyed him. 'You're not buying it, are you?'

Lomond took the bollard next to him. 'I think there's a ton about Webster being the Taxman that makes sense. I just don't...' He gestured like he was trying to encourage himself. 'I don't see it. But everything we know tells us it was him.'

Ross gulped. 'There's something I have to tell you.' He took a deep breath. 'Webster came to see me last night.'

Lomond was dumbfounded. 'What?'

'He broke into my back garden. He threatened me. Told me that if I got in the way today he'd hurt Isla and Lachlann.'

Lomond ran his hands over this head. 'And you never told me...never told a soul?'

Lomond had an *"I'm not angry, I'm just disappointed"* tone of voice.

Ross hung his head. He'd never made Lomond look or sound like that before. 'I'm sorry, boss. Really, I am. I didn't know what to do.'

'You come to *me*. That's what you do. Always. Christ, first Donna with that dealer dad of hers and now this. We're going to end up with loyalty points to spend with the Professional Standards panel at this rate.'

'I'm sorry. I wasn't thinking.'

Lomond thought it through, then let out a heavy puff of air. 'All right...Listen to me.' He waited for Ross to make eye contact. 'It never happened. You hear me?'

'Right.'

He didn't take his eyes away from Ross until he was satisfied the message had got through. 'Right. Go home.'

NORMALLY, Ross would have got the train from Central, but MIT's exploits on Union Street earlier on had made that a no go. The crossroads at Central Station, and the low-level platforms were still sealed off and shut down. He would have to jump ahead of Central and get on at Argyle Street instead to get back home to Cambuslang. It had been too long a day to face walking that far from the west end, so he opted for the subway.

When the train pulled into St George's Cross, he felt something urging him to get off. A proximity to something important.

The Webster thing about the hardware store was still nagging at him.

It would be a ten-minute walk to the Sichuan Feng, but it was a worthwhile detour. If for nothing else than to put a crazy theory of his to bed.

CHAPTER FIFTY-EIGHT

Ross FOUND A "CLOSED" sign hanging in the restaurant door when he got there. Checking the opening times in the window, they should have been open.

He took out one of his contact cards, then wrote on it "KENNY – CALL ME". He was about to put it under the door, when he thought better of it. Mr Wenbo, if he ever appeared again, might not take kindly to police officers imploring his restaurant manager to call.

He turned away from the door, caught between leaving and staying, when he spotted a dark figure moving quickly from the walk-in fridge through the kitchen.

'Hey!' Ross knocked insistently on the door. When he got no response, he called the restaurant phone line, but it went to an automated answer service.

In desperation, he tried the door handle. Whoever was in there hadn't locked themselves in, at least.

He called out, 'Hello?' from the front of the restaurant.

There wasn't a sound.

Ross tried again, calling out for Kenny this time.

No response still.

The kitchen was immaculate and had been wiped down thoroughly. Someone had told the staff not to come in.

But Ross knew that he wasn't alone in there.

He approached the walk-in fridge with trepidation. Before he tried opening the door, he looked all around him. Without the calming sound of the traditional Chinese music playing, and the tables bare, the restaurant felt barren. Empty.

He reached for the handle, which required some force to get it going. Then another sharp tug to disengage the rubber trim that formed an airtight seal around the door frame.

But as he pushed and pushed, it wasn't just the rubber trim that was holding the door back. There was something heavy leaning against the inside of the door. Something large.

Ross put his back into it, but whatever was in there was now lodged between the wall and the door. It wasn't a matter of force any longer.

He tried to squeeze through the small gap he had managed to create, but it wasn't enough for his entire body. He could, though, get an arm around.

He took out his phone and opened the camera. Holding it around the door, the only way of telling that his finger was engaging the button to take any pictures was the shutter sound effect. Once he heard three, he retracted his arm. He scrolled through the gallery, but he didn't see much in the first picture. It was blurry from the phone moving.

The next two pictures, though, were crystal clear. Lying in a heap on the floor in a puddle of blood was Kenny Fan.

He'd been shot twice in the forehead, execution style. His shirt collar was tattered, and there was a long smear of blood down the wall at the side.

The killer had hung him from one of the large industrial hooks normally used for strings of garlic. But the weight was too much for Kenny's shirt, and the body had fallen off.

Ross reached around the door again, this time crouching down to get low to the ground. From there, he could reach Kenny's ankle and manoeuvre him away from the door.

From touch alone, it was evident that the body hadn't been there long.

Once he had pulled Kenny out far enough, Ross got the door open all the way. He checked for vitals, but Kenny was definitely gone.

With trembling hands, Ross prepared to call 999.

Then the door creaked.

He didn't want to turn around, because he knew that

it would be over if he did. Instead, he looked for a weapon in the fridge. Something. Anything.

On a metal rack near the floor, was something that appeared heavy. Like a very large chicken leg, but with a little more heft to it. Thinking it might be a good option, Ross peeled off the kitchen towel wrapped around it.

Ross jumped at the sight of the bloody limb underneath. A foot.

George Melrose's? he wondered.

He was in need of a weapon, but a severed foot didn't quite fit the bill. Instead, he grabbed a food thermometer probe attached to the wall. It was long and heavy-duty. If he'd been able to take the temperature of the person no more than a few feet away behind the walk-in door, it would have said they were ice cold.

Ross grabbed the probe, preparing himself for the one chance he reckoned he had to get himself out of there.

Behind him, the door hinges squeaked.

It was time.

Ross swung the probe viciously around in an arc. But the assailant was much too fast. They kicked the probe out of Ross's hand, then brought a syringe stabbing down into his side.

Ross cried out in pain, then everything went black.

CHAPTER FIFTY-NINE

LOMOND SAT on the end of his bed, listening to the shower running. He felt nervous, like a teenager again, overanalysing each moment that had led up to every-thing feeling so right back in the taxi, and then in the fumbling walk up the stairs of his close. They'd stopped to kiss on every landing. Kissing hungrily.

Lomond lay back on the bed and put on 'Teardrop' by Massive Attack on his phone that was linked to a speaker. The room soon filled with the crackle effect of an old record. The slow, hypnotic beat of rim knocks on a snare. Then the fade-in of the harpsichord riff that made the song instantly like nothing else.

The shower stopped running, but the music filled the audible gap. He was relieved to not have to lie there in silence.

He felt himself drift away with the beat of the music, his smile fading as something occurred to him. It was the first time he'd slept with anyone other than Eilidh in that bed. He felt a sudden wave of panic. Of something that couldn't be undone. Never again would it be the bed that only he and Eilidh had been in.

He sat up, the moment of serenity now replaced with a crushing anxiety.

Ruth emerged from the bathroom wrapped in a towel. She moved swiftly. Like someone not planning on staying long.

Lomond noted that she hadn't got her hair wet.

She smiled sheepishly. The second her eyes left his, the smile disappeared. She picked up her phone and tapped out a message.

Lomond tried to keep his tone neutral. Light-hearted. But deep down, he was worried. 'Everything okay?'

She flashed her eyebrows up, and took a long drink of tap water from a glass. 'I drank too much.'

'You should eat something.'

'It's too late for that.'

Lomond's optimism about what they had done untethered itself from his heart. Now it was a balloon, drifting away on a breeze.

She could only have made her true thoughts clearer by saying "this was a mistake".

Lomond asked, 'Who could you be texting right now?'

She put the phone down. 'One thing you should

know about me...I don't do attachment. I don't have time for it at this stage in my career.'

Lomond struggled to digest her snippy tone. 'Hang on, are you dumping me for a second time...before we've even got back together?'

Ruth tutted as she pulled on her underwear and trousers with the towel still wrapped around her upper half. 'If this has any chance of working, it's important that you understand my boundaries. We're both working all the time on opposite sides of the country. Realistically, which one of us is going to compromise their career for this to work?'

Lomond didn't have to think hard about it. 'I'll do it.'

'You can't be serious.'

'I think Eilidh would want me to be happy. And this is all there is for me. You said it. We're both workaholics. That's the only type of person that's going to compliment me. Understand me. Understand either of us.'

Ruth tossed the towel onto the bed and got back into her shirt. She sighed. 'Moment to moment, I have no idea what John Lomond I'm going to get. Is it the romantic sweet one I got tonight, or the one who told me I wasn't good police?'

'I shouldn't have said that.'

'Because you were wrong, or because it gave away your true feelings?'

Lomond didn't answer.

She sat on the edge of the bed. 'Do you even *like* me?'

'I remember how we were together back then.' He took her hand. 'You're the closest thing I've felt to love before I met Eilidh. And I loved you before Eilidh.'

'I won't be your second best, John.'

'You wouldn't be.'

'You would be with me only because you can't still have Eilidh. There's a difference.'

Lomond didn't reply.

She put her hand to his face. 'I can see in your eyes how much you still love her when you say her name. I can't compete with that. You might not want to be alone anymore, but I'm not the one.'

On the bedside table, Lomond's phone rang. He always had the ringer turned up to max volume. Coming over the speaker, the sudden tone replacing the chilled music was piercing.

Lomond pushed out his lips, wondering how concerned he should be.

DONNA HIGGINS CALLING

'Donna, are you all right?' he asked.

She was walking somewhere fast, or possibly running. She was breathless, panicked. 'I can't get hold of Ross. I can't get him...'

'Whoa, whoa, slow down. What are you talking about? He was on his way home.'

'Isla can't reach him. He hasn't come home. His phone's ringing out. I think he's in trouble–'

Lomond checked the time on his bedside table clock.

'It's only been a few hours. He's probably stopped for another drink on the way home.'

Ruth paused, looking over in concern. She mouthed, 'What is it?'

Lomond shook his head to tell her not to worry. He tried to catch up to Donna's speed, but it was like trying to jump onto a speeding car from a standing start. 'Wait, wait, wait,' he said. 'Where are you?'

'Helen Street. About to get in my car. I ran a trace on his phone. The last signal was in Sauchiehall Lane about two hours ago. Right behind the Sichuan Feng.'

'What would he be doing there?'

'I don't know. But his phone's still there. It hasn't moved.'

Lomond pulled his legs down off the bed. 'Get uniform there,' he said. 'To be on the safe side.' He kicked his legs into his trousers, taking whatever clothes were to hand on the floor. 'I'll meet you at the restaurant.'

CHAPTER SIXTY

CONSTABLES ON FOOT nearby had got to the restaurant first, but they didn't have the exact location of Ross's phone. Donna hadn't been able to send it to them whilst racing in her car from Govan.

She headed straight for Sauchiehall Lane, where the phone had last transmitted a signal. The second her car stopped, she threw the door open and didn't bother closing it. She scoured the ground for the phone.

She called Ross's number again. Somewhere ahead the ringtone played faintly. The screen lit up, half-covered by a puddle that had been there for weeks.

Donna ran towards the phone, but after she hung up her own call, she was locked out of Ross's. And she didn't know the passcode. 'Shite.' She cursed herself for being impulsive, and not waiting to contact tech support at Helen Street in case there had been a way of keeping Ross's phone unlocked when she called. She needed in to his messages. His emails. For some kind of indication of what he was doing there.

One of the uniforms had gone in through the front of the unlocked restaurant. 'Donna!' he shouted. 'You'd better come take a look at this!'

Donna ran in with half-averted eyes, scared stiff that she might be about to discover Ross's body. At first, all she saw was the feet in the walk-in fridge. She breathed easier when she realised it wasn't Ross.

'Do you know him?' the PC asked.

She said, 'I'm not sure. But I think his name's Kenny Fan.'

HALF AN HOUR LATER, Lomond stood out in the lane with Donna. A light drizzle had been falling for several minutes, but Donna had only just noticed. When she touched her hair, she was surprised at how wet it was.

The rest of the Helen Street team was there, making sure nothing was overlooked. The Fettes Avenue team hit the streets, showing pictures of Ross to newsagents, chippy shop owners, homeless people, bus drivers.

Back at the office, Linda and Willie formulated a strategy with the other sub-teams of Glasgow MIT.

Lomond looked upwards into the rain, savouring the cool relief from the evening's mugginess.

From the Holland Street end of Sauchiehall Lane, DI Ally Corrigan's car crashed through puddles and nearly collided with a rubbish dumpster poking out into the cobbled road.

DCI Hunt and DI Corrigan got out of the parked car and jogged over.

'Any news?' asked Hunt.

'Nothing,' said Lomond.

Donna turned to Ally. 'You two came here to talk to Kenny Fan, didn't you?'

'Yeah, but Ross never said anything about coming back. We left here with the lead on Shaun's Volvo estate. He never mentioned any other questions he had.'

Hunt said, 'You don't think Ross–'

'No,' Lomond snapped. 'Of course not. Where the hell is Ross McNair going to get a gun, anyway. Kenny Fan was a gangland execution. I think Ross has found himself here at the wrong time.' He shook his head. 'I blame myself. I tried to warn him about you lot and your bloody cowboy unit.'

Ally took a step closer. 'Don't *even* try to pin this on us. Ross was a big boy. He knew what he was getting into with the Taskforce.'

'That's great DI Corrigan,' Lomond shot back. 'But if you'll excuse me, I now need to explain to a young mother that the father of her baby son is missing, and if she asks me whether he's alive, I'm going to have to tell her that answer that relatives of cops just love to hear: I. Don't. Know.'

Donna put a hand across Lomond's chest to push him back. 'Calm down. Let's all just calm down. This is nobody's fault but the person who took him.' She peeled away to answer her phone.

Lomond pointed at Hunt and then Corrigan. 'If I find out either one of you is withholding information from me on this, and Ross McNair turns up dead, you'd better have booked yourselves a decent burial plot. Because you'll be in it pronto when I'm done with you.'

When Lomond whipped away in the other direction, Ally was about to go after him, but Hunt held her back. He shook his head. 'Don't. You'd be exactly the same if it was one of ours.'

Donna hung up. She told Lomond. 'That was the Det Sup. She wants all of MIT back at Helen Street. She's sending uniform and two other sub-teams to take over here.'

'What about us?' asked Ally.

Hunt said, 'I'll go back to Helen Street. There should be someone from OC there to liaise.' He told Ally, 'Get the rest of the guys. Linda needs every available body she can get.'

'Cheers, Gordon,' Lomond said.

'You'd do the same for me,' Hunt replied. On his way past, he said to Ally, 'Meanwhile, if you've got any Hail Mary moves you can make, now would be a really good time.'

CHAPTER SIXTY-ONE

A TECHNICIAN from Gartcosh talked Pardeep through the process of getting into Ross's phone. A painstaking procedure that required software that looked alien, even to someone as tech-savvy as Pardeep. There was nothing suspect in Ross's messages or emails. The last items he had sent out were texts to Isla, promising to be home soon.

'We're going to help him keep that promise,' Lomond told the packed MIT room.

Help had been brought in from every resource the force had in the city. Even the full Organised Crime Taskforce was in attendance. They all stood around chewing gum, arms folded, carrying themselves like soldiers rather than police.

Ruth was only too happy to perform whatever menial task Lomond or Linda asked of her. Like Lomond, she just wanted to get Ross back.

Linda demanded that every camera in the city be studied. Every frame frozen and analysed. Every vehicle which passed through before or after Ross went silent was tracked and traced.

The room was buzzing. Phones ringing, every desk attended. People clamouring for various pieces of information, sharing intel from one side of the room to the other.

Lomond had never heard it so loud in there before.

Noticing Donna still wincing from her shoulder injury, Lomond asked, 'I thought you were getting that looked at.'

'I didn't in the end,' she said. 'I came back here instead.'

'Why?'

'That story that Ross said Kenny Fan told him about where the Taxman came from.'

'The shop fire? How many mouths has that story been twisted through over the years? Everyone adding their little twist to it. My dad used to call them stories with a bit of VAT.'

'It got me thinking, if the shop fire part is at least true, how many of them can there really have been over the years in Glasgow?'

'Shop fires? There must be a handful every year, surely. Across all of Glasgow? You think if you find the fire, you can use it to identify the Taxman?'

'I didn't get far into it because Ross went missing. I think it can be done.'

Lomond was on the verge of being convinced. 'But you don't know what year, or even the rough area. Or that it has anything at all to do with Ross's disappearance.'

'Clearly Kenny knew too much about something. He knew about Shaun's Volvo, and if he knew about the shop fire story, it might help find Ross. Somehow.'

'You think the Taxman has taken Ross?'

'I do.'

'All the evidence points to Shaun Webster being the Taxman.'

Donna paused. 'If I've got a pain in my arm, it could be evidence of having a heart attack. If a doctor amputates my arm, it doesn't stop the heart attack.'

Lomond snorted his approval. 'Okay,' he said, checking where Linda was. 'You don't need police reports. You need newspapers.'

'That means only one place.' Donna checked the clock up on the wall. 'It's too late, isn't it?'

'Normally.' Lomond started texting someone. 'I know someone who can open it up for you.' He glanced up from his phone, and widened his eyes. '*Go.* Before Linda sees you.'

Donna grabbed her bag and jacket and rushed off through the crowded office with steely purpose.

Lomond went to Willie, who had been orchestrating the rest of the team to pull together the bigger picture of everything they knew about the Taxman investigation.

'What have we got?' Lomond asked.

Willie held up a small whiteboard where he had collated the information. 'George Melrose – stole Gormley's money. Dennis Dunbar – among others, Barry McKenna's lawyer who set up the meeting that almost claimed Gormley's life, not to mention representing Lee Vickery in order to coerce him into informing on Gormley. Then there's Vickery himself, who had skimmed Gormley for years, then sold him out to McKenna. After that, all that's left is Damien Reid.' Willie wagged a finger in the air. 'This is where it falls down for me. Remember the scores the Taxman claimed. Lee Vickery was the first one that gave a point to us instead of the Taxman. Why? Because it righted a wrong going back years, which saw Vickery released early for the culpable homicide of baby Tyler.' Willie looked over to Ruth. 'Do you want to show him?'

Ruth presented a piece of paper bearing the insignia of Police Scotland. 'Don't ask because I won't tell. This is from the desk of Chief Superintendent Alasdair Reekie. Recommending to the parole board – in the strongest terms possible – for Lee Vickery to be released early. Billy McDonald was telling you the truth.'

Willie continued, 'As for Damien Reid, he was just a monster. No connections with Frank Gormley whatsoever. What we do know is that Shaun Webster tried to shoot Reid. Webster was the officer who found the Fultons. He was after revenge.'

Lomond said, 'Damien Reid was an outlier. The one victim who doesn't fit.'

'It wasn't a Taxman killing. It was never meant to be.'

'What was it then?'

Willie said, 'We've been talking it out, and...what if the Taxman knew – somehow – that Webster was going out to kill Reid. Someone who knew about Reid's day trip. If you know Webster's going to be there to get to Reid, you can hire the video screen to show the Taxman-versus-Police-Scotland score.'

Trying to clarify, Lomond asked, 'To make Reid's assassination appear connected to the Taxman killings.'

By way of agreement, Willie said, 'What did we *actually* see happen? It was nothing like the others. It was an old-school street hit. The only thing close to a Taxman kill was the scoreline. And, incidentally, I don't see how Webster could have afforded that.' Willie deferred to DC Foster.

He handed Lomond a quote printed from an email he'd just received. 'That's how much it costs to hire that screen just for ten seconds, on a two-minute loop with other ads.'

'Jeez...' said Lomond. 'Three grand?'

'And the Taxman score was up there on its own, playing continuously. No way Webster has that kind of cash sitting around. Did you know, also, he hadn't withdrawn one penny of his salary from his bank account for six months?'

'You don't say,' said Lomond, impressed with the find. 'And there was me wondering what you actually do. Now I know. Good work, Fraser.'

He nodded earnestly.

DS Erskine indicated she wanted to take over. She said, 'In the tunnel earlier on, Webster claimed to Ross to have no knowledge of the Taxman backstory. He was a patsy. When the Zodiac was killing for years across California in the sixties, there were dozens of murders and attempted murders wrongly attributed to the Zodiac.' She emphasised, 'Because everyone saw not what they wanted to see, but what they *expected*. If it was even vaguely similar to a Zodiac killing, that's who they assumed it was. In the end, San Francisco police think the Zodiac killed all of five people, but there were thought to be anywhere between twenty and twenty-eight Zodiac murders at the time. To this day, no one really knows.'

Jane's analysis gave everyone pause.

She concluded, 'We went out there yesterday expecting to intercept the Taxman, because Webster's dossier made it appear that way.'

Lomond said, 'You're making a very convincing argument for screwing up that one hundred per cent clearance rate, DS Erskine.'

She replied, 'I'll take the truth over a win any day of the week.'

Meanwhile, DCI Hunt very quietly went up the stairs to Linda Boyle's office. He knocked timidly on the glass, then opened the door.

Linda appeared stressed, but was willing to park it seeing as Hunt looked like he had something to say.

He was unusually hunched around the shoulders. A result of carrying a load he no longer wanted to carry. 'Have you got a minute?'

'Yeah, sit down,' she said with concern.

'I need to tell you something, and I'm sorry that I didn't earlier. But the landscape's changed considerably since Ross disappeared.'

Linda removed her reading glasses. 'Talk to me.'

As he gathered himself, he looked down into the office. 'It might be an idea if John hears this too.'

CHAPTER SIXTY-TWO

Linda called Lomond's desk. All she said was, 'Get up here.'

When he arrived, Lomond said, 'That Fettes Avenue crowd are not half bad. Shame that they're going to waste on the east coast. What's up?' He stood by the window, unsure what to expect going by Hunt's pensive expression.

Hunt stared into his hands. 'It's true that Shaun Webster went rogue from the Taskforce. I told Ross all about that. Him running his own operations and the like. What I didn't tell him was what Webster was doing before that. He wasn't just an ordinary member of the Taskforce who went undercover.'

'What was he doing?' asked Lomond.

'It was my idea...' he broke off.

'What was?'

'Putting Ally and Shaun together. They were a tight pair. Very tight.'

Reading between the lines, Linda asked, 'Were they sleeping together?'

'I took it very badly, because...because...'

Lomond and Linda shared a knowing glance.

Hunt said, 'Ally and I had been involved a little before then. Nothing too intense. But I wanted more. She didn't. I had no problem with her being involved with Shaun, until he encouraged her to go rogue as well.' He sighed. 'This was all Reekie's thing. I don't know why I went along with it...'

Lomond jumped all over the mention of the name. 'What was Reekie?'

Hunt looked a shell of himself. 'He told me that the Taskforce results could make him Chief Constable. That he could turn the organised-crime culture of Glasgow on its head. Provided we did things a little differently to how they'd been done before.' He took one last deep breath, then let it all out. 'Reekie was running Ally and Shaun off the books for two years. A two-man unit. Clandestine operations against organised crime. Highly secretive. Total deniability. No one else in the Taskforce knew about it. I had operational say, but Reekie was the sole point of contact. He said it was the only way to preserve the integrity of the mission. We all know the corruption issues that OC has faced over the years. It's endemic. And it will never change. It's the nature of the role, that you're given access to people who are excellent at selling things.'

Linda asked, 'Why are you telling us this, Gordon?'

'Because part of the operations involved safe houses. Lock-ups that no one else even knew existed. They couldn't. Reekie was the one who knew about them. After all, somehow they had to be paid for. I don't know exactly what Ally is into, but for a while, I've questioned whether she might have turned. Along with Shaun.'

'Working for organised crime?' asked Lomond. 'The pair of them?'

'For Frank Gormley specifically.' He looked down embarrassed. 'I've seen things at her house sometimes. Expensive jewellery. My wife had expensive taste. I know how much those things cost. And there's no way Ally could have afforded them. But I turned a blind eye and made excuses because I was...I was...'

'All right, Gordon,' said Linda, who rolled her eyes in Lomond's direction.

With no patience whatsoever, Lomond said, 'Do you know where any of these safe houses might have been?'

'Like I said, you'd have to ask Reekie. But please, I don't want any of this to sound like a criticism of Ally. It might all be perfectly innocent. If anything, she was the one who acted with restraint out in the field. Even though she of all people had every right to be out there breaking heads the way Shaun was.'

'What do you mean?' asked Lomond.

'Because of her childhood. She didn't tell me much.
But I know there was a lot of trauma there. A lot of grief.
Her dad ran a shop for a while. But it was burned down.
It wiped the family out. Her poor mother couldn't handle
it and took her own life. That was what sent the dad over
the edge too. He ended up killing himself the night
before the mum's funeral. Doesn't bear thinking about.'

Lomond stared at Hunt in horror. 'Ally Corrigan?'

'What about her?'

Lomond whipped around to Linda. 'Kenny Fan told
that same story to Ross. He said it was a rumour about
the Taxman's origins.'

'Ally told me that story last year.'

Lomond thought aloud to himself. 'Why wouldn't
she have reacted? Surely upon hearing someone telling
you that story, saying that it was how the Taxman
started, you would tell them they were wrong.'

Linda stood up, glowering over Hunt. 'Kenny's dead,
and Ross is now missing. Ally is the common thread.'

'But she can't be,' said Hunt.

Lomond didn't let up either. 'What if Kenny Fan
found out from Shaun Webster that Ally was the
Taxman? Kenny could have been blackmailing her. That
could be why he's lying dead in the Sichuan Feng right
now.'

'This is crazy...'

'Where is she, Gordon?' Linda demanded.

'I don't know!'

Lomond said, 'This is pointless.'

Hunt turned to Lomond to plead his innocence again. But Lomond was already throwing Linda's door open.

He yelled down the stairs, 'Ruth! Come with me. We're going to pay Reekie a visit.'

'What do you need me for?' asked Ruth.

'To keep me from killing Reekie.'

CHAPTER SIXTY-THREE

Ross woke up to a bucket of freezing water being thrown over him. It felt like being hit by a thousand shards of glass at the same time, the pain burrowing its way down through the nerves into his bones.

He tried to rock in the chair he was sitting on, but it wouldn't move. The chair was metal, and bolted to the floor.

His brain was trying to shuffle and organise a dozen sensory touchstones like playing cards that had fallen off a table. He wasn't getting anything visual yet because he couldn't open his eyes – he had been pressing his eyelids together so tightly during unconsciousness, they needed peeled apart. Whatever room he was in sounded cavernous. Echoey. The floor was rough, his shoes scraping and scratching at the uneven concrete.

Overhead, an aeroplane screeched by and it sounded very low down. Close enough that Ross figured that he had to be somewhere along the flight path of the airport – which narrowed the location down to either the outskirts of Renfrew, or most likely Linwood.

As for taste, all he could taste was metal. A common side effect of the tranquilliser that had been plunged into him. He couldn't touch anything other than the hand-cuffs that kept his hands together behind his back.

The place smelled of a work yard. Fresh timber somewhere nearby. The faint smell of petrol and diesel fumes.

Ross finally managed to open his eyes, and was greeted by the sight of DI Ally Corrigan standing in front of him with her fist pulled back.

There was nowhere to go.

She smashed her fist into his face, sending a wave of crisp, angular pain out from his nose, that darted around the inside of his head like a pinball. Ross knew now where she got her athletic build from. Boxing.

His mouth filled with blood again. He spat it away. It was hard to tell without looking or feeling, but he was pretty sure she had broken his nose.

'Where is it?' asked Ally, prowling in front of him.

Ross was still dazed from the punch. 'Where's what?'

She took two quick steps towards him and hit him in the same place.

He recoiled in agony, then made a conscious effort to exhale slowly. To breathe the pain away and gather his composure. 'I'm not resisting anything...please. Tell me what it is?'

His answer only enraged her further. She took three steps one way, then three steps the other way. Back and forth. Ready to strike again. She grabbed the empty bucket and tossed it further away. The sound of it tumbling across the rough concrete reverberated around the corrugated iron walls.

'The memory stick,' she spat. 'I know Kenny gave you a memory stick with an audio file on it. Tell me where it is, and I won't have to hurt you.'

Ross gave his head a shake. He wondered what she considered 'hurt' to actually mean, because he was pretty sure that he was already enduring multiple levels of torment.

His wrists were red raw from fighting his restraints for a while. The cuffs caked in dried blood.

Ally wiped her forehead with the back of her hand. All her nervous energy had led her to sweat. 'You saw what happened to Kenny. I can do it to you too.'

'I swear...' he pleaded. 'Kenny never gave me anything. I never saw him again after we met him together.'

'There's still time to come back in with us. I made six figures in pay offs last year. All cash. It's the wild west out there, and DCI Hunt wants to bring it all to a stop. He's got this notion that we can all live in peace and harmony together.'

'You enjoy your money, Ally. I'll enjoy my conscience, you fake-tanned snake.'

Ally pursed her lips, seemingly not rising to the bait.

'Frank will make you whole. He'll see to that. He doesn't hold grudges...'

Ross tensed his entire body as Ally pulled his head towards her raised knee.

'...that's what he pays me for.'

She drove her knee into Ross's face, landing right between his eyes.

She released his head, sending it straight backwards. Ross's vision darkened at the edges, then it slowly filled with white light. He felt faint. Sick.

Ally's laughter rang in his ears, taunting him. 'You know one of my favourite quotes? It's Mike Tyson. Everyone's got a plan until they get punched in the face.'

'Sounds about right,' Ross wheezed.

'Think you're so smart, don't you. Think you can come in and tear down what's taken me years to build?'

'I'm not trying to do anything except find the truth. To find justice.'

'Justice!' she raged. 'You don't know the meaning of the word. Shaun understood it. He was willing to do whatever was necessary to get the job done. Unfortunately, that didn't include my advice to take the bloody money.'

'Is that all this is? All this carnage, for what? A little bit of money?'

'Really? Morality lessons from the man who saved Damien Reid's life? Shaun knew more about real justice than you'll ever know. Now Reid's going off to an open prison, and Shaun's lying dead in a drawer in Gartcosh.'

'Spare me,' Ross said. 'All you cared about was setting Webster up. Playing up the vigilante angle, when all of this was just about making money for organised crime. For scum like Frank Gormley.'

Ally reached behind her back. She was holding something. 'Do you want to know something funny? Hunt invented the idea of the Taxman years ago. Until word of it spread and the gangsters we were pursuing actually believed the Taxman was real.' She stepped closer, and brought her hand out from behind her back. She was brandishing a knife large and sharp enough to carve a Sunday roast.

Ally continued, 'Tell you what, DS McNair. If you want to make me wait, I can make you wait too...'

She was so close to him, he didn't realise she was pulling her arm back. Then she thrust the knife into his stomach with a searing force that doubled Ross over in agony. She leaned in close to his ear.

She whispered, 'How long do you think before you bleed out?' She held the knife there. Then slowly released her fingers from the handle. 'I hope that's given you something to think about.'

Ross spluttered a desperate cry. He stared down at the knife in his stomach, in disbelief that it was really happening.

'It's the shock,' she said. 'That this can't possibly be happening. But it is.'

Ross's mind filled with images of Isla and Lachlann. All overlapping and playing like time-lapse photography.

Them growing old without him. Lachlann begging for his daddy again. Isla walking him in by herself for his first day of school. Growing up, asking to see photos of him because he was too young to remember him.

'Please...' Ross sobbed. 'Please...'

'I'll be back soon. Or maybe not.' Ally turned to leave. 'Looks like you're not cut out for organised crime, Ross.'

It took an age for her to reach the far end of the warehouse. When the metal door shut behind her, Ross had never felt so alone in his life.

He looked down at the knife in his stomach – the blood seeping from the sides of the blade.

And he began to drift away into the void.

CHAPTER SIXTY-FOUR

DRIVING down Ralston Road in Bearsden, it was hard to see any of the houses that lined both sides of the street. Huge trees overhung the road, and thick, tall hedges obscured the sight of any front doors. It was hard to picture a more serene, leafy, affluent suburb in the city. A place where privacy came at a premium.

Now Chief Superintendent Alasdair Reekie was about to discover its true cost.

Lomond parked on the street. The only car there. Everyone else had substantial driveways on which to park.

Reekie had two cars in his driveway. The garden immaculate. The sort of idyllic home a cop like Ruth dreamt of. For someone like Lomond, he couldn't imagine living in such a place. Living there would have meant he had compromised once too often. It was unavoidable. You don't get to live somewhere like that as a cop without bringing in a few skeletons in a cupboard.

Reekie answered the door dressed down in a variety of shades of brown. A checked shirt, a wool vest, brown cords, and brown slippers. In the background, Lomond could hear commentary from Sky Sports Cricket on the TV.

'John,' said Reekie. 'This is unexpected. And not entirely appreciated. What do you want?'

'We're trying to find Ross,' said Lomond. 'And your name came up.'

Reekie moved as if to shut the door. 'You're tired and upset. Ruth, take him back to Helen Street—'

She lodged her foot in the doorway, prompting a filthy, shocked look from Reekie.

'We're here about Shaun Webster and Ally Corrigan,' Ruth explained.

'You know I can't talk about that.' He went back inside towards the living room. 'Shut the door behind you. I'm got some monsteras growing on the stairwell, and I don't want them to suffer stunted growth from the cold.'

Lomond said, 'Ross McNair could be suffering far worse than that. Did you know he's missing, presumed abducted?'

'I heard.' Reekie returned to his seat, watching the cricket. 'Don't ruin the result for me if you know it.'

Lomond replied, 'I'd rather be waterboarded than watch cricket, so don't worry about spoilers from me.'

'I'm sorry, but I really don't understand how you think I can help you.'

Ruth handed Reekie a letter. 'That's the letter of recommendation you sent to the parole board on behalf of Lee Vickery. You also authorised a day release for Damien Reid. Why?'

Reekie sighed. He muted the TV. The most meagre gesture of cooperation he could think of. 'It's complicated. I don't expect you to understand.'

'Try me,' said Lomond. He moved in front of the TV. 'Were you running Shaun Webster and Ally Corrigan on clandestine organised crime operations?'

Reekie scoffed. 'This is so far above your pay grade. Laughable, really.' He picked up his mobile phone, then stood up. 'Excuse me.'

Lomond took a few steps to the side, seeing Reekie go into the bathroom. 'He took his phone, right?' he asked.

'I think so,' came Ruth's cagey reply.

Lomond overtook her, walking calmly towards the bathroom door.

'John? What are you doing?' she asked.

'Don't worry about it.'

The closer he got, the more concerned Ruth became. 'John?'

'Remember what I said about keeping me from killing him?'

'Yeah.'

'Now's probably the time to do that.' He lifted his foot up and drove it viciously into the door.

CHAPTER SIXTY-FIVE

RUTH YELLED at the top of her voice, 'John!' She lunged for him, trying to stop him.

But nothing was going to hold him back.

The thin plywood door and its equally lightweight lock didn't stand a chance against his size-twelve Oxfords.

Reekie threw his hands up in the air at the sudden crash of the door, dropping his phone as he did so. 'Have you lost your mind!' He looked with petrified eyes at Ruth. 'Help me, Ruth! For god's sake!'

She grabbed Lomond from behind as he stalked into the small bathroom.

'John, stop!' she cried.

Lomond kept her at bay with a forearm.

Reekie cowered by the toilet at the end of the room. 'You're not thinking straight, John...'

'Oh, I'm thinking *very* clearly, Alasdair,' he fired

back. He picked up Reekie's phone and saw the text message he'd been tapping out.

"Don't say a word."

'Who are you warning?' asked Lomond. 'Frank Gormley? You two must have been really close for this to have worked.'

Reekie held his hands up to his face. Nothing scared him more than being punched in the face. He'd never been punched in his life before. Something that Lomond didn't believe was a good thing in a man Reekie's age. There's only so much you can know about yourself if you haven't been punched in the face.

'You have to understand the position we were in,' Reekie spluttered. 'Organised crime has ten times the cash we have. We can't win, John. Can't you see that? When Frank Gormley was sent down, all hell broke loose. Barry McKenna had joined forces with some Chinese nationals who were ripping up the north of Glasgow. Extraordinary times require extraordinary measures. When you can't win the war, all that's left is to negotiate the terms of your surrender. We faced a simple and stark choice: keep throwing resources at the fight against organised crime and get nowhere, or join forces with Frank Gormley to negotiate a peace. Frank was the lesser of two evils. That's all.'

Lomond exclaimed, 'You chose appeasement over the fight? Call yourself police? You're Neville fucking Chamberlain, that's what you are. '

Ruth snapped, 'That's enough, John.'

'Don't be so self-righteous,' Reekie spat. 'Police forces have used safe spaces for prostitutes. There's no serious police organisation that doesn't secretly accept that legalising drugs would lower prison populations and save lives. Working with Frank was just an extension of that. Look at who's been killed, then look at who benefits. That explains who the real Taxman was.'

Lomond said with grim finality. 'Gormley.'

'Because he always makes them pay.'

'And you wonder why the public loses faith in the police.'

'We needed each other. Gormley had been informing for us for *years*.'

Lomond laughed.

'I'm telling you the truth,' Reekie said. 'The big guys, the really big ones like Gormley, McKenna. How do you think they've stayed at the top for so long? Luck? They're harder than everyone else? Please. They're all hard. All lunatics. What makes the difference is wiping out the competition before they get too big. It's what old-school gangsters like Barry Groves never learned. Hiding behind their pathetic notions of being "a grass". I don't admire men like Gormley, but I respect them, because they play it at it lays. Always.'

'So you decided to work together?'

'As a way of keeping the peace on the streets, yes. I brought in Webster to work with Ally. But he wasn't up to it. He lost himself in double lives. Ally tried her best to explain what we were trying to do, but he refused to play ball with any jobs that helped Gormley. Pretty soon, Webster got vindictive. Started targeting Gormley's people. Ambushing drug deals. Setting stashes on fire. Spiteful stuff. Gormley wanted him dead but I talked him down. I said instead that I could get rid of him. Ally hatched a plan that combined all of our needs in one go.'

Lomond said, 'The Taxman murders.'

'Gormley got rid of some enemies, and we made amends for mistakes in the past, like letting Damien Reid out early.' Reekie looked genuinely contrite. 'I know I fucked up with Damien Reid. I did. And it was my fault that the Fulton family died by that monster's hands. I have to live with that. It was Frank's idea to send Reid out into the open for Webster to wipe him out. I pulled a few strings to make it happen. It didn't take much convincing by Ally that it was the right thing to do. Shaun was besotted with her. He was shagging her, of course. That's what started all the problems. Gordon Hunt couldn't see her for what she is. A bent cop. Always has been. Always been on the make. Gordon was like a teenager around her. It reminded me of a bit of advice my mother gave me. When someone shows you who they really are, believe it the first time.'

'Oh, I know who you are. *Sir.* You were going to see Webster put away for the lot of it.'

'I would have made sure he was always safe. I saved his life! Gormley was going to throw him off a building!'

Lomond applauded sarcastically. 'What a *hero!*'

'I didn't get into all this for honest cops like Ross

McNair to end up in the firing line. I didn't sign up for that.'

'Neither did he.'

'Please,' he begged, clutching his leg which he'd clattered off the toilet bowl on his way down. 'Can you help me up?'

'No,' Lomond barked, immune to Reekie's whimpers. 'We're not done. I think you're forgetting how much and how quickly I've forgotten about you. Niven's only in the ACC West seat for a few more months. That's an exciting prospect for someone in your position. Assistant Chief Constable doesn't come up every year. Not in the area where you live anyway. You wouldn't even have to move out of this lovely house, with such a spacious bathroom that can fit three people in it. It would be a shame if an anonymous email detailing how you deleted Sandy Driscoll's file, and thus endangered the investigation into Jack Ferguson's abduction, were to make it to the Assistant Chief Constable selection panel. Say, the week before they made their appointment.'

Reekie was almost foaming at the mouth. His entire life's work was being dangled in front of him. 'You total bastard.'

Lomond went on, 'You also allowed a notorious paedophile to disappear into public life with a new identity after his release. A man that could have played a pivotal role in solving the Sandman investigation months, maybe years, earlier than we did. When you pile all that on top of this stuff with Damien Reid's parole...it paints a picture. And the picture kind of looks like you standing at the foot of a mountain, while an avalanche of shite comes racing towards you.'

Reekie recoiled at the imagery.

Lomond concluded, 'If I was in your shoes – and this is just me – I would probably be inclined to do that person a favour if they asked for one.'

Reekie was silent.

Until Ruth snapped, 'Just tell him, Alasdair! You know he's right. He might be an arsehole, but he's right.'

Lomond motioned at Ruth, and said to Reekie, 'Even she thinks I'm right.'

Relenting, and just wanting off his bathroom floor, Reekie asked, 'What do you want?'

'I need to know where Ally Corrigan might have taken Ross. Any safe house that she and Shaun Webster might have used.'

'I can't think, I can't...there were a few of them.'

Ruth tapped Lomond on the arm. 'Ryan Venables. He told us Shaun Webster had walked to Barnsford Road from somewhere nearby in Paisley. We stopped looking for whatever safe house Webster had been using because he showed up trying to kill Damien Reid.' She asked Reekie, 'Was there a safe house within a few miles of Paisley?'

Reekie didn't need any more working over to be convinced to talk. 'Linwood! Ally and Shaun had a lock-up in Linwood. Tucked away in the corner of the retail park with all the car dealerships. I never went there, but I'm sure it won't be hard to find.'

Satisfied that he was giving up everything he knew, Lomond pointed to the sink. 'Wash your hands. Looks like there's blood on them.' Then he left the bathroom, shoving aside the broken door hanging off its hinges.

CHAPTER SIXTY-SIX

AT NIGHT, it was hard to find a more handsome building in Glasgow than the Mitchell Library. It used to be lit by dense floodlights, which scorched the facade in a uniform pale yellow. Now, white uplighters dotted the balconies and pillars, and the iconic dome roof.

Sheila Christie ran up the steps from the Kent Road side, coattails flapping in the wind. When DCI John Lomond asked her to open the library for himself or a colleague after closing then it was serious.

There was only one person standing outside the iron-gates at the front.

Sheila called out, 'Donna?'

'You must be Sheila,' she answered. 'Thanks for doing this.'

Trying to interpret Donna's tone, Sheila asked, 'I don't need specifics, but how important is this?'

'My colleague's missing, and I think this could help find him.'

She raised an accepting hand. 'Say no more.'

Donna instantly liked her efficient but not unfriendly manner. She reminded Donna of a retired English teacher. The one that was stern but fair, and was lovely to you when you met her outside of school.

Sheila remained a few steps ahead of Donna the whole way through the marble reception area. 'You're better off in here rather than using the British Newspaper Online Archive,' she explained. 'Searching with that is like trying to find a picture of a particular grain of rice on Google Images.' She pointed up the stairs. 'You're in a hurry, so why don't you–' She broke off when she realised Donna was still trailing behind. 'Keep up, dear...'

Donna jogged a few steps to get closer.

'Why don't you tell me what you're looking for, and I'll do what I can to narrow things down. Firstly, do you know which newspaper?'

'I don't, sorry.'

'Do you have a particular year?'

'No.'

'How about a particular range of years?'

Ross had said it was about twenty years ago, but she added an extra five years either side for safety. 'Somewhere between fifteen to twenty-five years ago.'

'What's the story you're looking for?'

'A fire that burned down a shop.'

'Whereabouts?'

'Somewhere in Glasgow.'

Sheila gave a slow nod. 'Okay. I think we'll start with the British Newspaper Archive.'

'But I thought you said that it was rubbish.'

'Oh, it is somewhat rubbish. But the alternative you've given me is impossible.' She raised a jubilant finger in the air. 'Rubbish trumps impossible every time, Donna.'

Sheila brought her to a cavernous, decadent room with bookcases on two levels all around the walls.

'Pretty much every newspaper, ever,' Sheila said.

She took Donna to the nearest computer and opened the Newspaper Archive.

The search parameters were straightforward. That didn't mean the results they brought up could be easily skimmed.

The results ran into the hundreds, which took Sheila by surprise – pleasantly. 'Could have been worse,' she said. 'Do you want to run through these yourself?'

'I think so,' Donna replied.

Five minutes later, Sheila returned with coffee and two Abernethy biscuits on a plate.

'They're the best-kept secret in the biscuit world, don't you find?' Sheila said.

Donna smiled politely. Too embarrassed to admit that she was more partial to a packet of brownie-filled Oreos. Which she was certain would have horrified Sheila. Oreos were just a bastardised custard cream.

Fifty minutes later, Donna groaned and threw her

head back, stretching out her neck. If she lost concentration for even a few seconds, her shoulder was quick to remind her she was still actually in a lot of pain. But the possibility of finding the needle she was looking for in the most enormous of digitised haystacks was addictive.

After scrolling through page twenty-seven of three hundred and sixty-two, she remembered that Ross had mentioned a hardware shop specifically. It narrowed the results down, but not nearly as much as she would have liked. Sheila was right. The keyword search was too broad, and there was no way of narrowing it.

After another fifteen minutes of toiling, Sheila suggested, 'Have you considered an image search? It's a fairly new feature, but works quite well. I mention it because the sort of story you described probably would have run with a photograph.'

'I would have thought so,' Donna replied.

Recent advances in technology meant that the database was able to find photographs based on keywords picked out by an AI machine. It was able to recognise landmarks, words, human faces, and return results based on any of them.

Now the search results were narrowed down to just thirteen.

The first was a warehouse fire and obviously not the one. Then a car on fire on the Kingston Bridge.

Then the moment the next photograph appeared on the screen, Donna knew she had found it.

Sheila was about to direct her away from it, noting,

'Oh, look. You've actually searched for a date range going back as far as forty years. That's too far, isn't it?'

Donna stopped her. 'Wait. Show me that one. The shop.'

The photo was black and white, showing what little remained of a small independently owned hardware shop on Cathcart Road. It had been its own tiny, detached unit next to a patch of wasteland.

The date of the story was thirty-nine years ago.

The story had appeared the day after the event, so there was no mention of a connection to anything gang-land. But there was no confirmation of the cause of the fire.

Sheila pointed out a link to a connected story. The arrest of eighteen-year-old Barry McKenna over suspected arson.

Donna read at breakneck speed. 'Barry McKenna... his lawyer Dennis Dunbar said that there is no evidence of his client's involvement...'

It was all starting to make sense to her now.

What had really snared Donna's attention, though, was the name of the shop owner mentioned in the first story.

Harry Hunt.

The name of the shop: Hunt's Hardware.

CHAPTER SIXTY-SEVEN

THE ARMED RESPONSE unit was called in for the raid, such was the confidence that Detective Superintendent Linda Boyle had in Lomond's information, as well as how desperate she was to keep DS Ross McNair safe if he was indeed in a hostage situation with DI Ally Corrigan.

Lomond was in the back of a Ford Transit police van along with Ruth, Pardeep, Jason, and Linda. Willie and DC Lambie had drawn the short straws to stay back at the station to coordinate.

The Transit was part of a five-vehicle convoy, and it would be joined by a helicopter halfway between Glasgow and Paisley. Light was fading for the day, and the helicopter's thermal imaging technology could prove vital in any chase scenario – especially on the sort of terrain that surrounded the retail park, which wasn't easily accessible by vehicles.

Lomond had just wrapped up his story about what had happened at CSU Reekie's house. 'He took a little tumble in the bathroom. I helped him up quickly, and he told me that he remembered this lock-up in Linwood.'

'Bloody hell,' said Pardeep. 'Who would have thought – Reekie running OC officers like Judi Dench in them Bond films.'

Ruth said, 'I just hope none of you had stock in Reekie's career, because he is on his way out after this.'

'You think so?' asked Jason.

She nodded like it was a done deal.

Linda asked, 'What the hell does Ally want with Ross, though?'

'She's just a dirty cop doing it all for the money,' said Lomond. 'I don't care what Reekie has to say about common interests with Frank Gormley. The girl's a mercenary if ever I saw one.'

Pardeep pointed out, 'She'll get eaten alive in prison. Can you imagine? Ex-OC officer caught up in a scandal like this?'

Jason sniped, 'And they've got the gall to want to throw Donna out the force, when she helped save wee Jack Ferguson. It's shocking, man. Shocking.'

Pardeep asked, 'Am I right in saying that DCI Hunt is armed in the other van?'

Linda said, 'He's an authorised firearms officer. Has been for about fifteen years now. If I was an AFO going after one of my own team, I'd want to be carrying too.'

'It's just...I heard that he and Ally were a thing. For a while. Seems a bit...I dunno.'

'DCI Hunt's a professional,' Lomond replied. 'We don't see eye to eye on a lot of things, but let's show the man a bit of respect and not be gossiping about his personal life on the way to get Ross back.'

'Yep. Sorry, boss,' Pardeep said, putting his game face back on.

Linda asked, 'Donna had better be finding you gold wherever she is, John. I don't know why you think she doesn't need to be here.'

Lomond replied, 'Don't worry about Donna. She's following her nose.' He adjusted his earpiece, then did a radio check with everyone. 'Remember, folks. We're just MIT. This is armed response's op. That means when we're boots on the ground, it's DCI Hunt calling the shots.' He added, 'So to speak.'

CHAPTER SIXTY-EIGHT

LOMOND HAD NARROWED down the search for Shaun and Ally's old lock-up to a logistics centre in Linwood retail park that looked onto the A737 dual carriageway. Old shipping containers were piled up around an expanse of waste ground. Weeds growing up between the cracks in the concrete. Many of the containers rusted and decrepit.

Behind those was a warehouse with corrugated iron walls.

The convoy slowed only slightly for the final push through the Linclive Interchange roundabout.

Inside the warehouse, Ross was mouthing words but coming out with nothing. He kept saying 'how's my guy?', visualising Lachlann's beaming face and faltering walk towards him with his arms outstretched. Mouth wide open, guffawing with laughter at the mere thought of a cuddle from his daddy.

Ross was using it to keep him going. He didn't care about biology. He wasn't going to give up on Isla and Lachlann.

Faintly, he whispered, 'I'm here, John...Come find me...'

THE CONVOY PULLED up outside the perimeter fence and everyone from armed response filed out in regimented fashion, while the Helen Street MIT were only too happy to stay out the way.

After prepping his team, DCI Hunt sought out Lomond.

'How's it looking, Gordon?' Lomond asked.

'We're good. Listen, I'm going to go in first...'

Lomond was already sucking in his lips.

'Hear me out,' said Hunt. 'You want Ross back. I get that. But I equally want Ally to come out of there in one piece. I know her. And I know that going in hot and heavy is a recipe for disaster.'

Lomond winced as he received a loud crackle in his earpiece. He had to raise his hand in apology to Hunt and turn away. 'Sorry, what did you say?' Lomond asked the despatch back at Helen Street.

'I'm trying to connect a call to you from Donna Higgins.'

'Okay, go ahead.' He raised a hand in apology to DCI Hunt.

On the other end, Donna was frantic. 'Is it just us?'

'What?'

Insistent, Donna repeated, 'Is it just us? Can anyone else hear us?'

'No! What's going on?'

'It's Hunt. I just got word you're going after Ally, but it's not her. Hunt was lying. I think he's trying to lay this all on Ally and Webster. Hunt must have set Kenny up to relay that story in front of Ross. Hoping it would get back to us in time. Which it did. Hunt might be the one who killed Kenny, to silence him. He told Kenny to say the story was from twenty years ago. Thinking no one would be able to track down the real story of what happened. It was thirty-nine years ago. Barry McKenna was arrested on suspicion of arson, but his lawyer Dennis Dunbar got him off. The son of the shop owner was Hunt. He's been plotting revenge on McKenna. DCI Gordon Hunt is the Taxman!'

Lomond's insides were turning inside out. Hunt was only feet away from him.

In a neutral voice, Lomond said, 'Okay. Thanks. Cheers.' He turned back to Hunt.

'Everything okay?' asked Hunt.

Lomond stared at him a fraction longer than he normally would have. He couldn't help it. He needed time to process it, but now that Donna pointed out the theory, it made a lot of sense. 'Yeah,' Lomond said. 'Helen Street want me to check thermal imaging from the helicopter before anyone goes in.'

The moment Hunt's back was turned, Lomond waved at Linda and ran over to her.

'Give me another radio. A handheld,' he told her quietly, gesturing snappily with his hand while he pulled out his earpiece. 'Quickly, Linda.'

She handed him one from the boot of the Transit, then he was off again.

'Aye, you're welcome,' she said, writing off his abruptness as nerves over getting Ross back.

Hunt was giving his final instructions to the armed response team. He made it clear that he was to go in alone. Only when he gave the signal were the other AFOs to come in.

He was about to go, when Lomond called him back.

'Hang on...' Lomond said.

'Christ, John, what now?' Hunt complained.

Lomond reached behind Hunt and made an adjustment to a velcro strap on his bulletproof vest. 'Don't want that falling off at the wrong moment.'

'Cheers,' Hunt said.

He opened the metal door which clanged shut behind him. He made a show of raising his hands so that Ally could see he wasn't holding his handgun.

Ross was in the middle of the expansive warehouse, doubled over in the chair. He wasn't moving. And there was a sizeable puddle of blood at his feet.

'Tell me he's still alive, Ally,' Hunt said.

She was about to speak, then thought twice. Her eyes flitted around the metal rafters above. 'Can they hear us?'

'No, it's just us,' he replied.

'You said you could handle it if this happened. I counted two AFO teams. A helicopter. If I didn't know any better, I'd say you were cutting me loose.'

'I really was in love with you, Ally,' he said, creeping forward. 'We could have had it all.'

'It might have been having it all to you. Shagging a guy in his fifties who lasts ten seconds isn't my idea of having it all.'

'It's a mistake to get personal with me Ally. Barry McKenna's going to find that out soon enough.'

'You really think you can get to someone like that?'

'I know I can. I've been waiting since I was a sixteen to put a bullet in his brain for what he did to my family. That's why this is all so important. What we're doing in this Taskforce.'

Ally let out a vicious laugh. 'Do you even hear yourself?'

'You still don't know what this is, do you? You're not getting out of here alive, Ally. I can't let you.'

'What are you talking about?'

'Without the audio recording on that memory stick, it could sink us. If Ross dies, we'll never know where it is.'

'If Ross dies, it's over. We're in the clear. Job done. Shaun's dead. Kenny's dead.'

'Except,' said Hunt, 'everyone out there thinks you're the Taxman.'

'Why do they think that?'

'Because I told Lomond about your tragic backstory. How Barry McKenna's arson turned you into the blood-thirsty vigilante you are. You teamed up with rogue undercover officer Shaun Webster. Together, you killed George Melrose, Dennis Dunbar, Lee Vickery, and attempted to murder Damien Reid.'

Ally reached for the knife in Ross's stomach. 'You bastard! We had a plan. Why are you doing this?'

Hunt looked like he had a mouth full of bees. 'You shouldn't have shagged Shaun, Ally.' He pulled out his handgun from his holster and aimed it at her.

Ally pulled the knife out of Ross's stomach, unleashing a torrent of blood. Ross gasped as a fresh wave of agony took hold of him.

Ally swiped wildly through the air as Hunt kept marching towards her.

He shouted at the tops of his lungs, playing up an imaginary scene. 'Don't do it, Ally...!'

From fifty feet away, he fired once without breaking stride. A direct hit in her abdomen.

He kept coming. 'I tried to tell you...'

Now twenty feet away, he fired again. A direct hit in Ally's chest.

She catapulted backwards as if someone had pulled a rope attached to her back. When she landed, the back of her head cracked on the concrete floor. Ally spluttered blood from her mouth. It was full of it. Enough to gargle with it.

Hunt stood over her now, aiming the gun at her face. 'Any last requests?'

Then a deafening screech of feedback made him grasp at his ears.

'That's enough, Gordon,' said Lomond.

Hunt whipped around from where the voice came from, then he pulled at his bulletproof vest. It had a handheld radio set to transmit attached to it.

Lomond told him over the radio, 'It's over. We heard every word.'

AFOs flooded the warehouse from all angles, their orders countermanded by Detective Superintendent Linda Boyle. Now the only way out for Hunt was in handcuffs or on a stretcher with a blanket over his face.

Lomond entered the warehouse, flanked by Linda and Ruth.

From far away, Lomond asked, 'Was it worth it?'

Hunt scoffed. 'I don't expect you to understand. You ask me why I want to avenge my family? You're as well asking a tree why it grows.'

Facing the oncoming AFOs, Hunt stepped towards them.

The senior AFO called out, 'Stay back!'

Hunt kept coming. He knew there was no way out now.

'Hunt! Final warning...'

As Hunt fixated at the AFOs in front of him, he forgot about Ally a few steps behind him – and the knife in her hand.

She gurgled blood as she rolled onto her side. Then crawled up onto her knees. Her head flopped from side to side, barely conscious.

The senior AFO called out again, 'Put it down!'

Hunt smiled, raising his arms, encouraging them to shoot him.

'Put the knife down...'

Realising the AFO wasn't talking to him, Hunt turned on his heels. He walked straight into Ally who had the knife hoisted above her head. She'd already stabbed him in the side of the neck when the call to fire went up.

Two bullets struck Ally in the chest, sending her backwards once more. This time she wouldn't be getting up on her own.

Hunt sank to his knees, a hand raised impotently trying to remove the knife. But he never reached it. He fell forward onto his front. Blood shot out of his neck like a geyser and Hunt was unable to stop the flow. Ally had struck an artery. He had a matter of minutes left.

With Hunt already bleeding out, and Ally well on her way, there was one call that rang out through the warehouse.

'Medic!'

CHAPTER SIXTY-NINE

Ross was lying flat in his hospital bed, when he was woken by the sound of a little voice saying, 'Dah-*dee!*' When he opened his eyes, he saw Lachlann's face beaming back at him.

Isla held Lachlann up, then dipped him over so he could lean in and smush his mouth against his daddy's cheek. He made an accompanying 'mah' noise. His best impression of a kiss.

'Aw, thanks, little man,' Ross croaked. He smiled, but he didn't feel good. Not so much his stomach. The surgeons had fixed most of that. The issue was still the grogginess in his head, which had been hanging around since he first woke up from surgery several hours ago.

Isla kissed him on the forehead. 'Are you doing any better?' she asked.

'Oh, you know.'

In the corner of the room, where he had been sitting

for the last five hours waiting for Ross to wake up, Lomond said, 'False modesty isn't as attractive as you think.'

Ross smiled as he realised who it was. 'I'm just hoping you can go back to Helen Street and tell them how brave I've been.'

'They already know, Ross. Trust me.'

Struggling to stop him leaping out of her arms onto Ross, Isla said, 'Right, Lachlann, say bye-bye, Daddy, for a few minutes. Uncle John has to talk to daddy.'

Lomond smiled at his new name.

Isla put Lachlann down on his feet, then held her hand out for him to take it. He only seemed interested in an electric cart being driven past in the corridor. Lachlann charged out of the room, pointing in the direction the cart went. He yelled 'Caaah!'

Used to masterfully interpreting his gobbledygook, Isla replied, 'I know, it's like a car, isn't it...'

Once they were alone, Ross said, 'I wasn't awake for long last time. They wouldn't tell me. Did you get him?'

Lomond replied, 'Hunt's dead.'

Ross nodded solemnly. He took no pleasure in hearing the news. 'And Ally?'

'On a ventilator. The doctors like her chances. Hunt was trying to frame her for the lot of it.' Lomond took out his phone. 'Which would have been difficult with this kicking around.' He pressed play on the audio file.

It was a conversation between Kenny Fan and Hunt from weeks ago.

'What is that?' asked Ross.

'It's Hunt feeding Kenny the story of what happened to Ally Corrigan's family. Then instructing Kenny to tell it to you like it's the Taxman story.'

'Where did this come from?'

'It was a gift. From Mr Wenbo. Recorded in his restaurant.'

Ross exhaled as he remembered Kenny telling him about the microphones in there that he was so afraid of.

'Going by Kenny's bank account, he'd been black-mailing Hunt to keep quiet. Whether it was Ally or Hunt who killed him in the end, we might never know. Even if Ally does wake up, it would just be her word against a dead man's. That's the only thing keeping Frank Gormley out of custody.'

'We don't have anything on him?'

'Circumstantial at best. No forensics. Whatever lieu-tenants of his he used for the murders themselves will be well tucked away. The only people who could point the finger at him are either dead or in a coma. Frank's time will come, though. He'd best believe that.'

Ross stared at the ceiling. Just happy to be breathing. 'I want to come back, John. To MIT. Organised Crime was a mistake.'

'You can come back, Ross. But I can't say for sure what you're coming back to. Donna's hearing's been set for next week.'

'Next *week*? It was going to be at least a month away. Why so soon?'

'I don't know. But it's not a good sign.'

'Are you going to say a wee something on her behalf.'

'I'm sure I'll think of something.' He patted Ross on the leg. 'I should get out of here. It should be Isla and the wee man in here right now.'

Ross shook his head. 'It's strange. Now that this whole Taxman thing is over, I've had a bit of time to think things through. Reassess.'

Lomond laughed. 'You've been asleep for almost thirty-six hours, Ross!'

'I've got no interest in ending up like DCI Gordon Hunt. Or Ally Corrigan. Or Shaun Webster.'

'There are actually plenty of OC officers who haven't died in disgrace or gone rogue.'

'MIT's my home.'

For a moment, Lomond heard Ruth in his head:

'It's like emptying a loch one teaspoonful at a time. Except, it's always going to rain. That loch is never going to empty.'

Wondering why Lomond was staring so glassily, Ross asked, 'Are you okay? You look miles away.'

Lomond snapped out of his daze. 'Sorry. I'm great. But I should go.'

'Oh, wait...' Ross struggled to reach his phone on the bedside table.

Lomond hurried over. 'Whoa, I'll get that. Just ask. Remember you've got a big hole in your stomach.'

Ross scrolled through his contacts. 'Isla's going to be proud of me for remembering this, especially under these circumstances. The thing is – and don't freak out or go off on one...'

'That sounds like a guarantee that I will absolutely freak out and go off on one.'

'Isla's got this friend, Catriona, that she thinks you might like. She's really nice. Primary school teacher.'

Lomond waved his hand in a clear sign of 'no'. 'Ross, I can't.'

'Just take her number and think about it, at least. Let me tell Isla that much.'

'The thing is,' Lomond began. 'I'm sort of on my way to see someone. Just now.'

Ross smiled. 'Good for you.' He messaged the contact to Lomond's phone anyway.

Reacting to the notification ping as he walked towards the door, Lomond looked back with a smile, 'Tell Isla thanks.'

CHAPTER SEVENTY

HE LISTENED to 'Space Age Love Song' on repeat the whole way to Edinburgh. Each time, he liked it more. Felt it more. He could see it now so clearly. The future. And where he'd gone wrong after Eilidh.

He'd thought that running up hills and losing weight would help him make peace with the past. And it did for a while. It reminded him to treat himself like someone he cares deeply about. Lomond found it darkly amusing that people are far less likely to finish a course of medication prescribed to them than they are to complete a course prescribed by a vet for their pet. Because it was actually a responsibility to look after yourself. Not just shovelling in sweets and crap, and doing whatever you feel like. It was thinking about what's good for you.

And it didn't get more fundamental than recognising that if he was going to do that, he needed someone at home. Someone to care, and be cared for.

Only one person other than Eilidh had ever fit the bill.

He parked his car on Warrender Park Terrace, singing the Flock of Seagulls song all the way up until he opened his door.

The street was cobbled, and had a view across Bruntsfield Links, one of the nicest green spaces in Edinburgh.

Lomond looked around, grinning stupidly at everything. He imagined living around there. He had never lived in Edinburgh, and now that he had decided to take the leap and come through and tell Ruth how he really felt, anything seemed possible.

Linda had got Ruth's address from a friend at Fettes Avenue, but Lomond had been cagey about what it was for.

Lomond was still humming to himself when he got to her door and knocked.

When Ruth opened the door, her eyes widened in a panic.

Without her saying a word, Lomond knew that something was wrong.

In the hall behind her, a man appeared. He lingered. 'Everything all right?' he asked.

Ruth said, 'This is John Lomond...we were working together in Glasgow.'

Lomond gulped. 'Nice to meet you.'

A wee boy around two years old came running

through the hall. 'BAAAAH!' He stopped and hid behind his dad's legs.

Ruth stepped out in front of the door and closed it over behind her. 'What are you doing here?'

'Funny,' he said. 'I'm now asking myself the same question.'

'I warned you, John. I don't do attachment.'

'I made a mistake.'

'John...we're going to have to work together at times. I need to know this won't be a problem.'

'No. No problem.

'This here...this isn't my career. It's my life.'

As he turned to leave, she called his name.

'John. Before you find out some other way, you should know...I was the leak. For Colin Mowatt's story. I leaked the Taxman name and the information about Donna's enquiry.'

Lomond was so disappointed, he couldn't find any words.

Ruth went on, 'I wanted the case, and needed to pile more pressure on you to force Reekie and Linda's hand. It was greed. I knew that if I had experience with both Edinburgh and Glasgow, I would have a better chance of promotion.'

Lomond said, 'Your leak ramped up pressure on Professional Standards to bring the hammer down on Donna. She's going to lose her job tomorrow. Did you know that?'

Ruth shut her eyes in genuine contrition. 'That wasn't my intention.'

'And leaking the Taxman's name? What was that? Shits and giggles?'

'We'd just had that fight...'

Lomond scoffed. 'What are you, ten years old?'

'You said that I wasn't good police, John!'

After a long pause, he said, 'I don't know why I'm standing here surprised. Someone told me recently, when someone shows you who they really are, believe them the first time. I wanted to believe in you so badly this time round, Ruth. More fool me, eh?'

As he walked away, she told him, 'I'll fix this.'

'It's too late,' he said. 'There's only one thing I can do now.' At the end of her garden path, Lomond told her, 'Congratulations. Glasgow MIT will be yours in no time.'

'What are you talking about?'

He kept walking.

'John!' she shouted.

She kept calling his name, but he didn't respond.

CHAPTER SEVENTY-ONE

THE NEXT MORNING, Lomond and Linda were sharing an uncomfortable sofa that was too small for the pair of them, and too big for one. They had a coffee each, but had left them on the floor as they were undrinkably weak.

Lomond fidgeted with his armrest and shuffled around, trying to find a position that didn't hurt his back. 'What's the point in spending thousands on sofas you can't even sit on. It's like someone up the stairs went to DFS and said, hey, can I get a bunch of sofas that look Scandinavian, are horrible to sit on, and are wildly overpriced?'

Linda puffed. 'I was going to ask what sort of mood you were in. Thanks for letting me know. '

After a final tut, he gave up and opted to stand instead.

He had not long finished telling the story of what had happened the previous day in Edinburgh.

'So are we done talking about it, then?' she asked.

'What is there to talk about?'

'How big a plonker you are.'

'Oh, thank you. Thanks for that.'

'No, really. You thought that because you've been working yourself to death that what you need...is a fellow workaholic?' She snorted, baffled by his decision-making.

'I'm glad I amuse you,' he said.

Her smile slowly faded. 'You want to know why you and Eilidh worked, John? She was the "life" that complemented your "career". She balanced you out. Without Eilidh, all you've had is work. If you and Ruth got together, you would still only have work. Do you see where I'm going with this now?'

He reached down for his coffee. 'I get it,' he said.

She pursed her lips.

'Oh, don't make that face,' he said.

'What face?'

'That *oh, bless,* pitying face.'

'I can't help it. You are the dumbest smart guy I've ever met. Or maybe you're the smartest dumb guy.'

'You know what really sustains our friendship, Linda? The compliments.'

She chuckled. 'What were you thinking?'

He had no choice but to laugh at himself. 'I don't know.'

Both of them craned their necks as the doors opened

to the conference room where Donna had been for the last seventy minutes.

A woman holding a manila folder in her hand called to him. 'DCI Lomond. You're up.'

Lomond put his coffee on the floor again, then held his arms out for an inspection. 'My tie all right?'

Linda nodded. 'You okay?'

'Aye.'

'So you're really not telling me what you're going to say?'

He looked mischievous.

Linda knew the look well – and it often meant trouble. 'What have you done?' she asked.

As he buttoned his suit jacket, he said, 'You know what job I always thought I'd be good at if I wasn't police?'

'What's that?'

'Insurance.'

CHAPTER SEVENTY-TWO

Donna looked resigned and defeated next to her union rep, PC Nigel Skelton. With DCI Gordon Hunt dead, Donna had no one with authority or credibility from Organised Crime to speak on her behalf.

The only person left was Lomond.

He gave her a quick wink as he took a seat near the head of the long conference table. He was surrounded by suits from Professional Standards, while Donna was isolated much further down the table.

For Lomond's benefit, the panel chair, Karen Gilchrist, ran through the necessary introductions, and the reason for the hearing.

'Following a preliminary hearing of the Professional Standards committee, it has been decided that there is a disciplinary case to answer in the matter of Detective Constable Donna Higgins. This panel has been investigating the legality of how information was acquired to lead DCI John Lomond's Major Investigations Team to the address of Peter Lee, who was suspected of involvement in the abduction of Jack Ferguson. Were improper or illegal measures used in order to obtain that address? And was one of those measures the illegal unsealing of a Multi-Agency Public Protection Arrangements file that revealed information vital to the investigation. Now–'

Lomond lifted his hand to interject. 'Sorry, if I may.'

'DCI Lomond, I assure you that you will have every opportunity to provide a statement and answer the panel's questions.'

'But we can skip all that,' he said. 'Because Donna's not the one who should be in the firing line here. It's me.'

Karen sat forward in her chair. 'I'm sorry?'

'I'm telling you, on the record, that this panel is attempting to discipline the wrong officer with improper conduct. It's me who should be facing the charge.'

For a moment, Donna forgot that there was anyone else in the room. 'Sir, please. You don't have to do this.'

Lomond continued anyway. 'I took the file. It was me. DC Higgins may have appeared to be involved in this. But she was not.'

Karen knew exactly what Lomond was doing, and she wasn't about to see Donna walk out of the room unscathed. 'That may well be the case, DCI Lomond. But the panel has also been investigating DC Higgins' involvement in identifying a contact found on a money laundering gang's burner phone. When questioned by Specialist Crime Division as to how she knew the identity of said contact, she revealed that the contact was her estranged father, a known drug dealer named Barry Higgins. The issue is that DC Higgins acquired his address by participating in a drug deal, which concluded with her being taken to Barry Higgins' home. This was how she was able to give Specialist Crime Division his address.'

Lomond added, 'Which allowed SCD to arrest and charge him with a dozen different drug offences. You should be congratulating DC Higgins, not charging her.'

Karen was out of patience now. 'DCI Lomond, I'm going to have to ask you to step outside again, as–'

'I gave Donna the address,' Lomond said.

Donna suspected he might try to protect her from the MAPPA file charge. But now he was claiming responsibility for something he had nothing to do with.

He continued, 'I told Donna to make up a story about how we found his address, but it was all me. An informer on the street gave me it. I feared for the informer's life, so I told DC Higgins to come up with something. In the process, she mistakenly invented a story that's landed her in hot water.'

Karen took the temperature of the other panel members, who appeared beleaguered as to where to go now.

'DCI Lomond,' said Karen, 'are you aware of the charges you are now opening yourself up to?'

Lomond was as calm as a Hindu cow. 'I am,' he said.

Before she could continue, Karen looked over to the door, which had opened up without so much as a knock.

It was Assistant Chief Constable Brendan Niven. He was holding his hat under his arm in the formal style, on his way to an official function in Tulliallan.

Lomond was intrigued. In his temporary role as ACC, Niven had also been given the portfolio for Professionalism and Assurance – essentially, Karen Gilchrist's boss.

Pretending to have only just noticed proceedings were well underway, he said, 'Sorry to interrupt. Karen? A word outside?'

Donna looked at Lomond in confusion.

He was equally baffled. 'I don't know,' he mouthed at her.

A minute later, Niven took off and was immediately swarmed by cronies and advisors and assistants. Karen returned to her place at the table. Something had left her shellshocked.

'It would appear,' she said, 'that new evidence has come to light in this matter. The panel will of course be given the chance to review it officially over the coming days.'

Skelton couldn't believe their luck, and was terrified it might be wrenched away at any moment. 'DC Higgins has every right to be told what this new evidence is. Whatever its veracity.'

Lomond nodded. 'True,' he said quietly.

Karen shot him a look so acidic it could have melted

the ice around her own heart. 'Yes, thank you for that, DCI Lomond.' She cleared her throat. 'It would appear that Chief Superintendent Alasdair Reekie had misplaced the missing MAPPA file as part of a sensitive undercover operation. He has also provided a statement to Assistant Chief Constable Niven that DCI Gordon Hunt – since deceased – had provided the address of Barry Higgins to CSU Reekie during his time at the Organised Crime Taskforce on an unrelated enquiry. CSU Reekie has stated that DC Higgins' claim of uncovering the address was an attempt to cover up for him...' she said the word with neon disdain, '*forgetting* the episode.'

A few of the panel members shook their heads in incredulity.

They had heard some bullshit in their time. But this was on another level.

Karen concluded, 'This hearing will be suspended, until such time as ACC Niven can provide the statements in writing, in full. DC Higgins, you may go.'

Donna wanted to leap up and dance. Lomond wouldn't have been far behind her, if the rest of the panel hadn't shuffled so slowly out the room.

Skelton shook Donna's hand.

She then grabbed him and hugged him.

'You don't really have me to thank,' he said, being thrown around by her. 'I don't want to know how you did it, but you've got friends in important places.'

Once they were alone, Donna exclaimed, 'What the actual F–U–C–K?'

Lomond's head was still spinning.

'Was this you?' she asked.

'I didn't do a thing. Except throw myself on a sword that was apparently made of melted cheese.'

She still didn't believe him.

'Really, Donna. I've no idea how that happened or why.' He took out his phone as a message came through for him.

RUTH TELFORD:

"*A favour for old time's sake. Look after yourself, John. Glasgow needs you on the streets. Not on your knees.*"

Good old ACC Niven and his weekly curries with Ruth when they were in Aberdeen, thought Lomond. He wondered what Ruth had on ACC Niven to make him pull such a stunt on Professional Standards. It must have been juicy.

The next message to come through was from Reekie.

"*Consider us even.*"

EPILOGUE
THREE WEEKS LATER

LOMOND WAS PUSHING the trolley of his weekly food shop past the tills at the Tesco Extra in Maryhill, when he spotted a familiar face.

Shannon Muldoon.

It had just gone ten a.m., so Lomond expected to see a bottle of Glen's vodka sitting on the conveyor belt. But when he was along far enough, he saw a bag of apples, a box of Tesco's version of Rice Krispies, and a carton of blue-top milk.

Their eyes met, and she looked like she wanted to be anywhere else in the world but there in front of DCI John Lomond.

Lomond waved to her. 'Awright, Shannon.'

She waved back. Relieved to hear kindness in his voice.

It wasn't quite her turn to pay, so Lomond lingered by the end of another till.

'Did you move?' he asked.

'Three weeks ago,' she said.

It was apparent straight away that she wasn't drunk. There was a clarity in her eyes that he had never seen before. She was like a different person.

When it came her turn to pay, Lomond bagged her things for her.

'Don't bother with buying one,' he said. 'The boot of my car's packed out with them. You'd be doing me a favour.'

'Aye, awright,' she replied. 'Whit are you wantin'?'

'Wanting?'

'Aye.'

'Nothing.'

'Ah thought you wanted me tae grass someone.'

'I'm not working, Shannon. Just thought I'd say hello seeing as I saw you here. You doing okay?'

'Aye. Ah went tae a meeting the night after you came to the flat. Been dry since. It's no' much, but I'm doin' awright, I think.'

'Bloody well done. Seriously. That's great. One day at a time, right.'

'That's whit they say.'

Lomond glanced towards the cafe. 'I was going to get a tea. You fancy?'

Shannon had made a lot of changes in her life. But she never thought she'd be going for a cup of tea with a detective in Tesco.

A few minutes later they were laughing and joking at

a table by the window. Shannon mostly watched the buses going by. She had come a long way in just three weeks, but her confidence would trail far behind for a while yet.

'Ah did a share last week,' Shannon said. 'There's a meetin' ah go to down at Central Hall.'

'Aye? And how was that?'

'It was awright. But scary. Ah'm daein the steps. The twelve steps thing.'

'I know it.'

'Ah'm no' daein them in order because there's a few ah wanted tae get tae first. Ah was telt that wisnae how it's meant tae work, but fuck it.' She giggled, revealing sharp, blackened teeth. The smile came across like a wince, but after a few instances of it, Lomond realised: she wasn't used to doing it. There was something pure and joyful about it, though. Like seeing a dying plant come back to life. 'Ah've been thinking a lot about number five. The one about admitting wrongs. Ah was just thinking cos...you must think ah'm a terrible person. A terrible mother.'

Lomond said, 'No, Shannon. I don't.' It wasn't a lie.

'Ah know ah wisnae there for Tyler. Ah should have been. Ah wis too busy messed up on gear, knaw whit ah mean.'

'The thing is...that's all over. And now you have to move on. Because there's no changing what happened. It can't be undone. Think about it – what could you possibly do to change the sadness of losing a wee one?'

Shannon shook her head. 'Nuthin'.'

'It's called loss for a reason,' he said. He looked out the window. Grandparents walking grandchildren in buggies, despite the driving rain and gusty wind. Junkies wrapped up in multiple jackets because it was twelve degrees with some wind chill. A young man wearing a dress out walking his dog. Ladies in rain jackets pulling wheeled shopping bags. A man who had recently arrived from Somalia, dressed for deep winter. Some school kids who were bunking off class – or 'patching' as the kids now called it.

He watched the traffic lights change to green at the T-junction. But the lights changed faster than an old man with a shuffling walk could manage. He was still only halfway over the road. The traffic in both directions all waited until he had reached the pavement on the other side. He'd taken so long that the lights had turned red again for traffic, but no one blasted their horn or complained.

Lomond said, 'All that's left is to live a good life and be a good person. That's the only way to right a wrong.'

'You cannae live in the past,' Shannon agreed.

'It's true.' He drank the last of his tea. As he gathered up his things, he said, 'We only get one go at this, Shannon. And it doesn't get any easier. There's only three things I know for sure in this life. One – Billy Connolly is the funniest man who's ever lived. Two – Partick Thistle will never win the Champions League. And three – there's no such thing as justice.'

'Then what's the point of tryin'?'

Lomond shrugged. 'It's all we can do. If you try to fight it, it'll destroy you. It's tempting to fight it. But once you accept it, everything gets easier.'

On his way across the covered car park out the back, a message pinged on his phone. It was a confirmation for his new double bed being delivered later that day.

He felt both relief and sadness at the fact. It meant the end of something. But it also meant the start of something else.

He got into the driver's seat and hooked up his phone to the car. Before he had a chance to choose, the most recent track he'd listened to on his music app started playing. 'Comfortably Numb' by Pink Floyd.

He was about to change it, but instead he let it play.

There was something about the layers of strings and horns that he really wanted to hear in that moment. Yet there was something troublingly direct about the lyrics. Sitting in the car, with rain crashing down outside, he felt like the lyrics were being directed straight at him. Particularly the one about a dream being gone. So much of what he'd dreamt of had gone. His life with Eilidh. Being a dad. And now the notion of having a life after Eilidh with someone like Ruth.

At work, too, dreams were slipping away. He had been willing to lose everything in order to protect Donna. Ross had nearly lost his life because of corrupt OC officers. The whole Taxman case, in fact, had proven to Lomond that there was no such thing as justice in his line of work.

But as the song's orchestral arrangement soared leading into the first chorus, and then David Gilmour's first guitar solo, Lomond realised that he'd actually got it wrong. There might not have been justice – for baby Tyler, Damien Reid's victims, or even DCI Gordon Hunt – but Lomond being spared the consequences of the disciplinary panel, meant that he could continue fighting in his own way.

That dream was actually still very much alive for Lomond. A dream of doing what he could. Of little victories in the face of the cruelty of the world. He might have lost his job along with Donna. Ross might have died. All those good polis still out on the streets vastly outnumbered the bad ones. Even Shannon Muldoon had got her life together. Wasn't that a dream worth fighting for?

Ruth had said that as police, you could never empty a loch one teaspoonful at a time. It was always going to rain. Like chasing justice, you were on a hiding to nothing. But Lomond understood now, the point of being police wasn't to try and empty the loch. The point was to make sure that the loch never flooded. That's was Lomond's responsibility now. His purpose.

During Gilmour's second guitar solo, Lomond's thoughts turned to Eilidh, and his guilt about his night with Ruth. Wanting to rekindle things with Ruth hadn't been about trying to replace Eilidh. His intention had been to think of the future. His mistake was in trying to do that by looking to the past. It was time to take on board the advice he had just given to Shannon minutes earlier.

In his own words: *you have to move on.*

He picked up his phone and tapped out the start of a message.

'*Hi, Catriona, this is John Lomond. I don't normally do this sort of thing...*'

ALSO BY ANDREW RAYMOND